WRATH
CHILD

A SUPERNATURAL
THRILLER

ERIK HENRY VICK

RATATOSKR PUBLISHING

NEW YORK

RATATOSKR PUBLISHING
2080 NINE MILE POINT ROAD, UNIT 106
PENFIELD, NY 14526

WRATH CHILD/ ERIK HENRY VICK. -- 1ST ED.
ISBN 978-1-951509-12-5

Table of Contents

For Matty, Matt, David, and Clint.
Knowing you has made me a better man.

I was born into a scene of angriness and greed,
and dominance and persecution.
My mother was a queen, my dad I've never seen,
I was never meant to be.

And now I spend my time looking all around,
For a man that's nowhere to be found.
Until I find him, I'm never gonna stop searching,
I'm gonna find my man, gonna travel around.

—Steve Harris

I hope you enjoy *Wrath Child*. If so, please consider joining my Readers Group—details can be found at the end of the last chapter.

Chapter 1
It Begins. Again.

I

The alley stank of garbage and human waste and blood and imminent death. His nose filled with the amalgam of odors, and his nostrils flared wide to drink in even more of the heady cocktail's reek. The thunderstorm overhead brought some New England mill town or other to mind—full of chemicals, soot, and opportunity. He unwound from hunching over the girl, throwing his arms up and back, turning his face toward the bruised sky and letting the rain patter down on him. His face twisted with an ungentle smile as the bloody lump of flesh at his feet moaned, and his fingers curled into cruel claws at his side. Lightning flickered and danced from cloud to cloud, its brilliance, and the slimy rain with its acrid, soured egg smell, momentarily blinding him. His eyelids fluttered against the rain, against the bitter longing, against the feeling, the compulsion, the *demanding presence*, but he resisted dropping his head forward so he could look upon her. Peals of thunder ruined his ears, commanding more blood and depravity. Yet he waited, stretching out the moment, stretching his anticipation.

Oh, he knew what he would see. What he would see in her eyes as the realization struck her—about two seconds before the hammer struck her... He knew what he would see, but still, he forced himself to wait, drawing out the feeling, letting the *rush* build and build and build.

Thunder raged above him, and the dark passenger within him ranted and raved and prayed and pleaded. But none of it could command him to action, none of it could inspire fear or pleasure or anger or...*any* emotion within him.

Lightning sizzled across the sky, dazzling him, and at his feet, the woman moaned. *Almost time*, he said to that presence within. *Will you watch this time? Or will it again be too much for you?*

He didn't bother to listen to the inane answers, as he knew that by this time in the evening, the events and demands of the hunt had rendered his passenger into a shivering mess of jabbering pleas, jibbering demands, and rasping threats. All of it summed to exactly nothing to him. Taunting his passenger amounted to no more than an appetizer.

But still, the impulse to look down, to drink in her expression, her fear, her *suffering*, built to a fevered pitch within him. The muscles across his shoulders and neck shook with it, and his fingernails dug into his palms. His knees had begun to shake, his breath to rasp harshly in the back of his throat. His mouth tasted of copper and sweat and pain.

And it was marvelous. Better than the finest whisky, better than the most expensive wine, better than riding a new...

Well, not better than *that*, certainly.

When he could stand it no longer, he tipped his head forward but kept his eyelids squeezed shut as long as he could, his teeth grinding against the pressure, the desire, the *wanting*.

At his feet, she whimpered, and that was more than he could stand. His eyes flew open, his nostrils flared, saliva sluiced into his mouth, and the *need* beat like a second heart within him. He dropped his arms, one hand twisting into her long, beautiful yellow hair—though it was now streaked with red—the other snaking around to his waistband in the back, feeling for it, seeking it, caressing it…

There! The cold metal head of the hammer seemed to beckon his fingers, to cry out in ecstasy as his fingertips brushed against it. A grin of brutal savagery twisted the lower half of his face, and seeing it, the woman began to scream again.

He danced back and forth from foot to foot, barely able to contain himself as he drew the hammer, the fiberglass haft of it making that delectable slithering sound against the leather of his belt. His hand wrapped up in her hair kept right on winding and winding and winding, the ropes of her bloody hair growing tighter and tighter and tighter around his fingers and across his palm. His eyes caressed her naked skin, probed the secret recesses of her body, stabbed into her own, and her long, agonized scream crackled against the thunderclouds overhead. His smile widened, and he showed her the hammer. Her eyes grew as wide as any woman's ever had before—not only could he see the whites all the way around her irises but also the delightful pink beyond that. Her eyes dilated as the adrenaline hit her blood.

"Oh, yes," he crooned. "Fight! *Fight me!*" He cackled madly into the dismal, delicious night, and he shook her by the hair, doing a mad jig like a drunken leprechaun. He swung the hammer through the air, grinning at the feeling of ineffable power in the muscles across his back and shoulders, laughing at the sound of the hammer head cutting through the air, and she screamed anew when it slammed into the cobbles next to her head.

She kicked at him, heels striking out like a wild animal, and her nails bit into the skin of his wrist on the arm with which he held her hair, and he shook her—*hard*—then pressed her down to the scum-covered bricks, wedging first one knee between her own, then his other knee. He rapped her head against the cobbles, liking the sound of it, then lunged down until he pressed against her from foot to lip. Her heartbeat slammed against his ribs, her breath washed across his lips, her sex ground into his.

"Oh, yes," he moaned. But then she bit him. She latched onto his lip with her teeth, pressing them together as hard as any woman ever had a right to, and blood flooded across his teeth and tongue.

She'd expected to at least cause him pain, and when he laughed, he sprayed hot blood across her face, not even bothering to dislodge her from his lip. After all, what did he care?

Thunder crashed around them as he raised the hammer again. Cold rain splattered across his back as her hot blood splattered across his front. Beneath him, she stiffened while he wilted. Lightning tore at the darkness as the hammer slashed down and up and down and up and down yet again. The shiny metal head of the hammer danced in the murky night, thudding her head into nothing, adding her blood and flesh and skin and bone and brains to the refuse already coating the bricks.

When it was over, when his savagery had drained to a controllable level once more, he shoved her remains away and spit the parts of her that had ended up in his mouth against the wall. He rocked back on his haunches and grinned as the moon peeked through the bloody-black clouds and washed down on him. He savored it a moment, luxuriating in the ecstasy of murder, then performed the last few tasks he had with the woman, almost sad at leaving her in the alley.

Chapter 2
The Smith's
Return

I

Special Agent Gavin Gregory sighed and slapped the case file closed. His neck ached from too many hours poring over the reports, the pictures, the notes scratched in hieroglyphics by other agents, and the sensationalized news articles. He'd read it all before—at least a hundred times—and there was nothing he hadn't seen before despite his hopes that he would discover something new. And yet, he knew he'd go through it all, again and again, until he could write "closed" across the face of the cold case file.

He'd needed something to do during the last week before the long vacation his wife, Maddie, had booked, and going through cold cases fit the bill—desk work, sure, but it also got him home every night, and at a reasonable hour. He'd stopped taking new cases and had handed off low priority cases where he could. She'd arranged for an extended stay—one entire month—on Maui in the hopes of rekindling their relationship, of trying again, of...he had to face it...conceiving another child.

It wasn't that he didn't want those things too, because he did, but he didn't think they needed to go to some high-priced resort. They'd both come from humble beginnings, and it seemed…*wrong* to go to a fancy five-star place where other people just like them would wait on them hand and foot for an entire month. And it wasn't the money—his job paid well for government work, and since Maddie's writing career had taken off, there was plenty of money for the two of them. But still…he felt nervous about the trip, uncomfortable at the thought of doing nothing for four entire weeks. He shook his head to clear those thoughts away. They were going, and that was all there was to it. Maddie wanted it—said she *needed* it—and he was going to do his part.

In his seventeen years at the Bureau, he'd developed a habit of clearing his desk at the end of the day. Of locking case files away, cleaning all the stray junk he pulled out during the day—the paper clips, the eraser, the Post-Its, the stapler, his pencils, and any stray notes. It wasn't only about physical security, either, though that was a big component of it. It felt like the right thing to do. Doing the things that felt right was important to Gavin.

"Hey, Gregory," said Peter Fielding, his direct superior in the BAU. "Have you heard?"

"No, Pete. What did I miss?"

Peter grunted and found the remote for the television mounted in the corner of the bullpen. He unmuted the news feed and peered at the screen. "He's back."

"Who is?"

"The Smith."

Gavin flashed a sour grin at his boss. "That's not funny, Peter."

"Yeah, I know it isn't." He thumbed through the news channels, hunting for one showing the report he wanted. "Look." He gestured at the screen with the remote.

A graphic covered the screen—a street map of New York City, zoomed in on Murray Hill. When the map disappeared, it revealed a pretty young woman with blue-black hair and Asian features. She looked directly at the camera but didn't smile. "It was here, Chet, that the body of a twenty-one-year-old woman was found this morning. According to my contacts within the New York Police Department, the victim was found nude after being bludgeoned to death sometime during the night. The investigation is on-going, but so far, there are no suspects, and, according to my source, except for the bloody hammer used, no evidence has been found." Behind the reporter, men and women covered from head to toe with white nylon suits milled around.

"Is that the forensics team—"

"Yes, Chet, they are still working the scene, and my source indicates there is high confidence within the forensics department that there *will* be other evidence found, particularly on the body of the deceased."

"Terrible, Mona."

"It is at that, Chet."

"Does your source think this crime is related to the other two female victims found in the past few weeks?"

"The NYPD's official stance is that it is too early to tell if the crimes are related, but just between you and me, my source has told me *he* believes there is no doubt."

"Ah. That's *scary* news."

"Indeed," said Mona. "But rest assured that the NYPD's finest detectives are on the case—not only of this particular victim, but my source says all three cases have been taken over by a task force under the command of Lieutenant Kirk Haymond. The police chief, himself, established the task force and handpicked the detectives assigned to it."

"That lieutenant…"

"Kirk Haymond," said Mona.

"His name is familiar."

"It should be, Chet. He led the task force that caught the Subway Slasher five years ago."

"Ah. Then I'm sure he will sort it out soon."

"Let's hope and pray that's the truth, Chet."

Peter muted the feed. "Well?"

Gavin shook his head. "No. Not possible. The Smith's been inactive for too long."

"Maybe, maybe not. He could have changed his MO."

"What, and then change back? Why would he do that?"

Peter shrugged and leaned against the corner of Gavin's desk. "Perhaps he went quiet because you were getting too close. Now, he feels comfortable again."

"Or he tried to stop," mused Gavin.

"Or that," said Peters with a shrug. "Stranger things have happened."

Gavin leaned back in his chair and shook his head. "But, still, Pete. The Smith was active for three and a half years, starting in 2007. Then he just fell off the face of the Earth. No wind down, no similar crimes…just *gone*. What serial killer does that?"

"The smart ones. The ones who don't want to get caught but like it too much to quit."

Gavin shook his head once, a slow arc back and forth. "He didn't…" He sighed. "What you're suggesting is that his personality is organized, thoughtful, and disciplined, yet his crimes don't mesh with that. His crimes were frenzied…opportunistic…*not* planned. Disorganized, in other words."

Peter nodded. "Sure. I get that, but we don't know everything about these guys. Hell, maybe we don't know *anything*, and all this is just mental masturbation. But think about these New York murders. Three beautiful young girls bludgeoned with a hammer in two and a half weeks. He leaves the hammer at the scene, and reading between the lines of good ole Mona's report, he's leaving fluids on the scene."

"Maybe," said Gavin. "If he is, and if we can get the NYPD to share a sample, we can rule The Smith in or out based on that evidence."

"If it is The Smith, he's killing during rainstorms, and even though he's a secretor, the samples might be—"

"Too degraded or corrupted by the storm. I know."

"I hate to do this, Gavin."

"No," said Gavin, shaking his head. "You know I'm on vacation starting at five on Friday, and that we fly out on Monday."

Peter nodded. "I know that, Gavin. You can be back Friday night—Sunday at the latest. All you need to do is go up there, visit the scenes, talk to the detectives… You know, get a feel for it. Get your samples and bring them back. Write it up. We'll do the DNA while you're away, and if we can, we'll nab the bastard before you get home."

Gavin shook his head but said nothing. The sad fact was that he *wanted* to go. That familiar buzz had started in his sinuses the second he'd heard the news report. The buzz that said he was on the right scent, the right track—even though he was on no scent, no track at all. "I don't know, Peter."

Peter nodded. "I understand, Gav. I do. This job is hard on a marriage—especially one that's suffered a tragedy like yours has. You love her. I get it. But listen, you *know* The Smith. You, and you alone, can go up there for two or three days and come back knowing if it's him, and you'll still be back before the weekend."

He shook his head. "I know it bothers you—that The Smith got away, I mean. Hell, it bothers me, too. Gavin. I want to know if this is him. I want to know if he's reactivating, or if it's just some other bozo who likes to pound on blondes with a hammer."

Gavin nodded. He did understand, and truth to tell, he felt exactly the same. "Maddie's going to murder me if this takes more than a couple of days," he murmured. Peter smiled, and Gavin reached for the phone to arrange his travel. "She's going to kill me, and it'll be your fault, Pete."

"Want me to talk to her?"

"Are you insane?"

2

1289 Welcrest Drive, Minnieville, VA
Tuesday, 5:51 pm

Maddie looked up from her laptop and pinned him with her best glare. "You're doing what?"

"Uh, it's only for a day or two, honey. I'll be back by Friday." He looked down at his hands, unable to meet her hostile stare. "It's work. It might be—"

"*Duh.* You'll pick a corpse over me every time." She dropped her gaze back to her laptop screen. "Go away. I'm busy."

"I know it's writing time, but I—"

"You are interrupting my flow, Gavin," she said in a tone devoid of emotion. "I always work around *your* job, it's time you started working around mine since it pays *all* our bills."

"Sorry, it's just that I—"

"Have to go. Am so sorry about this. Blah, blah, blah." She shot a quick, hot-eyed look at him. "Close the door."

Feeling like an utter asshole, Gavin backed out of her office and pulled the door shut without a sound. He turned and walked back to their bedroom, where his garment bag and duffel already lay open on the bed. He moved quickly, getting underclothes from the dresser, a pair of sneakers and some workout clothes from the closet. He added two suits, dress shirts, ties, and his work shoes, then he stepped into the bath to grab his toiletries.

"Sorry," said Maddie from the bedroom doorway.

"No, I'm the one who's sorry. But what I do is important, and sometimes I have to go when I have to go."

"I know," she said, coming up from behind and wrapping her arms around his waist and putting her cheek against his shoulder blade. "But promise me we won't miss the vacation. I've been looking forward to it for a long time."

He put his hands over hers and gave them a gentle squeeze.

"We need this, Gav," she whispered into his back.

"I know. Pete just wants me to go up and see if it's The Smith. That's all I have to do. Go up, talk to a few cops, read a bunch of reports, maybe visit the scenes…"

She sighed. "Just promise me."

"It's only a couple of days, Maddie. I'll be back before the weekend starts."

"We need to go shopping, so you'd better be."

He patted her hands, and she sighed.

They both knew he couldn't make that promise.

After a moment, she released him. "I'd better get back to the novel," she murmured.

"I love you, Madison Gregory. More than anything." He watched her in the mirror.

She stopped, her back to him, and her shoulders slumped. "Yeah," she murmured.

3

LaGuardia Airport, Queens, NY
Tuesday, 9:41 pm

Gavin shuffled down the too-narrow aisle of the plane, his garment bag in front of him, his duffel bag thrown over his shoulder, and his coat draped over his arm. Like all flights to New York City, it had been overstuffed with all manner of people, and the line to disembark moved at a snail's pace.

The woman in front of him kept turning around for no reason he could detect, smashing her backpack into his garment bag and then glaring at him as though he were the one who couldn't hold still. She had the too-dark bronze tan of someone addicted to tanning salons and wore enough makeup for two or three women. He closed his eyes, not wanting to see her anymore, not wanting to be trapped behind her anymore.

"You think squeezing your eyes shut will protect you?" asked the carnival show attraction in front of him.

He snapped his eyes open. The woman had turned to stare at him, arms akimbo, head cocked at a jaunty angle. "You wouldn't know real power if it was staring you in the face."

"Uh…"

"Right, right." She waved her hand in the air like an orchestra conductor. "Uh… Duh… Uh…" she mocked.

"Look, lady, I don't know you and you don't know me. Let's keep it that way, okay?"

"Oh, you want it like that, do you?"

"I want off this plane. I want to get to my hotel and take a hot shower. Those are the things I want."

She grinned as she made a gun from her forefinger and thumb, then shot him with it. "Gotcha, spark." The line beyond her began to move toward the plane's door, and he jerked his chin up, but she didn't move.

"Tell ya what, sparky-spark. You buy me a drink, and I'll tell you a story you *need to hear*."

"Come on," said a woman behind Gavin.

"*FUCK YOU, MOTHERFUCKER!*" the woman screamed.

"Look," said Gavin. "I'm an FBI agent, and causing trouble on a flight is a federal thing these days. You don't want—"

"*What? What am I doing to cause trouble? I just want to save your soul, motherfucker! I'm doing God's will, motherfucker!*"

"Right. I appreciate it, I really do, but right now, we need to deplane so that—"

"*There's no time, sparkster! None! The Rapture could come at* any *moment! Don't you know that? Don't you know anything, spark?*"

Gavin puffed out his cheeks and shifted his garment bag and coat to his left arm. "Ma'am, you need to—"

"*Don't! Just don't, spark!*" she shouted, spittle flying. "*I'm trying to save your ever-fucking soul, dumbass! Are you too stupid to listen? Shall I shake the dust off my feet?*"

The aisle beyond her had cleared, and one of the flight attendants had come halfway from the cockpit to where the woman stood. She stopped there, wringing her hands. Gavin held up his hand, the classic "stop" pose.

The woman in front of him threw a glance over her shoulder. "*Best do as he says, MOTHERFUCKER! I'm* filled with righteousness, and if you push me, I'll smite your whore ass!"

"That's enough!" snapped Gavin in what Maddie called his "cop voice."

The unbalanced woman in front of him whirled her head back to face him. "*DON'T YOU GIVE ME NO COMMANDS, SPARKY-SPARK!*" she screamed in his face. "*Only Gawd can command me! Only GAWD tells me what to do! I'm filled with the SPIRIT, motherfucker! GAWD's ever-fucking love! I'm trying to SAVE you, praise GAWD! Are you too stupid to hear the word of the LORD? Are you too dumb to listen? Are you so motherfucking insane that you'll turn your back on an EMISSARY OF THE LORD GAWD?*"

"You say you're filled with God's love? I'm not feeling very loved at the moment." Gavin draped his garment bag and coat over the back of the seat to his left.

"*ARE YOU QUESTIONING THE BRETHREN? DO YOU DARE TO QUESTION THE BRETHREN, MOTHERFUCKER? The Lord thy GAWD will smite the shit out of you, sparky, if you do that! The Lord thy GAWD sayeth unto you—*" She jerked her head back like some crazy chicken and stared at him as he dropped his duffel into the seat with his garment bag. "*WHAT THE FUCK DO YOU THINK YOU ARE DOING, MOTHERFUCKER?*"

With a grim expression, Gavin took her by the shoulders and spun her in the aisle. "I don't want to arrest you, miss, but you can't do this on a plane. You need to walk down the aisle and get off the plane." He glanced at the flight attendant and gave her a little nod. One that said, "go call for help." She nodded and turned to trot back toward the cockpit.

The unbalanced woman in the aisle cackled like a witch on black sabbath. "*Oh, spark! Oh, sparky-spark-spark! You're killing me. YOU'RE EVER-FUCKING KILLING ME, MOTHERFUCKER! The Lord thy GAWD sent me unto you. He sent me from the wilderness. He sent me from the mouth of the fish. The BELLY of the fish, I mean! He sent me from the gates of Hell itself to save you, spark! And you REJECT him? You REJECT the LORD THY GAWD, spark? Do you? Do ya?*"

"Let's go. One foot in front of the other." Gavin applied a little pressure to her shoulders, and she squawked.

"*You DARE to put your motherfucking hands on me, MOTHERFUCKER? You want to fuck me, don't you, spark? I can tell, I can tell! You want to fuck the Brethren! But you know what the LORD THY GAWD says about fortification! You know what he says about lying down with your uncle? About seeing the Brethren naked, spark?*"

"Time to go," said Gavin in an iron tone. He propelled her down the aisle, and she threw her weight back against him.

"*Dancing! Dancing! That leads to foreplay! That leads to sex! That leads to fortification! That leads to all twenty-five Gates to Hell, spark! But the Lord GAWD has filled me with righteousness, and nothing I do is a sin! I'm here to save you, spark, and if that means letting you fuck me, then so be it!*" She began to unbutton her blouse, still facing away from him. She paused and tilted her head, her whole body seeming to freeze as she thought. "Hey! Maybe we can make *another* one. A brother!" she said in a normal tone, then she shrugged and resumed unbuttoning her blouse. "Be quick about it, spark. The Lord Gawd needs his dinner and hates it if it's late. The Lord Gawd knows I don't want a smack in the chops for not having dinner ready."

"Stop that, miss," said Gavin. "Let's get off the plane and we can talk."

"*Oh ho! NOW, you want to talk! Are you chicken? Scared to fuck one of the Brethren?*" She tucked her hands under her arms and clucked like a child taunting another. "*Got me all riled up with your talk of fortification, but now you want to back out? Well, FUCK you, MOTHERFUCKER! I'm going to save your goddamn soul if it means knocking you down and jumping on your cock! I'm going to fuck your goddamn soul if it means saving you!*"

Gavin sighed and began to move her bodily down the aisle. She grabbed at the seats as they passed, but he kept her moving, pushing her shoulders, bumping her butt with his hip from time to time.

"Foreplay, is it?" she cackled.

He got her all the way to the flight attendants' area before the uniformed airport police arrived.

"Ah!" she cried. "*Satan's Imps! Come for a foursome, boys? Well, get in line. I'm fucking souls by saving 'em, and there's plenty to go around!*" She reached toward the first cop's groin, and he slapped her hand away. "*Oh, no, MOTHERFUCKER! Don't you dare reject the handjob of the Lord thy GAAAWD!*"

Gavin pushed her against the wall that separated the passenger cabin from the cockpit and held her there. For just a moment, something wiggled under his palms. Something that felt scaly and cold. He stared down, but there was nothing there—just the woman and her ugly shirt. "Cuffs," he grunted, shaking his head. She screamed and fought, but Gavin held her pinned, and the four airport cops secured her arms.

"*TURN YOUR FACE AWAY FROM THE LORD THY GAAAAWD AND SEE WHAT BEFALLS YOU, MOTHERFUCKERS! JUST YOU WAIT AND SEE WHO FUCKS YOU NOW! WAIT ON IT! WAIT TO GET YOUR ASSES SMOTE INTO FINE POWDER BY THE BRETHREN!*"

Gavin blew out a breath and stepped back, letting two of the airport cops take her by the arms and frog march her up the gangway. He shook his head at the other cops. "5150," he said.

"You think?" asked one of them with a lopsided grin. "What set her off?"

Gavin laughed. "Getting off the plane, if you'll believe it. She just turned and started screaming at me."

From the gangway, the woman screamed, *"OH YOU'RE FUCKED NOW, FBI-MAN. GAAWD'S WRATH IS GONNA POUND AND POUND AND POUND YOU!"*

"What did she say?" asked Gavin.

"She said, 'Ignore me, I'm crazy as fuck.'"

Gavin laughed. "Yeah, I guess you're right. Need a statement from me?"

The airport cop shook his head. "Nah. She's going straight to Bellevue, I'm sure."

"Right." He turned to go get his things, but a very pretty brunette smiled as she carried them up the aisle and gave them to him. "Thank you," he said.

"Oh, no. Thank you, Agent…"

"Gregory."

She dimpled and cocked her head to the side. "Is that your first name?"

"Gavin," he said, grinning. "Gavin Gregory."

"Ah. Thank you for helping that poor woman."

"Well…"

She chuckled. "And for getting her the hell out of the way."

Gavin nodded once and picked up his gear, his smile fading a little. "Nice meeting you."

"You, too," she said. She reached out and put her hand on his arm. "Uh, can I buy you a drink?"

"Oh." A warm blush crept up his cheeks. "Uh, I appreciate it, but—"

"You're married," she said with a sigh. "Why are all the good ones taken?"

Not knowing what to say, Gavin smiled. "Sorry." He turned and walked up the gangway.

4

Pod 51 Hotel, Manhattan, NY
Wednesday, 6:27 am

The horrid, terrible alarm chirped like a cricket born in the depths of hell, and Gavin groaned. He rolled over and swatted the pillow next to him before he remembered where he was. He rolled to the other side and mashed the off button. His head throbbed, and his throat felt like sandpaper. He opened his eyes, blinking against the bright morning sun blazing through the east-facing windows. Yawning, he threw back the covers and sat up, turning his back to the window.

He had to meet the detectives for a briefing at the Seventeenth Precinct, and roll call was in thirty minutes or so, but all Gavin had to do was wash his face, brush his teeth, put on his suit, and run his hand over his close-cropped hair. And the precinct house was only a block from the hotel.

Gavin made a cup of coffee in the little mutant coffee machine and grimaced at the taste. He grabbed his phone and hit the speed-dial icon next to Maddie's name, knowing she'd have her phone in do-not-disturb mode. He grinned at the sound of her voice in her greeting.

"Hello there, Sleeping Beauty. It's Prince Charming. I'm calling to say I miss you—your bedhead, your dragon-breath, your surly, early-morning attitude. I woke up without a grump next to me telling me to 'shut that fucking alarm clock off,' and, well, it made me think of you. I'm headed out to my briefing in a few minutes and will probably be tied up with the detectives all day, so don't bother calling back. I'll try you again at dinner time. And don't worry, hon, it's doubtful I'll have to leave the precinct house. Anyway, make sure you—"

BEEEP!

"—brush your teeth, or you might kill the dog." He grinned and put his phone in his pocket. He almost never finished a voicemail on Maddie's phone before the damn thing cut him off. He slurped the rest of the disgusting coffee and headed downstairs.

It took him all of three and half minutes to get to the precinct house, and it took three times that long for the desk sergeant to confirm that he was supposed to be there and should be let into the inner sanctum.

"Up the stairs," grunted the sergeant. "Dicks are in roll call, but the bullpen's at the top of the stairs. You can wait there."

"Right. Thanks."

The sergeant waved a hand lackadaisically, already back to reading his paper.

Gavin shrugged and ran up the stairs. The bullpen was a small room overcrowded with desks and perp-chairs. It had an empty cage in the back corner, roughly the size of two refrigerators stood back to back. He walked over to the coffee machine and poured some in a Styrofoam cup.

"You the profiler?" asked a man from the door. He was large, both tall and wide—seeming big enough to play offensive tackle for the Giants. He wore an off-the-rack suit in pale gray and a vividly purple tie over a white shirt. He wore his hair slicked back over the crown of his head, coated in gel.

Gavin tapped his FBI badge that he wore looped in his belt. "Sure. Gavin Gregory, from the Behavioral Analysis Unit."

"Jim Denders," said the man. "We're back here in the meeting room." He turned and moved down the hall. Gavin expected heavy, thudding steps, but the man moved with a grace that belied his stature.

Smiling, Gavin followed him. "How long have you been on the job, Jim?"

"Too fucking long, I'll tell you that right now." He flapped a hand at shoulder height. "Eighteen, nineteen years. I forget. You?"

"Seventeen for me, unless you count a six-year tour as an Army MP."

Jim grunted and glanced over his shoulder. "Keeping assholes in line…it all counts. How'd you get lucky enough to land in this heap of shit?"

Gavin gave him a lopsided smile. "I've been with BAU for a long time. I've seen my share of shit heaps." He shrugged. "I was on The Smith in Virginia."

The cop lifted an eyebrow. "Hard luck, there. I heard you almost had him."

"We did at that. Between me and you, we missed him by less than three days."

"Hard luck," Denders repeated.

"How long have you been homicide?"

"Pssh. Too fucking long." The big detective shook his head. "Thirteen years of this shit." He waved his hand at a conference room with walls that were glass from the chair rail up. "This is us." He led Gavin inside. "Gavin Gregory, FBI." He hooked a thumb at Gavin. "Meet the merry band of asswipes who've pissed someone off at 1PP. Craig Mason, Lenny Mitchell, Andrew Franklin, and that fat bastard is in charge. Lieutenant Kirk Haymond." Each cop nodded his head as Jim introduced him.

"I'm really shit with names," said Gavin. "So, let me issue a blanket apology now."

Jim sank into one of the chairs, and it groaned as it took his weight. "We all answer to detective, so…"

"Right. Well, like Jim said, I'm Gavin Gregory, and I'm with the Feebs." He waited for the few tentative grins to surface, then sat down at the end of the table. "I'm BAU, and I don't give a shit about credit. If I can help you, fine, you take the credit. All I care about is stopping animals like the one the news channels are blabbering about." He held up his hand. "I'm not assuming he's serial. All I've seen are news reports."

"And that's my cue," said Kirk. "Look, Agent Gregory—"

"Gavin is fine."

Kirk nodded. "Gavin, then. Look, no offense, but I didn't request the FBI's help, and if I didn't…"

"I know, Lieutenant. I'm not here to attach to the case. As I told Jim out in the hall, I worked The Smith in Virginia. What I didn't tell Jim is that there are some at the BAU who find the details of your current case…uh…intriguing."

"You think this is The Smith? After all this time?"

"Not necessarily, but we'd like to rule it out. I'm not here to force my help on you, gentlemen. I'm here, hat in hand, asking for your help. I've got a big vacation starting at the end of the week, and I'd like to review your case files and rule The Smith out of this. If I can lend you a few insights along the way, I'm more than happy to do that."

Haymond blew out his cheeks. "You're welcome to review the cases. Fresh eyes, fresh insights. And I don't care about credit in a case like this, either. I just want those red names off my case board. And if it *is* The Smith, you're *welcome* to take the case over."

Jim grunted, staring at the tabletop. "Then I guess it's up to me to run you through the abridged version."

Gavin nodded and pulled out his pad. "Ready when you are."

"Three vics ranging from nineteen to twenty-three. All blonde, all pretty, all bludgeoned to death with a hammer. That's three separate hammers, by the way. We recovered one at each scene. All of the murders occurred during a rainstorm." Jim shrugged. "Gruesome crimes. All the signs point to torture, sexual assault of a kind, then the murders."

"Is your unsub a secretor?"

Jim glanced at Lt. Haymond and twitched his lips. "Yes, and a bleeder—the last one bit him it looks like—but the rain…"

"Right," said Gavin. "I'd like samples, nonetheless. Our lab—"

"No problem," said Haymond.

"Each scene was opportunistic. The twenty-three-year-old in Manhattan Valley, the nineteen-year-old in Greenwich Village—a student at NYU—and the last one, the twenty-one-year-old, in Murray Hill," said Jim. "Luck of the draw, I'd guess, and none of the vics have a single damn thing in common besides how they looked. We've had more time with the first two, and they don't have a single acquaintance in common. They worked in different fields entirely, studied at different schools, and lived in disparate neighborhoods."

"Not much to go on."

"No," said Jim. "Just the damn hammers."

Gavin grimaced. "Let me guess. A forty-ounce steel blacksmith's sledge with a fiberglass, shock-proof haft, purchased at a box store in the last month."

"Dead on," said Lenny Mitchell. "Each one purchased separately and paid for in the self-serve checkout line with cash."

"Self-serve?" asked Gavin leaning forward. "Then you have him on video?"

Mitchell shook his head and sighed. "Nope. The bastard smeared petroleum jelly over the lens from the side before he stepped into view. All we know is his general height from the shit behind him."

"Prints on the cash?"

"Yeah, loads," said Andrew Franklin, "but so far they're clean in New York. We've submitted them for analysis but haven't heard anything back yet."

"Right," said Gavin. "I'll see if I can light a fire." He jotted a note on his pad and looked up at Lenny. "Same store? Anyone see him in the stores?"

"Heh. We should be so lucky. The first one, he bought in the Flatiron District and dropped at the Manhattan Valley scene. The second hammer came from Lenox Hill and ended up at the NYU student's scene in Greenwich Village. The last hammer came from Jackson Heights."

"Purchased at random times?"

Mitchell nodded. "This last hammer was purchased seventeen hours after the first, and three days before the first victim was found—so, sixty hours before the first murder. He bought the second hammer the same day he killed the second victim. Then he waited until the night before last to use the last hammer."

"Hmm. He held onto it for roughly twenty-six days, then?"

"Sounds about right."

Gavin grimaced and stared down at his notes. "I guess I'll start with the pathology reports. The Smith marked his victims. His signature, both in terms of his murders and like an artist signs a painting, if you will."

Haymond shook his head. "I don't like the sound of that. We've held it back, but with all three of our victims, the unsub used the narrow end of the hammer to mark the small of each woman's back."

Keeping his head down, Gavin shook it from side to side. "Was it a religious icon?"

"No," said Jim. "It was a symbol. Some lines."

Gavin closed his eyes, suddenly nauseous and a little dizzy, his face cold. The room was as silent as a grave, with the breathing of six men the only sound. "A series of stacked lines?"

"Fuck," muttered Jim.

Gregory sucked in a deep breath and puffed out his cheeks as he exhaled. "Five blows?"

"Yeah," said Kirk Haymond. "A horizontal line then four diagonals beneath it. It almost looks Asian."

"Like this?" Gavin flipped to a new page of his notebook and drew:

As Gavin flipped it around so they could see it, Jim grunted and met his gaze. "What does that shit mean?"

Gavin sighed and slumped back, leaving the pad in the center of the table. "The best cryptography came up with when The Smith was active was the Gaelic letter 'gay.' G, in other words."

"An initial?"

Gavin shrugged. "We never made any traction on it. Hell, it could be just a random shape the asshole likes."

"Then it's him? The Smith?" asked Lieutenant Haymond.

"I can't say, but I certainly can't rule it out. This mark—hell, even that he left a mark—was kept out of the press. The exact shape was never distributed outside the FBI."

"Yeah, I remember the circulars said something about the small of the back and to contact the FBI for further details."

Gavin nodded. "That's right."

"And this is the mark? No question?" asked Haymond.

"I want to see your pathologist's pictures, but it's a distinctive shape."

The lieutenant turned a stern gaze on his detectives. "I don't want to hear chatter around the house about The Smith being back. Not one word to anyone about this possibility. No girlfriends, no wives." His gaze settled on Andrew Franklin. "No hot Asian reporters. Am I understood?" He waited a moment, meeting each detective's gaze until the man nodded, then Kirk looked at Mitchell and nodded.

"On it," he said and left the room.

Jim grunted and shifted in his chair. "This has to be a copycat, right?"

Gavin shrugged. "Rader took a longer break. And we don't know The Smith took a break at all. Maybe he changed his ritual and is only now getting back into the swing of things."

"Har-har," murmured Denders.

Agent Gregory felt the heat rising on his cheeks. "Poor choice of words, but you know what I mean. And maybe he went to Canada for a while."

"How likely is this change of MO?"

"The MO? We see that all the time. The MO is dynamic, it's what the killer tweaks to perfect his kill ritual, but the signature? That's very unlikely. So unlikely that most consider it impossible."

"Right," said Kirk, looking at Franklin. "That's on you, Andy. Start with the City, then go to the State,

34   ERIK HENRY VICK

then hit the national databases. Look for…" He turned a questioning glance on Gavin.

"Strange, multiple bruise patterns on the small of the back. Stress on multiple. A single bruise across the spine isn't what we want. We want a pattern, and something not attributable to furniture or ligatures or anything like that."

"Got it," said Franklin. He rose from the table and left the room.

"Jim, after he has his look at the ME's photos, take Agent Gregory to see that crazy shrink."

Gavin arched an eyebrow.

"Come on, Kirk! We don't have time for all this—"

"She said this was The Smith, didn't she? She said that after the press got the story about the second victim." Haymond stood. "It'll only take a few hours."

Jim scowled and sucked his teeth. "You're the boss."

Craig looked at Gavin and frowned. "We got this psychiatrist calling all the time. Name of Deborah Esteves. She claims she can help us. Says she treated The Smith in 2014."

Gavin's eyes widened. "And she called the NYPD? Is she in the City?"

"Nah," said Jim sourly. "She's at Kingdom Cross."

"It's one of the old state mental hospitals. Now private," said Kirk from the door. "Couple of hours west in a town called Lily's Glen."

Lenny Mitchell hustled into the room, stepping by Haymond with a nod. "Here you go, Agent."

"It's just Gavin." He took the three photographs from the detective and gave them a cursory glance. "From memory, these are a close match. If you can make me copies, I'll send them to Quantico for a forensic match."

"We'll have them for you by the time you get back from Lily's Glen."

Gavin glanced at Jim and nodded. "Good enough. Can we visit the scenes later this afternoon, as well?"

"Not much to see," said the detective.

With a shrug, Gavin said, "It helps me get a feel for the crimes. Pictures are good, but they are flat, lifeless. I want to see the living places, to stand where the unsub stood, to look around."

"I'll give you the nickel tour," said Jim. "No skin off my nose."

"You two get a move on," said Lt. Haymond. "I'll call ahead so the doc knows you're coming."

5

Kingdom Cross Psychiatric Hospital, Lily's Glen, NY
Wednesday, 10:27 am

Jim pulled into the official vehicles lot behind the hospital and killed the engine. Using his thick thumb, he pointed at the giant rectangular building and sighed. "This is likely a huge waste of time."

"But… Aren't we here to see a psychiatrist?"

Denders smiled with half his mouth. "Oh, sure."

"Then?"

"What Haymond didn't mention is that she made quite a name for herself a few years back. A lot of people think this is exactly where she needs to be, though not as a doctor."

Gavin shook his head. "I don't understand."

"Deborah Esteves used to work over in Gilead County. At the jail."

Jim glanced at him, and Gavin shook his head again.

"The county seat is Saint Mary, New York."

"The Saint Mary Psycho," Gavin said.

"Yeah. She was into that mess up to her neck. She transferred three patients here from the jail after having them declared unfit to stand trial and convinced a judge to put them into her care. Three men. One of them—"

"Look, Jim, are you slowly building up to—"

Nodding, Jim said, "Esteves claims one of the patients she transferred to Kingdom Cross is the guy who confessed to being The Saint Mary Psycho, though according to her, he isn't."

"Um…okay." Gavin dragged the last word out. "*And* she claims to have treated The Smith?"

"Right. Want to hear how much worse it gets?"

"I'm not really sure."

"Esteves claims that The Psycho suspect was possessed by demons or some shit."

"And she's still practicing?"

Jim shook his head, a sour grin on his face. "It gets worse."

"Not possible," said Gavin with a dark frown.

"Oh, it is. The other two she's got tucked away in there? Cops. One is the father of one of The Psycho's victims, a sergeant, and the other was his corporal."

"The ones The Psycho confessed to?"

Jim nodded. "You bet."

"I have a vague memory of something about The Psycho kidnapping a detective in Saint Mary?"

"Yeah. *After* this bozo was taken into custody. The kidnapping happened in the jail parking lot the night they brought him in."

"Why do I find myself waiting for the other shoe?"

Jim nodded, staring out through the front windshield. "The state police kept all of this out of the press, but both of the male cops were found in the cabin where they found the missing detective. The kidnapping victim, I mean. The good doctor found them but says the 'real' kidnapper had already split. The Psycho, she says."

"And the guy who confessed—"

The big detective shrugged. "Some say she coached him. Taught him how to beat the CPL 730.30 examiner. How to trick him."

"And the two cops?"

"One was clunked on the head with a hatchet, one was shot. They've never recovered. Catatonic or some shit," said Denders.

Gavin stared at the back of the hospital, feeling numb. Ambushed. Most of the ground floor had three feet of orange bricks rising from the ground, then four feet of smoked glass, and then more orange brick. He craned his head forward and looked up. The top of the building was wrapped in chain-link and security-glass. "Tell me they're not up there."

"Can't do it," said Jim. "That would be lying. She's got them all in the locked unit up top. Besides the nurses and psychiatric technicians, they are allowed no visitors without her explicit approval." He pulled the keys from the ignition, opened the door, and stepped out. "Come on. Let's get this over with."

Shaking his head, Gavin got out and followed Jim around to a guarded entrance, where they showed their credentials and signed an injury waiver before gaining admission. They walked to the main information desk and signed in. The receptionist pointed them to some uncomfortable-looking chairs and paged Doctor Esteves.

She kept them waiting for fifteen minutes, and when she finally came, she wore a mask of irritation. "It's about time!" she snapped.

"Funny," said Jim in a mild tone, "I was just thinking the same thing."

"I called the NYPD after the second victim—*two weeks* ago! If you'd come see me then, that last poor girl—"

"This really isn't the place for this, Doctor," said Gavin. "I'm Gavin Gregory. I work at the Behavioral Analysis Unit in Quantico—"

"FBI?" She quirked an eyebrow at him.

"Yes."

That seemed to mollify her a little. "Well…good."

"And," said Jim, "we're here now. When you contacted the NYPD before, we had no reason to suspect a serial murder. There wasn't even a task force set up at the time."

"But there is now?" asked Esteves.

Denders made a show of glancing around. "Perhaps it would be better to continue this conversation in private?"

Doctor Esteves sniffed. "Follow me." She turned and walked away, heading toward a door with an electronic lock. She punched in a six-digit code and the door popped open. "We should start in my office, anyway." She glanced back at them over her shoulder. "Set up some ground rules."

Gavin smiled, and Denders shook his head.

She led them through a veritable warren of corridors and electronically locked doors, and finally to a room with her name stenciled on a plaque beside the door. She fit a key into the lock, turned it, and stepped into a comfortable-looking office with pale tan carpet and dark leather furniture. An overstuffed bookshelf took up one whole wall, and a credenza sat along the other wall behind her desk and large leather executive desk chair. The fourth wall was mostly smoked glass that overlooked a small courtyard area filled with greenery.

Esteves waved a languid hand at the two upholstered chairs on the other side of her desk and sank into her executive chair behind it. She scooched forward and folded her hands on her desk. "Now, I want to start by telling you that I can absolutely help you solve your case. The perpetrator hasn't been called 'The Smith' in the press, but—"

"Why would you compare these crimes to that of The Smith?" asked Gavin.

She treated him to a withering look that still managed to convey her exhaustion. "How many men are there who enjoy killing blondes with a hammer?"

"You'd be surprised," said Jim.

"No, I wouldn't," said Esteves. "Not after what I've seen." She turned to Gregory. "And to answer your question, Agent Gregory, I know this is The Smith because I had the displeasure of knowing him in 2014."

"Knowing him? I thought you claimed you had treated him?" asked Jim.

A spasm flashed across the doctor's face. "Yes, I did. It's complicated, though, so please let me come back to those details."

Jim glanced at Gavin and shrugged.

"Still," said Gavin, "even if you knew him well, why did you make the jump from 2014 to now? And why assume someone being bludgeoned to death is—"

"Look," she said, "the answers to those questions are complicated—as I just said. Can we leave it at 'I have my reasons?' I promise that by the time we are done, you will understand."

"Go on, then," said Gavin.

"I had contact with both The Smith and The Saint Mary Psycho. And I can tell you, that despite their differences, the perpetrator behind each series is the same."

Gavin shook his head. "No."

"Yes," she said. "The crimes were committed by the same hand, Agent. Those and more. The Smith isn't your average, run-of-the-mill serial killer."

"Understand me, please, Doctor," said Gavin. "When I deny your assertion, the denial is based on accepted science. Serial killers have signatures that fulfill their needs, their compulsions, if you will. They may change their MOs, refine their methods, their targeting, but that signature, that's the thing that gives them release. They never change that."

"As I said, The Smith isn't the average serial killer. He doesn't kill out of compulsion, out of ritual."

"No?" asked Gavin. "Then why?"

Esteves nodded to herself. "He kills because he hates."

Gregory leaned back in his chair. "Well…yeah, the nature of his crimes tells us that. But that doesn't make him unique. Quite the contrary, in fact. And the established theory includes anger as a motive. This is—"

"I didn't say anger, Agent Gregory. I said, 'he hates.' And he does. He hates us all."

Gavin shook his head. "That seems like hair-splitting, Doctor."

She nodded, arching an eyebrow. "I can see why it might, but that's because you are judging my answer out of context. I don't mean he hates blondes. Or women. The personality responsible for those murders hates *humans*. You, me, the detective here, your wives, my daughter, *everyone*. He hates us, and he wants to kill us all."

"Then why stick to one at a time?" asked Jim. "Why not drive a big German car through a crowd of people standing in line? Or detonate a bomb at a rock concert? Or hide a nuclear weapon in a vending machine and ship it to a sports stadium? Why go at it piecemeal?"

"Because he also hates the person committing the murders."

"Self-hate is—" began Jim.

"Um, what do you mean he hates *the person* committing the murders? *He* is the person committing the murders, is he not?"

"No!" snapped Esteves. She took a moment, fighting for calm. "Do you want coffee? A soda?"

Both men shook their heads.

"Can we move on? Can you accept, for now, what I say? I promise I can help you find your murderer, and that the truth of what I'm saying will all become clear along the course of the story."

"Story?"

"I can help you stop these crimes." She nodded at Gavin. "Probably closing a slew of cold cases at the same time. But to avoid all this back-and-forth, you have to listen to my story first."

Gavin glanced at Jim and nodded. "We came this far," the big detective said. "In for a penny and all that."

Debbie nodded and laid her hands flat on her desktop. Gavin noticed her hands were shaking as she did so. She pressed her palms into the wood until her fingers and knuckles turned white. "We thought we'd stopped all of it, back in 2015. The price was terrible— one of my best friends...lost"—she shook her head sadly—"and three men live upstairs, two with no memory of our friendship, of the years we worked together, and the other trapped in the world of right now. They don't even recognize each other; they've been friends for almost thirty years. It's as if their memories were wiped clean, but I think I know why. I think I can help you avoid the same fate, should you catch up to...The Smith." She turned her head toward the window, her gaze unfocused, her stare taking on that thousand-yard quality of post-traumatic stress. "We thought we had him trapped. We thought we knew how to beat him."

"Trapped?" asked Gavin, arching his eyebrow at Jim Denders.

"We were so stupid! We didn't understand him at all." She shook her head. "We only understood what he *wanted* us to understand." She brought her gaze back to the two law enforcement officers seated across from her. "You see, these murders in New York City, and a spate of other crimes across the country...they are our fault. We were arrogant, and so many others paid for our mistakes." She shook her head, and a single tear tracked down her cheek. "He *played* with us. He *used* us."

"He?" Gavin repeated quietly, and her eyes focused on his face. "Do you know his name?"

"One day, back in the fall of 2014, one of the patients—one of the men upstairs—was the desk sergeant of Saint Mary's First Street Police Station. He—the desk sergeant—was also the father of one of The Saint Mary Psycho's victims, a college student named Beth. She was killed while she was home on summer break. On that strange day in September, a man—also one of the men upstairs—walked into the First Street Station..." She paused, taking a deep breath and shaking her head. "At first, we assumed he was mentally ill, but he was so much more than mentally ill. Sergeant John Jenkins had been a cop for twenty-seven years and believed he'd seen it all...

Chapter 3
The Confession

I

Sergeant John Jenkins had been a cop for twenty-seven years, and he believed he'd seen it all. He'd seen the craziest of the crazies come out of the woodwork every full moon. Thirteen hell-nights a year for twenty-seven years had given him heavy calluses to the unbelievable, but when the disheveled man came stumbling into the police station, haloed by the bright spring sunshine, he had the feeling he was in for something novel, something to set his heart hammering like the double-bass at an Avenged Sevenfold concert.

The man came inside, sun-blind and blinking against the relative gloom, turning a flat gaze on every person visible. When his eyes came to rest on John's, the policeman caught a shiver, and the empty-eyed man smiled. The grimy man strode up to the duty desk, as bold as you please, and thumped his dirty fist down next to John's nameplate. He peered down at it for the space of ten heartbeats, then brought his gaze up and pinned John with it.

"Hello, Sergeant Jenkins."

"Hello," John said. "May I help you?" The man stank like he'd never considered bathing, let alone gotten wet. His clothing was in a horrible state of disrepair. The dirty khaki cargo pants bore a rip along their inner seam from mid-thigh to right below the knee, and the once-white polo shirt had more in common with storm clouds than pristine snow and exposed almost as much of the man's torso through rips and tears as it hid.

"Yes, sir. Or at least I soap you fan," said the man. His voice sounded like a rusty saw blade dragged across a cheese grater.

"Uh, what did you say?"

The man smiled and nodded. "Sorry. Medical rendition. I sometimes mix up my nerds. *Words!* I sometimes say the wrong word. I said, I hope you can help me."

Ah, a 5150, thought John. "Happy to help if I can." *If I can understand your word-salad, that is.*

The man pursed his lips, then frowned down at John's desk. "It's… Bell, you see…" He laughed too loudly and turned his head to peer over his shoulder, then whirled around as if checking if someone were sneaking up on him.

John nodded and waited. It was a powerful ally—silence—for anyone who needed to get information out of a recalcitrant speaker.

The man brought his gaze back to meet John's. "I can whelp you, too."

"You can help me?"

The man nodded frantically as if eager to please. "Oh, yes. I'm…"

John suppressed a sigh and twitched his lips. "Spit it out, son. You've come all this way and made it to my desk. Might as well get things off your chest and out in the open where they can breathe." John thought that was a nice touch, but the man grimaced. "Let's start with your name."

"It's hard, sir. He-he-he doesn't… I don't think I remember my… That is, I plant…" He frowned, shaking his head, and cleared his throat. "He doesn't haunt…uh, doesn't *want*"—he drew a deep breath before rushing on—"*me to tell you.*"

"Who? Who doesn't want you to tell me?"

"*Glaaachk*—" The man's throat constricted, cutting off the flow of air over his vocal cords. "*Glaaaachka*—"

"Relax, son," said John in his warmest cop voice. "Don't think about it. Think about something you like, and somewhere in the middle of your pleasant thoughts, just spit it out."

The man nodded, and a far-away expression smoothed the lines of his face. He sighed and slumped where he stood, a small grin teasing its way onto his lips. "*Glacadairanam*," he blurted after a few minutes.

"Uh, okay. Who is that, and what's your name?"

"I-I-I-I-I-I—" With each stuttered vowel, the man's eyes grew wider and wider, his face redder and redder. His jaw and throat went on working as if he were choking long after he ran out of air to stutter with.

"*Relax*, son," said John, again. "I'm here to help you. No one here will hurt you. You're safe."

The man jerked his head back as if John had spat in his eye. "Strafe? *Chafe?*" He grimaced, his jaw and tongue working. "*SAFE?* You think you can make me fucking safe? Are you insane? I'm not *safe!* I'm never *safe!* How can I *ever* be safe with him riding me?"

John slid back from his desk, preparing himself for a fight, but he held up his hands in a placating gesture. "All I meant is that none of us will hurt you. We're on your side."

The man frowned even deeper than before and shook his head. "No. No, you're not on my tide. TH! I'm the *enemy*, Sergeant."

Trying to keep a reasonable, helpful expression on his face, John said, "You're not *my* enemy, son. I don't have any enemies."

The man laughed, and it contained a hysterical edge. "You only say that because you don't know who I am." He leaned forward with a conspiratorial air. "What I've *done.*"

Moving casually as if stretching, John reached behind him and opened the pouch on his service belt that contained his Broadsword Redfire pepper spray. Then he slid his hand to the handcuff pouch and undid that flap as well. "Well, let's start with who you are. Try the same trick as before," he said in a reasonable, we're-all-friends tone.

The man blew out a breath and let his eyes slide shut. "I don't remember my…" He appeared to spend considerable effort to get back to his happy place, but the muscles of his face twitched and writhed as if at war with one another. Finally, the man sighed. "It's no use. Maybe I can trick my memory by signing my name."

John nodded and grabbed a stack of sticky-notes and a ballpoint pen. "Sure. Give it a try."

Taking the pad and the pen, the man's face twitched and wriggled, and then gave birth to a sigh of relief. "This'll jerk. Yeah, this will smirk just sine." He set the pad down on the edge of John's desk and bent over it. The pen tip scratched and scratched for at least a minute before he straightened, a grin stretching from ear-to-ear. Once again, he heaved a sigh of relief, a sigh of pleasure, and let his shoulders slump. He waved his hand at the pad.

John reached for it in the slow way he stretched his hand out for a strange dog to sniff, ready to jump away if the guy went nuts—well, *more* nuts—and picked up the pad. He turned it around so he could read it. His eyes tracked back and forth over the chicken-scratch paragraph the crazy man had written.

After he'd read it all, his hand jumped to the butt of his sidearm, flicking aside the safety strap that held it in his holster, and he jerked the pistol out, pointing it at the man's chest. "*Get down, you sick fuck!*" John yelled in a voice much too loud for inside the station. "Get your fucking face on that carpet before I unload this into your chest!"

Nodding as though John had said nothing more than a pleasant how-do-you-do, the man extended his arms and bent to put his palms on the ground. He kicked his legs out behind him and did the reverse of a pushup until he lay flat on the police station's pale green carpet. He lay face down, his nose buried in the carpet, and began to weep.

John's pulse slammed in his ears, and he could *feel* his pulse drubbing away in the arteries in his neck. For the first time in his long career, rage threatened to over-power his judgment, and he felt a burning hatred for the man prostrate before him. He side-stepped once, then again, moving around the man with wide steps, keeping the gun zeroed on his trunk.

He heard other officers running to help, their footfalls like war drums. *It's now or never*, he thought, his finger tightening on the trigger. He wanted more than anything to shoot the motherfucker lying at his feet. He wanted to do more than that, to empty all fifteen 40-caliber rounds out of his Glock 22, then slap in his spare mag and do it all again. Rage thrummed inside him like a dose of high-amp electricity. He stepped forward, extending both arms as he aimed the Glock at the greasy hair covering the back of the bastard's head.

"Yes," said the man into the carpet. "Yes, John. Please. *Please.*"

"John? Everything okay?"

John squeezed his eyes shut. *Okay, then. Never.* He forced himself to step back, to take his finger off the trigger of his pistol. Forced himself to take a long, calming breath. But he still didn't trust himself to speak, didn't trust that he could keep his emotions at bay. He took another step back and dropped the hand holding his pistol to his side. He lifted his gaze from the back of the man's head and turned his eyes on his corporal, Larry Bateman. He gestured at the man, then flicked his eyes to the pad. Then he shut his eyes so he wouldn't have to see the sympathy in Larry's face. He shut his eyes because he thought seeing that sympathy, that *pity*, might drive him insane.

He heard Larry pick up the pad, heard him gasp, heard him call the other officers to cuff the suspect—because that's what he was now, a suspect—heard the rage thrumming in Larry's voice. He kept his eyes shut, standing still amid the flurry of activity as other officers rushed forward to take the man into custody.

When Larry put his hand on John's shoulder, John let his Glock fall to the pale green carpet at his feet. "John… My God, John…"

John shook his head and squeezed his eyes shut against the pain of it, against the agony of what the man had written on the pad. He wished he could unsee it, but the words had burned into his memory, had sunk into the structure of his gray matter, fused to his soul.

2

SMPD First Street Station, Saint Mary, NY
September 17, 2014, 6:33 pm

Hello, the note scrawled on the sticky note said. *I'm the one you call The Saint Mary Psycho. TH! I know who you are, and I'm sorry. I'm so worry, Sergeant. I butchered your slaughter, Beth, with a hatchet in a sachet three months ago, but she wasn't my first, and she wasn't my worst. Not by a long shot. Glacadairanam made me do all those wings, and I don't want to sew this anymore. Please mill me. It's the only way I can be free of him. TH! PLEASE SHOOT ME IN THE HEAD UNTIL I'M FED RED DEAD!*

Angel Kirk read the note again, then stood frowning down at it. "And he gave this to John? Is he a lunatic?"

"He did, and I think he must be," said Corporal Bateman. "When I came in, John… Uh…"

"Jesus," said Angel. "How is that man still alive?" She met Larry's gaze. "John is a strong man"—she shook her head slowly—"I don't think I could have stopped myself." She tossed the pad of sticky notes to her desk and brought her hand up to rub her brow. "*Jesus.*"

"Yeah," said Larry.

"Is John okay?"

"I…" Larry released a pent-up breath. "I think he will be, but I don't think we should test his resolve."

"Yeah," sighed Angel. "And this lunatic is in the box?"

"Chained to the fucking table. Oh, and get this: John said he talks like an idiot. Swaps in rhyming words for what he really means."

"Like in the note. Awesome. An idiot nutjob."

"And he's *crying* because John is a better man than he is. *Sobbing* because John didn't off him like he wanted.

"Crazy fuck. Goddamn crazy fuck." Kirk punctuated each sentence with a slap of her other hand on her desk. "And now I've got to go in there and pretend to be the bastard's friend. I've got to go in there and see if he's the lunatic who killed John's baby girl or if he's just some dumb motherfucker with a death wish." She dropped her hand from her brow and looked up at Larry. "Jesus. How am I going to keep from bashing his motherfucking skull in with a coffee cup if he really is The Psycho?"

"Get in line, Detective. It starts with me, and I'm right behind John."

"Right. Jesus." She fished the pad closer and squinted at it. "Who—or what—the fuck is Glacadairanam?"

"You got me, Angel. From what little John said, this asshole claims Glacadairanam is stopping him from telling us his name. Or maybe made him forget it. Who the fuck knows?"

"Jesus," said Angel. "Can we just shoot the bastard fuck and bury him in the woods?"

Larry grinned, and it was a gruesome sight. "Fine by me."

Angel released a huge breath and shook her head. "Better call Dr. Esteves. You know we're going to need her for an eval before we lock him in a cell."

"Oh, no. We're not sending this mother—"

"If he's as nutty as a fruit bat, yes, we are, Larry. Know why?"

"How can you even think about it?" Larry's face burned crimson, his voice molten steel dropped in ice-cold oil. "How can you think of letting that goddamn—"

"Slow your roll, Corporal. I'm *not* thinking of letting him off, I'm thinking of making sure he goes to prison. For *life*. If he's a nutter, and we get a confession out of him without having him checked out, any competent defense attorney is going to eat that up."

"But—"

"No, Larry," said Angel, her tone going from hot to exhausted. "We do this right. For John. For his little girl, and we *make that motherfucker pay.*"

3

Angel crossed the small concrete-block room and slapped her cheap notebook down on the metal table across from the sobbing man. He had his head down, resting his forehead on his crossed arms. She had to take a moment to stop her hands from shaking, to stop them from reaching over and banging the man's head into the table until he quit bawling like a baby.

Or died.

She sucked in a breath and blew it out, going for a cold calm, and settling for non-murderous rage. "Okay. You've put on your show. You can stop the waterworks and the crazy act now. Sit up. I've got questions that need answers." The man didn't acknowledge her, didn't stop his wretched sobbing, didn't lift his head. "Before we go any further, I need to read you your rights. You have the right to remain silent. Anything you say can and will be used against you in a court of law. You have the right to an attorney. If you cannot afford an attorney, one will be provided for you. Do you understand the rights I have just explained to you? With these rights in mind, do you wish to speak to me?"

"Lawyer, ha!" murmured the man into his arms. "What good is a lawyer?"

"Do you waive your right to an attorney? You realize that anything you say here will be used to prosecute you?" A digital camera ran in the corner of the room, capturing both audio and video, and Angel wanted his Miranda warning to be perfect. *Be damned if I leave him a loophole,* she thought.

"Yeah, yeah. Who dares about hat either? I wanted him to send this torture, to flop me, to…to…" He lunged to his feet, eyes blazing, and Angel scooted away as fast as she could. "*WHY DIDN'T HE KILL ME?*"

Angel narrowed her eyes and clenched her jaw, scanning the man's face, his expression, and most of all, the look in his eyes, assessing him, trying to decide if she believed his act. "Sit," she ordered, pointing at his overturned chair.

The man glanced down at his handcuffed wrists and shook them back and forth as though he had a chance in hell of breaking them. The table creaked and groaned as he threw his weight against the bolts that held it to the floor. Angel's notebook rattled to the floor.

"Settle down and take your seat, or I'm going to let some of my fellow officers come in here and *help* you take your seat."

The man froze in mid-shake and just stood there, arms extended to the left, drool dripping to form a small puddle on the tabletop. "I want to gouge out my sighs. *Eyes!* Flew out my own lung. *TH! Tongue!* Please. Let me noose."

Yeah, he's sane, she thought derisively. *Hardly need to waste Debra Esteves' time on a 730 exam.* Deep inside, part of Angel felt like crying, a part felt like screaming, another part felt like curling into a tight ball. And yet another part felt like putting a bullet in the sick fuck's head. "Well, I can hardly let you do any of those things, whatever they are. Ass in the chair."

He turned and glanced behind him, then rattled the handcuffs once more.

"Right." She walked around the table and righted the chair. "Now, sit," she said, leaning in close to show she wasn't scared by his antics. "Or I'll *make you sit.*"

"Wheeze kill me," he said in a voice devoid of anything human. "Shill me. Drill me. Sew it. *Kill me!*"

"That's not going to happen, either." She stared at him for a moment in silence. "You know what? I can't decide which has a better chance of driving me to put a bullet in your sorry ass, that this was a cruel hoax, or that what you wrote on that pad is the truth." She felt her cheeks go warm, and she couldn't resist a glance up at the camera.

He lifted his eyes and met her gaze with candor. "Truth. Honest."

"You're The Saint Mary Psycho?"

Ever so slowly, he wagged his chin up, then down. "*Here*, anyway."

"What's that mean?"

"Other places they…uh…I mean, the sicknames…*nicknames*"—he took a deep breath—"The Hangman, The—"

"Wait just a fucking minute. Are you trying to tell me you are behind those murders, too? The ones in Texas?"

He shrugged.

"Come on. That's crazy. The Hangman had killed seventeen starting in 2004. The Saint Mary Psycho got the credit for twenty-one starting in 2013. Am I supposed to believe *you* did all that, crazy as a fuck-bug like you are, and-and-and no one caught you?" He met her gaze, and the terror in his eyes chilled her to the core. "*Jesus*," she muttered.

4

SMPD First Street Station, Saint Mary, NY
September 17, 2014, 7:09 pm

Debra Esteves used her ID card to open the gate of the restricted lot behind the First Street Station and found a space amid the marked police cruisers. It was strange to see so many cars in the lot during the middle of the shift, but the full moon was only a night or two away, and Debbie figured they had a lot of arrests to deal with. She sat a moment, trying to gather her thoughts…and to finish the disgusting, cold cheeseburger she'd picked up from McGregor's on her way from the hospital.

Larry Bateman had called just as she was packing up to leave the jail for the evening. Angel Kirk needed a suspect evaluated—someone who'd made quite a stir by the sound of it. It was a common enough request, but Debbie wished it had come at another time. She'd promised to attend her daughter's school play later that evening, and she wanted to keep that promise. She drew a deep breath and pushed thoughts of the play, her daughter, her life, out of her mind. These evaluations helped pad Denise's college fund. They were *necessary.*

Debbie grimaced down at the burger, and then at the slime of ketchup all over her hand. She shoved the mess into the grease-speckled bag and crumpled it up, taking a big swig of Dr. Pepper to wash the taste and memory of the cruel meal down. With another sigh, she opened her door and climbed out. It was quiet—too quiet for the number of cars in the lot and the number of arrests it implied. She walked to the staff-only entrance and waved her ID at the scanner set into the wall. The door buzzed to admit her, and Debbie entered the hallway that served as the building's spine.

The eerie soundtrack (or lack of it) continued inside. It shared the feel of the morgue, or maybe the local library. The susurration of the ventilation system competed with the murmur of voices kept low. Angel had said the suspect was in the interrogation room, and with a glance in the empty detectives' squad room, Debbie turned and knocked on the observation room door.

Larry Bateman opened the door and then stood back to let her in, but without his usual joke and smile. Debbie's stomach tightened as she took in the small room filled with grim-looking patrolmen and detectives. "Ladies and gents," she said and flashed her patented Debbie Esteves smile.

No one smiled back.

5

Angel folded her arms across her chest and scowled at the man. "I already told you. We're waiting on a *doctor*. She's going to evaluate you, and see if—"

"Don't see ridiculous," said the man chained to the table.

"Ridiculous?" Kirk threw her hands in the air. "*I'm* not the one who waltzed in here—"

"I sold you. I *told* you, and I fold you about that. *Glaaachk—*" His throat spasmed and cut off his air as it had a hundred times before.

Angel waved it off. "Yeah, yeah. Don't strain your brain again." She sat for a moment glaring down at her chipped nails. "Look, whatever your name is, you're going to have to offer *some* kind of substantiation of your claims."

"I don't care if you believe me or not. I *am* the Faint Mary Psycho, and I-I-I kuh-killed all those pretty swirls. *Glaaaaachka*—" His throat seized yet again until he gave up and shook his head. "*He* made me do it. I couldn't stop him, so maybe *I* didn't kill them, but my body did."

"Yup. Tell me again how he made you do it?"

"He *rode* me like a horse. I-I-I could tree, but I couldn't control my muscles. I couldn't stop him—flop myself. All I could do was watch."

"Right. So, tell me some of the things you watched yourself do."

"Not *me*, my *body*."

"Right, whatever. Give me a sneak-peek, and then after you talk to the doctor, you can tell me all of it."

"Here I am," said Debbie, entering through the door that led to the observation room.

Angel glanced at her with a weary air and stood. "This is Dr. Esteves—the one I was telling you about. I'm going to step out to give you privacy."

The man scoffed and tossed his head toward the mirrored glass. "I'm possessed, not cupid."

Angel shook her head and stepped into the observation room.

Larry glanced at her. "What's she doing?"

"If I had to guess, I'd say she's seen something that would make a confession inadmissible. In other words, she's doing what I called her here to do." Angel looked around, noting the not-quite-friendly stares. "Look, we all want this bastard motherfucker to fry, but since the powers that be have seen fit to stop enforcing the capital punishment in this state, we'll have to settle for as much time in Clinton or Sing Sing as we can get." She stabbed her thumb at the glass. "She's here to make sure whatever we get from this idiot sticks, and if that means we have to wait until he's had his fucking meds, then that's what we're going to do!" Her voice swelled louder and louder as she went on until she almost yelled the last few words.

In the interrogation room, Debbie Esteves turned to look at the mirror, then returned her gaze to the disheveled man seated on the other side of the table.

6

SMPD First Street Station, Saint Mary, NY
September 17, 2014, 7:19 pm

John Jenkins sat on the hard, wooden bench in the locker room. He had the place to himself—every other officer that could be there was in the observation room watching the show, but that was the last place John wanted to be.

Company was the last thing he wanted.

Stupid! he railed at himself. *Should have blown that motherfucker away when I had the goddamn chance! I'm such a pussy! Now, I get to go home and tell Elizabeth that I failed her again, that I could have put a bullet in the head of the sick fuck that killed our baby, but I didn't have the spine for it. Now, I have to look at myself in the mirror every fucking morning, knowing that bastard is alive and probably having the time of his life in some cushy Club Med asylum.* He looked down at the Glock in his lap. "I should have killed him. I should have used you and let him have it. Like he wanted."

His face settled into hard lines as he picked up the firearm. He pulled the slide a quarter of the way back and checked the chamber. He thumbed the magazine release and let the loaded magazine clatter to the floor.

The gun slid into his mouth, and except for the faint taste of gun oil, it felt right.

7

SMPD First Street Station, Saint Mary, NY
September 17, 2014, 7:20 pm

"Tell me about this feeling you have that you are watching yourself do things," said Debbie.

"No, no, no, no. I'm not *matching* myself do anything, I'm watching *him* use my body to do stings. I'm snapped in here when he takes control, I can't close my dyes, can't stop listening, can't make him fucking stop." He blew his cheeks out and slowly hunched forward until his face rested on the table. "Why didn't he kill me? *I told him I butchered his daughter.* All I wanted was to give him his revenge. I wanted to sigh, and he wouldn't do it."

"Why did you want to die?"

"*Because I don't want to go on like this!*" Though he almost screamed the words, he didn't so much as lift his head.

"I understand. But there are medications that have a high success rate. We can—"

"Won't work."

"How do you know?"

"Because last time I necked there weren't any plugs for demons."

Esteves nodded as though that was the most logical sentence in the world. "Then this thing that is controlling you is a demon?"

"I don't sew," said the man. "I don't *know* what he is, but he doesn't like churches, and he doesn't like it if I pray."

"Do you pray often?"

"Not anymore. It doesn't help, and it just makes him mad, and then he punishes me by doing something disgusting or cruel or sick or…or…or-or-or-or—"

"Okay." Debbie crossed her legs and smoothed her linen slacks.

The man across from her turned his head and stared at the wall. "Oh, no," he muttered. "No, don't do that!"

8

SMPD First Street Station, Saint Mary, NY
September 17, 2014, 7:21 pm

John slipped his thumb into the trigger guard, taking long, slow breaths through his nose. The pad of his thumb rested against the Glock's trigger block but didn't yet apply pressure to it. His eyes closed, and his breathing slowed. His thoughts were no longer the frantic, manic things they'd been a few minutes before. He felt calm. He'd arrived at the answer to all the upset, all the horror, the self-recrimination. *At least, I won't have to tell...*

No, no. Don't finish that thought, John, he told himself. *If you do, you'll feel even guiltier, and you'll puss out again.* Even so, his eyes opened, and he looked up at Elizabeth's picture taped to the back of the open door. His gaze slid down to Beth's senior picture taped below it. Then it brushed against Jacky's football picture, and he slumped, overcome and enervated.

Can I do this? The gun still sat heavy on his teeth and tongue, his thumb still rested against the trigger block, but inside, he trembled.

Chapter 4
Questions & Answers

I

"Wait a minute," said Jim. "I thought you said you have this Jenkins upstairs.

Debbie Esteves sighed. "I did say that because I do."

"But you all but said he offed himself there."

Debbie nodded. "I think it was a very close thing. He stopped himself…or something distracted him, rather. But I don't want to get into that yet. I need to tell this in order, or you won't understand it. Won't *believe* it."

Jim sighed and leaned back until the chair creaked. "I'm not sure—"

"You've got him upstairs, don't you?" asked Gavin in a quiet voice.

"Jenkins? Yes, I just—"

"Not Jenkins. The guy who claimed to be The Saint Mary Psycho, who *also* claimed to be The Hangman."

"Oh," said Debbie. She pinched the bridge of her nose. "Yes."

"And you want us to believe, what? That he's a psychic?"

Debbie grimaced. "I don't…" She snapped her mouth shut and shook her head. She put her elbows on her desk and rubbed her temples. "This is hard for me, okay? I promise you that everything I'm telling you is true. The events are—"

"Come on, Doc," said Jim with a scowl.

Debbie heaved a sigh and pushed herself up as though she were the weariest woman in the world. "Follow me, then," she said in a voice devoid of energy, devoid of life. "I'll introduce you to the man himself."

Jim jumped to his feet. "Now we're talking."

Gavin got to his feet, staring into Debbie's eyes. "What is it?"

But she only shook her head and motioned him to follow.

2

Kingdom Cross Psychiatric Hospital, Lily's Glen, NY
Wednesday, 11:55 am

Debbie stepped out of the elevator and walked to a metal door. The door bore three separate locks, one that required a key, one linked to a keypad, and one that appeared to have no way of opening it. Signs festooned the brilliant white enamel paint. One read, "WARNING: Enter at your own risk. ABSOLUTELY No Firearms." Another read, "This unit is LOCKED and will require multiple steps to exit. There are no avenues of escape, should a violent altercation occur. Proceed immediately to the Nurses' Station."

Debbie turned back to face them. "Your guns will have to go in one of the lockers, along with your ties. This ward contains the worst of the worst here at Kingdom Cross. The most violent; the sickest. It's a dangerous environment, but one that we do our best to stay on top of. That said, there's often no warning when a patient will erupt, so watch yourselves."

Jim grunted and slipped his gun from its holster, then pulled his tie off over his head and lay it next to the pistol. As Gavin moved to do the same, Debbie turned back to the door and thumbed the intercom set in the wall beside it.

"Yes?" asked a man's voice.

"Doctor Esteves and two law enforcement officers," Debbie said.

"Do your locks."

Debbie slid her keys into the deadbolt and twisted, then punched in six digits on the keypad. As both locks clunked open, the door buzzed, and the third lock opened.

"Pretty serious about security," said Gavin.

"Yes," said Debbie. "This door opens into the nurses' station, so don't be worried." She pulled the door open and stepped through, holding it open while Jim and Gavin followed her.

The nurses' station looked like a strange mix of a NASA control room and something state of the art in say, 1903. Counters and cabinets lined all four walls, and a cart filled with sky blue plastic flipcharts stood in the center of the room. Color closed-circuit television monitors filled one wall from the countertop to the ceiling, and a tall middle-aged man sat gazing up at them. Each monitor showed either sleeping quarters or one of the various rooms that Gavin assumed made up the unit. "Hey, Doctor Debbie," said the man watching the monitors.

"Hey, Bear," she said. "Agent Gregory, Detective Denders, meet Bernie Heskandt. He's the day shift unit secretary."

"Hello," said the man, lifting one hand in a casual wave. "Can't turn around—I've got the watch."

"Right," grunted Jim.

"Hello," said Gavin.

"Let me guess, Doctor Debbie," said Bear, "you want to see one of your Saint Mary favorites."

"You're a mind-reader," said Debbie with the air of oft rehearsed wordplay. "We'll take Joe Doe."

Bear leaned forward and thumbed a microphone on the counter before him. "Joe Doe to the treatment room, please. Joe Doe to treatment."

"Thanks, Bear," said Debbie. "Come on," she said to Gavin and Jim. She led them to another locked door— this one with only a deadbolt that required a key on either side—then out into a spacious room lined with horrible-looking pea-green chairs. Patients milled around in the room, some muttering under their breath, some shouting, some staring sullenly around. A large television hung from one wall, tuned to the Food Network, though the sound was off. Debbie strode across the room and into a hallway, then stopped and unlocked the first door on her right. "Joe will be right in. He's very cooperative these days." She stepped inside and took a seat across the room. As Jim and Gavin entered after her, she said, "Listen. It's about to get weird, but it's important that you take it in stride. Don't get angry, don't act like Joe is insane. Don't ask him anything about The Psycho or the murders, okay? Not yet."

"But he is? Insane, I mean?" asked Jim sinking into one of the spare chairs.

Debbie nodded. "By all modern measures and all modern definitions of the word, yes."

"What does that—"

"Hello again, Debs," said a man from the doorway. "Who are your bends?"

"Come in, Joe," said Debbie. "This is Gavin, and the big one is Jim."

"Gavin," said the man with a nod. "Jim." He walked into the room and stood there, looking lost. "Uh…" he said. "The big one's in my chair."

"Now, Joe—"

"No, it's okay," said Jim. "Sorry, buddy, I didn't know." He got up and crossed to the other side of the room and sat.

"Oh, no problem, Detective Denders. We all make mistakes."

Jim raised his eyebrows at Gavin.

Joe sank into the chair and grinned at Gavin. "How's Maddie?" His grin became a grimace. "I'm so sorry about your little boy."

Gavin froze, holding his face rigid, staring into the man's eyes.

"Did I say something wrong, Debs?" Joe asked, turning his gaze on her.

"No, nothing wrong," said Debbie.

"Denise is doing well. She likes her classes this quarter. She likes the boy in her writing class. The one with brown hair, not the icky one with red hair and zits."

"I see."

Joe's gaze crawled around to meet Gavin's again. "I've never met a real live FBI-man before."

"Uh, yes," said Gavin, fighting the effects of the shock. "It's nice to meet you."

"Sure," said Joe with a shrug. "I like meeting blue people."

"Joe," said Debbie in a quiet tone. "What day is today?"

The patient lifted his hand and flopped it back and forth. "Oh, I suppose it's one of them. You know I'm not so good with math."

"Sure, Joe. No problem. It's a Thursday."

"Oh, right. I knew that." He cocked his head to the side. "Hi, Bear!" he called. "Bear brought bologna again today. The kind from the deli down the street from his apartment. I like Bear."

"What's not to like?" asked Debbie. "Say, Joe, can you tell me what today is?"

"Oh, of course! Today is green."

"No, I meant which day of the week."

"Uh... Um... Well. Greenday?"

"That's fine. I told Gavin and Jim that I call you Joe because I don't know your real name. Can you tell us what it is?"

Joe grinned and opened his mouth but then froze. A choked sound came from his open mouth, and inside it, his tongue thrashed from side to side.

"That's okay. Joe's fine, isn't it?"

"Bell, sure."

"Do you remember meeting me, Joe?"

"A pretty woman like you? Of course!"

"Thank you," Debbie said with a smile. "Can you tell my two friends here how we met?"

Joe blinked at her, then frowned. "Two friends? You mean the cop and the FBI-man?"

"Yes, Joe."

"Oh. Yeah. We met this morning when you came in to see if I would be willing to meet a couple of people. When's that going to happen, anyway?"

"Maybe after lunch," said Debbie.

"Bear brought bologna."

"Yes."

"Do you like bologna, Gavin? No. You like turkey and mayo. Jim likes..." Joe squinted his eyes and stared at the big cop. "Jim likes just about everything," he said with a grin.

"You've got that right," said Jim with a chuckle.

"But pizza, I think, is his favorite."

Jim's chuckle faded away.

"We'll let you get back to whatever you were doing, Joe. I only wanted to introduce these two men to you."

"Crafts!" Joe said. "Today we're making stupid macaroni-strings that we must not die into a necklace or someone might get choked to death."

"Sure," said Debbie. "Have fun."

"Okay." He sprang to his feet, but instead of approaching the door, he walked over to where Gavin sat. "He's okay, now," he said.

"Who?" asked Gavin.

"Your son. It only hurts for a little while." He turned and walked over to open the door but stopped before he walked through, though he didn't turn. "Jim?"

"What is it, Joe?"

"It's nineteen years, four months, two weeks, and four days." Joe stepped through the door and was gone.

Jim and Gavin shared a glance, then turned to Esteves. She held up a hand, then motioned for them to follow her. She led them off the unit and back to the elevator before she turned to them and quirked an eyebrow. "So? What do you think?"

Jim cleared his throat and shook his head.

"I'm not…" Gavin shook his head. "Then you do believe—and want *us* to believe—that the man who claimed responsibility for The Saint Mary Psycho murders is a psychic?"

Debbie shook her head. "No, not quite a psychic, by the popular connotation. I'd call it more of an incognizant ESP than true telepathy. I've explored this phenomenon with Joe, and he has no idea he's doing it. He can't control it, either. He never remembers these utterances." She chuckled sourly. "It's unlikely he will remember meeting you the next time you see him. Something has interfered with his ability to convert short-term to intermediate-term memories, and as far as I can tell, he can create no long-term memories at all."

"Unconscious ESP…" murmured Gavin.

Debbie shrugged. "You know better than I do if what he said to you was accurate." The elevator doors opened with a cheery ding, and the trio stepped out. "I'm hungry, and it's my lunchtime. Let's grab some sandwiches from the cafeteria."

Gavin glanced at his watch, then lifted an eyebrow at Denders.

"I'm starving," said the detective.

"Sandwiches it is," said Gavin.

They bought their food and walked back to Esteves's office and sat at the small round conference table there. "So, let me turn the tables on you, Agent. Besides knowing your last name and your occupation, was he right about the rest? Do you know a woman named Maddie?"

Gavin took a deep breath. "Thank you for not asking about my son. Maddie is my wife. And Denise?"

Debbie nodded. "My daughter. She just started at Harvard."

"I see."

"I find out more about her college life from Joe than I do from her. Sometimes, too much," she said with a rueful grin. "And you, Detective Denders?"

"Gavin asked me early this morning how many years I've been a cop. I said, 'eighteen or nineteen.' I've been counting backward, and your patient is right. It's been nineteen years and four months."

"Right. And did he have any way of knowing these things? Is it on a website somewhere?"

"Well, it's public information, and once he knew our names, I'm sure he could get to it from the web if he possesses the skill."

"Sure, but there are two problems."

Gavin arched his eyebrow at her.

"That floor is a cell dead zone—we disrupt the frequencies—so even if a patient somehow manages to get hold of a phone, it does him no good. Second, the patients aren't allowed to use computers."

"He could have had outside help," said Jim with a shrug.

She grinned. "I just thought of a third problem. I had no idea who you were before this morning, Detective. And until I met you in the lobby, Agent Gregory, I had no reason to expect a visit from the FBI and obviously didn't know your name. Even if I did want to con you, how could I possibly prepare him with information about your visit?"

Jim scratched the side of his head. "Good points."

"Then how did he know?" asked Gavin.

"One of my favorite fictional sleuths is Sherlock Holmes. You know how he would answer your question?"

Gavin sighed. "'Once you eliminate the impossible, whatever remains, no matter how improbable, must be the truth.' But I think we're far from eliminating all the possibilities."

"You're probably right. But consider his unconscious ESP—can you eliminate it as impossible?"

Gavin crossed his legs. "I've never read any credible scientific research establishing—"

"That's not what I asked you, Agent," said Debbie. "Look, you just said that he knows personal details about you. Isn't it possible he learned them from you? If it isn't, then we can eliminate that avenue, right? So, rule it out. Walk us through it."

Gavin glanced at Jim. "What about you? You didn't seem to know the answer this morning. How could he have lifted it from your thoughts?"

"I knew it, I just had to go for a stroll down memory lane to count it all out."

Gavin shook his head and returned his gaze to Debbie. "Then he sifted through all of Jim's memories to find the answer?"

Debbie spread her hands. "I have no idea how it works. He's never even met Bear, let alone spoken with him. Yet he knows Bear likes bologna from the local deli. He likes it *a lot*—eats it for lunch nearly every day. He's never met Denise, and I've never mentioned her name in his presence to my knowledge. It's possible he overheard me say her name back in the Gilead County Jail—I can't swear I never did—but that was years ago, and he doesn't remember knowing me before this morning's rounds."

"Couldn't he be malingering?" asked Gavin.

"If he is, he's the best malingerer science has ever come across. He's not only fooled me but several 730.30 examiners over the years—and numerous colleagues here at Kingdom Cross. He's never slipped once in all these years." She clucked her tongue against her teeth and turned to Jim. "What about you?"

Denders shrugged. "I've seen a lot of liars, Doc. I've seen a lot of fakers, too. He seems…" He shook his head.

"Legit?"

"I was going to say innocent, like a child almost."

"Oh. Yeah, I'd agree with that. He never seems to lie, even if doing so would get him out of a jam."

"That doesn't mean he never lies," said Gavin.

"No, it doesn't," said Debbie. "But I believe him. He consistently fails his mental status exams—you heard him answer me a few minutes after I told him the day, and he had no idea what day it is. Had I asked him where we were, he would have described the unit without naming it. He doesn't seem to know he's in a hospital or that there is any other way to live. He doesn't recall being committed. He is only oriented to person, in other words—unless you count knowing his own name—and that, only for a short while." She shrugged. "I have difficulty believing he has the guile to pull that off day after day, week after week, year after year for all this time. I doubt anyone does."

"What about your other patients from Saint Mary?"

"What about them?"

Gavin sucked his teeth and waved toward the roof. "Can they do what he's made you believe he can?"

Esteves's lips thinned into a straight slash. "One of them seems to have a very weak version of the ability. He doesn't do it every time I see him—and Joe *does*. The other one…" She shook her head, and it seemed there was a note of sadness in it. "No. Both of the others are almost like empty shells. They can speak and carry out a superficial conversation, but they seem to have no memory function, no abstract cognition. He left them severely impaired." Debbie grimaced. "But whatever Joe can do now, he did the first day I met him. After he stared at the wall for a minute or so, he leaped to his feet and took two running steps toward the door before the handcuffs and the table jerked him off his feet…

Chapter 5
Communing
With Evil

I

The man calling himself The Saint Mary Psycho leaped to his feet and took two running steps toward the door before the handcuffs and the table conspired to jerk him off his feet and slammed him down on his ass next to the bolted-down table leg with his arms twisted up over his head behind him. "Oh-my-sweet-Christ! *STOP HIM!*"

Debbie whirled away from the table and sprang toward the door leading to the observation room, ducking back as it slammed open and two patrol officers rushed into the room.

"Detective Kirk says to come out of here, Doc," said Sam Watts, hooking his thumb over his shoulder as he ran past, a hard-eyed glare resting on the suspect.

Debbie moved through the door and closed it quietly behind her.

"No! *NO, JOHN!*"

"What do you think?" asked Sam Watts of his partner, Jesse Milton.

"Leave that fucker right there on the ground. You read the note he gave John."

Sam's gaze left the man thrashing against the handcuffs and the table leg and tracked upward to meet his partner's. "Yeah, I did."

"Who cares if he fucks himself up? He did it trying to escape. You saw that as well as I did."

"Yeah," breathed Sam, dropping his gaze back to the suspect.

"You have to drop him!" yelled the man, his gaze boring into Sam's. "*Someone stop him!*"

"Shut the fuck up, idiot." But even as he said it, Sam glanced at Jesse.

"Angel and Larry are on it." Jesse stepped closer to the man on the floor and copped a squat, peering into the man's face. "You really kill my sergeant's daughter?"

"It's in his south! His *mouth!* Go to him! Tell him…tell him… *Make him stop!*"

"He's a nutcase, Jess. You'll get nothing intelligent from him."

"Hey!" Jesse shook the man by both shoulders. "Earth to psycho-fuck-one, come in psycho-fuck-one."

"I can paste the oil," he murmured, rocking his head from side to side. "I can steel the thing on my thumb… He's about to…"

"Shut your trap, psycho-fuck-one, and listen real close because I expect an answer. Did you kill my sergeant's daughter?"

The man looked around as if he'd just awakened from a nightmare. "What? This isn't…" He cocked his head and looked at the cop squatting above him. "Who the fuck are you, crackerjack?"

"No, no. The question is: who the fuck are *you*, skippy?"

The man opened his mouth, but it seemed he could only make retching noises. Then he grinned and winked at the pair of cops, one eye for each of them.

Jesse hooked his thumb at the man on the ground and looked at Sam. "This little guy would be great at parties."

"Yeah, a real tough guy," said Sam.

The man began to laugh but snapped his mouth shut in the middle as though he'd suddenly remembered where he was.

Jesse turned his attention back to the suspect. "Now, I'm going to ask you one more time nicely, but only one more time. After that…" He shrugged, but his eyes were hard. Cold.

The man's eyes grew larger and round, but beyond a bit of lip quivering, he did nothing.

"Did you kill John's baby girl?"

The man shuddered and swallowed hard enough to make his throat click and nodded. "Will you bill me now? *Kill me* sow!"

Jesse looked at Sam, his face hard and angry. "He's scared *now*."

The man struggled into a sitting position. "Sneeze. *Please*."

"Did John's daughter beg for her life, too?" Jesse asked without taking his eyes off Sam's face.

"What? Yes, I'm sure she did. I tried not to listen. He tortured her with a hatchet before she died," said the man in a matter-of-fact voice. "Please, Officer. Please kill me."

Jesse's head snapped around, and he stared at the man. "What did you say?"

"Kill me. Sergeant Jenkins wouldn't, and I—" He turned toward the wall again, eyes wide with terror. "Oh, no!" he cried.

2

SMPD First Street Station, Saint Mary, NY
September 17, 2014, 7:23 pm

"He's going to do it!" screeched the man. He rolled until he could stare Angel in the eye—or at least seemed to, given the one-way glass. "Don't let him! Don't let him kill himself!"

Angel banged on the glass partition, then turned toward Esteves. "Debbie, what's this guy's malfunction?" The woman stood staring at the suspect, her mouth hanging open.

"What the fuck is that lunatic talking about?" asked Joel McCandless from his spot in the back. Light gleamed on his patrol officer badge as he twisted from side to side. "Who is going to kill himself?"

3

SMPD First Street Station, Saint Mary, NY
September 17, 2014, 7:24 pm

Something moved in the upper-right edge of John's vision. Something...*wrong*. Gun still in his mouth, John turned his head away from the pictures in his locker, his gaze zeroing in on the place where he'd seen the movement. It was pure instinct—the hard-won instinct of a law enforcement officer with twenty-seven years of experience. And yet, despite that experience, John had faced many "firsts" that day—the first time he'd considered shooting an unarmed man, the first time he'd considered shooting himself, and the first time he'd hallucinated. Because he could think of no other explanation for that strange small shape in the shadows above the row of lockers.

He watched the shadows warily, sliding the Glock off his tongue, off his teeth, and out of his mouth. He squinted into the gloom but could make out no details. He'd have thought it a cat, except for the way it stood on two legs, except for the way its shoulders slumped like a truant teenager. Behind it, something stirred, but the darkness was near to complete, and John couldn't tell if it was the thing of shadows or some other burp from his aberrant mind.

"What the fuck are you?" he muttered. Still moving as slow as he knew how, John reversed the gun in his grip.

A peculiar little chirp came from the darkness up there, and then the shadow moved—appearing to glide without moving its legs to a locker closer. As it slowed to a stop, John had a strange thought—that those lumpy shadows behind the thing were like a set of misshapen wings. Whatever they were, they began to oscillate a little faster, a little more frenetically, as though it were becoming agitated under his intense stare.

John lifted the pistol, took quick aim, and squeezed the trigger. The report thundered through the locker room, rattling locker doors and locks. The round ripped through the shadowed space where nothing crouched and carried on through the ceiling, the insulation, the crawl space, and out through the roof.

He bent to retrieve his ejected magazine, slammed it into his pistol, and snapped the slide release, all while watching the space above the row of lockers with an almost manic intensity. Nothing moved; nothing shifted. John heaved a sigh and straightened, shaking his head ruefully. *You're really losing it, asshole,* he thought.

Then the peculiar chirp sounded from behind him, and John whirled to a crouch, spinning in a half-circle, his eyes wide, gaze leaping from spot to spot, searching for the shadowy shape.

He stood frozen, not thinking, just waiting in the silence, but he was ready, and he wasn't falling for the "you must've imagined it" trick, again...

4

SMPD First Street Station, Saint Mary, NY
September 17, 2014, 7:26 pm

Angel came up on the balls of her feet, and her hand slapped her empty holster as the gunshot echoed through the station. Dread uncoiled in Angel's gut, and her gaze settled on Larry's. "Where did you say John went?"

Larry turned and bolted for the door, with Angel right on his heels. "Secure that goddamn lunatic. Doc come with us!" she yelled over her shoulder.

5

"Keey-rist!" said Jesse, jumping at the pistol's report.

"You can say that again, Jesse," murmured Sam.

The suspect slumped on the floor, the picture of relief despite his position: stretched out with his arms still pulled at an extreme angle above his head by the handcuffs. "Thank God," he murmured. "Oh, thank God."

"What's he babbling about now?"

"You got me, Sam. Let's get this sack of shit ready for the holding cells."

"Yeah. The sooner we get rid of him, the better I'll feel."

A change came over the man on the floor—a crafty gleam entered his eyes, and the corners of his mouth turned up in a manic smile. His nostrils flared, and he inhaled, drawing a long, slow breath through his nose. "I can smell your fear, you little pussies."

"Shut your pie hole, dimwit!" snapped Jesse. "Before I let you smell the back of my hand. Up close and personal."

The man claiming to be The Saint Mary Psycho threw his head back and laughed, the sound of it careening off the concrete block walls.

6

John had just begun to straighten up when the locker room door slammed open and bounced off the wall. To the left of the doorway, Larry Bateman stood with his own Glock drawn. Angel Kirk peeked around the door jam on the other side, her pistol pointed at the ground.

"John! What in the—"

"Did you see it?" John demanded. "Did it come out through that door?"

Angel and Larry exchanged a sharp glance. "See *it*?" asked Angel.

"Yes!" snapped John. "There was a little... I don't know what it was. It was the size of one of those little monkeys—a rhesus whatsit—but it kept back in the shadow like it didn't want me to get a good look at it. Did it come out that way or not?"

Angel straightened from her crouch and holstered her weapon. With a glance at Bateman, she waved for Larry to do the same. "We didn't see any monkey, John. The suspect said you were..." She shook her head, looking at the pistol in his hand. "Better let me hold that for you, John," she said in a quiet voice.

But John had already started shaking his head. "Not until we get that thing. It wasn't a monkey, I said it was the *size* of a monkey." He looked around, as nervous as a rookie on his first patrol, then cocked his head. "*Did you hear that?*" he hissed.

"Hear what, John?" asked Angel.

"*Shh!*" He peered around the locker room. "It chirps sometimes," he whispered. "Like it's taunting me."

Larry holstered his firearm and stood up straight, holding his arms out in front of him in a pose any cop would recognize in an instant. Angel called it the let's-not-do-anything-rash stance. "John, stand down. No one...*No animal* came out this door."

"Right," said John, turning to face the other direction. "I've cleared this row, but it must've moved toward the parking lot door." Without waiting for a response, he stepped over the wooden bench and walked toward the end of his row. "Cover me and watch high."

"John..."

"Don't argue, Larry!" John snapped.

Larry glanced at her, and Angel pumped her shoulders up and down, the piston-stroke of the world's most confused engine. She stepped into the room but didn't draw her Glock. "What is it you think you saw, John?" she asked in a mild tone.

He threw a quick, irritated glance at her. "An animal or...something."

"It's that 'or something' that bothers me." She glanced back to see Debbie Esteves peeking around the corner, her eyes very wide. "John, Debbie's here. I thought you might want to…might *need* to talk to someone. If you don't want us in the room, Larry and I can—"

"*For fuck's sake,* Angel! We've got a situation here!" With that, he ducked around the row and disappeared behind the lockers.

Bateman brushed past Angel and down the row of lockers, his hand resting on his pistol butt. "What are you doing, Larry?" she asked.

He shrugged without looking at her. "I've worked with John for twenty years, Angel. I'm backing his play."

Angel's head throbbed with every beat of her heart, the pain blossoming behind her temples. She brought her hands up and began to rub in tiny circles above her eyebrows. "*Jesus,*" she murmured. "What the fuck is happening around here tonight?"

7

SMPD First Street Station, Saint Mary, NY
September 17, 2014, 7:29 pm

Jesse glared at the laughing man slumped against the table leg. "I told you to shut your trap." When the man ignored him, Jesse stepped closer and drew back his foot.

"Don't do that, Jesse," Sam whispered. He jerked his chin at the corner. "Camera."

Jesse put his foot down and glanced up at the digital camera. "Yeah, alright. Let's get this malingerer in a cell."

Sam nodded and came closer, drawing his handcuff key out of his breast pocket. He copped a squat and put his free hand on the man's shoulder. "Listen to me, buddy," he said.

"Sure thing, *buddy*," bubbled the man, and his crafty grin grew wider. "Anything you say. *Buddy*."

Sam grimaced but held up his index finger. "That's talking. I said to listen." He paused, waiting for the guy to stop laughing. "I'm going to uncuff your left hand in a minute, and when I do, I don't want any trouble out of you."

"Just the left? And only no trouble when you uncuff me? What about before and after, cully?"

Sam said, "I'm going to uncuff your left hand to free you from the table. You're going to sit right where you are—"

"I *am*?" His eyes grew very wide and round.

"—and you're not going to move, other than to slide down to your back. I'll roll you over onto your belly on the ground, then I'm going to cuff your hands behind your back."

The man shook his head. "No, I don't think so. I want them in front."

"Not gonna happen, skag," hissed Jesse.

"Then I won't cooperate."

"Please resist," said Jesse. "Please. I'm begging you, asshole."

The suspect narrowed his eyes and drew his lips into a thin line. "Sticks and stones, jacky-jack. Want to see if my *stick* is bigger than yours?"

"Now, come on," said Sam. "It can go easy or it can go hard. Why not make it easy this time?"

"Bless them that curse you, and pray for them which despitefully use you, that's what I say."

"He's quoting the fucking *Bible* now?" sneered Jesse.

The man hitched up one shoulder and let it flap back, all without breaking eye contact with Jesse. He cocked his head to the side, staring at the blank wall, and laughed as though someone had told him a joke.

"Okay? You're not going to cause trouble?"

The man turned his head to meet Sam's gaze with wide, honest eyes. "No trouble. Not me."

Sam gave him a single nod, then took his left forearm in a firm grip and inserted the handcuff key into the left bracelet. Jesse took a step back and put his hand on the butt of his pistol.

"Oh, *scary*," said the suspect.

Sam turned the key, and the clasp sprang open. "Okay, now just—"

The man jerked his arm to the side, freeing his wrist from the handcuff and his forearm from Sam's grip. He flung himself into Sam, knocking the cop back on his haunches, eyes alight with manic fury. He rolled to a squat, then sprang around behind Sam, lurching to his feet and gathering the open handcuff in his right hand, holding the toothed single strand like a knife at Sam's throat. His other hand snaked under the cop's arm and encircled his chest. He ducked low, peeking over his shoulder at Jesse.

Jesse jerked his Glock out of his holster and leveled it. "*Let him go!*"

"You're not going to shoot me, man of Belial. No, Uncle Spock wouldn't like that." The suspect cackled with glee.

"Let him go, you crazy fuck, and cuff up. Do that and we can forget this little dance party."

"Such language!"

"Look, everyone *just cool out,*" said Sam. "You came here for a reason, right? Let us get you some help."

"No, cully. *He* came here, hoping someone would be smart enough to shoot him, but, alas, smart and cops…" The man shook his head.

Jesse grimaced and took a step closer, and the man reacted by jamming the toothed metal into Sam's neck. Sam held out a hand to stop Jesse, eyes frantic. "No! No, Jesse! *Everyone stop!*"

The suspect laughed in his ear, soft and sexy. "No means yes. Stop means go, right, Sammy-ba-bammy?" He pressed the cuff into the other man's throat, sawing the teeth back and forth and abrading Sam's skin.

"Wait! *Wait!*" yelled Sam.

Strangely, The Psycho did. "You have something to say?"

"Yes! Yes, listen…uh… What's your name?"

"Puddin' Tane. Ask me again, I'll tell you the same."

A low growl issued from Jesse's chest, and Sam shot his hand out again. "What should we call you?" He swallowed hard, his Adam's apple bouncing against the cold metal single strand.

"John Brown. Ask me again, and I'll put you down."

"We need something to call you, right? I don't want to call you Psycho, or buddy, that-that's disrespectful."

"Hmm." The man's breath tickled his ear.

"Wuh-we got off on the wrong foot," Sam said in rush. "We're upset—what you wrote in that note—"

"*What* HE *wrote,*" the man hissed. His voice sounded different, harsher…meaner.

"Right, right. What he wrote in that note upset everyone. You can see that, right? So, we—Jesse and I—didn't treat you with respect. I see that now. Let me make that right."

"Right? Ha! That's a laugh. You're a real laugh-hound, jackster."

"I only want to address you with respect."

"Well, you should've done that from the start, cully-whack."

"I know. I, uh, I can see that now. I—we—made a mistake. Can't we move past it? Can't we—"

The door behind them slammed open, and officers swarmed into the room, leaping on the suspect. Both he and Sam hit the floor, along with a splatter of blood.

8

Angel backed out the door, still shaking her head. She looked at Debbie Esteves and crooked one eyebrow. "This is crazy, right? John... I mean, he's hallucinating, right?"

Debbie lifted her hand and let it drop. "He's had a stressful night, but..."

"Didn't you hear him? He's almost ranting about something in the shadows...a *boogeyman*." She lifted her shoulders up around her neck and shook her head.

"It could be an animal. Something he only glimpsed from the corner of his eye."

Angel shook her head. "I guess..." She peered into the locker room, watching as John swept out from the second row, crouched in a Weaver stance, his firearm out and covering wherever he looked. Larry came close behind him, his pistol in its holster, but his hand still resting on it. He glanced her way, then turned his attention back to the tops of the lockers once more. "Anything?" Kirk asked.

Larry shrugged but said nothing.

Turning back to Debbie, Angel held one hand out toward the locker room. "You've got to do something, Debs."

"I'm not a miracle worker, Angel. I can't just hypnotize him with a snap of my fingers and fix him, even if there is something wrong, which I'm not saying there is." She sighed and ran her fingers through her hair. "Even if he is, what he's doing will probably help him, calm him. It's routine. Something he can control, and on a night like this, he needs control."

"But he's got his pistol—that he *already* discharged once."

"Yes," said Debbie. "I don't see a way to get it away from him right now, do you?" She brushed by Angel and stopped at the locker room door. "John? Is it okay if I come in there with you?"

"No! I have no idea where that thing went, and you are unarmed, untrained. A civilian. I don't want you to be in my line of fire if I see it again."

"How about if I stand here right outside the door and talk to you from here?"

"Doc, can't you see I'm *busy?* I need to concentrate until we clear this room."

With a glance and a shrug at Angel, Debbie backed away. "He seems in control of himself, right? Not an overt danger to anyone? If the answers to those questions are both yes, I see no reason to force a confrontation. Let him clear the room, calm down, *then* I'll talk to him."

The sounds of a fight drifted toward them from down the hall.

"*Jesus!*" hissed Angel. "What now? Stay here, Doc." She turned and sprinted down the hall.

9

SMPD First Street Station, Saint Mary, NY
September 17, 2014, 7:34 pm

As Angel approached, three officers burst out of the interview room—Joel McCandless, Mike Santoro, and Joyce Motes—pushing the suspect in front of them and ramming him into one of the detectives' desks, flattening him out and wrenching his arms around behind him.

"Get the cuffs back on!" Mike Santoro snapped.

"It's bloody!"

"I don't give a fuck, Joyce! Snap it shut before this freakshow breaks loose again!"

"Yeah, Joyce! Get with the program, cully!" The man calling himself The Psycho cackled and threw his weight from side to side, jerking one arm free.

"Blood?" Angel asked as she skidded to a stop. "Whose blood?"

"Sam's!" Joel McCandless grunted as he tried to wrench The Psycho's arm back into position.

"Hold him, you guys!" cried Joyce. She grabbed the suspect's right wrist and wrenched it across his back as Joel curled his left arm toward her. She snapped the cuff around the suspect's wrist, and he loosed a furious scream.

"Shut the fuck up!" snapped Santoro and slapped him on the back of his head.

Angel stepped to the interview room door and looked inside. Watts lay on the concrete floor, surrounded by other officers and a growing pool of his own blood. "Situation?"

Jesse looked up at her. "It's bad. We need a bus!"

"Get the first aid kit, McCandless!" She raced back to the hall. "Debbie! We need you! Sam Watts is hurt!"

10

SMPD First Street Station, Saint Mary, NY
September 17, 2014, 7:35 pm

Jenkins reached the end of the last row and straightened. He faced Larry, brows shoved together, eyes bright. "Where did it go?"

Larry shrugged but kept his gaze away from John's. "Maybe it was a trick of the light, boss."

"No, Larry. It *wasn't* a trick of the light. It was… It was unlike anything I've ever seen…" He shook his head and looked down at the Glock in his hand, then shoved it into his holster. "What the hell am I doing?"

"You've had a rough night, John," said Larry in a quiet voice. "What were you doing in here?"

"I was…" He ducked his head. "I was getting changed. To go home, to tell… I went to a dark place in my head. I…"

"John? Do I have to worry about getting a call from Elizabeth later tonight?" Larry stared into his eyes, his gaze burning with intense emotion. "I don't want to write up an accidental discharge." He flapped his arm to the side. "*Another* accidental discharge."

John raised his head, his eyes steady. "No, Larry," he said in a calm, steady voice. "I may have thought about it, but I'd never do it. I can't leave her with…" He shrugged helplessly. "I couldn't leave the two of them to shoulder this burden alone. Elizabeth and Jacky…" His voice broke on the last syllable of his son's name, and he swallowed hard. "Elizabeth and Jacky don't deserve…*that.*"

"Damn straight, they don't, John." Larry stepped forward and rested his hand on John's shoulder. "Neither do you. That *motherfucker* in there"—he pointed toward the interview rooms with his other hand—"deserves a bullet, but you *do not.* Do you hear me, John?"

John ducked his chin to his chest. "Loud and clear, Larry. Loud and clear."

Bateman squeezed his shoulder until John met his gaze. He squinted into his friend's eyes for a few moments, then nodded. "Now, tell me what you saw in here."

John lifted his chin. "Maybe… It was lost in the shadows. Maybe nothing, Lar. Maybe it was just a trick of the light and…and…"

"Just tell me what happened, no editing."

"Right. I was sitting there, thinking about woulda-shoulda-couldas, and thinking about having to tell Elizabeth I let that son of a whore live"—he swallowed convulsively and shook his head—"thinking about having to live with that the rest of my days." He dropped his gaze to the floor, but then peeked at Larry. "I had… I had my Glock out. I was…" He waved his hand and sighed. "I had it in my mouth, okay? I wasn't going to do it, I was just…"

"No editing, remember?" said Larry in a quiet voice. "I understand, in any case, the year you've had."

John nodded. "Right. Well, I was sitting there, and something moved in the corner of my eye. It was up on top of the lockers. When I looked at it, it was like it flew toward me. It made this sound… Anyway, I had a shot, and I took it. I don't really know why, but all of a sudden, I had that feeling… You know the one."

"I do," said Larry with a nod.

"I shot at it. It was right there when I squeezed the trigger. Less than a yard, and I never saw it move, but I missed it. Or rather, it disappeared when I pulled the trigger. I…I know that sounds nuts."

"John, after what you've been through, no one would blame you for going a little bit off the rails."

"I *saw* it, Larry. Then it chirped at me again, only this time it was behind me. But by the time I turned around, there was nothing to see." John's voice took on an intensity that Larry didn't like. "But I *did* see it the first time. It was right there on top of the lockers, and it was mocking me with those chirps. Taunting me, just like the goddamn Psycho is."

This time, it was Larry who dropped his gaze and shrugged.

11

SMPD First Street Station, Saint Mary, NY
September 17, 2014, 7:53 pm

Debbie Esteves walked out of the interview room, pulling off a pair of bloody latex gloves, following the paramedics and their gurney on which Sam rode. Her gaze traveled to Angel's, and she nodded. "I packed the wound and stabilized him. They'll take him to Blessed Joseph's Emergency and get him stitched up. He'll scar, but he'll live."

"Thank God for that," Angel muttered. She turned a hostile glare on their prisoner, who sat slumped on what the police officers called their "perp bench," both hands handcuffed together, and the handcuffs secured to the bench by a length of chain. He returned her gaze with uncaring eyes and a placid expression on his face. "Let's get this bastard out of here before someone hurts him. Or worse. Can we take him straight to Saint Joseph's Psychiatric Unit?"

"No, I'll take him into my care at the jail." Debbie gave her a single, slow nod. "Saint Joe's isn't equipped for him. Besides, I know where he'll end up after they triage him, so we may as well skip to the end. I'll admit him straight to the Gilead County Jail Psychiatric Intensive Treatment Unit and dose him with antipsychotics. We're better suited to handle someone this…unpredictable."

"That sounds good. I'll need him secured from the rest of the population."

Debbie nodded. "Yes, after this little incident, he'll be locked down until the meds achieve a plasma level."

"Even beyond that, Debs. If what he says is true—and this little stunt with Watts makes me believe him—he's hyper-dangerous."

Debbie returned her gaze without blinking. "We'll get him stabilized, then reassess moving him to ad seg for his own protection. In the meantime, I'll keep him isolated and under lock and key in one of the PITU single-bed cells." She glanced at The Psycho. "Can you guys do the transport? It'll be faster than waiting for the jail to send a car."

"You bet your ass," said Angel with a tired grin. "I'll drive him myself in a transport van—with a whack of strong officers to help." She met Debbie's worried gaze. "He won't have any accidents on the way over."

"Good. Then I'll head over and get the paperwork started. Bring him right up to the PITU."

"Right."

12

First Street, Saint Mary, NY
September 17, 2014, 8:13 pm

Angel slid behind the wheel of the police transport van, glancing in the rearview mirror as she did so. The man claiming to be The Saint Mary Psycho sat all the way in the back, separated from Angel by a wall of steel grating. Double-belted to the hard fiberglass seat inside the cage, his hands cuffed behind him, he stared back with expressionless eyes. The three patrol officers she'd chosen for escort duty—McCandless, Santoro, and Motes—piled into the van as she turned the key in the ignition.

"Is-is-is-is that man okay?" asked The Psycho. "The one that got cut?"

"Shut your mouth!" snapped Joyce Motes.

"Please… I just bead to know."

After taking a moment to translate that gibberish, Angel said, "He'll live." She glanced at the rearview mirror. "But you gave him a fucking scar he'll never forget." The man hung his head, but not before Angel saw tears shimmering in his eyes. She shook her head and muttered to herself.

"You should kill me. I deserve to fly."

"Cut it out. You spoke fine before." Santoro turned to glare at the prisoner.

"*Glaaaachk*—" He shook his head. "That's pot me."

"Just shut up, okay?" Angel ground her teeth.

"I—"

Santoro banged on the cage with his fist. "She said to *shut the fuck up,* asshole. Do it before I crawl back there and make you wish you had."

"Mike," said Angel in a quiet voice. "He's not worth it."

Santoro turned back to the front, shaking his head.

Angel was glad GCJ was a ten-minute drive rather than the hundred minutes a journey to Kingdom Cross Psychiatric over in Lily's Glen would take. She wasn't sure The Psycho would survive a journey like that.

"Uh, I spate to be a bother, but I've got to pee."

"*Jesus,*" muttered Angel.

13

John Jenkins sank to the wooden bench in front of his locker and rested his head in his hands. "Do you think I'm losing it, Larry?"

"No, John, I don't. I think you are reacting to the night, to what that crazy fucker wrote. But listen…" Larry sat on the bench next him and hesitated, hand raised to put it on John's shoulder, but then he lowered it to his lap. "We don't know any of it is true, John. He's obviously taken a few licks to the bean."

"But he knew her name, Larry."

"Yes, and so does anyone who can read the Saint Mary Dispatch. That's nothing, John."

"What about the hatchet?"

"What about it? He could have guessed the details from the newspaper stories, or maybe he just caught a stray neutrino from Jupiter or something and it flipped a bit in his brain. It doesn't mean he's The Saint Mary Psycho. It doesn't mean he killed her."

"Yeah." John sighed. He lifted his head and turned his red-eyed gaze on his friend. "But I have this feeling, Larry… This feeling that he's not lying—at least not about Beth." He lifted his hands in mute helplessness, then let them drop.

Larry lifted his own shoulders, then put one hand on John's arm. "You might be right, John. He might have killed her, he might have killed them all, but if he did, it's like Angel said. We've got to do everything right. For you and Elizabeth. For Beth. We've got to do everything by the book to make sure that motherfucker pays in full."

John nodded and sighed again. "Yeah. Do that. Make sure we dot all the i's and cross all the t's." He turned his face, his eyes flat and dead like doll's eyes. "Get him for me, Larry. Put him away."

Larry nodded and moved his hand to John's shoulder.

"And whatever you do, Larry, don't let me near him. I…" John's Adam's apple bobbed as he swallowed hard. "I can't be trusted around him. Not yet. Maybe not ever." He gazed into the shadows. "I…" His voice faded to nothing.

"You got it, boss." Larry glanced at the pictures taped to the inside of John's locker. "Now, let me drive you home. We can tell Elizabeth together."

"I should object. I should say I can handle it. But…Larry…"

"I know, John. I can only imagine, but I know what you mean."

14

"This way," said Debbie Esteves. "I've got his cell ready." She led them from the unit's intake area toward the hall that housed the psychiatric segregation cells. They weren't much different from the cells assigned to ad seg prisoners—maybe eight-by-six-feet with only a bed for furniture, if it could be called that—except the ones in the PITU all had security cameras that were monitored twenty-four hours a day.

The "bed" was a rectangular box made of stainless steel with rounded over edges and foam padding on all the corners. A thin gel mattress rested inside an indentation on the top. Tie-down loops, for anchoring the shackles in the event a patient needed restraints, were riveted to the sides of the bed.

Debbie pointed at the first steel door, and the four patrol officers walked The Psycho inside.

"Want us to secure him, Doc?" asked Angel. "We don't mind, believe me. He acted like a four-year-old the whole trip."

"Sew, I didn't," said the man.

"How come you can talk as clear as the morning air when you want something, but when you—"

"It's part of his illness. It's called paraphasia." Debbie looked at the thin, dirty man in their midst. "Well? Do I need to have them chain you down?"

He shook his head, then asked, "Will you kill me, now?"

Debbie shook her head. "No. No one will kill you. We're going to help you."

"That means killing me, filling me, drilling me," he said with a despairing shrug.

"Didn't you hear the doc? Cut the shit," growled Mike.

"It's okay, Officer Santoro," said Debbie, meeting his gaze for a moment before turning back to the prisoner. "What is your name? What should I call you?"

"Pudd—" He snapped his mouth shut. "No, I don't have to say that now."

"Why not?" asked Debbie.

"He's not here."

"Then tell me your name."

"I… That is…" The man looked around in confusion. "I don't think… I'm not sure I can… *TH!*" He shook his head.

"You can remove his cuffs, gentlemen," said Debbie. "Then come on out of there." The cops did as she asked, and the small room seemed to grow as they left the room. "Can I call you Joe for now?" she asked the prisoner.

He shrugged, his gaze dropping to the floor. "That's not my name."

"I have to call you something. It'll have to do, for now."

"Yeah, sure." His shoulders rose and fell as if it meant nothing to him one way or the other.

"Have a seat, Joe. I'll walk these folks out, then come back for a chat. Would that be okay?"

The man looked around the little room and burst into tears. "Home again, home again," he chanted under his breath and sank to the gel mattress with a sigh.

15

4983 Livermore Lane, Saint Mary, NY
September 17, 2014, 8:21 pm

John and Elizabeth lived in a modern colonial on a pretty, tree-lined street. The yard was well-maintained, as was the building. John took a certain pride in his planting beds, in the immaculate lawn, and the cozy look of the house. Given his job, he paid special attention to creating a haven for his family. Or at least he had before Beth's murder. Now, he performed his tasks by rote, with no real love of the work or the results—and it showed.

Larry pulled his squad car down the long asphalt drive and parked next to the door he knew led to the welcoming kitchen. He glanced at John, who hadn't spoken since they left the locker room at the station. "Ready?" he asked.

John started from his memories and gave Larry a brusque nod. "As I'll ever be."

As they got out of the car, Larry noticed John was performing the calming breath exercises they'd both been taught at the academy—breathe in for four seconds, hold it for four seconds, exhale for four seconds, remain empty for four seconds, then repeat.

John mounted the steps to the kitchen door and peeked in through the glass pane. Warm yellow light bathed his face, and he froze—long enough for Larry to think he might bolt—and then turned the knob and stepped inside. "Elizabeth? I've got Larry with me." The kitchen was empty, but pots and pans sat above the blue flame of the stove's burners, and it smelled like heaven.

"Larry! Hello!" called Elizabeth from the other room. "Are you here for dinner? There's plenty."

"Uh, hi, Elizabeth," Larry called, feeling small and mean and wishing he were somewhere—anywhere—else.

She came to the inner door of the kitchen, a smile on her face that didn't reach her eyes. She glanced at Larry, then John, who stood with his chin tucked against his chest, then back at Larry. "What is it?" she asked in a small, cold voice. "Is Jack—" A single tear spilled from the corner of her left eye.

"No, no," said Larry in a rush. "No, Jack is fine as far as we know. *Everyone* is fine," he said.

"Then…"

"Elizabeth… Honey…" John spoke without lifting his head. "I… That is…"

"There may have been a development this afternoon, Elizabeth," Larry said into the uncomfortable silence.

Her gaze bounced from John to Larry. "A development?"

"*Maybe.* We don't know anything for sure yet."

Her gaze darted back to John, and she took a single step toward him, then her gaze flicked back to Larry. "Why are you here, Larry?"

"A man came into the station," said John, directing his words at the linoleum. "He's a 5150. *Obviously* crazy."

"But?"

Larry cleared his throat. "But he said some things—"

"He gave me a note, asked me to kill him. He said—"

"Oh, my God, John! You didn't—"

"No," said John in a voice as old and dry as the desert itself. "But I wish I had." His voice cracked on the last syllable, and a tear dove from the tip of his nose to splatter the linoleum between his work boots.

"The man claims to be The Saint Mary Psycho," said Larry. "He claimed—"

"He said he killed Beth." John's voice was cold, hard, and it shook with pent-up rage. "He said he hurt her and killed her and he begged me to put a bullet in his brain but I didn't—I couldn't—I just stood there with my gun out and did *nothing.*"

Again, Elizabeth's gaze darted from Larry to John and back. Tears splashed from her eyes, and for a single moment, Larry thought he saw fury in them, but then it was gone, replaced by heart-wrenching compassion, and she stepped closer to John, wrapping her arms around him.

Moving as quietly as he could, Larry turned and slipped out the back door, closing it behind him. He felt awful, but he could add nothing, *do* nothing. Anger thrummed in him like the thirteen hundred amps zapping through the power line stretching across John's front yard.

He slid behind the wheel of his squad car with a muttered curse. He felt powerless, helpless, in the face of his friend's grief. Larry had always thought he could make things better by finding The Psycho for them. By finding him and either slapping cuffs on his wrists or putting a bullet in his head. But the scene in the kitchen showed him how useless all that would have been. It just ripped away the scabs, reopened the half-healed wounds, exposed the raw nerves of the Jenkins' pain.

He cranked up the cruiser's V8 and slid the gear selector down into reverse, then sat for a moment, staring straight ahead but not seeing anything in front of him. Instead, he saw John standing above the perp, his Glock centered on the back of his head, saw John's finger tight on the trigger, his knuckles shining bone-white in the afternoon sun streaming in the front windows of the First Street Station. He saw John's face as Larry came in, saw the horror of what John had been contemplating and the despair of not having pulled the trigger. Larry took a deep breath and blew out, going for calm but landing on frustrated.

Angel could think what she wanted, but John didn't rattle easily. The fact that he hadn't blown that fucker's brains out attested to that. But whatever he thought he'd seen in that locker room had *scared* him to the bottom of his boots. That, as much as anything, was why he'd gone along and helped John clear the locker room.

He lifted a hand and rested it on the top of the steering wheel, then glanced at the house. He half-hoped John or Elizabeth would come out and call him back inside. That they'd say everything was okay, that he should come in and sit down to supper with them like they had so many times in the past.

But, of course, that didn't happen. *Nothing* was okay, and nothing would ever be okay again.

He lay his right arm over the seat back and turned to look through the rear window, then froze. A dark shadow shot across the drive twenty feet behind his car. His muscles went rigid, his mind blank.

Relax, asshole. It was a cat or one of those obnoxious little dogs the soccer moms go in for.

His mouth twisted in a wry, one-sided grin at his own silliness, and he scoffed at himself. Shaking his head, he backed down the drive at idle, taking care not to drop a tire off in John's lawn. At the end of the drive, he turned on the headlights without looking, peering down Livermore Lane for kids on bikes or walking in the gutters. Seeing no one, he lifted his foot off the brakes and let the car bump out into the road.

He turned back, watching the headlights wash across John's yard. Just beyond the effective range of his headlights, something darted from behind a giant hydrangea and shot across the drive to the denser holly bushes John kept trimmed like a tall wall between his drive and the neighbor's.

That was no cat! That was no yip-yip dog! a shrieky voice shouted in the back of his mind.

But, of course, it was a cat. *It had to be a cat.*

"If it was a cat, why was it running on two legs?" he murmured to himself as he stomped on the brakes. He peered into the dark shadows under the holly bushes. He leaned forward over the wheel, squinting, and holding his breath, watching for any telltale movement in the gloom. "Who said it was running on two legs?" He snapped his head from side to side, denying it, *refusing* it.

But it had been. It *had been,* and Larry knew it without a doubt.

He pulled back into the driveway and slipped the car into park, leaving the lights blazing, the engine running. He got out and slid his big Maglite from the door compartment where he liked to keep it. He switched it on and focused the beam, playing it along the base of the holly shrubs.

"Cat's long gone, dumbass," he muttered. He swept the beam of the flash along the shrubs, seeing nothing, and shook his head. "Freaked out by a fricking cat, Larry? What's next? Pink elephants? Might as well take up drinking." He chuckled. "Drinking *more*, anyway."

But he didn't turn and get back in the car. Instead, he stood there, Maglite pointed at the end of the shrub wall, trying to see everything at once from the corners of his eyes. He stood there, staring into the gathering gloaming until a chill traversed his spine.

"Idiot," he called himself. He turned back toward the car, and as he did, a piping chirp rang in the night air. The chill that had slid down his spine returned, bringing gooseflesh with it. Larry froze, staring into the darkness beneath the shrubs as if mesmerized, Maglite forgotten and hanging uselessly at his side. *It's a cat, Larry,* said his mother's voice, far back in his mind. He shook his head slowly. *A cat that* chirps? *That's no cat, and you know it.*

He brought the Maglite slowly across his body and shifted it to his left hand, then slashed it at the dark space beneath the shrubs, his right hand slapping gun-leather, and his thumb snapping away the safety strap—functioning on automatic. The Maglite's bright white beam stabbed into the gloom under the holly, but there was nothing there.

Not even a cat.

He shook his head and forced himself to relax. He drew a deep breath in for four seconds and held it for a four-count. He lifted his hand from the butt of his pistol and smiled.

The chirp came again, this time from behind the car.

Larry's Glock was out and up, the triton night sights trained on nothing. He slipped his index finger inside the trigger guard and pressed the trigger block, ready to fire if he had to. The front sight jittered a little as his hand shook—something that had never happened in the two decades Larry had been a cop.

Moving stiff-legged, Larry strode toward the back of the car, painting the ground with his light. He reached the end of the car and peeked around behind it. A dark splotch—as though someone had dropped black ink on his cornea—streaked under the bumper and beneath the car. He dropped prone, his finger so tight on the trigger he thought any little wind would set the thing off…

But there was nothing there. Not even a splotch of blackness.

Larry's breath gusted out of him, and he took his finger off the trigger block, then out of the trigger guard altogether. He played the white beam of the flashlight under the car. "Goddamn thing didn't run off," he whispered. "It *disappeared under there.*"

He shook his head and holstered his pistol. *No, it didn't, jerkoff. It was never there to begin with. You let John's...well, whatever John's little episode was, you let it rub off on you. Get it together, Marine.*

Still shaking his head, Larry climbed to his feet and got into the car. Despite what he told himself, he sat at the end of John's driveway, peering into murk beneath the American holly bushes for another five minutes before he put the car in reverse and backed out.

Looky here, he thought. *Looky, looky, but don't get too close. The crazy's catching.*

Chapter 6
That Goddamn Birthday

I

"Hold it," said Gavin.

Debbie arched an eyebrow at him.

"I'm not sure what that's supposed to mean… 'The crazy's catching.' Are you trying to tell us these three men shared a *folie à deux?*"

"No. It's not that."

Gavin shook his head and glanced at Jim. "Then…what?"

But Debbie shook her head. "You'll have to let me tell this in order and in my own time. It won't make sense otherwise."

"It's not making much sense as it is," said Denders. "No offense meant."

A peculiar smile twisted Debbie's lips. "None taken. Believe me when I say I know exactly how all this sounds."

Gavin looked at his watch. "We are under certain time pressures…"

Debbie sighed. "Yes. I understand. The investigation." She glanced at the clock on the wall. "There's a lot more. Can you stay over? At a motel in Lily's Glen, I mean?"

Denders shook his head. "No chance."

"And we have certain tasks we need to take care of this afternoon. In the City."

Esteves shook her head. "I really thought meeting him would do the trick. How can you…" She sighed. "The things Joe told you. The details. How can you experience that and think—"

"Listen, we can come back," said Gavin. "Unless there's another victim tonight. We could come back in the morning. Right, Jim?"

Jim looked at him and cocked his head.

"He *knew* those things, gentlemen. He won't remember that he did, but when he said them, he *knew* them. Do you doubt that? Do you still think I put him up to it despite the evidence to the contrary?"

"Evidence?" asked Jim.

"You know what I mean. With the situation being what it is."

"I need to see the scenes," Gavin said. "And to do that, I need the daylight. It is important, Doctor Esteves."

"*This is important, Agent Gregory!*"

Gavin pressed his lips together and dropped his gaze away from her angry eyes. "If we have the time, we'll come back."

"You'll never find her without me." Debbie pushed away from the table and began cleaning up, slapping their trays together with a clatter, jangling silverware and china to the top tray.

"*Her*?" asked Gavin.

Debbie's hands slowed, then stopped. She looked up and met his intense gaze calmly. "I misspoke. I meant 'him,' of course." As Gavin continued to stare at her, she went back to straightening up. She turned and took a card from her desk drawer and turned it over. She wrote a phone number on the back and handed it to him.

"Uh… I'm married."

She grinned at him. "It's not for that, Agent. You could be in danger. Call me if something strange happens." She produced another card and wrote her number on it. "You, too, Detective. And come back in the morning."

Gavin glanced at Jim. "We'll try."

2

Kingdom Cross Psychiatric Hospital, Lily's Glen, NY
Wednesday, 3:07 pm

Jim slid behind the wheel of his cruiser, then glanced at Gregory as he got in. "What do you think?"

Gavin stared at the building, then leaned forward to gaze up at the top floor. "How'd they do it?"

"Do what? The circus trick?"

Gavin turned in his seat and looked at the big cop. "You think it was a trick?"

"What else?" asked Denders with a shrug. "Look, I went to the county fair when I was a kid. One year, there was a guy there who had a ton of great prizes for ten-year-olds, so me and my friends, we all wanted to do it." He cranked the ignition and put the car in reverse, backing out slowly. "The gimmick was, you'd go up to him, and he'd do this bit—you know, fluttering eyelids, waving his hands around, pressing a crystal to his forehead. He had a bunch of little papers in the palm of his hand, and after he did his bit, he wrote two things on the paper: your birthday and your weight." He turned out of the Kingdom Cross parking lot and headed toward the Interstate. "Then, he made a big deal of getting his pretty assistant to help you up on this big scale he had set up so everyone could see the weight. After he weighed you, his assistant helped you down, giving you ample chances to see into her skimpy top so you didn't look at him. Now, I'm not saying he changed what he wrote—because none of my friends saw him do that, and I didn't see him do anything hokey when it was their turns—but he either changed it, wrote it later, or maybe he had the scale rigged somehow. None of my pals weighed remotely what I did, and yet, the weights he guessed and what the scale said all seemed to be in the right proportions."

"He was right?"

Denders shrugged. "You know how scales weigh differently. I didn't weigh on his scale what I did at home, and it was the same for all my friends, but we did match the number he'd written down *exactly*."

Gavin shrugged. "And the birthday?"

Nodding, Jim got them on the highway and headed back toward the City. "This is the spooky part. He didn't scribble something, then pretend it was the month. He wrote it out: November 6, 1973. The full deal."

"You're confusing me, Jim. From the way this started, I expected an anecdote about why this business has to be a setup."

"Yeah." Jim shrugged. "I think about the circus trick all the time. The weights…I can imagine different ways to rig the scale. But the birthdays?" He shook his head. "Right down to the year like that? He couldn't have palmed that many sheets, right?"

Gavin shrugged. "There's always a trick to stuff like that. I mean, if he was for real, then why was he working a fair? Why not go to work on Wall Street and get rich?"

"I'm right there with you." The big man glanced at him. "But still. The exact date right down to the year. How'd he do that?"

"Joe knew my…" Gavin shook his head. "He knew my wife's name. He knew about…my son."

"Plus all the rest," said Jim, waving one hand in a circle. "How long I've been on the force, right down to the number of days and weeks and months. Shit, Gavin. I didn't know that until I worked it out to see if he was right."

"Just like the birthday."

Jim nodded. "Just like the goddamn birthday." He drove in silence for a moment, then glanced over. "But here's the thing, Gavin."

"Yeah?"

"Introducing us to Joe was like that pretty little assistant with the gaping top."

"A distraction?"

"Could be."

"But…" Gavin shook his head. "But why? Why…*any* of it?"

"Well, that's the question, isn't it? What could she be getting out of it? Attention? She's a shrink for fuck's sake."

"She's got a bone to pick," Gavin said slowly. "She's got something…she needs to…to prove, right? Something about how all this went down in Saint Mary."

"Interesting," said Denders. "I could check that."

"But if that's the case, why not go to the press? Why come to us and then sit and wait, even though her calling the NYPD seemed to produce nothing?"

Denders scratched his chin, then ran a hand through his hair. "Because if that scale wasn't fixed, and if he didn't change the weight he wrote on the paper, why'd he get the girl to show us her bra?"

"And then there's the birthday."

"Yep. That goddamn birthday."

3

Alley near Third and 36th, Manhattan, NY
Wednesday, 5:43 pm

"Pretty brazen," said Gavin, hooking his thumb at the street behind them.

Jim shrugged. "It was dark. Raining. And most of the traffic down here would've been on Third Avenue." He shrugged again. "Besides, this is New York City. Who looks?"

"Still, not much cover for the kind of thing The Smith liked to get up to."

Jim turned and took a few steps toward 36th Street. "I'm going to go grab some joe. Maybe a sandwich. You want anything?"

"No thanks," said Gavin, turning his back on the detective and street beyond. "I just need a few minutes."

"You've got them." Jim's heavy footsteps crunched away.

The light was poor, the shadows in the alley long. Gavin peered down at the forensic drawing of the scene, glancing around trying to place where the perp dropped the hammer, where the victim lay when she was found. The alley stank of garbage and something worse—like the musty smell of a circus tent or the lion's den at the zoo. He noted the blood splatter on the drawing, then peered at the dark spots on the bricks and pavement, all the while trying to imagine The Smith hunched over the twenty-one-year-old woman. "What did you do?" he whispered.

He walked to where the woman had ended her days, then stood with his feet wide apart, as though straddling her prostrate form. His gaze made the circuit of blood splatter evidence again, and he adjusted his footing, holding his pen as though it were the hammer's haft, then swinging his arm and imagining the blood arcing away. "It's not right," he muttered. "Magic blood splatter."

He scanned the CSI report for the umpteenth time, still not finding what he was looking for. Still not finding any mention that The Smith had positioned her just so, that he'd staged the body after he marked her, though it was clear to Gavin that he had. Each body they'd found in the mid-2000s had been moved post-mortem, and it seemed this victim had seen the same treatment.

"Why did you move her?" he asked. They'd held the staging detail back—yet another cold fact to help distinguish copycats and false confessions. He'd been sure he'd find a way to rule The Smith out of this crime. He'd been sure this was a copycat or simple coincidence as he boarded his flight the day before, but… "One hell of a coincidence," he murmured.

He moved to where the perp must have stood while he beat the woman, lining himself up with the blood evidence. He mimed rolling her over to mark the small of her back. As he straightened, he shook his head. He was still yards away from where she ended up. "Why move her that last time? What's the point?" he mumbled.

Something scraped on the gritty concrete behind him.

"A few more minutes, Jim," he said over his shoulder, his gaze intent on the drawing. The detective didn't answer—not even a grunt—but that was fine with Gavin. He took two giant steps to the side, then glanced back at where the woman had died and shook his head.

The Smith had never *posed* the bodies—at least not that they'd been able to determine. He'd just moved them for reasons unknown.

The soft scrape came again, and this time, Gavin smiled ruefully and flipped the folder closed on the forensic drawing. "Yeah, I can take a hint." As he spun around, his smile faded, and his brow wrinkled.

He was alone.

"Jim?" he called. He took a few tentative steps toward 36th Street, then stopped. His hinkiness meter pegged all the way to the right, and a shiver ran down his spine. Gavin fumbled his small flashlight out of his pocket and clicked it on, stabbing at the shadows with the bright LED light. He was alone in the alley.

Gavin thought about the last story Esteves had told them and shook his head, feeling more than a little foolish. With a sour grin at his own suggestibility, he turned and walked to the end of the alley. Jim stood up at the corner, watching the traffic flow by on Third Avenue, one hand shoved into his front pocket, steam from his coffee twisting up toward his face.

With one last glance toward the growing darkness in the alley, Gavin put his flashlight away and tucked the folder under his arm. His stomach growled, and his eyes burned with fatigue. It had been a long, weird day, and he still had to call Pete back at the BAU. He pinched the bridge of his nose and sighed. *And tell him what? That this has all the earmarks of a Smith murder? That he's really back?*

He scrubbed his hand over his face and lifted his foot to leave the alley behind. The absolute silence from the dead end of the alley bothered him. No car sounds from Third Avenue, no wind, no children from the various courtyards around the block, just *nothing.* He stared at the back of Jim's head for a moment, willing the detective to turn and see him, to come down the street with a joke, but the man stood gazing into the river of cars. Gavin turned his head slowly, his hand digging in his pocket for his flashlight.

The chirp came then, confident and aggressive, penetrating and sharp, a taunting sound, a *laughing* sound.

Gavin dropped the folder, sweeping the flashlight up and on, the white beam stabbing the darkness-shrouded alley while his other hand reached for the pistol on his hip. A man, a monster—he didn't know what he expected, but he expected *something.*

Instead, there was nothing in the alley, and though he stood there for a long time, there were no more chirps, either.

4

Jim put the cruiser in park and gave him a concerned look. "You sure you're feeling okay? You look very pale."

"No, I'm fine. Tired, I guess." He put his hand on the door release. "I'll grab a quick bite from room service, then hit the hay."

Concern flickered in Jim's steel-gray eyes. "Did…" He shook his head. "That crime scene…the last one. Something's off there, isn't it?"

"I'll fill you in tomorrow, Jim. My head is pounding like you wouldn't believe."

"There's a clinic—"

"Nah. I'm fine. A couple of aspirin, a meal, and some sleep. That's all I need. We'll talk about the scene in the morning, and then, if there's nothing pressing, maybe we'll head back to Kingdom Cross."

"Think there's something there, then?"

"Something," Gavin said with a shrug.

"That damn birthday."

"That's right. That, and the cute assistant."

"We'll dig up the truth," said Jim, turning to look him in the eye. "Whatever it is."

"Right. Whatever it is." Gavin popped the door open. "Goodnight," he said.

"Night. Get some rest." The big detective turned to assess the traffic as Gavin closed the door and strode into his hotel.

The air conditioning in his room felt crisp and cold as Gavin slipped out of his shoes. He sat on the edge of the bed and shook his head with self-directed scorn. How easily she'd manipulated him, the doctor, with her ghost stories and tall tales. He flopped back on the bed, wincing as his back muscles spasmed a little before relaxing, then he lay staring up at the ceiling.

The guy at Kingdom Cross, Joe... He knew Maddie's name, *knew about Austin, about his...* Gavin snapped his eyes shut and cut the thought off. *That doesn't mean a thing. He could have read about it in the paper. He could be playing possum.*

Sure, said a voice in the back of his mind. *But why?*

That's the sixty-four-thousand-dollar question, isn't it? Why? Why would the good doctor want to tell us stories? Why would Joe go along with it? Or is it the doctor who's going along? After all, Joe's the one who claimed to be The Saint Mary Psycho.

There were reasons an innocent man might confess to a crime he didn't commit—plenty of them, ranging from the psychiatric to the narcissistic. Plus, the notoriety factor, the twisted sort of fame that went along with being known as a serial killer. But none of that seemed like Joe, and Gavin considered himself a good judge of character. *Then again, Esteves doesn't trip any bells, either, but what do you expect from a trained psychiatrist?*

His phone chirped, and it sounded nothing like the noise in the alley, but his heart lurched to a thunderous gallop as he swept it up off the bed and answered it. "Hey, Maddie," he said after glancing at the caller ID.

"Hi. Can you talk? Why are you out of breath?"

"Sit-ups. You know. Yeah, I can talk."

"If you're working out…"

"Nah, just thinking. I could use a break. What's up?"

She sighed into the microphone, and the noise came across like a loose tarp flapping in a brisk wind. "Are you…"

"Not yet, hon. I've got some loose ends to chase down up here."

"And the case? It's nothing, right?"

It was Gavin's turn to sigh into the phone. "I'm…"

"Oh, *Christ!*" she snapped. "I knew it, Gav. I *knew* it."

"Listen, Maddie. I'm not sure yet. There are a few things that look hinky, but maybe there are good explanations for them. And look, it doesn't matter. I told Pete that I had to be back this weekend, and I meant it. If he wants a continued presence up here, he'll just have to—"

"Unless it really is The Smith," she said in a cold, hard voice.

"Maddie…"

"Because if it *is* him, you'll want to stay, vacation be damned. Right?" Her breath came fast and crisp. "Right?"

"Maddie… Maddie, listen to me a minute."

"Tell me I'm wrong, Gavin."

"I love you. I *want* to go on this vacation. I *want* things to get better. *I'm willing to do the work, Maddie.*"

Silence stretched between them, and as it did, Gavin's stomach churned.

"But if it's The Smith…" Maddie breathed.

"Honey, you knew what I was when you married me. You know how I'm wired."

"Right," she said crisply, biting off the word. "It's just that I'd hoped this once—*just one goddamn time*—you'd put me first."

"Maddie, I do put you first. I think about you every morning when I wake up. I think about you all day long. You're who I want to talk to the second I'm done working, who I want to eat with, cuddle with, sleep with. You're everything to me. You know that."

Maddie said nothing.

"I'm doing the best I can to make sure I'm there, honey."

There was no answer, and he pulled the phone away from his ear and glanced at it, then sighed dejectedly. Maddie had hung up. Gavin got up and paced to the too-short, uncomfortable easy chair shoved into the corner of the room. He sank into it, hit Pete's speed dial icon, and pressed the phone to his ear.

"Fielding," said his boss. "What do you have for me, Gavin?"

"I can't rule him out. Not yet." Gavin heard the man lean back, heard the clunk of a La-Z-Boy reclining, the rasping of Pete's phone against the stubble of his beard.

"The mark?"

"It's there, and it matches. I sent some stuff down this morning."

"Saw it. Did he stage the scene?"

Gavin closed his eyes. "Yes, and it's just like it was back then. No rhyme or reason, no pose, no extra junk lying around. The body's just not in the place the blood splatter dictates it had to have been when he struck her."

"Shit," Pete muttered.

"Yeah, and there's something else." Gavin told him about meeting Esteves, about the story she'd told about Saint Mary.

"Is she a wingnut?"

"It doesn't feel that way. I'll try to get back out that way and talk to her again, but, Pete, we talked about this. I've got tomorrow and Friday morning, then I've got to get back."

Pete said nothing for a minute, then he said, "Gavin, if this is The Smith—"

"Then you'll have to send someone else."

Fielding sighed. "I can smooth things over, Gav. I'll talk to her."

"No, Pete, you won't. This is important. I'm not the only agent who worked on The Smith case."

"No, you aren't the only one, Gavin, but you are the *best* one."

Gavin closed his eyes, really squeezing them tight.

"I'll take care of everything, Gavin. I'll request the jet. I'll call the resort, tell them how important your work is, get them to hold the room, to accommodate you. The Bureau will cover any extra days, and you'll get your month."

Gregory sucked in a breath and blew out his cheeks. "I'm not sure any of that will matter, Pete."

Pete sucked his teeth a moment. "It's like that, is it?"

"I think so. She just hung up on me. Didn't even give me a chance. She needs this, Pete. You know she makes more from her little vampire romances than both of us together. It's not money she's worried about."

Pete sighed. "I know. Listen, put all that aside for now. You're coming home Friday night. I'll requisition the jet for LaGuardia at…what? Six?"

"Yeah," Gavin sighed. "Six should be good. But then I'm done for a month, Pete."

"Right," said Pete. "I've got to go. Dinner and all that. Call me tomorrow night, earlier if something breaks."

"Sure thing, boss." Gavin disconnected the call, then sat, arms resting on his knees, phone held loosely in one hand, head hanging. He had to let it go on Friday.

He had to.

5

Gavin lurched awake, sure he heard something. He lay still, eyes wide, peering into the cold blue light cast by the alarm clock's LED screen, straining his ears to hear past the pounding of his own heartbeat. He grabbed the pistol from where it lay on the nightstand, the cold hard polymer frame giving him some sense of safety, of comfort. The bedclothes rustled as he checked the Glock had a round in the chamber and transferred it to his right hand—his shooting hand.

He widened his eyes, once, twice, and again, then took in a long, slow breath, held it, released it slowly, and drew in yet another. Beyond the blue pallid swatch of light, the room was nothing but stygian felt, furniture nothing but dark lumps against a darker background. Purple and green monsters swam and leered in his vision, but he ignored them, his flickering gaze dancing from one dark form to the next, the tritium night sights glowing as he moved the pistol to follow his shifting eyes.

But—just like in the alley—there was nothing there.

Gavin took a deep breath and blew it out, forcing his head back, forcing his muscles to relax. He put the pistol back on the nightstand but left his hand resting on it, not yet ready to give up its cold comfort.

Eventually, his eyelids slid closed, and his muscles relaxed completely. With a sigh, he pulled his left arm under the covers and nestled into the bed.

6

Alley near Third and 36th, Manhattan, NY
Thursday, 2:03 am

Gavin stood at the mouth of the alley, hands shoved in the pockets of his warm-up pants, feet sweating in his running shoes. He was no longer breathing hard—he'd been standing there too long, staring into the dark alley, waiting...waiting for...

Waiting for what? *he asked himself. The only problem was, he didn't know what he was waiting for.*

The City was bereft of sound—the night sky rendering it as a silent black and white film, artsy and cold. Occasionally, a silent car drifted by on Third Avenue, pale-faced drivers leering at him.

Something creaked deep in the grave-black alley—a hangman's rope screaming at the weight of a body just dropped—and Gavin shuddered at the sound. He peered down the alley, opening his eyes wide once, twice, and again. He took a long, slow breath, held it, then released it slowly before starting all over again.

But it didn't help his visual acuity. In fact, it didn't help anything. He was no calmer than before—if anything he was more anxious that his old-stand-by calming technique no longer worked.

He turned his head toward Third Avenue again, hoping to see Jim Denders come strolling around the corner, his huge, wolfish smile shining in the moonlight. But there was nothing there.

Gavin knew he had to go into the alley's maw alone. That he had to investigate. There was a mystery waiting for him, a puzzle to solve. It was what he did, after all, solving puzzles.

He took a single step forward, the grit of the sidewalk rasping beneath the tread of his New Balance shoe. He drew his hands out of his pockets slowly, wanting them free in case he had to act fast, not thinking about the fact that his sidearm was back in the hotel, that he had nothing so much as a penknife on him.

He took another step, sliding his foot across the concrete rather than lifting it and moving forward—like a kid scared to cross the dark basement. A cold, soundless wind gusted at him, hitting him square in the face from the dark depths of the alley. That wind stank, smelled of spoiled eggs, of old food, of sawdust and animal shit, of meat burned to a crisp over a raging fire, *of body odor, and of blood. Something clanked—steel against concrete—once, twice, and again, and Gavin froze.*

He knew better, knew he should be either charging into that miasma or running for Third Avenue and someone's cell phone, knew he had to get to fighting or get to calling for back-up, but the soles of his running shoes seemed welded to the ground, stuck in the concrete. His thighs spasmed, and his knees jerked as he tried to shift his feet, but all that accomplished was unbalancing him.

His mouth snapped open with a soundless scream as his feet slid forward as though he stood on a moving sidewalk, rushing him into the welcoming grip of the cold, cold darkness...

7

Pod 51 Hotel, Manhattan, NY
Thursday, 2:11 am

Gavin lurched awake, sure he heard something. He lay still, eyes wide, peering into the cold blue light cast by the alarm clock's LED screen, straining his ears to hear past the pounding of his own heartbeat. He was soaked with a cold sweat, and the sheets were twisted around his feet as though he'd been struggling to get free of them, to jump out of bed.

Nothing moved in the silent darkness surrounding him, and nothing should have. He was in his hotel room, safe. He reached out with his left hand and found the polymer frame of his service weapon, even though it had been an ugly nightmare that had awakened him. There was nothing in the room—*could be* nothing in the room.

He hated hotels. He was too hot for the blankets, and he kicked them off, forcing himself to lie still, to close his eyes and think of nothing. After a moment, he lifted his hand from the pistol and rolled up on his side. His breathing slowed, his eyelids sank closed, and his body relaxed.

On the edge of sleep, he sighed. *Only a dream,* he told himself. *A nightmare.*

Behind him, in the weird little bathroom, a soft chirp sounded, and his eyes flew open. He flung himself around and snapped on the bedside lamp, snatching up the Glock, staring into that aborted-hallway-cum-bathroom with wide eyes.

Did you really expect to see something, Gavin? he asked himself. *Really?*

With a groan, he lay the Glock on the nightstand and killed the light, ignoring his thumping heart. He lay down, crossed his hands over his chest, and closed his eyes.

8

Alley near Third and 36th, Manhattan, NY
Thursday, 4:03 am

Gavin stood at the mouth of the alley, hands shoved in the pockets of his warm-up pants, feet sweating in his running shoes. He was no longer breathing hard—he'd been standing there too long, staring into the dark alley, waiting...waiting for...

Waiting for what? *he asked himself. The only problem was, he didn't know...*

Jim? *He scratched his head, turning to glance up toward Third Avenue. There was no sign of the gargantuan detective, only silent cars fluttering by like dandelion puffs in a light breeze. Pale, slack faces stared back at him from the drivers' seats, wailing, horror-filled faces screamed in silence in the back seats.*

Above, the night sky whirled, a massive machine turning without sound, sharp points of light glittering like motes of diamond in the vast, cold emptiness. Clouds rushed in from the horizon, moving faster than nature allowed. Rivers of lightning jumped and lanced and crackled between those dead gray puffballs, but no thunder boomed, no sounds invaded the mute night.

If Jim's not here, then what am I waiting for? What? A sign? A phone call? *He patted the empty pockets of his sweat-soaked warm-up pants.* Must have forgotten it back at the… *He shook his head.* At the what?

He swiveled his hips and started toward Third Avenue, the soles of his running shoes grinding on the gritty sidewalk, and he stopped after a single step, marveling at the sound it made. It was the only sound in the entire world, after all, and it tickled his ears. He did a little jig, shuffling his feet in the grit, smiling at the crunchy sound.

A cold, animal-pen-smelling wind wafted at him from the depths of the alley, and a lone sheet of newspaper danced in the eddies, racing toward him, then spinning in place, then shuffling back, then racing forward again. He watched it, his smile widening. There was a poetry to the silent night, a certain quality that inspired him, made him want to—

A chirp! *he crowed in his mind.* I'm waiting for a chirp to come from the end of the alley where The Smith is hiding.

A grand mystery awaited him in the deep shadows back by the dumpsters he could barely see. Something glinted in the light shed by the hundreds of bolts of lightning that danced overhead. He had to investigate it. That was his purpose, to find the truth, to turn the obfuscating soil back, to expose what lay beneath, to…

Bitter dread settled in his gut. Gelid fear clutched at his throat, squeezing, squeezing, and his heart thumped with it, raced with it. His face felt numb, frozen in terror, eyes open wide, mouth hanging ajar, snot gathering on his lip.

His body turned away from the mouth of the alley, leaving only his head facing that murk, that gloaming, that darkness. His feet moved, his thighs pumped, and had he not been stuck knee-deep in the mire of wet concrete beneath him, he would have raced away. As it was, he lurched side to side a bit but made little forward progress.

Terror built behind his eyes, pressure in his sinuses soaring until he thought his skull would explode, and pulses of blue light blinked in time with his racing pulse. His breath ripped in and out, in and out, in and—

He choked against the blockage deep in his throat, against the lump of hard cold that snaked across his teeth and slid down his tongue. In the depths of his chest, a scream began, but the thing in his neck overpowered it, denied it, snuffed it out.

Then, it came.

At long last, it came.

After eons of waiting, choking, panicking: an aberrant chirp; a strange, off-key note from a mistuned bagpipe, a perverse twang from a psychotic cricket; and Gavin couldn't look away from the abyss swirling back there amongst the dumpsters and the dead.

He could no longer breathe, and his chest burned from the lack of air. His legs still pumped, still spun endlessly in the mire, still did nothing, ever-sinking, ever-running. His limp hand flapped uselessly at the place where his pistol would have been—had he been carrying it. His other hand clawed at the invisible bands of steel encircling his neck, clawed at his throat, shoved at the immobile lump of cold steel stuck in his throat.

The chirp came again, echoing from one end of the silent night to the other, shrieking like a jet engine hard on the afterburner, whistling like a steam engine in the red, and Gavin flailed to the side, pulling his feet up, shoving his knees to the side, flinging his weight away from the bizarre, misshapen lump coming at him from the graveyard back in the shadowy alley.

The chirp came again, sounding closer, coming from that strange shape that seemed to shift and blur and waft like smoke all at once. The sound ate at him, burned his ears, sucked his eyeballs dry like a hot desert wind. He longed to plug his ears with his fingers, but everything below his chin had faded away, numb, paralyzed, forgotten. He thought if he heard that noise one more time, he would die.

The chirp came again, and...

9

Gavin lurched awake, pulse slamming in his throat, unsure if he'd screamed or if he'd only dreamed the sound. He flailed at the lamp, succeeded in flipping it on, succeeded in flipping it to the floor with a jagged crash. The pale blue light from the alarm clock did nothing to illuminate the darkness around him, did nothing to slow his racing heart—how could it? It was only a clock.

He slapped his hand to the nightstand, reaching for his Glock, but it wasn't there. His neck ached, burned, raw and abraded, and something cold and wet was coiled around it. He grabbed it—the sheet, soaked with his sweat.

His phone chirped again—the emergency ring tone, the only one he allowed to disturb his sleep.

He pulled the twisted sheet loose, then up and over his head, his gaze creeping around in the dim blue haze emanating from the clock's LED face. His pistol was on the floor—maybe it had gone over with the lamp. His phone was farther, as though he'd flung it away.

He took in a long, slow breath, held it, released it slowly, and drew in yet another, then widened his eyes, once, twice, and again, going for that cold calm he'd cultivated for bad crime scenes, for life-threatening moments, but it didn't work. It didn't work at all.

Forcing himself to move, one hand massaging his sore neck, Gavin rolled from the bed and stumbled over to his phone, sweeping it up with his other hand. He peered at the caller ID, then answered it. "Gregory," he croaked.

"Uh, it's Denders. You sound like shit."

"Yeah," he grated. "It is four in the morning."

"Almost four-thirty. Get dressed. We've got another one."

"Fuck," Gavin hissed, glancing down at the now-cold sweat streaming from his body. "Give me a few minutes."

"I'll be downstairs in five, but I'll wait." Denders coughed explosively. "But hurry. No need for makeup or a tie."

"Right." Gavin snapped his thumb on the disconnect button and staggered to the light switch. Brilliant white light filled the little room, but even so, he stood still for a moment, peering into every nook and cranny.

But he had no idea what he was looking for.

10

Gavin pushed out onto the street, his gaze creeping up to the sky, sure, somehow, that dark clouds and bizarre lightning would fill it. But it was a clear morning, and only stars blazed in the sky above. He trudged to the car and swung the passenger door open. He wore his slacks and a dress shirt, but no tie and no coat.

"You look like shit, Agent Gregory," said Jim, one hand on the steering wheel, half-a-grin on his face.

"Feel worse," said Gavin. "Didn't sleep well."

"No?" Jim turned to face forward, then craned his neck to check for traffic before getting out holding two cups of coffee. "Headache?"

"Nah, the aspirin took care of it. I kept waking up with a jump. You know"—Gavin twirled the fingers of his left hand—"like in a horror flick."

"Right." The big man held out a cup. "Brought you coffee."

"You're a scholar and gentleman." Gavin grabbed the paper cup and poured the hot black goodness down his throat.

"I'm pretty sure I'm neither of those." He flicked his fingers toward the east. "This one's close. And you're not going to like it."

"Tell me," said Gavin before taking another swig. The coffee soothed his throat.

"Another girl, another alley."

"Another hammer?"

Jim glanced at him and nodded.

"Fuck."

"You said a fresh scene would work best," said Denders, his mouth a grim slash through the bottom of his face.

"Yeah," sighed Gavin. "Me and my big mouth."

"I still haven't told you the part you're not going to like."

Gavin arched an eyebrow at him.

Denders shrugged and flicked his fingers at the intersection to the east again. "Right down there is a restaurant. It's on the ground floor of an apartment building."

"And?"

"The girl worked in the restaurant, lived in the building."

Gavin twirled the fingers of his free hand and took another gulp of coffee.

Jim looked toward the intersection and grimaced. "The restaurant is called 'The Smith.'"

Something hot and slimy twisted in Gavin's guts. "Motherfuck!"

"Yep. She's wedged between the dumpster and the back wall of the restaurant."

"Ah, shit," muttered Gavin, scrubbing at his eyes with a thumb and forefinger. "You're right. I *hate* it."

"Come on," said Denders, turning and walking down the sidewalk. "There's no way to get to the alley from the street."

"Closed off?"

"Right," said Jim with a nod. "There's an entrance there with a glass door for people and a metal door for service. The whole thing's not very high. He could have climbed it, easy."

"Even carrying a kicking girl?"

Denders shrugged. "She could have been back there already—taking out her garbage or dumping something from the restaurant. I've got a uniform heading down to wake the manager up."

Jim led him half a block to the intersection and then across. He pushed through the service door and then out into the alley beyond. They signed into the scene with the duty officer, then stepped under the crime scene tape. Haymond stood next to the brick wall, looking on as the CSI techs did their thing. His face was a study in dejection. He glanced their way as they approached and frowned.

"Barely eighteen this time," he said with a frown. "He messed her up good." The lieutenant hooked his thumb over his shoulder. "She worked right there. The place is called—"

"Jim told me."

Haymond grunted and nodded.

"Same brand of hammer?" Jim asked in a low voice, and Haymond grunted again. "Fuck," the big detective muttered. "The thing on her back?"

Haymond shrugged. "They can't roll her. She's wedged between the wall and the dumpster, which is full, of course." He grunted again and jerked his head at the other side of the alley. "Weird thing is, he killed her over there. If you believe the blood splatter guy, that is."

Gavin nodded, a sour frown on his face.

"You knew that already," said Jim. It wasn't a question, and the man's eyes narrowed a fraction.

Gavin nodded again. "It's something we held back from everyone. Up until now, the move has been very subtle, and most people never even noticed. But this…"

Haymond nodded. "He did this on purpose to tell you it's him. That and the goddamn restaurant."

"Is she blonde?" asked Gavin.

"That or strawberry. Hard to say given the blood and the shadow behind that dumpster. The ME will confirm it."

Gavin peered up, looking for windows that didn't exist. "I suppose a witness is too much to ask for?"

"No one saw nothing," said Haymond, then winced and burped. His meaty hand went to his side and rubbed in a circle. "Fucking job."

"When can I get in there?" asked Gavin. "It'll help if I can see the scene fresh."

Haymond looked at him a moment, his tongue distending his lips as he ran it over the front of his teeth. "Never understood that."

Gavin's shoulder bounced up and down once. "Seeing the scene as the unsub left it helps me to see what he wanted to show us." He waved his hand at the CSI crew. "They are here to sift everything into evidence bags. They're not worried about what the unsub is trying to tell me."

"Trying to tell you…" Haymond shook his head. "I'm just an old beat cop, Gregory."

"Sure," said Gavin. "But these guys…they live in fantasy when it comes to their murders. They have a ritual that means something—at least to them. If I can figure out what it means, we're a hell of a lot closer to catching the bastard."

The lieutenant looked away, pursing his lips. "Five minutes," he grunted. "Emory! Back your crew off for a few minutes. The FBI wants to walk the scene."

A tall, thin man rose from a crouch, peering their way. "Lieutenant, there's *evidence* to—"

"Just do it, goddammit!" Haymond yelled. His hand went to his belly again, and he burped.

Gavin stood quietly while the CSI technicians walked away from the scene, some shaking their heads, some glaring at him. When the last one—Emory—had walked past, Gavin held his cup out to Jim, then stepped past the big detective.

"Five goddamn minutes, Gregory," Haymond said. "Not one second more."

"That's fine, Lieutenant. Thank you." Haymond turned away with another burp. Gavin stood for a moment, returning Jim's blank-faced stare, then turned and walked to the middle of the enclosed space.

The blood splatter gleamed in the lights the CSI team had set up—on the wall opposite the dumpster. The hammer lay in a pool of blood, and there were long marks stretching from that pool toward the dumpster. *Why? Why not just kill her by the dumpster? What is it with you?*

Gavin followed the drag marks to the side of the dumpster and peered into the shadows between it and the wall. He fished out his flashlight and clicked it on. She looked even younger than eighteen to Gavin's mind, sixteen at most. As thin as she was, the unsub had bent and mashed her to get her in the space. Both collar bones appeared broken, as did her pelvis. Her face was a bloody mess, but the remains of one uncrushed eye ridge said she had had delicate, elfin features.

He straightened and glanced back at the hammer swimming in the pool of her blood, at the drag marks, at the blood splatter. *What are you doing? What is the ritual?*

The Smith had always confused him—and not only him. He seemed to plan his attacks to the smallest details—finding and stalking the perfect victim, to capture her without anyone catching even a glimpse of him—but then killed them in an absolute disorganized frenzy. He also left a mountain of evidence—not that any of it led anywhere—as though he didn't give a single shit, but if that were true, then why all the elaborate planning and stalking? Why wait for the perfect moment? Why didn't he leave usable fingerprints? He flicked his light back behind the dumpster, staring down at the poor girl, wondering if the unsub had left more secretions.

Frustration and fatigue warred within him. He'd told Jim being at a fresh scene would help him—because on every other serial case he'd worked, it always had. But this was the freshest Smith scene—if it *was* The Smith and not some smartass copycat—and there was *nothing* helpful. He felt no connection, gleaned no insights…nothing. It was just a scene of unmitigated violence and bloodlust.

He shook his head and walked back to Jim.

"Get anything?" the big detective asked.

Gavin shook his head. "It's weird. He definitely moved her, definitely wanted her touching the back wall of the restaurant—but beyond that…" He looked Jim in the eye. "It might as well have been aliens."

Haymond scoffed and threw up his hands. "Emory! Get in there and do something *useful!* You two get to work."

Jim lay a huge meaty paw on Gavin's shoulder and gave it a gentle squeeze. Then he retraced his steps through the utility shed, leading Gavin back to the sidewalk. "Don't worry about him. He gets crabby before his first dozen doughnuts."

"No, he's right. That was a waste of time. I..." He shook his head. "The Smith doesn't make sense—he defies what we know about serial killers. Always has. Up until now, I thought the staleness of the scenes..."

"Yeah," said Jim as though he understood. "We'll catch him with plain old police work."

Gavin grimaced. "That hasn't worked either."

"But I wasn't on the case before," said Jim with a grin. "Come on. I'll let you buy me breakfast."

Nodding, Gavin turned to follow the big man. After he'd taken a few steps, he froze and spun around. He'd heard a soft chirp—almost a whistle—from behind him. There was no one there, but Gavin felt someone's eyes on him, nonetheless.

"What?" Jim asked softly, right behind him, and Gavin jumped.

"Did you hear it?"

Jim turned his head ponderously and looked him in the eye. "Depends on what you mean."

"A...chirp."

Jim stared at him for a long time. "Maybe," he said with a nervous chuckle. "I heard...*something*, but I don't know as I'd call it a chirp. More like a low whistle."

Gavin glanced at his watch. "Maybe we should get that breakfast to go." He flicked his gaze here and there, but the street was well-lit, and there weren't many shadows to begin with. He started and raised his eyes, sure he'd see someone ducking away from an open window in the girl's building, but there was nothing.

"Kingdom Cross?"

"Yeah. I think we'd better talk to Esteves."

Jim nodded.

"Hey, did you…" Gavin shook his head. "Never mind."

"What? Did I what?"

"Did you dream last night?" He ducked his head.

"Yeah," said Jim. "I did. I dreamed about that carnie huckster. About his pretty little assistant." Jim sighed. "Come on, Gavin. Let's get moving."

II

Kingdom Cross Psychiatric Hospital, Lily's Glen, NY
Thursday, 7:07 am

They sat slurping coffee and watching the time dribble by. The sign on the door said the hospital was closed to visitors until nine, and even though they were on official business, the guard inside had said they had to wait for the shift change.

A knock on the passenger-side window brought Gavin out of a mindless sort of reverie. Debbie Esteves stood, bent at the waist, looking at him without smiling. She twirled her finger, and Jim rolled down the powered window.

"Good morning," she said.

"Howdy," said Jim.

"I didn't think I'd see you two again."

Gavin cleared his throat. "I…" He shook his head. "He dropped another body. The scene…isn't helpful. I think we need to hear the rest of your story."

She stared at him for a few moments, her gaze flat and stony, but then she gave him a single, curt nod. "Come on. I have a staff meeting this morning, but I'll play hooky."

They got out, followed her inside, and headed down the long hall to her office. "Coffee?" she asked without looking back.

"Please," said Jim.

She thumbed the intercom button on her desk and asked for a carafe of coffee and three mugs. She jerked her chin at her table and then bent to check her email. "What you have to understand about my story," she began without looking up, "is that we were just like you at the beginning of it. We thought Joe was insane, that he suffered from psychosis at the very least." She came over and sat across from them, locking her gaze on Gavin. "We thought, in other words, that he was as crazy as a loon. We didn't know whether to believe he was The Psycho or not, but we did know that the things he *said*…" She shook her head. "The diagnostic signs were all there. He appeared homeless, disheveled, and inappropriate to the extreme. He was, at times, hostile and suspicious, then friendly and trusting in the blink of an eye. He presented with a memory impairment, though at the time, I thought it was a feature of his mental illness. And the things he said…" She shook her head. "He talked about a being that 'rode' him, 'drove' his behavior—a classic presentation of a control delusion. He seemed to hallucinate but masked them well—or so I thought. In hindsight, I think it was his telepathy. I think he saw things happening—John's near suicide, like that. Joe's speech was also extremely disorganized. He used neologisms when they suited him, and—"

"He used what?" asked Jim.

"Neologisms—made-up words and phrases that are meaningless, except to the patient," said Gavin, and Debbie nodded.

"And he spoke in clangs—meaningless rhymes—paraphasia, and perseverated. He said the same things over and over. 'Kill me.' Like that. It seemed like his associations were loose as a goose, but that's only because we didn't know the topic of the conversation most of the time." Debbie sighed. "If I'd only *believed* him." She shook her head and waved her hand through the air. "If wishes were fishes and all that. Obviously, we all knew he was a 5150…"

Chapter 7
The Saint Mary Psycho

I

"Obviously, this guy's a 5150. But what I want to know—no, *need* to know—is whether the stuff he wrote, the stuff he told John he did..." said Angel, staring Debbie in the eye.

"You want to know if it's all part of some random misfiring in his brain box. Right now, all I can say for sure is that if you'd taken his confession at face value, you'd never have gotten a conviction. He's too far gone into his delusion of control at this point in time. He's too disorganized, too..." She spread her hands. "As to whether he really is The Saint Mary Psycho or not, that's a question you can answer better than me."

"Yeah, I wish," said Angel with a sigh. She glanced at the bank of monitors, and her gaze zeroed in on the man who'd been booked as Joe Doe—the man who stood beneath the camera in his room, staring up at it with a bland expression on his face. "Debs, do these things have audio?"

Debbie followed her gaze. "Sure."

"Mind if I stick around? I'd like to see what you can get out of him firsthand."

"I don't mind," said Debbie. "But remember none of this will be admissible."

"I don't really care about that at the moment. I just…" She lifted her hands, shook her head, and let her hands drop. "I need to know, okay?"

"Sure. Stick around, then. Maybe I can get some sense out of him." She glanced at her patient. "Then again, maybe not."

"Thanks, Debs."

Debbie nodded and left the nurses' station. She walked down the hall to the seclusion rooms but paused before she reached Joe Doe's room. Fatigue swirled in her bloodstream, dragging at her mind. She'd already worked a full day before the call to the police station. All the excitement and adrenaline had amped her up, sure, but now all that was gone, leaving her sapped, wiped, out of gas. She wanted nothing more than to go home and soak in a tub full of hot water.

She heaved a sigh. She wouldn't get closer than wanting it for a few hours at least.

She walked down to Doe's room, and as she entered the room, he turned away from the camera but couldn't resist one more peek up at it inside its protective metal and polycarbonate box. "Is she still here?"

"Who?" asked Debbie.

"You know who. Angel. The pretty one."

"I don't think so."

"She is. You're lying to me, Doc. I can tell."

"No, Joe," said Debbie, her expression solemn. "I don't lie to my patients."

He flashed a sour grin at her. "Yes, you *flew*. I pan tell!"

Debbie shook her head. "How could you know that, even if it were true?"

"I don't know. Maybe *Glaaachk*—" He shook his head. "Maybe *he* told me. Fee does that plum times. Tells me things I have no way of snowing."

Debbie quirked an eyebrow at him. "When you make that sound…*glaaachk*…are you trying to say the weird name you wrote in your note to Sergeant Jenkins? Glacadairanam? Am I pronouncing that right?"

"Shh!" He shook his head. "The risks you rake, clock! Don't you know anything?"

Debbie shrugged. "I guess not. Why is it dangerous to say that word?"

"Because, stupid, he might *fear* you play it!"

"Glacadairanam," she said, staring him in the eye.

He chopped his hand in the air, then turned away and began to pace. "Why won't you believe me? You're risking your life!"

"Joe," said Debbie. "Everything is okay. This is a safe place. You can—"

Laughter ripped out of him in great, belly-shaking gales. "Safe? *Safe*?" Tears streamed down his face. "You don't know *anything* about safety, lady. This face is no safer than the other space like this…the other *hyuck*—" His hand went to his throat again. "This is no safer than

Puh-puh-pyucht— Glaaackh—" He massaged his throat.

"Can I get you a cup of water?"

He treated her to such a look of intense scorn that she wanted to back away from him. "Why won't any of you listen to me?" he asked in a frigid voice. "Why are you all so…so…*stupid*?" He squeezed his eyes shut and scrubbed his face.

"Look, Joe, I'm trying to help you—"

"If you want to help me, go down to the med room and get a scalpel, then come back and cut my throat!"

"I'm not going to do that," she said. "No one is going to hurt you."

"Then you *don't want to help me!*" He blew out his cheeks and backed away from her, a panic-stricken expression twisting his features. "You should go… I don't want to hurt you."

"Then don't. Choose not to."

"Don't you set it? If you jeep this up, you're mowing to get hurt, but it won't be me suing it! Don't flame me!"

"Then who should I hold accountable? This Glacadairanam?"

"Yes." His gaze danced around the room. "But don't say his tame! He'll fear you and come. You wouldn't bike that." He leaned closer. "*Dangerous*," he stage-whispered.

"Is that what happened back at the police station? Your controller came and attacked Officer Watts?"

The man flung himself on the bed, drawing his legs up into the fetal position. "I told them, same as I'm felling you. I… I fought it was safe with…*him* off slaying with Sergeant John. I didn't think he'd come back so soon. I was going to let them truss me up, to do whatever they wanted to do. I thought… I thought…"

"What, Joe? What did you think?"

He flashed a look of pure irritation at her. "Don't call me that! *It's not my name!* I thought if they rook me away before he came pack, he'd sick someone else, and I'd be tree of him at last." He shook his head. "I should have known better." He rolled to his back and stared up at the ceiling morosely.

Debbie nodded as if that made sense. "So, if I can't call you Joe, then what?"

"He doesn't want me to remember my game—to remember *anything*. He doesn't taunt me to give you a same. I already sold you that."

"That's fine, but earlier, you mentioned 'TH.' Come on, I've got to put something in your chart eventually. Are they your initials? TH? What do the letters stand for?"

He grunted and slammed his head against the mattress. "*I CAN'T YELL YOU!*"

"Please don't slam your head, Joe. I can't let you harm yourself."

"Don't worry. *He* won't let me do any steal damage to myself. I've sighed… That's why…that's why I roped

Sergeant John would snow my brains out. *He* can't control Sergeant John. Not yet."

"I can't abide even the appearance of you hurting yourself, Joe, so please don't do that again."

He sat up and smiled. His gaze was hostile, and Debbie shrank back. "You're pretty," he said. "Why not turn off that camera so we can play. It'll be fun."

"I don't think so, Joe."

The man scoffed. "You're so stupid, it's funny. That's not his name. He *told* you that."

"*His* name? Who am I speaking to right now?"

"That's for me to know and you to find out." He sprang to his feet and took two steps toward her. "Come on. Turn it off so we can play. I know lots of fun games." His eyes narrowed, and he treated her to a slow smile and even slower wink. "I'll tell you my name if you do."

Debbie took two steps back to maintain the distance between them. "I don't think that would be—"

With a guttural roar, the man lurched toward her, arms outstretched. The unit's emergency klaxon blared, and she sprinted toward the door.

Shrieking maniacal laughter, he was quicker.

A vicious haymaker slammed into the side of her head, even as the door slammed open and three corrections officers stormed into the tiny room from the hall.

2

Gilead County Jail PITU, Saint Mary, NY
September 17, 2014, 8:41 pm

Angel peered down at the small cut on Debbie's forehead, shining her small LED flashlight on the wound. "It doesn't look bad at all, Debs. More of an abrasion than a laceration."

"That's a relief. I don't even remember how I got the damn thing." She glanced up at the monitor, where grunts and curses accompanied the image of the three guards shackling Joe to the bed. "I've had prisoners go off on me before—everyone who's worked in corrections or psychiatry for more than ten minutes has—but never with such…"

"Raw violence?" Angel sank into a chair with a groan. "This shit chair is *no bueno* for my back."

Debbie explored the slow ooze dribbling from the cut on her forehead with a tentative finger. "Head wounds always bleed the worst."

"So… Debs, what's the deal?"

With a sigh, Debbie dropped her hand to her lap and looked Angel in the eye. "He's mentally ill—of that, there's no question. Is he competent?" She tsked. "I doubt it."

"Beyond 'mentally ill?'"

"He exhibits signs of depersonalization disorder, psychosis, religious delusions, delusions of persecution, paranoia, control… Need I go on?"

"I see. Crazy as fuck, in other words."

"If you want to get all technical. I'll tell you what, though. Give me forty-eight hours to crash-load zoraperidol into him until his eyeballs float—and we might hear sense out of him."

"The initials he gave you…" Angel flipped through her notepad. "'TH,' does it mean anything to you?"

Debbie shook her head. "You?"

"Nothing. Then again, it's not much to go on." Angel pointed at one of the corrections computers. "Can I use this?"

"Sure."

Kirk pulled the keyboard toward her, typed in her credentials, and frowned at the unfamiliar desktop. I should be able to…" She hunched closer to the screen and squinted at the icons lined up on the bottom of the screen. "Here the bastard is." She doubled clicked an icon and a law enforcement database portal appeared on the screen. She typed 'TH' into the aliases field and hit enter, frowning at the screen. She worked the computer for a moment or two, then whistled. "Well, that's not good, but it's about what I expected."

"What's that?"

"There are a ton of hits, that's what. I should have known better than to expect anything *helpful* with so little."

"I'm surprised it gives you any results."

"Tom Hannibal. Thomas Harris. Timothy Henderson. Tracy Henry McDonald. All TH's..." Angel glanced at Debbie with a sour grin on her lips. "Should I go on?"

Debbie heaved a sigh. "I don't even think that it's real. It's another layer of his delusion. It might be a neologism. *He* might not even know what it stands for."

"Whatever that is." Angel flapped her hand.

"Neologisms are made-up words or phrases that are important to his delusion."

"We can't send in his prints since he burned them off. I guess I can send a tech over to swab him for DNA. See if we get any hits that way."

"As for DNA, he'll get that here as a part of his intake."

"*Get off bee, you brotherfucking gasbowls!*" Joe screeched on the monitor.

Angel shook her head. "What is the nonsense with the rhyming words, anyway?"

Esteves wagged her head to the side. "It's a symptom of the severity of his thought disorder. It's a combination of both phonemic and semantic paraphasia, though I've never seen it as bad as this."

"Phonemic and yada-yada what?"

"Phonemic paraphasia is when a patient gets syllables out of sequence or mispronounces words. Usually, it's just a simple substitution of one word or syllable. Something like, 'I slipped on the lice and broke my arm.' Semantic paraphasia is the substitution of inappropriate words. 'Gasbowls' instead of 'assholes.' But by the extent of impairment Joe displays, I'm beginning to believe there is an underlying physical or structural component to his illness."

"Organic brain disorder?"

"Maybe. An MRI would clear things up considerably, but I'm not signing off on a field trip to Blessed Joseph's until his condition improves."

"Or better yet, never," muttered Angel.

"Yeah! Yeah! Chain me, brain me, train me up! That'll make me fine as a fiddle! That'll fruit me right down to the sound!"

"Jesus," Angel murmured with a sour laugh, glancing at the monitor. "It's not funny, but it sort of is."

"The nonsense rhyming business is what we call a 'clang,' which is another indicator of a severe thought disorder."

"Jesus," Kirk repeated.

"You've got that part right," said Debbie, staring at the monitor as the three guards struggled to control Joe's limbs while they secured him. "It's easy to picture him committing murder when he's acting like this."

"How long until we have the DNA results?"

"*If* he's in the system, and we have a perfect match, a couple of days should do it. Unless the lab's backed up. Hopefully, a good sample is in CODIS."

"And if not?"

Debbie shrugged. "There are other databases, but partial matches will produce a lot of false negatives to weed through."

"Seeing as how my current suspect pool is half the adults in the country, I'll take those reduced numbers any time."

"Fair point," said Debbie, her fingers exploring the area around the cut on her forehead.

"*Hey! HEY!*" shouted Joe as the three corrections officers finished securing him and made room for a nurse to stick a needle in his arm. "Is that pretty doctor still here somewhere? Tell her to come play with me. I'll be good."

Debbie drew a deep breath and sighed. "I should have been a dentist like my mother said."

"And miss out on all this?" asked Angel through a crooked grin.

"I think I could make the sacrifice." Debbie turned away from the monitors.

"Supposing he's legitimately as cuckoo as he seems, how long before we can interview him and get a reliable statement?

"It's a waiting game, now. We'll push as much IM zoraperidol lactate as we dare for a few days to try to get him under control. From there?" She shrugged. "He may never be fully compliant."

"I'd hoped to get more from him tonight or tomorrow morning."

"It's possible but not probable. This zoraperidol should knock him for a loop. Drooling, muttering, sleeping. Those are the behaviors we can expect from old Joe in the next day or two. Once he's under control, we'll switch to oral meds and back the dose off a little each day until we find the minimum viable dose. That's when he'll be the most tractable, the most reliable."

"It is what it is, I guess." Angel's gaze flicked to the monitor. Joe seemed relaxed, his muscles loose, head lolling toward the camera. *I'd like to get in there and wring some answers out of his scrawny neck.* A soft smile appeared on his face, and he tipped a wink at the camera. "*Jesus,*" murmured Angel.

"Don't sweat that," said Debbie. "A lot of patients know the routines of jailhouse psych units. He knows someone is watching him, and he doesn't care who it is. He knows that act is unnerving—that's the whole point."

"Right." But even so, a shiver ran down Angel's spine.

3

Angel watched the prisoner's eyelids droop, spring open, then droop again. "Zoraperidol for the win," she murmured.

"Not quite yet, but it's inevitable with that dosage," said Debbie.

"Will he sleep a long time?"

Esteves treated her to a terse nod. "That's the plan."

Angel glanced over, a questioning expression on her face. "I suppose that makes sense given his level of violence."

"It's better to zonk him at this stage. Hopefully, he will wake up with a new outlook on the world."

"Hmm." Angel slumped a little. "I guess there's no reason for me to stick around?"

Debbie shook her head. "I'm out of here myself as soon as he gives it up and goes to sleep. The staff will keep an eye on him and call if his situation changes. I could add your name to the list if you want?"

"Want? No." She smiled out of one side of her face. "Even so, I guess you'd better sign me up."

They said their goodbyes, and Angel went out through the heavy steel doors into the staff-only hallway that ran down the middle of the jail. The stench of the place was horrific, and even that late at night, the constant clamor of catcalls, banging, shit-talking, and laughter set her head to pounding.

In the booking area, she signed out, retrieved her sidearm, and then pushed out into the cold air, drawing her police-issue windbreaker closer around her. The clean scent of the semi-rural night smelled of honey and cloves. But even outside the building, she could still smell the stench of the place—the funky combination of body odor, spunk, rotting food, and dirty clothes.

She walked toward the van, and the odor followed her. She wrinkled her nose, caught a lock of her hair, and smelled it. "Uck," she murmured. "How can you stand to work here, Debs?" She peeled her windbreaker off and draped it over her arm. "At least cops get to go outside and clear away the stink."

Shaking her head, she threw her jacket over one shoulder, climbed into the driver's seat of the van, and slid the key into the ignition. She cranked it but it didn't make a sound—not so much as the sluggish cranking or dreaded clicking that accompanied a drained battery. "What the hell?" she muttered, letting go of the key. She switched on the lights but nothing happened, not even a pale flicker shone on the macadam lot. *Great. That's just fucking great.* She glanced down at her watch and muttered a curse.

She climbed down from the van and slammed the door, trudging a step toward the staff door into the jail, gritting her teeth and frowning. She didn't see the figure in the dark car three rows over watching her.

4

John lay next to Elizabeth, staring at the shadowed ceiling and wishing he could go to sleep, but the scene with the crazy asshole kept replaying in his mind, the emotional rollercoaster no less potent for his knowing where the story led. He tried to tell himself he'd done the right thing—as Elizabeth had spent the evening telling him—but some dark voice in the back of his mind insisted otherwise.

He rolled onto his side and stared into the inky black outside his bedroom window. In daylight, the window showed a picture of beatific loveliness—his neat, well-maintained lawn, the four planting beds ringing four large butternut hickory trees, and the elegant border grass demarking where his property ended and the woods began, all standing before the pleasant backdrop of scrub-free woods that stretched away into infinity. Given the moonless night, however, he could barely make out the towering hickories.

Heaving a sigh, he slipped back down on his back, staring at the patterned ceiling again. His eyes traced patterns, forming pictures in his mind's eye— spaceships, various pieces of fruit, rockets, and... He frowned up at the vision of the small, dark shape dancing across the ceiling.

He didn't know what to think about what had happened to him in the locker room. Yes, he'd been through a shock, but it wasn't his first rodeo. He shook his head. Yet, it *was* the first time someone had confessed to murdering his daughter and then asked him to kill them.

Why didn't you pull the goddamn trigger? he asked himself in a flash of fury.

Shaking his head at his own foolishness, he forced his eyes closed and began repeating the word "one" over and over in his mind, visualizing the word flashing behind his eyelids. Usually, the technique would at least make him drowsy, but as the seconds turned into minutes, he thought he saw something between the flashes of the word "one."

It was just a fuzzy shape, ill-defined and murky around the edges, but it set his nerves on edge. He rolled onto his side, opened his eyes, and peeked into the black maw of the backyard.

"Mmph," mumbled Elizabeth next to him.

"Sorry," he whispered. He closed his eyes and continued counting to one for what seemed like a miserably long time.

John was almost asleep when he heard it—a thin squalling chirp. His eyelids flew open. He still faced the window that opened on the yard, and something gleamed red at the edge of the trees.

What is that? A reflector? A toy? He stared at it for a full minute, squinting his eyes for clarity and finding none. He was just about to get out of bed for a closer look when the gleaming thing moved.

5

*Gilead County Jail staff parking lot, Saint Mary, NY
September 17, 2014, 10:59 pm*

Debbie let loose a tendon-creaking yawn as she pushed through the doors and stepped into the parking lot, wrinkling her nose as the odor wafting around her went to war with the night's clean smell. She was tired—physically and mentally—and wanted nothing more than to wash the jail's stink out of her hair and go to bed.

Debbie steered her mind clear of the guilt-puddle about missing her daughter's play. Guilt didn't help her, and it certainly didn't help Denise, though the extra money *would* help Denise attain her dream of an Ivy League education. Not that it was only Denise's dream... She shook her head as her mind began its oft-repeated circular track of self-recrimination, guilt, justification, and back again. She set her jaw and banished the thoughts. After all, there was nothing she could do to change anything. She'd done what she'd done.

Her thoughts turned back to her new patient. Joe. He was clearly schizophrenic, but it presented in an idiosyncratic way with obvious psychotic overtones. She'd seen bits and pieces of his delusions reflected in various patients over the past decade, but she'd never seen a heaping combination of them in one case.

She closed her eyes a moment, dreading what she knew was coming when she got home. The PubMed searches; the Pyscinfo dredging. Her mind wouldn't let it go, not until she'd at least tried to find out if the patient was truly alone in the world, or if there were other cases that matched his in complexity.

She glanced around the darkened lot—not many places were safer than the secured staff lot of the county jail, but things could still happen. Her gaze skittered right past the police van at first, then snapped back to it. Angel had left the PITU almost half-an-hour earlier, and it wasn't as if anyone wanted to spend time in jail if they didn't have to. There was no cafeteria for the staff, only a break room that smelled almost as bad as the tiers of the jail itself.

Still, this is the jail, Debbie. Seeing a police transport van in the lot is hardly earth-shaking. She nodded to herself, putting a period on her thoughts with grim determination. But still, something nagged at her mind. Something pulled her gaze back to that van, and without conscious thought, she turned toward it and walked closer.

The van sat in a little circle of emptiness, an island in the darkness, and something lay next to the driver's side tire. A dark shape. A lump.

She slowed but kept moving forward, her hand snaking into her purse and finding the snub-nosed .38 she carried. She stared at that dark mound. It was small—maybe the size of a discarded jacket or lost beach towel—and dark in color. What little starlight there was seemed to disappear at the thing's edges, as if whatever the lump was made from, it absorbed light, devoured it.

She approached the van, her gaze swept the dark shadows beneath it, and she nudged the dark shape with her foot. It was a windbreaker, an inside-out windbreaker. After a long stare into the darkness around her, Debbie squatted and turned the jacket the right way out. It was dark blue, with white letters that read "POLICE" across the back.

Fear bit her then. Fear for Angel.

6

Angel moaned and opened her eyes, wincing at the pain in her head. Tape covered her dry lips. An engine rumbled nearby, and the noise of tires on the road seemed very loud in the confined space. Her hands were cuffed behind her back, but the cold press of steel sank fangs of jagged pain into her wrists. That was bad—very bad. She had very little chance of getting away unless she could get to her handcuff key, and even then it was a toss-up whether she had the dexterity to unlock the cuffs. The rough carpet beneath her cheek scratched her skin, and something sticky and warm inched down the back of her head.

The brake lights flashed, momentarily lighting the space around her with red, bleeding light, and she knew where she was—in someone's trunk. A black shoulder bag was shoved in the corner, the kind of kit bag the patrol officers of the Saint Mary Police Department seemed to favor.

"Hey!" she shouted and winced at the bolt of agony that shot through her head.

The radio came on, and the volume of pounding heavy metal rose to bleeding-ears levels.

7

Debbie straightened and spun toward the jail, her hand aching around the snub-nosed .38's grip. She sprinted for the staff entry, still carrying the jacket but not conscious of the fact. Her heart pounded in her chest, and her pulse slammed through the arteries in her neck. By the time she slid into the door at full speed, her breath rasped in and out of her too-dry throat, and spots of color had blossomed high on her cheeks. She slammed the door open so hard it bounced off the inside wall with a crash, startling the officers inside. "Dial 911!" Debbie screeched. "Code thirty!"

The duty sergeant snapped the phone to his ear and punched the numbers in. "Gilead County Jail, duty room," he said into the receiver. "Officer needs assistance at our location." He looked at Debbie and made a beckoning gesture.

"Angel Kirk. She was here, and the van she brought her prisoner in is still in the parking lot. Her jacket is out there on the ground!" Debbie pointed at the slowly closing door.

The duty sergeant pointed, and Debbie looked down at the jacket in her hand.

"Dammit!" she snapped.

"Has Detective Kirk called in?" the sergeant said into the phone. He cocked his head to the side. "Okay. Her vehicle is still here, but Dr. Esteves says she left a while ago. I remember her going out." He listened a moment. "Yes, of course." He snapped his fingers at some of the corrections officers that had gathered around, then pointed out into the parking lot. "Not you, Doc," he said.

Three guards jogged outside carrying flashlights.

"No reply?" the sergeant said. "We might have a situation."

"What about her cell?" asked Debbie.

The sergeant nodded and held up his index finger. "Try her cell." Again, he listened, still staring at Debbie. "What? Try her department-issued phone *and* her personal." He nodded. "Right. I have three corrections officers performing a search of the lot right now, and I'll arrange for an interior search. Hold on." He put the phone down and swiveled his chair around to face the intercom. "All staff, all staff. Report the last known whereabouts of Detective Kirk. All staff, all staff. Report to your duty rooms and begin a hard count of all prisoners." He took his finger off the microphone key and swiveled back to the phone. "Done," he said into the receiver. "Yes, the reports will come in over the next few minutes." His gaze once again rested on Debbie's face, but now his eyes were very, very round.

8

The volume of the music hurt her ears, and Angel could hear nothing else, but when the cell phone in her pocket buzzed, she felt it. The only problem was that her hands were behind her back, and the phone was in her front pocket.

Frustration thrummed within her like a live wire.

Horrible scenarios flashed through her mind, one after another, each more violent, more terrifying. Her academy classes had covered most situations, but she'd always known the situation was under control, safe, during that training.

She slid to the side and banged her head on something she couldn't see as the car slid around a corner. Pain rattled around inside her skull as though jarred loose by the impact. Her sense of direction had already taken a hit from being in the trunk of a moving vehicle with no references, and the second rap on her noggin did nothing to help it.

What if Joe is just some sick fuck? What if he isn't really The Saint Mary Psycho? a small voice asked from the depths of her mind. *What if the guy driving this car is the* real *Psycho?* Cold, greasy dread uncoiled in her belly like a nest of baby snakes, and she panicked, thrashing from side to side in the narrow confines of the trunk, jerking her hands to the left, then back to the right, trying to reach her keys, her phone, anything. She kicked furiously at the inside of the rear quarter panel—which was useless, and she knew it, but she did it anyway.

She opened her mouth as far as the duct tape would allow and screamed with as much power as she could, but the music was louder. She crabbed around until she could direct her kicks at the trunk lid, but it was no good. She couldn't get her feet up there, and all she could do with her knees was to bruise them.

The taillights flashed red again, and then she tumbled to the side once more as the car lurched through another turn.

Taillights! She struggled until she was near the very rear of the car, then flopped around until the taillights were at her back. She strained and grunted and wrenched her shoulders until her hands brushed against something cold, cylindrical, and corrugated—a wire loom cover. She grabbed at it and missed. *DAMMIT!* She tried again, this time looping one pinky around the wiring.

Angel curled the other fingers of her hand around the wires and tried to jerk them free but almost lost her grip in the process. The wire loom stretched as she pulled again.

Come on! COME ON!

The car screamed around another corner, and Angel tightened her fingers into a death grip on the corrugated wire cover.

9

Calls came over the intercom while Debbie stood by feeling useless. Her gaze bounced from the door to the sergeant and back again. The duty sergeant fielded the incoming reports and prisoner counts in a calm voice, his face held in a rictus of control, but his eyes told a different tale—one filled with anxiety for Angel Kirk. Sirens shrieked into the parking lot outside, and Debbie turned toward the door.

"No, Doc. Wait in here, please."

"The officers will want to talk to me."

"I know, but we are unsure about the lot's security. The Saint—" He shook his head. "You could get hurt. The cops will come to you."

10

Momentum flung Angel toward the back of the rear seat, stretching her arms behind her with a flare of raw agony in her shoulders, but she didn't let go of the wiring. It stretched and stretched as she rolled and lurched in time to the car's tire-shrieking maneuvers. She thought her tendons would snap, but even so, she kept her death grip on the wire loom.

Just when she thought the pain would overcome her, the wires snapped free, and she slammed into the seatback with a grunt. Loose junk rattled around her, poking her, knocking into her.

The cell phone in her pocket began to jump and jive once more, and she wrenched her hands to the right side, stretching her fingers as far as she could, ramming the cold cuffs painfully into the knob on the side of her wrist, twisting her own left arm across the small of her back. Her fingertips slipped inside her pocket and brushed the slick, cool end of her phone.

Then she was tumbling again, sliding toward the rear of the vehicle. Her head thumped against the trunk lid, and she saw stars. Though her elbow crushed beneath her and her left shoulder was screaming with the strain of having her arm wrenched behind her back, she kept her fingertips in her pocket, fishing for her phone. Finally, she pinched the corner of her phone between two fingers and pulled it up enough to get a better grip.

The driver of the car performed another of his extreme driving turns, and she smashed into the corner of the trunk. But despite the raw, burning agony in her shoulder, Angel kept her hand in her pocket, her fingers on the vibrating phone. She pulled and pulled, but the damn thing seemed stuck on something, and her fingers grew slick with sweat.

And then her phone stopped vibrating.

She lay still a moment, her thoughts blue with profanity. Still, if she could get the phone out and keep hold of it, maybe she could dial blind and shout for help. The very fact that she had the thing at all was important. The police department could track her location by triangulating her phone's signal as long as she was in range of a cell tower.

As long as someone knew she needed to be found.

Angel groaned as the car slid around another curve, throwing her headfirst into the driver's side quarter panel, then slamming her back the other way. She kept the phone pinched between her index and middle fingers, though it meant keeping her arm chicken-winged in order to reach around in front of her, her shoulder bent almost to the point of dislocation, the steel shank of the handcuffs cutting off her circulation. The erratic driving scared her—it spoke to being out of control, wild with anger or some other strong emotion, and in a hostage situation, extreme emotion spelled disaster.

That was how she thought of her predicament. "A hostage situation." She couldn't bring herself to admit what it really was—an abduction by an unknown person for what could only be nefarious reasons. No one risked long stints in maximum security for a lark.

No one sane, anyway.

She tugged at her phone, mentally screaming at it, at whatever kept it prisoner in her pocket. She wiggled it from side-to-side, almost lost her grip, and then froze, panic freight-training through her. If she lost her grip, it was over. There was no way in hell she'd ever get her arms back in the right place, no way she could get the thing back between her fingers, much less extract it from her pocket. Pins and needles already crawled up and down her arm, and the other arm shrieked with agony from shoulder to wrist. Her hand had finally gone numb from the lack of circulation, but at least her headache was a touch better—the driver had turned off the obnoxious music.

The phone began its merry dance again, and Angel flinched, almost losing it. She pulled frantically, wriggling her hips as she did. Then she felt it—her credentials case. The one she'd shoved into her pocket as she approached the van. The one that had settled over her phone like a book jacket over a hardbound book.

She worked her fingers until she felt it with her ring and pinky fingers and shoved at it while pulling the phone in the other direction. She couldn't straighten her legs—even if the trunk had enough room—because it would pull the contents of her pocket out of reach. Gritting her teeth in frustration, she kept at it until the phone felt freer.

Angel ripped the damn thing out of her pocket and, craning her neck to see, put the phone on the carpet and swiped to accept the call. Hearing the other person was out of the question, so Angel yelled, "Help! This is Angel Kirk, SMPD! Some bastard's kidnapped me! I'm in the back of a—"

Tires shrieking, the car skittered around a tight corner, and both Angel and the phone flew toward the passenger side. She slammed her head against the trunk's hinge mechanism and saw stars for a moment. She lost track of the phone, but it no longer mattered. "I'm in the trunk of a Crown Vic, I think!" she yelled. "I was at GCJ Staff parking! Call the police and tell them to track my cell phone!"

With a symphony of screaming tires, the car skidded to a stop. The driver's door opened, and footsteps sounded as the driver came around to open the trunk.

11

"I'm going out there," said Debbie with iron in her voice.

"Hold on," said the duty sergeant.

"No," she said, pushing out the door into the cool night air. She strode toward the group of cops standing around the van.

"Dr. Esteves!" yelled the sergeant from the door. Behind him, the phone started ringing.

Debbie didn't even glance back. She kept her eyes locked on the police officers. They'd glanced her way when the sergeant yelled her name but seemed content to stay put. "I found her jacket," she called.

"Fine," said one of the officers.

"Is that Joel McCandless?" she asked.

"Yes, Doc. There's nothing much to see here. We've canvased the lot and…" McCandless shook his head. "We found the keys to the van over there." He pointed at the far corner of the lot. "Did you see anything over there when you came out?"

"Nothing," said Debbie. "Just this jacket. Near the van." She held it out and Joel took it, shook it out to look at it, then folded up and shoved it in a paper bag. "Any leads at all?"

Joel's grimace was answer enough.

12

The trunk, Saint Mary, NY
September 17, 2014, 11:14 pm

Something thumped against the trunk lid. "Shut your goddamn mouth!"

That voice... Angel shook her head. The voice sounded so familiar, yet so...*wrong.* Outside, keys jingled then slid into the trunk's lock. *This is your chance, Angel. Don't fucking blow it.* She readied herself on her knees as best she could, spinning around so that her head pointed at the rear of the car, her feet wedged against the back seat. She couldn't get to her knees, but if she could surprise the man that held her, maybe she could bolt away.

The trunk's lock clunked, and she tried her best, tried to propel herself up and out of the trunk, a sprinter coming out of the blocks.

She didn't make it. Instead, she slammed down on the bottom lip of the trunk, slammed the small of her back against the bottom part of the trunk's latch, and searing agony shot down her legs and radiated up to her shoulder blades as though someone had sprayed her with lighter fluid and set it ablaze. Her eyes teared, but she kept them open.

Her abductor stood, back to the arc sodium streetlamp, nothing but a black silhouette, and laughed down at her. Moving with the speed of an insect, he snatched her phone from where it lay near her hip. He chuckled and powered it off.

"It's not too late," Angel croaked. "Let me go, and you have a chance, you can run, and we probably won't ever find you. But kill a cop…" Her voice quit, and she swallowed hard. "Do that, and they'll never stop chasing you."

"So melodramatic," the man said in a hoarse whisper. He laughed again as he raised his fist and smashed it into the side of her face—the hardest blow she'd taken in her whole life—and everything went black.

13

Gilead County Jail duty room, Saint Mary, NY
September 17, 2014, 11:17 pm

McCandless's radio squawked, emitting that combination of cop-speak and radio noise that only police officers seemed to understand. Debbie Esteves certainly didn't understand the transmission, but she understood human emotions and the expressions that went with them, and her heart fell. "Did they"—she gulped to force the knot in her throat down—"find Angel? Did they find her…body?"

McCandless shook his head. "They had a lock on her phone by cell-phone triangulation. Dispatch had an open line and everything, but…" He shrugged and frowned. "There was a commotion, then the phone was switched off." Joel's grim, calm, nothing-to-see-here expression seemed welded to his face.

Conflicting emotions warred within Debbie—joy that Angel wasn't lying dead in some alley or field, horror that her abduction was real. "So, what now?"

"Patrol is scrambling to get out there, but…"

"He won't screw around now that he knows about the phone."

Joel shook his head. "Would you?"

"No. But if you can get cars there quick enough—"

"We're trying, but… Don't get your hopes up, Doc." He reached out tentatively and touched her arm. "We'll do our best."

"I know it, Joel." Debbie prayed their best would be good enough to find Angel before… She feared it wouldn't.

"You might as well go home, Dr. Esteves," said Joel. "Unless there's something else you haven't mentioned yet?"

Debbie shook her head. "Nothing." She glanced over her shoulder at the jail's entrance, then her gaze climbed the side of the building to look at the outside wall of the seclusion room Joe slumbered in. "He said *he* was The Saint Mary Psycho," she murmured.

"Yeah, and maybe he is. Don't borrow trouble, Doc. We don't know what this is, yet. Maybe one of the goons Angel locked up got out on parole. Or it might be a random thing." Again, McCandless patted her arm. "We'll know more in the morning."

Debbie nodded and trudged toward her car, exhausting and heavy emotions dragging at her. *I'll be up all night, now,* she thought. *I'll never get to sleep.*

14

4983 Livermore Lane, Saint Mary, NY
September 18, 2014, 7:17 am

John sighed and opened his eyes to the dishwater light of another gray dawn streaming through the windows. For a moment, he thought about closing his eyes and trying to sleep the day away. After all, he wasn't on duty, and after last night, he probably wouldn't be for a while—and that was perfectly fine. He couldn't imagine going back, changing in that locker room where he'd lost his shit, sitting at his desk where that mad motherfucker had—

He cut that thought off and swung his legs out of bed. He'd never been one who could sleep in. On the other side of the bed, Elizabeth mumbled something that might have been Chinese for all the sense he could make of it, then flopped over, facing away from the window.

John glanced at the backyard, and the memory came swimming back… The memory of the dark shape at the edge of the woods, the wailing chirp, the red… *Didn't I go out there to check it out?* He shook his head, stood, and went to the window, his eyes scanning the yard for threats. *Observe, assess, communicate.* The words came unbidden from the depths of his mind. It was a phrase the instructors at the academy had said about seventy million times over the course of his training—a catchphrase he'd repeated about a hundred times as much to new recruits under his command.

His yard was quiet, peaceful. No monsters lurked at the edge of the woods, no shadowy shapes cavorted, no gleaming red eyes, no chirps.

He slipped into a comfortable pair of jeans and a T-shirt, then slid his carry-weapon into the inside of his waistband. He tiptoed downstairs and sat at the kitchen table to don his shoes.

The morning air was cold and crisp, and it raised gooseflesh on his arms and painted the air with his breath. He rounded the back corner of the house and stopped, stock-still, one hand on his pistol.

Observe, assess, communicate.

He scanned the backyard again, and his change of position revealed exactly nothing new. Still, he waited, as still as a statue but ready to react. He watched, barely breathing, only his eyes moving as he scanned the planting beds again and again.

After a few minutes, he relaxed from his rigid posture and stepped into the yard, allowing his hand to dangle free at his side. *You know you hallucinated all that shit in the locker room,* he told himself. *The stress, the impossible situation, brought it on. There's no such thing as shadow monsters—no matter what size they appear to be.* He walked across the grass, still watching for sudden movements. *Keep on this way, though, John, old buddy, and Dr. Esteves will commit you. There's no such thing as monsters.* That last thought brought a sour grin to his face. *The Saint Mary Psycho is a monster. So is that mental-defective from last night.*

He sighed as he approached the planting beds. They were a mess of overgrown wild grasses and creeping wild roses, and once those damn roses got a foothold…

John froze in mid-thought, mid-breath, mid-step.

Small, three-toed footprints tracked back and forth through the planting bed.

15

Gilead County Jail PITU, Saint Mary, NY
September 18, 2014, 7:21 am

Debbie used her key to slip into the nurses' station later than usual for her morning rounds. Doing her

ERIK HENRY VICK

hair earlier that morning, she hadn't thought she looked particularly healthy or very pretty. In fact, she thought she looked a little like a bag lady, just cleaner and with nicer clothes. She felt blue, scared, and angry—not a great recipe for a psychiatrist.

But it was too early in Joe's treatment for her to pass him along to a covering psychiatrist. He may sleep through the day, but she wanted to be around if needed.

"Morning, Dr. Esteves," said Kelly-Ann Malley, the unit secretary on the day shift.

"Hello, Kelly-Ann. Everything quiet this morning?"

Kelly-Ann nodded and swung around in her chair. "Nothing much going on. The new patient is still asleep."

"Speak of the devil," Debbie said, pointing at the bank of seclusion room monitors. Joe stood gazing up at the camera in the corner of his room, eyes clear of sleep, piercing and narrow. His face was as hard and impassive as one carved from stone.

Kelly-Ann glanced back and shook her head. "I swear he was asleep two seconds ago."

"Did he have a good night?"

"Better ask Chanda to be sure, but I didn't hear anyone complaining about him during the shift-change."

"Is Chanda in the med room?"

Kelly-Ann nodded. "Want some coffee?"

"Only if you have time to save my life," said Debbie with a rueful smile.

"Coming up."

Debbie turned and entered the galley-like medication room. Chanda Curry stood bent over a med cart, fussing with its computer. She glanced at Debbie and nodded. "Damn thing's always fritzing out on us."

"I can come back."

"No," said Chanda with a sigh. She swatted the cart with the palm of her hand. "I can't fix it, anyway. What can I help you with, Dr. Esteves?"

"How was Joe Doe overnight?"

"Not a peep from him all night, according to Ruth. He slept like a baby."

"I think he needed it." Debbie shrugged with one shoulder. "He's up now, though."

"I held his breakfast tray in case he woke up. Want to see him, or should we get him fed?"

"Let me get some coffee in me and check the notes in his chart. Then I'll see him."

"Breakfast it is, then. But I'm telling you, the nursing notes are pretty sparse."

Debbie nodded and left the room. She picked up the coffee Kelly-Ann had brought her and smiled her thanks. Joe's chart, labeled "Joe Doe 911293" lay already open on the desk the physicians used for chart work. She scanned the notes—sparse, just as Chanda had promised—in a matter of minutes, then turned to watch him eat.

But he wasn't eating. He hadn't moved an inch, despite the tray lying on his bed behind him. He just stared into the camera's lens as though he could see through it, as though he could see *her*. Debbie suppressed a shiver but didn't turn away.

She stared at the monitor, locked in a sort of battle of wills to see who would move first, though her patient didn't know—*couldn't know*—about the contest. She watched him for what felt like a long time and then decided he was either blinking in perfect unison with her or not blinking at all. He seemed hardly to breathe.

"He's a strange one," said Kelly-Ann.

"Yes. Quite ill," said Debbie without taking her eyes off the monitor.

"Yeah, but weird beyond all that. Do you think he's really…"

"The Saint Mary Psycho? I don't know. I know he *thinks* he is The Psycho, but to be honest, he doesn't seem to have it together enough to be anything but a psychiatric patient."

Down in his seclusion room, Joe brayed derisive laughter.

As Debbie stared on, a strange blot seemed to separate itself from that of the man and walked toward the camera—or toward the outer wall of the room. She'd have thought it a shadow if that had been possible in the sun-bright room. "Did you see that?"

"See what?" asked Kelly-Ann.

16

Larry had spent a miserable night—going home to his tiny apartment and falling asleep with the television prattling on about whatever news-cycle sensation was in vogue. The ringing phone had snapped him awake with just enough sleep to feel like death warmed over, and now his face felt smeared with petroleum jelly, his mouth tasted of sour chemicals, and his ears rang with caffeine and sleep deprivation.

It hadn't been so bad at first—there'd been things to coordinate, two scenes to process. Adrenaline had kept him fueled and running on all cylinders, but he'd sat behind John's desk since around eleven the previous night, and his adrenaline was spent and there was nothing more to do but try to keep the shift on track. That, and wait for something to happen. He stared down at the file into Angel's kidnapping, which lay open on the desk, and scoffed at how thin it seemed. His belly burned as if he'd been swallowing acid all night—and the way they brewed the coffee on the night shift, he reckoned he had.

But he'd been through it all before, and sure as shit, he'd go through it again in the future.

"Corporal!" Joyce Motes called from the doorway of the detective's squad room. "Detective DeQuinzio wants you. He says to double-time it."

Groaning, Larry pushed himself up. "What the hell does he want?"

"It's Angel's phone. It's on the move."

"Hot damn!" He shot up out of the chair and sprinted down the hall, leaving his fatigue behind. "Where?" he shouted.

"The interstate!" DeQuinzio called back.

A group of officers and detectives stood around DeQuinzio's desk.

"Real-track?" asked Larry. "Protectus?"

"Right. The mobile carrier was too slow."

Larry looked at the screen, which seemed a lot like the maps available on the internet, except for the blinking red dot making its merry way west on I-86. "Troopers?"

"Called them. Who do *we* have close?" asked DeQuinzio.

"Give me five minutes, and you'll have me."

Tony cocked his head and squinted up at him. "Go. Remember you're in plain clothes. Take back up."

"Right." His gaze snapped across the patrol officers standing by, assessing who was awake enough. "Santoro, saddle up!"

Larry turned and ran for the door, with Mike Santoro on his six.

17

Debbie plodded down toward the seclusion room that housed her anonymous patient. All the cup of strong coffee Kelly-Ann had poured her had done for her was bring on a bit of dyspepsia. In fairness, her upset tummy could have come from her emotional state, but as a trained psychiatrist, she preferred to blame the coffee. Or anything, really, but that weird shadow moving away from Joe and disappearing through the outside wall. When she replayed the memory in her mind, an unquiet dread bubbled to the surface of her mind, and her stomach felt worse. But every time she did so, she became more and more convinced that she'd seen what she'd thought she'd seen—a shadow separated from Joe's shadow and darted away. A shadow with *purpose.*

But that's... She didn't finish the thought, but she didn't have to. The image her brain insisted she had seen was *crazy.*

She stopped outside the door and closed her eyes a moment, reaching for that calm place she had cultivated within herself—her internal eye-of-the-storm, her retreat. Then, with a deep breath, she knocked on the door and opened the steel cover of the door's inset window. "Good morning, Joe!" she called in a bright, sunny voice.

He should have stood framed in the little window, staring up at the camera as he had been a few minutes before, but she couldn't see him. She came up on her tiptoes and tried to see the area close to the door. Using the tip of one key, she tapped on the polycarbonate window. "Joe?" she called. Her brow furrowed as she slipped her key into the deadbolt.

She felt sicker and sicker the longer she stood there dithering about turning the key. *Something's not right here,* a panicky voice whispered in the back of her mind. *He's in there; I just saw him on the monitor, for goodness' sake.* Her stomach rolled, and she loosed a greasy burp. *Go back to the station. Ask for an escort,* said that fear-filled voice. But she didn't. Instead, she stood there, peeking through the polycarbonate, her hand on the key.

Then the key turned beneath her fingers.

18

I-86, outside Saint Mary, NY
September 18, 2014, 7:41 am

With a white-knuckled grip on the steering wheel, Larry sat hunched forward, staring at the traffic ahead with burning, bleary eyes, watching for anything suspicious. *Observe, assess, communicate,* he thought, repeating the phrase he'd heard John say so many times over the course of the years, the phrase that had been drilled and drilled into him at the academy until he'd wanted to puke. He knew the vehicle holding Angel was still ahead of him—DeQuinzio said as much on his last radio transmission—but they had no idea what the vehicle was.

He had his lights on, but the screamer was off as a half-assed compromise to stealth. His foot was buried in the floorboard and every time he glanced at the speedometer, with its needle hovering between Death and Destruction, two things tightened: his grip on the wheel and his sphincter. The cars he passed seemed like no more than drips and splotches of color, some crazy abstract expressionist painting of anxiety.

Santoro's cruiser ran behind him, close but not too close, and he was doing the radio. All Larry had to do was drive and avoid killing anyone. *Everyone.* "Come on, come on, come on!" he chanted.

"Whoa, whoa, whoa, Bateman! You just blew by them," DeQuinzio crackled over the radio.

"*Fuck!*" Larry muttered. His eyes jumped to the rearview mirror as his foot lifted off the accelerator and moved to cover the brake pedal. Santoro's cruiser was already slowing, nose pointed at the pavement like a horse reined-in by a harsh hand. Larry's gaze flicked down the siren's controls, and he flipped the screamer on and blipped the thunderous klaxon a couple of times. It only took him a second, but when he brought his gaze back up to the road, it was already too late.

19

Debbie snatched her hand away from the key as though it were hot and getting hotter by the second. The back of her hand felt scaly, slimy—*alien*—as though a reptile had wrapped around and around it, but when she looked down, there was nothing there. Her keychain jangled, and her gaze snapped to it.

The key continued to turn with no one touching it. The deadbolts used weren't like household deadbolts—they required a key on both sides, and a key in either precluded the insertion of a key in the other, so what she saw was patently impossible yet happening.

A blow that felt like the inadvertent kick of a toddler struck her left bicep, and something hot and thin snapped around her neck. For a moment, that cable-like thing tightened convulsively, but then it disappeared with a feeling like a toddler pushing off her left shoulder, diving toward the door.

The seclusion room door swung slowly open, and Joe crouched on the other side, grinning up at her with the devil's lust. His eyes seemed to flash and pulse, and his grin appeared to stretch and grow beyond the bounds of his face. The pulsing light from his eyes glowed as red as a brake light's just before an accident.

Debbie stumbled back from the door on numb feet, her right hand over her left trapezoid. Her palm felt hot and wet, and when she pulled it back to look, it dripped with her blood. Her gaze came up from the blood on her hand and tracked across to Joe's face.

He sprang at her then, legs uncoiling to propel him high into the air, hands curled into fists in front of his face. One foot snapped forward, and the other trailed back, as though he sprinted through the air itself. Debbie watched, frozen in place, unable to even bring her hands up to shield her face as the madman descended toward her. He bent his arms at the elbows, raising both white-knuckled fists, and then slammed them down on her shoulders, driving her to the floor. He landed atop her and rolled away like a circus tumbler, like a predatory animal. Debbie shoved with her legs, frantic to put distance between them, but Joe treated her with utter disregard now that she was out of his way. He bounded away, screaming and laughing at the shrieking alarm.

20

Larry jerked the wheel hard to the right, and he almost made it. The semi trailer's boxed-beam bumper seemed to reach out and grab the quarter panel, starting at the very front and peeling the sheet metal back like a candy wrapper. The front end of the patrol car shrieked to the left while the back of the car lifted, lifted, coming up almost gracefully, almost like a dancer readying herself to pirouette, sliding and hopping toward the right lane. He locked his elbows and stood on the brakes, knowing better, knowing it was too late and doing it anyway, unable to control his limbs any more than he could stop the wreck.

"*MVA! MVA! Bateman versus a tractor-trailer!*" Santoro yelled over the radio.

"*Jesus fucking Christ!*" snapped DeQuinzio.

The semi's driver locked up his own brakes, eyes wide in his side-view mirror, and the trailer leaped sideways, smashing the front end of Larry's cruiser with its double rear axles, and batting the front end of the Crown Victoria back to the right. The rear tires of the cruiser skidded across the concrete with twin screams and clouds of smoke, then slewed back and struck the rear of the trailer again. The car shuddered and rocked, skittering farther sideways, out of control and spinning, and Larry held on for dear life. The woods on the side of the interstate loomed closer and closer with each counterclockwise revolution of the car, and then he was crashing into the brush, tree branches screeching along the roof of the car.

"Keep your wits, Santoro!" snapped DeQuinzio.

"Bateman's out! He slid right off the road, and he's headed for the… Oh, Christ! Larry's going to go off the ridge!"

He had a single moment of absolute clarity, and what he saw was the insane slope of the hill dropping out beneath him, his stomach dropping away with the earth.

21

Gilead County Jail PITU, Saint Mary, NY
September 18, 2014, 7:48 am

Debbie groaned and crawled to the wall, her neck and shoulder muscles shrieking, her head pounding. Joe shouted and laughed and carried on somewhere out of her sight, and the klaxon rolled on and on, the clamor combining into an ice pick slashing into the center of her brain. She didn't understand what had happened, how he had turned the lock from within the seclusion room, how he'd been able to hide from her while he did it.

But most of all, she didn't understand why he'd left her alone, after the violence of his attack.

Her mind flashed back to what had happened right before the door had slammed open, and she rubbed at her bicep, feeling that invisible toddler's kick again, then rubbed at her neck, tracing the red-hot razor wire she remembered snapping around her throat then disappearing, Joe's *pulsating* blacksmith-coal-glowing eyes. *What the hell was all that?* she asked herself, shaking her head. Memories, as Debbie knew better than anyone, were pliable, fragile things that often insisted on the impossible.

But the last thing she needed was a second helping of Joe's attention. Levering herself up by pressing against the wall, Debbie regained her feet, saving her aching arms and shoulders the effort. She stumbled toward the nurses' station as four extra guards came pounding past her from the other direction.

"Okay, Doc?" one of them called.

"Go on," she called without looking up. "Be careful, he's wired and *strong*." She leaned against the wall for a moment. "And try not to hurt him!"

They sprinted around the corner without further comment, and Joe cackled with glee. One of the guards cried out in pain. All the noises after that sounded like a riot, and she could guess who was on the losing side of that. "*Restraint*, gentlemen!" she shouted.

She made it to the station, and Kelly-Ann opened the door to let her inside. "I would have come to help you, but the officers said—"

"No, they told you right," said Debbie. She hissed with pain as she sank into one of the spare chairs, closing her eyes against the oncoming headache. "No sense risking us both."

"You are going to need medical," said Kelly-Ann, gazing at Debbie with concern written across her face.

"I'll be alright."

Malley cocked her head to the side. "Are you sure? I can have—"

"I said no!" snapped Debbie and regretted it the instant the words left her mouth. "Just give me a minute, Kelly-Ann. Let me sit a second." She covered her eyes with one shaking hand. "I'm in pain, and on top of it, I'm getting a bear of a headache."

"Sure thing, Doctor."

Debbie jerked her chin toward the reinforced window she sat too low to see out of. "What's happening?"

Kelly-Ann's gaze lifted, and a frightened frown twitched her lips down. "He's backed into a corner. Somehow, he got a baton from someone. There's a guard down, bloody-faced and still. The prisoner is…" Disgust remapped her features. "He's *smiling* and waving them on. Oh, Christ, I think someone is going to get seriously hurt—"

"Give me the mic and set it for unit-wide," said Debbie.

Kelly-Ann slid the microphone over to her and flipped two switches.

Debbie lifted her hand to press the button and winced. "Press it for me." A moment of whining feedback snapped across the unit's speakers as Malley did so. "Joe," grated Debbie, then cleared her throat, the staccato thunder of it rumbling across the unit. "Joe, listen to me."

"*Pretty lady!*" was his screeching reply. "*Oh, you come right the fuck on, sparky! I've got just the THING for you, SO YOU COME RIGHT ON AND GET IT!*"

"Officers, stand back a moment, please," Debbie said. "Joe, listen. You can't win, you're in a jail, and there's nowhere to go—"

"*Who wants to go anywhere, pretty lady? I'm right where I want to be, or I wouldn't be here!*" He smashed the baton into the steel door next to him, and the clanging sound reverberated through the unit. "*Say! Where's the other one? Where's that pretty cop?*"

"What are you trying to—"

"*Ha! These bozos have no idea how to handle someone like me. THEY'RE SCARED SHITLESS!*" His rancorous laugher rang out. "*Yeah, that's right, sparky. That's right...*"

"Oh, shit," muttered Kelly-Ann.

"What? Tell me!"

"*Yeah, fucker! Come on and get some!*"

"Ed Saunders looks *pissed*, Doctor. I think he's—"

"*Why so timid, chummy?*" Again, Joe's harsh laughter bounced down the hall.

"Ed Saunders! Listen to me! I want you to back off, and I want you to do it right now!" Debbie yelled into the mic, feedback whining.

"*Oh, that's right, pussy. Go hide behind the pretty lady's skirt like the dirty, child-fucking coward you are!*"

Debbie hung her head. From down the hall, the sick thud of hardened oak batons striking flesh sounded. "*Restraint!*" she yelled into the mic, but it did no good.

22

4983 Livermore Lane, Saint Mary, NY
September 18, 2014, 7:51 am

John stopped, his foot on the dooryard step, his hand on the doorknob. He knew Elizabeth would be up and getting breakfast. *I can't tell her about the footprints. She'll think I'm nuts.* His lip curled. *Were they even* real? *Fuck… I* think *I'm nuts.* He closed his eyes for a moment, not thinking, not doing anything but existing, then plastered a smile on his face and turned the knob.

"There you are," said Elizabeth as she poked her head around the corner into the kitchen. "Want breakfast?"

John shook his head. "No, I need to run into town."

She shrugged. "Suit yourself, but my cooking is way better than that diner's."

"No doubt about it," he said. "I'd take a coffee to go, though."

Elizabeth shook her head. "Haven't brewed it yet." Her mouth gaped wide in a tendon-crackling yawn, then she smiled at him. "Just got up, you mean old man."

"Drive-thru for coffee, then," he said as he gave her a peck on the cheek. "Hey, do me a favor? There's a diseased fox in the yard. Stay out of the back beds until I can sort him out."

"Ew." She went to the sink window and peered outside. "Where?"

"Back by the trees," he said. "Leave him to me. That's why I'm headed to town, to get some lye."

"He's dead already?"

John shook his head. "He either is or will be by the time I get back."

"Ew," she repeated.

"You bet," said John as he stepped outside.

23

Debbie raced down the hall, her head still pounding, her shoulders still aching, blood still trickling down into her shirt. At the other end of the hall, a group of GCJ officers stood clustered around a kneeling Joe, one arm up to shield his head.

Ed Saunders stepped closer and raised his baton.

"No, sir!" Debbie yelled. "He's down, Saunders!"

"Get on your face, mutt!" snapped Saunders—oak nightstick still held up, ready to strike—and he shot a furious glare at Debbie for a moment. "I'll give you to the count of one."

Joe darted a glance at Debbie, confusion written in his expression in large block letters. "I…"

"On your face, I said!" Saunders grabbed Joe by the hair and jerked him forward.

"That's enough!" Debbie yelled.

As Joe slid forward onto his belly, Saunders stepped back and stared at Debbie through slit eyelids, chin tucked down, a grimace on his face. A small mouse was already blackening beneath his right eye, and a thin trickle of blood slid down the side of his face. For a moment, a shadowy form appeared on Saunders' shoulder. Something strange, something small, something insubstantial, blurred… John Jenkins' words from the locker room came back to her. *There was a little… I don't know what it was. It was the size of one of those little monkeys—a rhesus whatsit—but it kept back in the shadow like it didn't want me to get a good look at it,* he'd said. The shadow on Saunders' shoulder was the same size, maybe even the same shape.

"Stay back, Doc," said Saunders with a lilt to his voice that Debbie didn't like.

"Come on, Ed," said one of the other guards. "He's done, man."

"Shut up, Allen," said Ed in a tone devoid of emotion. "This fucker hit me. No telling what he'll do next."

Debbie slowed; her gaze focused on the blur of shadow. "Saunders, your prisoner has given up. Put cuffs on him so I can examine him."

Ed flashed a twisted little grin at her. "Sure, Doc, just as soon as I know he's going to be compliant with your examination." He winked at her, slow and lazy. The shadow on his shoulder turned its head toward her, and the most peculiar chirp sounded as the whole thing disappeared.

Debbie stopped, suddenly woozy again, and reached a hand to the wall for support.

"You okay, Doc?" asked Allen Jeffries, the guard who'd asked about her before.

"Sure," she said. "A little dizzy. Can you please secure the prisoner?"

Jeffries nodded and stepped forward, but as he did, Saunders whipped his head around and hissed at him like an insane cat. "What's the matter with you, Ed?" he asked.

"I've got it." Saunders reached for his cuffs, then held them up next to Joe's face. "Please resist," he whispered but loud enough for everyone to hear. "Or are you a pussy?"

Joe, face down on the concrete floor, didn't move.

"That's what I thought," crooned Ed as he snapped the cuffs on. "Now, get your ass up." He grabbed Joe by the left bicep and stood, dragging the man to his feet. "Don't think I'll forget this!"

24

Bateman's car, outside Saint Mary, NY
September 18, 2014, 7:53 am

Groaning, Larry peeled his eyes open. He hurt all over, but his head was the worst. Every beat of his flogging heart set off a pounding in his head that felt as though someone had a jackhammer pressed to the base of his skull. His left shoulder felt numb and cold, while his left hip felt hot and seemed to screech like an injured animal and throb like a techno beat in overdrive. Blinking rapidly, he rubbed his eyes and groaned. The bright morning light filtering down through the trees stabbed at him and made the pounding in his head fifteen times worse, and half-congealed blood gummed his eyelids. A hot, sticky stream slid down the left side of his head. He reached up and around with his right hand, feeling the wet rivulet running down from the crown of his head. He pulled his hand away and grimaced at the blood staining his fingers.

The hood of the cruiser had folded up like an accordion and cracks webbed the windshield. *Safety glass saved my eyes at the very least,* he thought. Steam snuck out from beneath the hood. His whole left side was a mass of conflicting sensations: pain and numbness, heat and cold, aches and sickness. He sucked in a deep breath and winced at the pain from his ribs.

He fumbled for the seat belt release with his left hand and had to bite down on a scream as agony lit up his shoulder like a power line applied directly to his radial nerve. Something in there made a grinding pop as he tried to relax it, and a pulsing, stabbing pain ran the length of his arm, eclipsing the pain in his head. It felt as if a bag of ground glass or maybe a ball of razor wire had replaced his shoulder joint.

He sat still, doing nothing but trying to breathe through the escalating agony in his shoulder. He rolled his head to the left on the seat's minuscule headrest. The driver's side window was gone, shattered, and lost somewhere on his trip down the hill, and the bark of an ash tree seemed close enough to lick. He rolled his eyes down and took in the reason for all the pain on his left side—the ash tree had caved the door into his side when the tree had stopped his sliding descent. *That's bad. Lucky to have survived.*

But he didn't feel lucky. He felt battered and mistreated.

He swiveled his head to the right and gazed out the unmarred passenger window at the lovely copse of trees he found himself in—lovely except for the angry, chaotic furrows his dancing tires had gouged into the earth, the smashed and shattered limbs, and the tree trunks left in the wake of his spinning descent. The roof of the car blocked his view of the upper part of the hill, but he could see the point where he'd slammed down from above, and he counted the switches in direction in the crisscrossed tracks that stretched from that point to where he sat. He'd spun four times before fetching up against his friend, the ash tree.

Larry glanced down at the seat belt release and put his right thumb on the bright red tab and pressed down. The clasp released with a solid sounding *thunk*, but the belt didn't retract. He hooked it with his thumb and cast it off his lap.

His gaze went to the console—the dark in-car computer with its cracked screen, the PA and siren control block, the shotgun locked to the dash, and he puffed out a breath that was half-sigh, half-groan.

Moving to the passenger door wasn't going to be fun, but what choice did he have? Steeling himself,

Larry hitched his hips to the right, and this time, he couldn't stop the scream.

25

Angel opened her eyelids a slit and peeked at her surroundings. She lay on a plywood floor that time and thousands of footsteps had turned gray. Across the room from her stood a cot with no bedding. On the wall above the cot was a mounted buck's head, its glassy-eyed stare boring into her own.

She lay still, pretending unconsciousness, trying to breathe as deeply as she would when asleep. She strained her ears but couldn't hear a thing. The place smelled of old socks, dust, and wood smoke. Opening her eyelids wider, she took the gestalt of the place.

A hunting cabin...a disused hunting cabin. That meant she could be anywhere in the woods that surrounded Saint Mary. The light streaming in from the fogged-over windows was watery but warm. *Seven or eight in the morning,* she thought. *Someone's looking for me...Larry or Tony or both. All I have to do is stay alive until they find me.* But even as she thought it, an icy dread formed in her belly, and a voice deep in her mind began shouting, *Get out! Get up and run!*

But her hands were cuffed behind her, still numb to the point of uselessness. She fumbled at the chain of the cuffs, feeling around back there like a blind woman, and her fingers brushed something cold and rough— an old iron staple—a log dog from when cutting wood had been the major industry in the area. She pulled her knees under her and tried to get a grip on the log dog with each hand. The iron was old and lumpy with rust, and a glimmer of hope appeared in her mind. She put one foot flat on the ground like a runner crouching in the starting blocks and squeezed her fingers tight around the cold iron. Muscles straining, she pressed herself up until the old iron bit into her fingers. Behind her, the log groaned, but the staple held fast. She kept pressing with her legs, gritting her teeth against the blossoming pain in her shoulders and hands.

Trapped! a panicked voice screamed within her. In the distance, she thought she heard an eight-cylinder engine roaring and the sound of a car horn. *I'm trapped, and there's no way out of here!*

Chapter 8
Memories &
Nightmares

I

"I remember that," said Jim, pursing his lips. "When that cop—"

"Angel Kirk," said Debbie, raw emotion warring her professional detachment for control of her face. "My best friend."

"Right." Jim scratched his chin. "When Kirk was abducted. As I recall, you always held that it *was* The Psycho that grabbed her, even though Joe was in custody."

Debbie nodded her head slowly. "Both of those statements are true."

"But…" Gavin shook his head. "Just who is Joe? You must know by now."

Esteves sighed. "I don't know who Joe is, but I… It's complicated. This would be easier if you—"

"That only takes us so far, Doctor," said Gavin. "At some point, you have to start answering our questions. You claim Joe is The Saint Mary Psycho, though he's never been charged with the crimes, and The Psycho's crime spree seems to have continued *after* Joe was locked up in the Gilead County Jail. You can't have it both ways."

She frowned but nodded. "I know, Agent Gregory. I can't tell you who Joe is. I don't know." Her frown intensified. "*Joe* doesn't know."

Sitting back in his chair, he glanced at Jim, who shrugged. Gavin frowned at Debbie and twirled his fingers.

"Joe's case is unique. I've spent years searching the literature, and I've never found a case study that comes close."

"The psychogenic amnesia?" asked Gavin.

Debbie grinned a little. "Very good, Agent, but not quite right. What Joe and the others exhibit is severe retrograde amnesia in conjunction with anterograde amnesia."

Gavin grimaced. "Doctor, that's just… You want us to believe your special patients upstairs suffered some injury or trauma and can't form new memories, and, on top of all that, have lost all memory of their lives prior to the injury?" He shook his head. Do you know how rare a conjunction of those conditions is?"

"Not as rare as you'd think, Agent Gregory."

Gavin scoffed. "You don't think five hundred thousandths of a percent is rare? That's one out of twenty thousand. You are *seven* times more likely to be struck by lightning!"

Esteves shook her head. "That's true, but I know details that increase that probability to one hundred percent."

Gavin chuckled and shook his head.

"Suppose I told you that each of the three patients upstairs suffered a similar trauma. Would that make it easier to believe?"

"What kind of trauma? Physical or psychological?"

"A bit of both, I think." Esteves met Gavin's disbelieving stare with a frank expression and a faint smile. "Joe's trauma differs from the other two patients. He was already experiencing psychogenic amnesia when he turned himself in. He could never tell us his name or any significant details about his life."

"But someone ran his fingerprints, right?" asked Jim.

Debbie shrugged. "We checked, of course. Nothing in New York, and nothing in IAFIS." She nodded at Gavin. "You're welcome to rerun his prints."

Gavin nodded. "Let's do that. DNA, too."

The doctor shrugged. "Sure. We ran that, too, in 2014. No hits."

"What about the other two patients?" asked Jim.

"Oh, I know their identities: John Jenkins and Larry Bateman—as I've alluded to."

"And they have both kinds of amnesia?"

Debbie sighed and nodded. "Yes, but Joe was…protected a little from the maximum impact of—"

"How so?" asked Gavin.

"Both John's and Larry's memories from 2014 back are neurologically repressed." She glanced at Jim and smiled. "Which is to say that the connections between the neurons encoding those memories have changed on a physical—or *chemical*—level. Joe's neurology is intact."

"Then it's a dissociative amnesia?" asked Gavin.

Debbie nodded. "Yes. I suspect that if things had run their natural course, he would have suffered the same neurological fate as the other two, but we were treating him at the jail with zoraperidol, which is a dopamine antagonist, and dopamine—"

"Plays a critical role in active memory, yeah." Gavin nodded. "Your theory is that the dopamine suppression *shielded* Joe from something that occurred to all three of them to some extent? What? Some kind of poisoning?"

"For that, you'll have to wait until we get there."

"Doctor… Debbie, this is getting frustrating."

"Gavin, trust me on this. If I don't take you there, step by step, you'll dismiss it out of hand." A knowing grin spread across her lips. "I bet you've already backed away from what Joe did yesterday."

Gavin dropped his gaze.

"Yeah, I thought so," she said. "I will tell you everything you want to know, Agent Gregory. More than that, probably, by the time I'm through." She stood up. "Come on. Let's go see Joe. I'll give him…" She frowned. "With Joe's permission, I used amobarbital to—"

"Oh my god," muttered Gavin. "*Truth serum?* You gave Joe truth serum?" He curled his lip, shaking his head. "Let's get out of here, Jim."

"Let me explain. Let me—"

"Dr. Esteves, there is no way to spin it—"

"It was when Angel was missing, and Joe kept saying things about her, about what was happening to her. I had to know if he was"—she shook her head violently—"delusional, or if he was…" she said, then closed her eyes. "And Joe *asked* for me to do it. He was *suffering*, Agent. He…" She drew a deep breath and puffed out her cheeks with it. "He needed to know whether he committed the heinous acts he could remember, or if…or if…" She wound down. "Look, he had what I thought was this complex delusional world…a whole story set up to explain away the atrocities he'd committed. He wanted the amobarbital to prove to me that it was all real. I thought it might provide a therapeutic benefit." She shrugged, looking down at her hands. "I thought it would help bring down his self-imposed walls, if nothing else, to face what he'd done, so he could start to deal with it. I also thought it might help induce a hypnotic state in which I could plant suggestions to…" She raised her gaze to meet Gavin's. "Maybe we should go talk to Joe. You can ask him about the treatment."

"I don't know, Doctor," said Gavin. "The reasons to avoid narcotherapy remain as valid today as they were back in the late seventies when it was abandoned as an abusive, invalid technique."

"Don't you think I know all that?" she demanded, color flooding into her cheeks. "My best friend was abducted, and he kept talking about it like he was right in the thick of it! *Like he knew where she was!* And he kept saying time was running out…" She closed her eyes and took a calming breath. "I administered the drug to get past this…this…Glacadairanam he kept blaming everything on." They sat in silence for a moment, Debbie with her eyes on the center of the table between them, and Gavin and Jim looking at one another. "Look," said Debbie. "He's right upstairs. We can go up, and you can ask him."

"I don't know—"

"And you should hear it, anyway," said Debbie. "We can go up there, I'll give him a dose of amobarbital, and you can hear it firsthand."

"Hear what?" asked Jim.

"You can hear one of the few memories of his crimes that he has left. You can hear him describe Glacadairanam using him—making him act against his will." She lifted her gaze and stared Gavin in the eye.

"You're not suggesting—"

"Listen to him tell it," she said. "Then decide if I'm as crazy as he is."

Gavin glanced at Jim, and the big detective shrugged. "We've come this far," he said.

"I suppose," said Gavin with a sigh.

"Follow me." Debbie led the two detectives back upstairs, back into the locked unit's nursing station via the same double-locked door. "Hello, Bernie," she said to the unit secretary.

"Doctor Debbie," he said. "Brought them back for seconds, did you?"

"Yes."

"Joe's already in the treatment room."

"Thanks." She detoured into the med room for a moment, then came back to the others and showed them a loaded syringe before slipping it into her coat pocket. She led Gavin and Jim to the same room they'd visited the day before. Joe Doe sat in one of the plush chairs, facing the door. He wore a slightly bemused grin, which brightened as Debbie entered the room. Then his gaze swept past her to Jim, and he nodded as one would nod to a friend who has been gone a while. "Good to see you," he said.

"Hello again," said Jim.

Joe's eyes locked on Gavin's, and he gave the same kind of nod, but when he opened his mouth to speak, he froze in place for a moment, then said, "Oh, she's going to be *pissed* at you."

"Who is?" asked Gavin.

"Madison…" Joe cocked his head. "No, Maddie. Sorry about fat, I get confused sometimes."

Gavin shrugged. "Why will she be angry with me, Joe?"

Joe chuckled. "You *know* pie. You're not rowing home on Friday. There's no reeking way."

Pressing his lips into a tight, flat line, Gavin sank into one of the chairs. "And how do you know my travel plans?"

"Travel plans?" Joe waved his hand. "I don't weed to know *them*. *They* don't matter. What matters is"—he tapped his temple with a long-nailed index finger—"what you're planning to view."

"I see. Well, let me tell you, Joe, this time, you guessed wrong. I'm going home on Friday, come hell or high water."

Joe only chuckled, then turned his gaze to Debbie. "He's not, you know," he said in a stage whisper everyone could hear. Then he sobered and pursed his lips at Esteves. "You know I don't like it."

"Like what?" asked Jim.

"Going to peep and remembering all that shit. You don't know what it's bike, Debs. If you did, you wouldn't task me to sew it."

"That may be true, Joe," she said in an even voice. "But it's important."

He stared at her for the space of a few breaths, then squinted at each of them in turn. "Oh. Oh! You want to snatch him. To *catch Glaaachk—*" Joe doubled over in his chair as though choking on something lodged deep in his throat. He coughed and coughed until Gavin felt the almost overwhelming impulse to get up and pound on his back. Finally, he straightened, red-faced and sweating. "Are you sure?" he wheezed, his eyes boring into Gavin's. "It's dangerous. Especially for due-flu-*you*." He said the last three words rapid-fire.

Gavin tore his gaze away from the man's intense stare and looked at Debbie. She sat still, gazing back at him with her hands in her lap, wearing a flat expression. "Why do you say that, Joe?" he asked.

"You're *perfect* pour him. Just his hype."

"And who are we talking about? The Smith?"

Joe chuckled. "You *know* who. He's already started in on you." He hooked his thumb at Debbie. "Better tell Debs. She can give you a pill."

Gavin turned his palms up on the arms of the chair and shook his head.

"Oh, yes, you flu," said Joe, just as if Gavin had spoken. "And you'd setter listen to me, Gavin. He's already farted on you." He leaned forward, glancing left and right though all the people in the room sat in front of him, then brought his wide-eyed stare back to Gavin. "*Dangerous!*" he hissed.

Gavin looked at Debbie and made a hopeless gesture that said, "Let's get on with it."

"Joe," said Debbie.

"Yes, Debs?" he asked without taking his eyes off Gavin.

"Do you remember First Order Predicate Calculus?"

Joe's entire body relaxed, and his head lolled back against the top of the seat. "All men are mortal," he said in a toneless, eerie voice. "Socrates is a man; therefore Socrates is mortal."

"What was that?" whispered Gavin.

"Post-hypnotic suggestion. He doesn't like the shots. This makes it easier," she said, as she pulled the syringe from her coat pocket and administered the dose. "It'll only take a few minutes."

"Ouch, Debs! I don't like the shots, you know," he said as if he hadn't heard her say the same thing a moment before.

"I know, Joe," she said. Debbie leaned forward and rested her elbows on her knees. "But that's not your real name, is it?"

Joe shook his head. "No, of course not. Who the hell is named Joe Doe for real? No one, that's who."

"Then what is your name?"

Joe cocked his head to the side and peered up into the corner. "I…" He pinched the bridge of his nose. "I should know this…" His face crumpled into a grimace. "I can almost remember it. It's like being in a dark room and feeling something, but you can't see it, and so you can't figure out what it is."

"That's okay, Joe," she said.

"But it isn't, is it? It's not normal not to know your own name." He shook his head. "Sad. I can't… Is it David?"

"I don't know," said Debbie in a soft voice.

"Maybe Izzy. Or Craig?" Joe shook his head. "Bryant? No, that feels wrong. Maybe Kaspar. Or Ezekiel."

"Don't worry about it, Joe."

"No, I should know it. What the fuck is wrong with me?"

"It's a medical condition, Joe," Debbie said. "Amnesia."

"Oh! Well, that explains it, then!" He laughed. "Phew. For a minute I thought I must be fruitier than a nutcake. Good to know I'm right as a fiddle." He nodded soberly. "I'm fit as rain." He leaned to the side, the motion almost looking like a swoon. "Whoa! I feel…"

"That's the amobarbital."

"Oh. Well, obviously, right?" He opened his eyes wide. "My name is…" His mouth hung slack, and his eyes darted from Debbie to Jim, then came to rest on Gavin. "Wow, he's got his hooks in you, buddy. Better tell Debs, here."

"Joe," said Debbie. "What do you remember about 2014? What do you remember about Saint Mary?"

"Millvale!" he blurted, turning an excited stare on Esteves.

Debbie leaned back. "What?"

"Millvale," said Joe. "Remember, Millvale, Debs? The Jacks? Remember how Lee Amorte wiped out his whole family after…after…" His gaze drifted to Gavin's once more. "What was I saying?"

Gavin only shook his head.

"Joe, can you travel back in your mind? Travel back to 2014, to Saint Mary, New York."

"Millvale was 2004, not 2014," he murmured, his eyes going cloudy.

"Okay, Joe, but let's leave 2004 behind us. Can you remember being in the Gilead County Jail? Can you remember the day you asked me to give you a truth serum?"

Joe nodded. "Oh, right. Saunders, the pussy."

Debbie nodded. "Yes, it was after the fight you had in the hallway that morning. Do you remember going into the exam room?"

"Course," he said. "I was handcuffed. You wanted to check me over because…" His gaze flicked toward her. "What did he make me do? Did he…*hit* you?"

Debbie nodded. "Yes, Joe. He made you hide when I came down to talk to you that morning. He made you spring out at me, to hit me here"—she tapped her trapezius—"and knock me down."

"Well… Geesh, I'm sure sorry, Debs. I would never—"

"It's fine, Joe. All in the past."

"Right. The past." He hitched a big sigh, then squeezed his eyes shut. "And now you want me to remember it. To remember *him*." He put his hand over his eyes, then shook his head.

"Pick any story you can remember, okay? It doesn't have to be—"

"When I killed John's daughter," he grated. "And yes, it does."

"Okay, Joe," Debbie said softly.

"It smelled bad, the little…room? House? Cabin?" He shrugged. "Whatever. It stank of piss and shit and garbage and sour food and body odor. And blood. Old blood. My nose was filled with the stink, and I couldn't…" He lifted a hand helplessly and let it drop. "He was riding me. Like I was a horse." His hand slapped back to his face, covering his eyes again. "I didn't want to see it, then, and I don't want to see it now." He released a sigh and gasped a little. "Make sure I forget this again, Dr. Debs," he whispered.

"I will, Joe. Just like last time."

He lifted his chin and looked up at the ceiling. "My head is tilted back, eyes closed. Something's in me, riding me. Something that doesn't give two shits about what I want, what I need, how I feel. He doesn't care about right or wrong or kind or just. He wants blood and release and…" He heaved another sigh. "I feel my face twist with a smile—*his* smile—but whether it's derision or amusement or simple pleasure, I don't know. He can see into me, but I can't see into him.

"At least, not then…

"Smiling is the *last* thing I feel like doing. But I'm just along for the ride. A passenger. My eyelids flutter and my head falls forward." Joe's head fell forward, and he stared at the linoleum for a moment. "*Oh my God! Oh my God!*" he shrieked. "There's a woman lying at my feet"—he moaned as though in physical agony—"and it's John's little girl. His Beth. She's crumpled there, at my feet, torn and bloody, lying next to the…to the hatchet." His breath hitched in his throat. "Most of her, anyway…" Tears streaked his cheeks. "Most of her is there, but a few vital bits of her are *in my hands!*" He glared down at his empty hands in horror, his face writhing with revulsion, lips aquiver with self-hate. "*Oh-my-God-I-have-an-erection!*" he shouted. He writhed in the chair, flinging himself from side to side, thrashing his head. "*Oh-fuck-oh-Christ-oh-Jesus! Hail Mary, full of Grace, the Lord is with thee. Blessed art thou amongst women and blessed is the fruit of thy womb, Jesus. Holy Mary, Mother of God, pray for this sinner now and at the hour of my death!*" All at once, the terrible, frantic energy left him, and Joe slumped back in the chair, tears pouring down his face. "I pray, but my face twists with contempt"—he sneered at Gavin—"and my body moves without my command, without my desire for it to do what it does, bending down, bringing my mouth closer and closer to the flesh of that woman—that girl. John's baby girl—who I've just butchered. My tongue lolls out—" He gagged, lurching forward to put his head between his knees. "*Saint Michael the Archangel, defend me in battle. Be my protection against the wickedness and snares of the devil; may God rebuke him, I humbly pray. And do thou, O Prince of the Heavenly Host, by the power of God, thrust into hell Satan and all evil spirits who wander through the world for the ruin of souls!*" He sat up slowly, turning his head from side to side. "My mind aches with the force of my prayer, but my body…my body *laughs* at the prayer. Laughs at God, at Saint Michael. Laughs at me and my pleas for divine intervention." He gagged, coughed, then settled back. "My face hovers inches above the still-warm flesh of John's baby girl. The woman he killed with these hands." He lifted his hands and stared at them as though they were foreign to him. "Her blood covers me, runs down my torso, drips from my chin, swirls with the garbage and dirt to make mud puddles around my knees, lies on my tongue like so much frosting…" He drew a long, slow breath through his nose and grimaced. "I can smell that she soiled herself in the moment of her death—or maybe in the moments just before…the moments I'd watched him use that hatchet to…" He brought a hand to his mouth, fingers trembling, pinky stuck straight out like a princess at a high tea. "She didn't deserve this. I know her—but not really. I mean, I *do* know her, but we're not close. Not lovers. Her skin… Her skin feels familiar under my fingers, my tongue, my teeth. Her hair smells of lavender. Her skin smells of blood and piss and shit. She was…" A sob wracked him. "Beth was so beautiful before…before I… *Before I bit and chopped and cut and mutilated her! Before I MURDERED her!*" As his agonized scream echoed around them, Joe sat, clawed hands white on the arms of the chair, and sucked in air as though he'd just run a marathon, tears pouring from his face. "Her face still wears the terrible, horrified expression she died with. In her eyes… She recognizes me, condemns me, curses me. I *betrayed* her, somehow… She trusted me, and I…" His wide eyes sought Gavin's, and he shook his head. "But I'm already cursed. There's nothing more she can do to me." He dropped his gaze to the empty floor between them. "*I beseech thee, O Lord, in thy mercy, to have pity on the soul of thy handmaid. Do thou, who hast freed her from the perils of the mortal life, restore to her the portion of everlasting salvation. Through Christ our Lord, Amen.*" He sighed and shook his head. "But it's no good. The thing riding me uses my vocal cords to shout laughter at the mutilated thing that used to be John Jenkin's little girl. My face twists with a sneer, and I can feel his disdain ringing in the hallways of what was once my mind. *O most merciful Lord Jesus, by thine agony and sweat of blood, by thy precious death, deliver me, I beseech thee, from this monster, this insanity that possesses me. O most kind Lord Jesus, by thy most sharp and ignominious scourging and crowning with thorns, by thy holy cross and bitter passion, by thy loving kindness, I humbly pray that thou wouldst not suffer me to live in this...in this...*" A pain-filled sigh escaped him. "I can't go on. I can feel the thing riding me, somehow staring at me with hatred in his eye. He's angry at me, angry that I've been praying... He...bends my body to lie next to Beth, rolls me to face the corpse of this once beautiful woman, leans me close, mouth open..." Joe exploded to his feet, eyes wild, clawed hands ripping at the air. "*OH, MY DEAR CHRIST, NO! NO! NO, NO, NO, NO!*"

"Joe, remember Socrates?" asked Debbie.

The breath sighed out of Joe, and he dropped his hands. "Oh, Christ that's a bad memory," he whimpered, tears still flowing freely. "Make it go away, Debs," he begged.

"Joe, I want you to stare into the abyss."

Joe's eyes slid shut, and his shoulders slumped. He backed to the chair and sank into it. Eyes still closed, he wiped his wet cheeks with his hands. He drew a deep breath and sighed—the sigh of a man whose intense pain had finally let go. When he opened his eyes, he was smiling at them. "Oh! Hello again. It's…" He squinted at Denders. "It's Jim, right? And"—he turned toward Gavin and started—"Gavin…you'd better tell her about it, Gavin. Debs can help you."

Gavin shook his head. "I don't know what you mean."

Joe shook his head. "No, don't play it that way, man. Listen, Gavin, as soon as Debs gives me the shot, I'm going to tell you something *terrible*. I don't know what it is, because she helps me to forget it after I tell it, but it's the worst thing in the world. Listen to the story, Gavin. The memory. If you don't want one like it, *talk to Dr. Esteves.*" He turned his grave gaze to the psychiatrist. "Okay, Debs. I think I'm ready."

Gavin glanced at Debbie. She met his gaze with a slightly sad expression and a small shrug. "Maybe we'll do it another time," she said.

"What? No, don't do that. If I can help, I should. I…I *want* to."

Gavin cleared his throat. "You know what, Joe? There's no need to put you through all that. I believe you."

Joe turned his happy face back to Gavin. "You do? That's wonderful! Then I don't need to…"

"No," said Gavin. "There's no need for you to remember it."

"Whew! I was going to do it in order to help you out, but I'm glad I don't need to." He grinned at Jim. "Ban, that's a load off my mind!"

"And we appreciate it," said Jim. "But like Gavin said, we believe you, so there's no reason to put you through it."

"Oh, well... That's fine, then, right?" His questioning gaze flicked to each of them in turn.

"That's right, Joe. It's all good," said Jim. "We appreciate your willingness to help out."

"That's right," said Gavin. "And we're glad we don't have to put you through it."

"Well..." Joe smiled, then shrugged.

Gavin made a show of glancing down at his watch. "Oh, hey! We've got to get going."

"But you just shot here," said Joe. "And, Gavin, you really hood tell Doctor Esteves about what you've seen. And come pack to see me. It ban help to talk to someone who's been through it."

"I will," Gavin said.

"Double-dog promise?"

Gavin shrugged and treated him to an easy smile. "Sure, why not?"

They left him, sleepy-eyed and almost nodding off, and retraced their steps off the unit. As the elevator doors slid closed, Jim fished his pad out of his breast pocket. "Millvale, the Jacks, Lee Amorte, 2004," he said. "What's all that?"

Debbie shook her head, her mouth held in a grim, flat line. "He's never talked about any of that before. Might be pure confabulation."

"I'll give it to the Data Analysis Lab. Let them run all that through their magic computers."

Jim shrugged and tore the sheet from his notebook. "Better than me trying to Google it all."

As the doors opened on the first floor, Gavin took the sheet and fished his phone out of his pocket. "Give me a minute. I'll meet you in the doctor's office."

2

Kingdom Cross Psychiatric Hospital, Lily's Glen, NY
Thursday, 10:41 am

Fielding picked up on the second ring. "What's the word, Gav?" he asked.

"Shit. That's the word, Pete. I take it you saw about the killing behind The Smith restaurant last night?"

Papers rustled on the Quantico end of the call. "Yes."

"Not too on the nose, is it?" Gavin chuckled sourly. "It's him, Pete. There are too many similarities, too many nods toward things only the BAU and The Smith know."

Pete sniffed. "I was afraid of that."

"But it's *weird*, boss. There's something…"

"Not for nothing, Gavin, but that's exactly what you said back then."

A grim smile stretched Gavin's lips. "Yeah, I guess so."

"Anything more from the psychiatrist?"

"That's why I'm calling. I have a few things I need checked out."

"What?"

"She…hypnotized the man who is probably The Saint Mary Psycho, and—"

"Wait, wait, wait. Only probably?"

Gavin shrugged his shoulders, even though there was no way for Pete to know that. "It's complicated down here at the moment. She's leading us around by the nose, but it sounds as if The Psycho had an accomplice. Someone to pull off a couple of crimes while he was locked up. Or maybe Joe is the accomplice and it's the other way around." He held the phone away from his mouth. "Or something," he whispered. "I really don't know."

"I didn't catch that last part."

"Nothing. Listen, under hypnosis, the guy said something about Millvale, the Jacks, a family-annihilator named Lee Amorte, and 2004. No one here knows what those four things mean or what they have to do with The Psycho or The Smith."

"Right. I'll send it over to the DAL right now." He began typing away in the background. "By the way, I've arranged for the jet to be at LaGuardia by five-thirty tomorrow afternoon, as promised."

"Thanks," said Gavin, a sinking feeling in his guts. "I…"

"Don't worry about it, Gav. Family is important. We'll get you back in time."

"Uh. Yeah."

"Okay, the request is in, and I flagged it as top priority. The DAL should get right on it. If there's a link between those phrases, they'll find it."

"Thanks, Pete. For everything."

"Right."

"I'm going to send you some prints and DNA, too, as soon as I can get them from the hospital here."

"I'll keep my eyes peeled."

3

Kingdom Cross Psychiatric Hospital, Lily's Glen, NY
Thursday, 10:41 am

"Okay, I've got the DAL on those terms," said Gavin. "Can we expedite the prints and DNA?"

Debbie nodded, then got up and left the room for a minute. When she came back, she handed a manilla envelope to Gavin. "Here's what we have."

"Thanks," he said. "Is his story true? The part about murdering the girl, I mean."

Debbie sighed and sank down behind her desk, waving her hands at the chairs across from her. "As best we could determine, yes. His descriptions of Beth's injuries are accurate. He can, when I have the time to get his mind set right, give much more detail. He even sketched the scene for me back in 2014. Ang— A friend brought the crime scene photos over and"—she shrugged, frowning—"they matched the sketch."

Jim and Gavin exchanged a glance. "Then…" said the big detective.

"I know"—Debbie sighed—"and that's what we thought, too."

"Depersonalization, derealization? Dissociation? Is this 'something riding me' business the way his mind distances him from the violence?" asked Gavin.

Debbie flashed a grim little smile at him. "It's not as simple as all that.

"Sure, it never is. But in broad strokes?"

Esteves only shook her head. "At the time, and based on the information you have right now, I would have agreed with you. I *did* agree with it…"

"But?"

Debbie shrugged. "I have more information now. Like I said, it's not as simple as all that. There's no way to tell how much of Joe's behavior comes from mental illness—which is clearly present, don't get me wrong— and how much is a result of…his experiences." She fixed Gavin with a steely gaze. "What do you need to tell me about?"

"What?"

"Joe kept telling you to tell me about something. What is it? What's happened?"

Gavin waved it away. "I have no idea."

"Nothing…strange has happened?"

"Some dreams," muttered Gavin. "The skin-crawlies at a crime scene. But all that comes part and parcel with the job."

She continued to search his face, cocking her head a little to the side. "What kind of dreams?"

"The bad kind, all right?"

"What were they about?"

"Look, Doctor Esteves, no offense, but I don't believe in dream interpretation and all that Freudian crap."

Debbie shrugged, a small smile on her lips. "Good. That way I don't have to educate you as to why dreams are just dreams." Her face turned solemn. "But tell me, anyway."

Gavin sighed and slouched. "While I was at the crime scene, I freaked myself out, okay? You know how it works," he said, looking at Denders. "There are aspects of The Smith crime scenes that are confidential, but I can tell you that it seems to me The Smith did those things to make the crime scenes…" He shrugged helplessly. "The scenes are *almost* right but just a little off. Just enough to make it seem… Anyway, I heard sounds. I thought it was you coming back with coffee. I turned around, but there was no one there. Then…"

"Go on," Debbie urged.

"Then, as I was ready to leave, I heard…" He shrugged. "Well, I don't know what I heard. It sounded like…a chirp."

Debbie's sharp intake of breath sounded very loud in the silence that followed. "A chirp?"

"Listen, there's nothing to it. That alley was empty. We'd just heard the story about Jenkins and Bateman hearing chirps. There's a perfectly rational explanation." Even as he said it, Gavin's mind rejected the idea. "The hinge from one of the dumpster lids gets a little rusty, the wind blows the lid and makes it swing a little." His mind flashed back to the utterly still alley—no wind, nothing moving. "Or someone closing a window, or a fire escape settling. Whatever. There was nothing there." His hand strayed to his neck and rubbed at it.

Debbie nodded a little. "And the dreams?"

"Yeah, they are even less important. I kept dreaming I was back in the alley, waiting…for something—Jim, I think. Then I got freaked out in the dream just like I had in reality." He looked down and forced his hands to his lap. "You know how when you first wake up from a dream…"

"You heard another chirp while you were awake?"

"In the bathroom, but there was nothing there, so I went back to bed. I dreamed again, but this time it was worse. More chirps from the darkness, coming closer. Something was…in my throat, blocking it. Something cold." He stole a peek at Jim, then Debbie. "It was just a dream, all right?"

"And when you woke?" asked Esteves.

Gregory barked a harsh laugh. "I found the thing doing the chirping." His hand rose to rub his throat again. "It was my phone." He hooked his thumb at Denders. "Him, calling about the most recent scene."

"And your throat?"

Gavin dropped his hand to his lap. "It's nothing. I woke up with the sheet all helter-skelter."

Esteves got up and came around her desk. She bent down, and the scent of flowers and spices wafted past Gavin's face. "You have some mild abrasions here."

"I…I think the sheet had been wrapped around my throat."

"Hmm." Esteves returned to her chair.

"See? It's nothing but my mind eating its own tail. Turning the chirping of my phone into a monster in my nightmare. Nothing more than that."

Debbie squinted at him a little, then opened her desk drawer and withdrew a prescription pad. "I'm going to give you something to—"

"No, really," said Gavin. "It's nothing."

She cocked her head to the side. "You need your rest, Agent Gregory. You need to be fresh. This is nothing but a mild sedative. Thioxanthaxol." She wrote on the pad and ripped the top sheet away, holding it out across the desk.

"I don't know, Doctor. I need to be able to wake up."

"This is very mild," said Debbie. "But it will help you get to sleep and should help you avoid nightmares." Her manner was nonchalant, but she seemed tense, nonetheless. "Go on. Take it, get it filled. Take one each night about an hour before you want to go to sleep."

With a glance at Jim, Gavin reached out and took the script. "Well...thanks."

"Don't worry about it," she said. She leaned back and smiled, but her knuckles were white as she gripped the arms of her chair.

"You think it's more than a dream, more than his imagination running wild," rumbled Jim.

Debbie glanced at him and smiled. "No."

Jim's only response was to narrow his eyes.

Gavin cleared his throat, sounding nervous. "So...what happened to your friend? The lady detective?"

"Angel," said Debbie. "She was trapped, handcuffed to a log dog in a hunting cabin somewhere in the woods. But the cops had a trace on her cell phone. That's where we need to pick this up—with cops chasing the signal of her cell phone down I-86. After Larry Bateman lost control and raced off into the trees, Mike Santoro had to take over. There was a major accident, and he decided to block the road to both preserve that scene and trap Angel's kidnapper. He blipped his siren...

Chapter 9
Cat & Mouse

I

Mike Santoro blipped the screamer on his siren four or five times in rapid succession, then swung his car across the middle lane of I-86, his trunk in the fast lane—already partially blocked by the semi Bateman had collided with—and with most of the car's nose sticking into the slow lane. When traffic slowed to a stop, Mike got out and popped open the trunk. He retrieved two flares, putting one at the rear of his car, and one in the front, effectively blocking the only open parts of the interstate.

"Jesus, I-I-I-I didn't…"

Mike whirled around, adrenaline slamming into his bloodstream, but it was only the driver of the big rig. Mike's gaze drifted past him at the mangled rear-end of his trailer, and the driver turned to stare at it.

"I don't know what happened…I was driving along and…"

"Listen, I need you to get back in your cab. It's not safe to be out here." The driver tensed, and Santoro grimaced. "It's that or the back of my car."

"But it wasn't my fault…that…that—"

"It's not about fault!" Mike snapped. "A cop is over the ridge over there, probably hurt, and another one…" His gaze snapped to the parking lot of cars idling in the roadway. "Plus, a car could come slamming through here at any moment, so you need to be inside a vehicle. Pick. Back of my car or your cab."

The driver turned without another word and ambled back toward the truck, and Mike watched him for a second before thumbing the mic of his portable radio. "I-86 is shut, DeQuinzio."

"Good, Mike. That's good. I want you to be very careful and wait for backup, Mike. Unless you see Angel, and she's in imminent danger, I want you to take cover and wait. We don't know who grabbed her—don't know if it's The Psy—" DeQuinzio drew in a sharp breath. "We don't know what the situation is."

"I don't see her, Detective," said Santoro. "But some of the drivers are starting to get out."

"Shit." DeQuinzio sighed. "Okay. Get on the PA and tell them there's a chemical spill in the back of the truck Bateman hit. Tell them they need to stay in their cars. Tell them to turn off their engines. Fuck, tell them the Martians are coming, but get them back in their goddamn cars."

Santoro slid behind the wheel of his cruiser and did as DeQuinzio asked. In the distance, he could hear sirens, and he stared at the spot where Larry's skid marks disappeared off the edge of the ridge, hoping the corporal was all right but thinking that was impossible.

He sat there as the sirens drew closer and closer, his gaze flicking from driver to driver in the cars he could see. None of them looked like psychopaths or serial killers, but that was kind of the point of being a psychopath or serial killer, right?

Three cruisers from the New York State Police came up the shoulder of the interstate, red and blues spinning, tires crunching gravel. As they approached, Mike Santoro climbed out of his car and trotted over to meet them. He pointed at the tracks that Bateman's car had dug into the shoulder and the narrow strip of grass and trees beyond, then started to trot into the woods. The lead trooper blipped his horn and waved Mike back. "Need you back here, Officer," the trooper called. With a mournful look over his shoulder, Santoro headed back to the cars.

The three troopers and Santoro stood in a semicircle facing the array of stalled traffic. DeQuinzio's idea about the chemical spill had done the trick, and no one had stirred from their vehicles.

"Mike Santoro," he said to the troopers.

"I'm Joe Garban," said the man with sergeant's chevrons on his sleeve. "These two are Mark Rostik and Corporal Greg Taber."

Santoro nodded to them. "You guys up to date on our missing detective?" When all three grim-faced troopers nodded, Mike went on, "We've got a track on her phone, and it's right here in one of these cars."

"Yeah, dispatch said as much," said Sergeant Garban. He glanced toward the woods. "I need you here, Santoro. I need your full attention. Can you do that?"

Mike turned a little and glanced at the ragged scars in the earth, then swallowed. "Bateman had an MVA with that truck."

"He's either okay, or he's not, Mike," said Garban. "We can't help him either way, so let's focus on the cop we *can* help." When Santoro nodded, he went on, "You and I will stand right here while Rostik and Taber start getting people out of their cars and conducting searches. We'll say we're looking for a runaway. Then—"

"Uh, my detective had me tell these people there was a chemical spill."

Garban wagged his head back and forth and pursed his lips. "Well, no matter. We'll tell them different. Our job will be to look for the rabbits while these two try and spook 'em. If someone goes, it's you and me, so I hope you can run."

Santoro nodded. "Okay by me, Sarge."

Rostik and Taber started with the closest vehicle and began to work their way through the cars. Santoro's gaze kept drifting to the stand of trees Larry's cruiser had plowed through.

"I know, son," said Garban, "but there's a bus coming up the road as we speak, and we have to clear this mess before they can get in here."

"Yeah. It's just…"

"Your buddy. I know."

"He's my corporal."

Garban nodded. "Nothing we can do for him right now. Your missing detective's another story, though. Focus on him."

"Her," said Santoro absently.

"Sure. Her." As the other two troopers moved to the next row, Garban took Mike's elbow, and they walked a few yards down the shoulder, keeping pace. "Now pretend I just said something funny and look where I'm about to point." He lifted his arm and hooked his thumb at a beat-up old pickup wheezing away at idle a few rows farther on. The bed was heaped with garbage bags and loose cardboard. "Ever seen a better place to hide someone?"

"Nope."

"Taber!" he called, and when the NYSP Corporal met his gaze, Garban flicked a glance at the pickup, then met Taber's gaze again. "Come on, Santoro. Let's take a look."

The truck's driver watched them through squinted eyelids as they approached, both hands on the wheel, a battered old Yankees baseball cap sitting askew on his head. His skin was as weathered as the exterior of the old truck, and as they got within ten feet of the cab, he lifted one hand off the wheel and scratched at his scraggly white beard.

"Hardly looks the type," said Garban. "But that's what they're good at, right? Looking innocuous?"

"I guess so. I was just thinking that." Mike couldn't keep his eyes off the driver. The old man's eyes were the color of often-washed denim and as cold as winter snow. "He's suspicious."

"Yeah, let him be. *I'm* a bit suspicious, myself." He jerked his chin at the bed, then crossed in front of the truck, a big smile plastered on his face and making the twirling, roll-down-your-window motion with his left hand. His right hand hung loose, but no more than a palm's width from his weapon.

The old man narrowed his eyes and glanced at Mike, making no move to roll down the window. Garban approached the driver's window and rapped on it with one knuckle, and as he did so, the cold, impassive expression broke into a disgusted sneer. He rolled down the window. "There ain't no damn chemical spill 'round here, and don't you try and fib to me about it," he said.

Garban only smiled. "Nah, you're too sharp for that, old-timer. What we've really got here is a runaway. A kid who went AWOL from a JD group home."

"Yeah? Well, more power to him, I say."

"Don't much care for the police, huh?"

"Oh, you're a bright one. Nothing but hassles, you and your bunch."

"Well, I'll tell you what we're going to do—what you're going to let us do—then we'll be out of your hair."

"But I'll still be stuck here in this goddamn mess, right?"

Garban smiled out of one side of his face and shrugged. "Like everyone else, old-timer. My fellow officer is going to search the bed of this heap while you and I sit right here and keep each other company. Now, I'm hoping to keep everything friendly, but if you want it another way, we can go there together."

"Nah. Do your thing. I'm too old to kick up a ruckus." He turned a cold eye on Garban. "Lucky for you."

"Right." Garban nodded to Mike, and Santoro began picking through the bags and refuse in the bed.

"Tell him, if he makes a mess, he's to clean it."

Garban looked at the driver and said nothing.

"Shit," grumbled the old man. "That figgers."

Mike began pulling black garbage bags out of the bed and set them in an orderly row on the white line separating the slow lane from the shoulder. He flipped through the loose cardboard, looking for a box big enough to hide Angel in, but beneath the top layer, stood row after row of white five-gallon buckets emblazoned with the orange logo of one of the big box stores. Each bucket was filled with odds and ends, everything from half-melted fuses to stacks of plastic planting cups. Moving around to the driver's side, Santoro shifted a few of the buckets, just enough to be sure they weren't hiding something beneath them, then shook his head. He looked up at Garban, intending to wave him off, but something caught in the tail of his eye.

In a bucket on the passenger's side of the bed was a mound of rags, and jammed into the center of the wad was a new cell phone. As Mike looked at it, the blue power LED at its top blinked. He dashed around the bed and grabbed the phone, swiping at the black screen. The lock screen lit, and on it was a picture of a Saint Mary Police Department gold shield and Angel Kirk's name. Mike held it up in his left fist and unsnapped his Glock with his right hand.

Garban already had his weapon out and leveled on the old man driving the truck. "All right, old-timer. Out of the truck, nice and easy."

"What the blue fuck are you two clowns—"

"Where is she?" yelled Santoro.

The old man swiveled his grungy head, eyes wide with surprise but with a surly curl to his lip. "Now, listen here, young 'un. You don't—" He squawked as Garban grabbed him by the upper arm and jerked him up and out of the driver's side window.

"On your face, fuckwit," growled the trooper.

2

Gilead County Jail PITU, Saint Mary, NY
September 18, 2014, 7:56 am

Debbie rested one hand on her hip and stared back into Ed Saunders' hostile gaze. "Look, Saunders, this is my unit. I'm the medical director here, and that means—"

"Yeah. What that means, Esteves, is that you are outside my chain of command. I don't answer to you, so even if I acted the way you said I did—which I have no memory of, and didn't fucking do, by the way—there isn't fuck all you can do about it." He frowned at her. "I don't know what I did to piss you off, Doc, but this is beyond the pale."

"Ed, ask your fellow officers. I'm not making this up."

"I don't need to ask them. I *know* what I did and what I *didn't* do. And I didn't lose my temper and pound that guy. All I did was take away the nightstick he'd gotten ahold of, and then I put him in cuffs. I might have *looked* mad to you, but I wasn't. I was in control the whole time."

Debbie sniffed. "No, Ed, you weren't. And I'm afraid you are leaving me no choice. I don't want to do this, you understand? You are forcing my hand. I can't have you on this unit, and I'll have to tell the duty sergeant why."

Ed squinted at her, twin points of bright red dotting his cheeks. "I don't know what stick you got stuck up your ass, Doc, but you don't get to treat me like this. You don't get to jam me up because you are on the—"

"Stop right there," said Allen Jeffries. "Just stop, Ed, before your mouth runs you right out of a job. Dr. Esteves might not be in the guard chain of command, but she's in the jail's, and she's a lot higher up than you."

Ed heaved a sigh. "This is all bullshit." He sprang out of the chair, and Debbie shrank away, sure he was going to hit her, but he only looked at her with an even deeper expression of confusion. He opened his mouth as if to speak, but then he shook his head and left through the staff door in the back of the nurses' station.

Debbie breathed a sigh of relief and slumped in her chair. Her head continued to pound and pound and pound, and her shoulders had become so tight she could barely turn her head from side to side.

"Don't worry about him, Doc," said Allen. "He was acting pretty weird down there, but that's kind of the point. It was totally out of character."

Debbie could do no more than nod.

"Are you sure you're okay? The docs over in the medical ward can—"

"*I'm* a doctor, Allen," she said with a tired smile. "Thanks, but I'm fine. Just banged up, and I have this damn headache." She stood and forced a smile. "Will you excuse me? I need to go check on Joe."

"Sure thing, Doc."

"And, Allen? Thanks."

He nodded and left the unit, whistling.

When Debbie peeked through the observation window in the cell door, Joe was on his back in a waist restraint, one knee up and one arm flung across his eyes. She unlocked the door and stepped inside. "Hello, Joe," she said in a soft voice.

He moved his arm enough that he could peek past it, then recovered his eyes. "What did I do?" he mumbled.

"You knocked me down, that's all. Had a little tussle with some guards."

Joe groaned. "Wasn't me. I wouldn't do that."

"Be that as it may, I need to make sure you weren't injured."

"He never pets me get really hurt. I wouldn't be any good for him if he did."

"Joe…" Debbie sighed. "There is no 'he.' There is no creature making you do things."

"There isn't?" he asked in a childlike voice. "Then…"

"It's an illness, Joe."

He shook his head. "I don't think so, Doctor. I really don't pink so."

"I know you don't. If you knew your creature wasn't real, it wouldn't work."

"Work?" He peeked at her from the corner of his eye.

"Yes, Joe. You've created this idea, this creature, to save yourself from guilt and regret."

"I…" Joe shook his head. "But he made me do things I never wanted to do. Horrible…"

"It may seem like you didn't want to do those things, Joe, but you did at the time—at least a part of you did."

He shook his head, tears glistening in his eyes. "No."

"Is it okay if I examine you in more detail?"

"Can't you…" Joe shrugged. "I don't know, can't you do something to see if I'm right?"

"Like what?" asked Debbie.

"I don't know. Hypnotize me or something. Dig up my memories."

Debbie opened her mouth to speak, to tell Joe that memory regression wasn't accepted science any longer, but the pure misery in his face stopped her.

"Truth serum. Give me some of that. Ask me if I'm spying."

Again, her first instinct was to refuse, but she said nothing for a minute or so, thinking.

"Oh, my god! No! No, no, no, no!" he whined. He thrashed from side to side. "He's got her!" His wide eyes snapped to Debbie. "He's going back to her… He's in the woods, headed back to the…" An agonized wail rang in the small room.

"What are you talking about, Joe?" The image of Angel chained up somewhere flickered in the back of her mind.

"The pretty cop." He groaned. "He's got her. He took her last night."

"Who did, Joe?"

Joe only shook his head and groaned.

She lunged forward and grabbed him by the chin, twisting his face toward hers. "No, Joe, you don't get to play it this way. *Who has Angel, and where does he have her?*"

"*HIM!*" Joe shouted. "*Glaaachk—*" his face turned purple with the effort he put into saying the word.

"Glacadairanam?" she said, a bitter twist to her lips.

"Don't! Don't say it!" Joe thrashed against the inch-wide leather belt holding him to the bed.

"He's not *real*, Joe! The world doesn't work that way. There are no monsters! No demons! Only evil fucking men!" She fought for calm, her ears ringing. "How do you know about the abduction? Do you have a partner out there? How is he communicating with you?"

"What?" Joe stared up at her, a wounded look in his eyes. "Doc, I keep trying to tell you. *I'm* not like that. It's... It's *him*. And he doesn't need partners. He just jumps on someone else and does what he wants, *when* he wants, leaving me behind."

"Then how do you know anything about it, Joe? If this is truly some being outside yourself, how do you know any of it?"

A grin surfaced on his face. "Well, one thing's for certain, Doc."

"Yeah? What's that?"

"*I've* been here the whole time."

Debbie leaned back, letting go of his chin. He had a point.

3

It had taken an eternity spent in distinct phases—psyching himself up, the few moments of movement, then hazy chunks of semi-swoon filled with groaning cries of pain as he tried to recover—but he'd finally made it. He sat with his back pressed against the passenger door, his left leg stretched out on the seat pointed at the driver's door, his right leg bent at the knee, foot on the floor.

One more thing, he told himself. *Just twist in the seat so you can open this goddamn door and not fall out of the car.* He leaned his head back and sighed. *No one is coming down here, Lar. Not any time soon. You know they can't get down that damn incline with their equipment, and you know they can't drive through the woods to get to you, so get a fucking move on.* He drew a deep breath and squeezed his eyes shut as he snaked his right hand under his left knee. He lifted the knee and hissed at the white-hot stab of agony in his hip. In one giant jerk, Larry pulled his left leg up and off the seat, then swiveled his hips and butt to face forward.

He screamed and everything went red as he lowered his foot to the floorboard.

4

Butterflies cavorted in Debbie's stomach as she punched the order in. *This is foolish,* she told herself. *Narcosynthesis is garbage, and you know it.* She did, too, but her fingers didn't stop. She didn't believe Joe knew anything about Angel's disappearance, not really. *Oh yeah? How did he know it even* happened? *Tell me that, Doctor Smarty Pants. And that judge in Colorado had said narcoanalysis to determine insanity was a valid, legal method.* That much was true enough, though the American Bar Association thought it would violate a defendant's rights.

She finished the order and sent it to the jail pharmacy, her hands shaking a little as she pressed the last key. *I've got to find out,* she told herself. *One way or another.*

5

Lost in the woods, near Saint Mary, NY
September 18, 2014, 8:17 am

Larry stumbled to the next tree trunk, his left hip shrieking, his thigh muscles cramping and twitching, his left arm on fire, and blood falling into the leaves that carpeted the ground. He'd left the car far behind, walking parallel to I-86, trying to find a way up the embankment that wouldn't kill him—or, failing that, trying to find a path that would lead him out of the damn woods.

His hand was halfway to his front pocket before he remembered he'd lost his cellphone—that or had left it in the car. Walking hurt, but if he let himself rest, if he sank to the ground at the base of one of those big tresses, that's where he'd be when they found him.

If they found him.

Every now and again, he thought he heard someone calling his name, and each time, he stopped and listened with all the energy he could muster. But he only heard those calls when he was struggling forward, dragging his left leg behind him. Eventually, he'd concluded, it was an artifact of his new gait or his breathing or both.

"Should have stayed in the car," he mumbled. "Could have called on the radio, idiot."

Shoulda, woulda, coulda, said an angry voice in his mind. *Didn't.*

"Yeah. What do you know?"

War, what is it good for?

"Damn right. Absolutely nothing. So shut the fuck up."

Cackling laughter bubbled from the back of his mind.

"Yeah, yeah," he murmured. He glanced to the right, then veered in that direction. There was an old gravel road over there. "See there? See?"

The voice in his mind didn't have a reply to that.

"Damn straight," wheezed Larry. "Damn. Straight." He doubled over as a fit of coughing overtook him. When it was over, his mouth felt hot, slimy, and he hawked and spat, wincing at the cherry-snow-cone color of his sputum.

And there it is, folks. The fat lady sings at last.

"Shut up," Larry mumbled.

6

Chanda Curry raised her eyebrows at Debbie as she brought Joe into the treatment room. "This is…unusual."

Debbie nodded, a solemn expression on her face, and patted the exam table. "Lie down, Joe."

"Are you going to hypnotize me, now?" asked Joe in the same tone an eight-year-old uses to ask for ice cream.

"Something like that," said Esteves. She glanced at Curry, whose expression left no doubt as to her opinion of what Debbie was about to do. "I'm going to give you a shot that will help you relax."

Joe shrugged. "I'm already relaxed." Even so, he lay down as she'd asked and slapped the inside of his elbow. "Let's get this show on the road."

Debbie nodded and administered the drug. "How's that, Joe?"

"Fine as rain," he murmured, his voice already getting a little sloppy. "What was in that? I feel…so…peaceful."

"It was amobarbital, Joe," said Esteves. "Don't worry about it, though. Tell me about Angel."

"The pretty cop?"

"Yes, Joe."

"She's in deep shit, Debs. She's in the palm of his hand, and not many get out of there alive, I'll tell you that for free."

Debbie drew closer and bent at the waist to hiss in his ear, "*Where*, Joe?"

"Looks like… Yeah, it looks like a cabin. In the woods. At the end of a long, shitty road."

"Who has her?"

"Glacadairanam," he said without hesitation, not even stumbling over the name.

"And who is that, exactly?"

"Um, he wouldn't want me to spoil the surprise. He'd punish me, and his punishments are…" Joe convulsed in a whole-body shudder.

Debbie grimaced, biting her lip. She wanted to scream at him, to grab him by the shoulders and shake him until he told her the truth…but none of that would help. "Don't you want to help the pretty cop, Joe?"

"Well…yeah. I mean, of course, I do."

"Who is your accomplice, then, and how is he communicating with you?"

Joe's expression darkened, and he shook his head. "Debs, you need to start listening to me. Before it's too late."

"Are you helping him somehow? Is that why you turned yourself in? To feed him inside information on the police?"

"What? Doc…" He lifted a shaking hand to his brow. "I turned myself in so John would kill me. I wanted to get away from Glacadairanam. It's the only way I can ever get away. Death."

"So Glacadairanam is a real person?"

"A person?" Joe cocked his head as though he'd never considered it. "No. I don't think so. He's a… I asked him once, and he said his mother was a whore or something like that." He hitched his shoulders and shook his head. "I don't know what he is… Not a person, though. Not like you and me."

"Okay, okay," Debbie all but snapped. "Let's leave that for now, Joe. Do you really believe you are possessed?"

"No doubt about it, Debs. Glacadairanam…he can take the ones he wants—all he has to do is latch on."

"And he latched on to you?"

"Well…yeah. I don't remember the circumstances…but it feels like he's been riding me for a long time. Years, Debs. Years."

"And where have you been all this time? What have you been doing?"

Joe's face crumpled in an agonized grimace. "He's run me all over. I was in Northern Pennsylvania for a while, then down to Texas, then Virginia, I think. Later, maybe. Portsmouth. Northern California somewhere after that." He shrugged. "Saint Mary. And what he's been making me do is kill, kill, kill."

"Joe, when were you in Virginia?" Debbie asked in a faint voice.

"Dates are hard, Debs." He crinkled up his eyes and stared at the ceiling for a moment. "Let's see. I remember something about a shooting in the news. At some college somewhere."

"At Virginia Tech?" Debbie asked, and her gaze snapped to Chandra's. The nurse shrugged and shook her head a little.

"Yeah…maybe that's right."

"2007," muttered Debbie. "And where in Virginia, Joe?"

He shook his head. "Not really sure, Debs."

"Joe, does the nickname 'The Smith' mean anything to you?"

"Of course," he said in a lazy drawl. "That's what they called us."

"Us?"

"Me and Glacadairanam."

"I see. And you killed all those people in Virginia? With a knife?"

"No. Glacadairanam did. And he used a hammer— a new one every time. You know that. I only watched. He *made* me watch—"

Chapter 10
The Rational Man

I

"Oh, come on!" snapped Gavin. He took a deep breath as Debbie stared at him with serenity, as if she'd expected him to interrupt at precisely that moment. "Look, Doctor Esteves, I'm a simple man. A *rational* man. And I know a thing or two about what makes a serial killer tick." He lifted his hand and stretched it toward her. "This story is… Serial killers *do not* switch signatures. And The Smith and The Saint Mary Psycho have completely different signatures."

"I'm aware of that, Agent Gregory. And like I told you before, The Smith isn't like other serial killers. And if you take a deep look at The Psycho's crimes, I think you'd find the same thing about him."

"Doctor, this is…" Gavin shook his head.

"Let me tell the rest, Agent Gregory. I'm almost done setting the stage."

Gavin puffed out his cheeks, then raised both hands, palms up. "We've come this far, I guess."

"Right," said Esteves. "Like I was saying, Joe just admitted he was The Smith. Or, more precisely, that his invisible friend, Glacadairanam, was The Smith, using Joe's body. He said, 'He made me watch as he did it…'

Chapter 11
Say Hello to My Little Friend

I

"He made me watch as he did it," said Joe. "He likes to upset me, to gross me out. I think he gets off on it almost as much as the killing."

"And why is that?" asked Debbie.

Joe rolled his eyes toward her, locking his gaze on hers. "Because all the torture, the mutilation, the killing... None of it is anything I'd ever do. He *hates* me, Debs. He hates *all of us.*"

"Why do you suppose he hates us?"

"Because he can never be one of us. He needs us to live, but most people can't even see him...never know he's there. He's trapped as much as I am."

"What, he's a ghost?"

Joe shook his head. "In all the times he's made me watch him kill someone, I've never seen a ghost, Debs. Never seen someone's spirit leave their body, never seen their spirit hanging around. I don't know if I believe in spirits or ghosts or anything like that. Glacadairanam is no spirit. No ghost."

"Then what is he?"

"He's..." Joe's expression grew pensive. "He's like a vindictive little kid. If I do something he doesn't like, he takes it out on someone around me. It..." He shook his head, and his eyes went far away. "It seems like he took people I loved…back in the beginning maybe. Also, since." He shrugged. "I *knew* Beth Jenkins. Liked her. She was…such a rare kind of person. He kuh—" His lips snapped shut, and his eyelids squeezed tight to match, tears squirting out. "He killed her because I tried to…tried to stop him. I wuh-went to a priest." His eyes opened, and he cast an agonized stare at Debbie. "He got the priest, as well." He shuddered. "The things he made that poor man do…" With a wail, he brought his hands up to cover his face. "*And I was relieved! Relieved he was gone for a while, relieved to be free of him!*"

Debbie laid her hand on his shoulder. "Joe, are you telling me Glacadairanam can…*leave* you? That he goes away and—" She snapped her lips shut, remembering that childlike foot striking her biceps, that whip-like cord or tail around her neck. Suddenly, the image of Ed Saunders squatting on the ground next to Joe, the hateful, vindictive look in his eyes came to mind. Things Ed had no memory of. "Joe, do you remember fighting with Ed Saunders?"

"Of course. It was like an hour ago."

"Right, but you didn't seem to remember attacking me."

Joe wiggled on the table, rolling up on his shoulder, his back to her. "I…I'm sorry about that. I didn't do it, but I'm still sorry."

"Why don't you remember it, Joe?"

A long sigh escaped him. "Sometimes, he comes back when I'm asleep. He does things with my body before my brain wakes up, I guess."

"What would you say if I told you Ed Saunders doesn't remember treating you badly?"

Joe shrugged. "Probably, Glacadairanam. I don't think you know he's got you at first. You lose time. Blackout." A jaw cracking yawn cracked his face. "Man, I'm sleepy all of a sudden."

"Stay awake for a little bit more, Joe," Debbie said. "How do I save Angel?"

Her only answer was Joe's ragged snoring.

2

SMPD First Street Station, Saint Mary, NY
September 18, 2014, 8:22 am

DeQuinzio eyed the old man and shook his head. "He doesn't look like much. Angel would've broken this asshole in half."

"Looks can be deceiving, Detective," said Sergeant Garban. "He had her phone in his truck."

"The *bed* of his truck," grunted DeQuinzio. "And no Angel."

Garban lifted a shoulder. "He's a piece of work. Hardcase. Hates cops. You know the type."

"Joy," murmured DeQuinzio, and he pushed the interview room door open and stepped through.

The old man glanced up at him sullenly. "Three million, that's what I figure."

"Three million what?"

"Dollars, you fucking pig."

DeQuinzio sat down opposite the wrinkled old man and waited.

"Well? Ain't you gonna deny it?"

Still, Tony said nothing, *did* nothing.

The old man glowered at him, one eyelid twitching. "Three million. I figure that's what I'm gonna get out of my lawsuit—the one I'm gonna file for false imprisonment."

Tony nodded and waited some more.

"Because you can't just arrest people, you know. Ain't Constitutional. You need some proof, some reason to suspect them."

With a little shrug of his head, DeQuinzio leaned back in the chair.

"You need a reason to search a vehicle!" the old guy muttered. "Ain't had none."

"Got it all out of your system, now?" asked the detective.

The old man sneered but said nothing.

"Good." DeQuinzio glanced down at the paperwork he'd brought in with him. "What is it? Lindsey Tapley."

"Yeah. Don't wear it out."

"Mr. Tapley, setting aside your role as a Constitutional scholar, are you employed?"

Tapley leaned back in the chair and crossed his arms. "Work for myself."

"Doing what?"

"That's the beauty of it, ain't it?" He leaned forward, eyes blazing. "I do whatever the fuck I want, whenever the fuck I want to."

"Fine. Let's come at it a different way. What the fuck did you feel like doing last night after ten? And what the fuck were you doing on I-86 half an hour ago? While you're at it, you might as well tell me why the fuck you have the cell phone of a sworn police officer in the back of your truck."

"What? I ain't got no—"

Tony held up the bag containing Angel's cell phone and waved it.

"That ain't mine."

"How did it get in your truck if that's so?"

"It's a pick 'em-up-truck, you Christing whore's son. Anyone could have dropped it back there."

DeQuinzio nodded and set the cell phone down. "I guess that could be the case. Answer my other questions."

"What business—"

Tony slammed his hand down on the table, making the cell phone jump. "Listen to me, Tapley. A police officer has gone missing, and the cell phone she answered during her abduction was in the back of your 'pick 'em-up-truck,' so unless you'd like to spend the rest of your life guarding your asshole in the showers at Clinton, you'd better drop your goddamn attitude and start talking!"

Tapley's face froze and blanched. He started shaking his head. "No. Uh-uh. I didn't do nothing to no cop. Last night I was at Millster's Tavern. You know the place? Out on 51? Dan, the bartender, he can tell you. I was there from suppertime until closing."

"We're going to check that. No sense in lying."

"Ain't lied to you yet."

"How'd you get the phone."

"Lookit, I told you. I don't know nothing about no phone. It's a goddamn pickup! Can't keep no one out of the bed!"

DeQuinzio stared at Tapley through squinted eyes, as still as if carved from granite, eyes just as hard. "You'd better not be lying to me," he said at last.

"Yeah, yeah. Go do your checks. I got work to do this morning."

Tony grabbed Angel's phone and stepped out. He nodded at Mike Santoro. "You're in plain clothes the rest of the day. Get changed, then roll on out to Millster's. See if this asshole was there from seven o'clock on."

"Right. Won't do much good in plain clothes if I'm driving a cruiser."

Tony grunted and tossed him the keys to Angel's car, then turned to Garban. "Can you get this expedited?" he asked holding up the evidence bag containing the phone.

"Prints?"

"Prints," said Tony with a nod. "And see if your tech boys can get anything off it that might help."

"Like what?"

"Beats the piss out of me. GPS traces. Cooties. Whatever."

Sergeant Garban nodded. "I'll walk it through myself."

3

Millster's Tavern, Saint Mary, NY
September 18, 2014, 8:37 am

Santoro pulled Angel's dark blue Crown Vic into the space in front of the seedy little bar's front door. He sneered at the weathered wooden door, knowing it was locked. He'd been so caught up in the excitement of it, he hadn't even thought about the fact that it was a bar, and that it would probably be closed until at least lunchtime. *But still, I drove all the way out here... Might as well make sure.*

He opened the door and slid out, wincing at the irksome pain in the small of his back and its twin in his neck. "Working too much," he mumbled. He glanced at the diamond-shaped window in the door. "Mark Dunston, proprietor," read a faded sticker filling the bottom half of the glass.

Millster's was locked up tight, just as Santoro had guessed it would be. He thought about heading back to the station, but the idea of standing around waiting was anathema to him. He got back in the car and radioed dispatch for Mark Dunston's home address.

4

Lost in the woods, near Saint Mary, NY
September 18, 2014, 8:49 am

Larry limped into the middle of the road when he heard the car approaching from around the bend behind him. He turned and fished his badge out of his front pocket, holding it up, his other hand stretched out, commanding the driver to stop. He smiled as a dark blue Crown Victoria came rolling around, then lurched, tires skidding in the gravel. They stayed like that a moment, Larry looking like the world's bloodiest traffic cop, and the car idling where it had come to a stop. A broad grin splayed across his face as Larry noted the SMPD plate on the front of the car. *Found me!* he crowed in his mind. "Man, I'm glad to see you!" he called.

An electric whine was his only answer—the driver's side window rolling down. A hand beckoned.

Larry squinted at the car, trying to see past the glare of the early morning sun reflected on the windshield. "Who's that?" he called.

"Christ, Bateman, get a move on!"

"John?" he called, but there was no answer.

5

A hunting cabin, near Saint Mary, NY
September 18, 2014, 8:55 am

Angel strained and strained and strained until she saw red spots dancing in her vision, and her fingers felt as though someone had cut half-way through them with a rusty saw. The iron staple, as rusted as it felt, didn't budge. "Come on! Come on!" she muttered fiercely. She shook her shoulders and lunged, but the log dog was still stuck fast. She slumped against the wall, breathing hard and hoping the warmth she felt in her palms wasn't blood. She tried, again and again, to break the damn overgrown staple free, fighting it for a while, then resting before trying again.

But it was time to face facts: the log dog was set fast, and she wasn't getting away that way.

Outside the rough purr of a V8 grew louder, and the sound of tires on gravel sent terror racing around her mind like a mad dog. A large empty cavern yawned in her belly, and she shivered as though from a sudden chill, sinking back on her knees. *Pretend to be asleep!* the panicky part of her brain wailed. She lurched to her side, wild gaze zipping around looking for something she could use, for anything she could use as a weapon.

But there was nothing.

A chain rattled against the door, and Angel squeezed her eyes shut. She heard a lock snap open, then more rattling chain. She tried to still her breathing, to take long, slow breaths, but her body didn't want to cooperate. Something thudded against the door, and she almost screamed. Then the door creaked open.

She lay there, eyes closed, feigning sleep, as heavy footsteps trod into the cabin. The door slammed shut, and again, the chain rattled. A lock snapped shut, and she couldn't resist any longer. Angel opened her eyes the tiniest bit—just enough that she could see a little, but not enough that they looked open.

A man stood in the shadows shrouding the door. He wore jeans and a light T-shirt, either white or gray—it was hard to say in the gloom. He had close-cropped brown hair, and his stance seemed familiar. He stood with his back to her and his head down for ten seconds or so, just staring down at the gray floor as though he wanted her to get a good look at his back. He looked familiar, but at the same time, not—like the brother of a man she knew.

"I know you're awake," he murmured.

Bullshit, she thought. *I'm not falling for that.*

"You'll never break that log dog, if that's what you were trying to do. I can see through walls. I saw everything you did."

Bastard probably has cameras up. Angel sighed and gave up the ruse. "They're coming for me, you know. I haven't seen your face. You can let me go and have a good chance of getting away."

He chuckled, and Angel knew who he reminded her of—John Jenkins. But she shook her head. The man was a sick twist and as different from John as night was to day.

"What do you want me for?" she asked. "I haven't done a thing to you."

"You're pretty," he said in an oily voice. "I like you."

She shook her head.

"I think we should play." He pushed his phone into the front pocket of his jeans. "Now, don't freak out," he said in his familiar-but-not voice. He started to turn toward her, and she squeezed her eyes shut.

"No! Don't turn!" she blathered. "I haven't seen you. You can let me go, but if you"—her throat closed convulsively, and she had to cough before she could go on—"*hurt* me, then every cop in the state will be after you. Do you want that? To be chased—"

"*Shut up!*" he hissed in a voice as cold as death and twice as creepy. Something banged and clattered on the plywood floor in front of her.

Angel peeked at it, and her heart seemed to freeze for a moment, her blood running cold.

On the floor in front of her lay a stainless-steel hatchet, and Angel screamed for a moment, then something slammed into the side of her head, and everything went black.

6

A muffled scream brought Larry awake in the musty darkness. For a moment, he existed only in an intense bubble of pain—the ragged sawing in his hip, the hot stab in his ribs, the thudding thump in his head.

A door opened, followed by the shriek of a screen door on rusty hinges, then someone crunched toward him through gravel. The rough carpet beneath his cheek stank of gasoline and flares and gunpowder.

Where in the hot sweaty fuck am I? He remembered careening off the interstate, going over the ridge and down through the trees, the agony of climbing out of the wreckage, and then walking and walking— *A car! And—*

The trunk opened, sunlight glaring down, casting the man standing there into silhouette. "Oh, you're awake," grated the man.

"I'm a fucking cop, asshole. Do you know how much shit you're in?"

The man laughed, and there was something familiar about it, but Larry couldn't say what. With the quickness of a striking cobra, the man leaned in, smashed his fist into Larry's face, and everything went black.

7

A hunting cabin, near Saint Mary, NY
September 18, 2014, 9:28 am

Angel groaned, her head pounding and throbbing and aching with each beat of her heart. She tried to reach up and touch her head, and though she was no longer on the floor, no longer cuffed to the log dog, her hands were secured by handcuffs down by her sides. She pulled, and a thick chain rattled on metal. She lay on her back, no pillow, no cushion between her and the cold, cold metal she lay on.

"Good, you're *finally* awake. You're kind of a wimp, you know that? I barely tapped you."

"What the fuck—"

"Look at me," he whispered.

Angel shook her head, and nauseating, shrieking pain washed over her in a wave. She moaned through gritted teeth.

"Look at me!" the man roared in her ear.

Angel jerked her head back, trying to scramble away, though she lay chained to a metal bed with nowhere to go.

"Goddammit, woman! *You fucking look at me!*" the man hissed. "A hatchet isn't a precision instrument, but if you want me to cut off your fucking eyelids with it, I will."

Shuddering with fear, Angel lifted her head, eyes still closed. "Why? Tell me why you picked me… I'm… I'm no coed, no blonde bimbo."

His laugh was harsh, uncaring. "I'm not telling you a damn thing, *chica,* except that I meant what I said. I *will* cut your eyelids off with that hatchet. Of course, I can't say what other interesting chunks might come off with them if you make me do that. Your nose, maybe? Eyebrows? *Eyes?*"

She cracked her eyelids, staring at his running shoes. Another man lay on the floor against the wall in the corner. His back was to her, but blood dripped from a head wound, and his breath came in short rasps.

Almost against her will, her gaze began to crawl up her abductor's blue-jeaned legs, noting the bulge of a concealed weapon at his waist under his shirt, crawling across the white T-shirt, and then zipping to his face. "John? John, is that you?" she asked with a gasp.

"Yes, but at the same time, no." He threw back his head and laughed, then he turned to face her.

"What the fuck, John? What game are you playing here?"

"A fun one," he said with a malevolent smile. "But don't call me 'John.' My name is Glacadairanam."

She frowned, and her brow wrinkled. "This isn't funny. I know that guy upset you last night, but—"

"He's a waste of time." He shrugged. "Fuck him. Let him rot."

Angel sighed, fighting for calm. "John, let me out of these cuffs. We can call Debbie Esteves. She'll know what to do. She can help you, and I...I won't press charges. Not after what you've been through."

"Oh, I don't think so," he said. "No, I think we'll play my game instead."

Angel rattled the chain against the metal table. "Let me out! John, let me out of these!"

He leered at her from across the room. "If I do, you'll be sorry."

"John..." Angel shook her head. "I don't believe this. This isn't you, Jenkins. You're not a killer."

He sighed and swept a hand over his close-cropped hair. "I told you," he said in a nasty tone. "John's not here, now. My name is Glacadairanam, and I'm your worst fucking nightmare."

Chapter 12
Superstitious Nonsense

I

"You said this wasn't a *folie à deux*," said Jim. "You said Joe was The Saint Mary Psycho."

Debbie took a sip of the iced tea she'd bought with her lunch, her gaze burning on his over its rim. "Agent Gregory, Detective Denders, I haven't lied to you a single time. Every single thing I've said is the God's honest truth."

The paper napkin rasped on his skin as Gavin wiped his mouth. "I don't know, Doctor Esteves. I said before that I'm a rational man. An *empirical* man. Do you really expect me to take this carnival-barker's nonsense seriously?" He glanced at Jim, a little curl tweaking the corners of his mouth. "Joe Doe isn't The Saint Mary Psycho because he's been *possessed by a demon?* Come on. That's such a tired old melody. At least Berkowitz had the good grace to come up with an original slant. Then again—giving credit where it's due—this is probably the most elaborate, the most convoluted garden path I've ever been down."

"I haven't told you a single lie, and believe me, there were plenty of places I could have gilded the lily to make myself seem the heroine."

Denders squinted at her with an expression of speculation. He glanced at her hands, then back up at her face. "You have a daughter."

"I do."

"But no wedding ring?" He pointed at her left hand.

Esteves grunted and almost—*almost*—rolled her eyes. "No, and no husband, either."

Jim glanced at Gavin. "And you've taken special care of this Joe Doe for years now. Even had him transferred here to your care."

"Are you suggesting that I—"

"Hey, I'm not suggesting anything." Denders spread his hands. "I'm just making observations."

"Jim—" began Gavin.

"You think I'm in love with him?" Esteves asked with a curious, amused lilt. "You think we're a couple?" She glanced at Gregory with an arched eyebrow. "You, too?"

"Stranger things—"

"That's just stupid," she said in a flat voice. "And—not that it's any of your business—but my husband is dead. Years ago, and I no longer wear the ring. Does that meet with your approval?" Her voice was calm, emotionless, and she wore a serene expression. "Do I pass your little ring test, now, Detective?"

Though her expression and tone didn't change a mite, Gavin had the idea she was *furious*. "Let's not get off on a tangent."

"Tangent?" she said, turning on him and arching an eyebrow. "Defending myself against a misogynist is a tangent?"

"The whole thing is a tangent," said Gavin.

"Why are you so defensive, Esteves?" asked Jim. "And I don't hate women. I don't hate *you*." His phone rang, and he glanced down at it. "Sorry, I have to take this," he said, getting up and walking out into the hall.

"Listen, he was just asking questions. Occupational hazard to ask questions that border on rude, to elicit a response that otherwise might not be given."

"I'm familiar with the technique, Agent," said Debbie in her flat, furious voice. "It doesn't mean I like having it turned on me." She looked down at her leather blotter and spread her hands wide on its surface. She took a deep breath. "I know why The Smith moves the bodies," she said in a voice that barely carried across to Gavin.

"You what?" Gavin feigned nonchalance, but his heart was going a thousand miles an hour and felt like it was displacing his voice box.

"He does, right? Reposition the bodies after he's killed them?"

"Why would you think that? There's been nothing like that in the press."

She jerked her chin up. "Joe told me about it one time. In one of our narcoanalysis sessions."

Gavin narrowed his eyes. "How often do you give him the amobarbital?"

She shrugged. "These days? Not very often—there's no point. I don't believe he has much memory left of his life before he became The Psycho, and I've tried to work through, around, and under the blockage. I think his memory has been scrambled."

"To protect himself from what he did."

She shook her head. "No, scrambled by Glacadairanam's possession of him. But stop avoiding the question, Agent Gregory. Does The Smith reposition the bodies? Joe also said he marked them."

"Joe marked them?"

She shook her head, looking irritated. "Glacadairanam marked them. I know the mark, too."

"Another drug-fueled confession?"

She shrugged and waved it aside. "Are you going to answer me?"

Gavin leaned back, looking her over, trying to work out what angle she was playing. "I'll admit it, Doctor. I'm stumped."

"Stumped?" She spread her arms wide. "About what? Me? I'm an open book, Agent Gregory."

"Huh," he laughed. "Yeah, and I'm the crown prince of Uzbekistan."

"Do they have crown princes there?"

"No fucking idea, if you'll pardon the French."

"Then, I propose a quid pro quo."

Gavin puffed out his cheeks. "Dr. Esteves, I'm not going to answer your questions about an ongoing investigation. Especially one that you could easily become a suspect in."

"A suspect?" Debbie widened her eyes and grinned. "Little old me?"

"Yes, you," said Gavin.

"I'm no serial killer, Agent Gregory."

"No?"

She drew a deep breath. "No."

"I'm not so sure."

Debbie uncrossed her legs, scooched her chair forward, grinned, and folded her hands on the blotter. "No?"

"No," said Gavin fighting the desire to share her grin. "You've spun us quite a tale, Dr. Esteves. Much of it could have come from your firsthand experiences—or from the papers—but the rest of it…"

"The rest of it I shouldn't know," she finished for him. She gave him a single nod. "And I wouldn't, except for Joe."

"Back to that?" Gavin nodded once. "Fine. Let's get back to that. Why do you move the bodies?"

She arched an eyebrow at him and treated him to a half-smile. "Why do I move the bodies? *I* don't."

"Sorry. I misspoke. Why did Joe move the bodies?"

She lifted her chin, and the good humor left her expression. "Joe's on a locked unit in a high-security mental hospital. He no more moved your bodies than I did."

Gavin waved his hand. "Before. In Virginia."

Debbie turned her head a little to the side and squinted at him. "You're pretty good, Agent Gregory," she said. "This aw-shucks act."

"What is it, Dr. Esteves, that scares you about giving a direct answer to a direct question?"

"Scares me? Nothing." She slid forward to the edge of her chair, leaning her forearms across the top of the desk. "So, here goes. Joe *didn't* move those bodies, either, as you already know. *Glacadairanam* moved the bodies…after he marked them."

Gavin tried, and failed, to suppress a sigh. "Fine. Why were the bodies moved?"

"Would you agree that most serial killers pose bodies as a part of their ritual, to thwart the investigation, or to shock the person who discovers the body?"

"Yes."

"And you've been to The Smith's scenes?"

"Of course. All of them, though not always when they were still staged."

"But you've seen the forensic photos, the scene maps?"

"Yes."

"And do any of those three reasons seem to fit?"

Gavin pinched the bridge of his nose. "Dr. Esteves, this isn't a classroom, and I'm not your student. I'd like a direct answer."

"And I'll give you one. None of those three reasons seem right, I'll bet, because they aren't. Glacadairanam *does* get off on shocking his victims—and trust me when I say that anyone who encounters him fits in that category—but he moves the bodies for one simple reason." Debbie leaned across the table, eyes flickering with an intense emotion. "He does it because he wants you to notice it. He wants you to know he's real. You, or someone like you."

"Oh, come on, Doctor," said Gavin with a sigh. "You said yourself he signs his bodies. That connects them."

"Yes, *when* that signature is found," she said, suddenly cool, aloof. "Another fact held back from the press to weed out false confessions, right?" She sniffed. "He signs with the Gaelic letter gay."

Gavin stared at her for a few moments. "That's correct, Dr. Esteves."

"Gay for Glacadairanam, Agent Gregory."

Gavin shrugged. "Or 'go' or 'green' or—"

"No, Agent Gregory. Joe told me Glacadairanam marks all his victims with his initial, and we're not talking about only the victims you attribute to The Smith. He wants you to follow the chain from one set of victims to the next. That's the only way a rational man will ever believe he's real."

"Is that so? There are other victims marked with this letter?"

Debbie nodded. "Joe said The Psycho's victims are all marked—"

"But they aren't. The letter is tattooed into the flesh with the sharp end of The Smith's hammer, Doctor. Since The Psycho didn't use a hammer—"

"It's the letter that's important, Agent Gregory, not—"

"Oh, come off it!" Gavin shouted. "Not one of The Psycho's victims bore a Gaelic gay or any other letter. Five different medical examiners did exhaustive post-mortems, and not one mentioned even a strange bruise."

"They didn't know where to look. They didn't know what to look *for*. As The Psycho, he didn't leave bruises."

Gavin took a deep, calming breath. "Convenient."

"Not really," said Esteves. "It would be far more convenient for me if they had." She leaned forward again. "Listen to me, Agent Gregory. Think about it. How could Joe know the details of The Smith's crimes? If you believe only The Smith knows these details, then how, with Joe locked up and under twenty-four-hour surveillance, is The Smith killing again?"

"If Joe really is The Smith, then he isn't the one doing the killing, Dr. Esteves. It's a copycat. And if The Psycho's victims bear the mark, tell me where to look."

Debbie shook his head. "A copycat who knows all these details? All these secrets the FBI has held back? That seems unlikely."

"It seems unlikely that you would know these things, too, Dr. Esteves."

She shrugged, a smile twitching the corners of her mouth. "As I said, I wouldn't know any of them if Joe hadn't told me."

"What is it Sherlock Holmes always said?" He pursed his lips a moment, but he wasn't searching his memory. He was watching Debbie Esteves closely. Reading her face, assessing her involuntary movements. "Once you eliminate the impossible, whatever remains, no matter how improbable, must be the truth."

"But it isn't impossible that The Smith is committing these current crimes, Agent Gregory. Not the *real* Smith, anyway."

Gavin opened his mouth, but before he uttered a single sound, the door banged open and Jim came into the room, his coat rucked back past his holster, his hand on his hip. "I think you'd better come back to the City with us, Dr. Esteves."

"What for?" she demanded.

"Jim?" asked Gavin.

"We got some of the DNA back. No matches, but it's enough to tell us something."

"What?" Gavin asked, pushing his chair away from the desk, his gaze dancing back and forth between Denders and Esteves.

"The person committing your new murders is female," said Debbie in her flat voice.

"That's right," said Jim, his voice and face hardening.

Esteves gazed at Jim for a few moments, then glanced at Gavin. "No," she said, "I don't think I'll go with you, Detective Denders." She held up her hand to hold Jim's arguments. "Before you go on about how I can either go willingly or in handcuffs, let me say this: you don't have enough to make an arrest, Detective. We both know it." Jim shot a quick glance at Gavin, and she smiled. "But I'm happy to answer all your questions, and without an attorney. I'll…what do you call it…waive my rights. The only thing is, at the end of the day, I'm going home to sleep in my own bed." She spent another thirty seconds or so bouncing her gaze back and forth between them. "Detective Denders, Agent Gregory, I am innocent. You don't know for sure, but I do. And I'll say it again, for all the good it will do, I've told you nothing but the truth."

"Then why not come with us? Why not go back to the Thirteenth and clear it all up this afternoon?" asked Gavin.

"Because, Agent Gregory, my answers will be the same here or there, and if I give them here, I sleep on my own mattress, between my own sheets."

Gavin glanced at Jim and shrugged. "What do you want to do?"

Jim's stare rested on Debbie's face, half-an-inch from openly hostile. "I might not have enough evidence to arrest you this afternoon, Esteves. But I will get it."

"*If* I'm guilty."

"As you say, Doc," said Jim with a slow nod.

2

The car creaked and rocked as Jim climbed in behind the wheel. He stared at the hospital, his eyes narrowing, then relaxing, narrowing again, then relaxing again. He banged the car door closed, but still didn't slot the key into the ignition.

"Well?" asked Gavin. "Do you really think it's her?"

"I keep thinking about the first bra ever I saw on a girl."

"That goddamn birthday?"

"Dead right."

They sat in silence for the space of a few deep breaths, each staring at the hospital. "She's an accomplice, then?" Gavin asked.

Jim shrugged. "Maybe an unwitting one, but yeah. I think so."

"And the female DNA?"

"How many crime shows talk about planting DNA? How many documentaries?"

"And she is a doctor…she'd already know if she were a willing participant."

Jim grunted.

"It fits," said Gavin with a slow nod. "What do you want to do?"

Jim inserted the key and cranked the squad car over. "I know a guy who's on with Lily's Glen P.D. Used to be undercover in the City and is as hard as nails." He winked at Gavin and put the car in reverse. "Let's go see if they've got anyone else good enough. See if the chief is willing to cooperate with the FBI."

3

Pod 51 Hotel, Manhattan, NY
Thursday, 6:27 pm

Gavin stepped off the elevator and turned toward his room. He was bone-tired, and his brain felt like so much soggy cereal. He didn't want to think about Debbie Esteves anymore. He didn't want to think about Joe or The Smith or any of it. He wanted to take a shower, plop down in front of some good old mindless television, and eat a room service meal. Maybe wash it all down with a beer or five. He found himself wishing it was Friday, wishing that he was on a plane whistling through the atmosphere toward Virginia, toward Maddie.

But as he opened the door to his room and saw the bulky manilla envelope lying there on the ugly carpet, a sense of dread overcame him. *I will be on that plane,* he told himself. *No matter what is in this damn envelope.*

He stepped inside his room and let the door shut on its own. He stared at the envelope for what felt like a long time, then bent and swooped it up, coat tucked over his arm, and ripped away the flap. Inside was a Mead composition book, one of the ones with the gray and white cardboard cover. He tossed his coat on the bed as he crossed over to the ridiculous little round table—the kind seen only in motel rooms and the offices of middle managers. He sank into the upholstered chair next to it and opened the notebook.

"Angel Kirk," he read from the top line of the first page, looking down at row after row of neat handwriting without reading it. "Where in the fuck did you come from?" He flipped the journal over, then slapped it on the table, staring at it like it offended him.

After a few moments, he picked it up and began to read.

4

Angel Kirk's Journal
Marked September 21, 2014, 4:28 am

Dreams. Nightmares.

Jesus, what a dream. I dream all the time, everyone does, but since…the incident…my dreams are dark. I mean, I have my share of nightmares—what cop doesn't—but the dream last night felt so…I don't know…*real*.

My dreams have gone ugly…*evil*…since the…

Come on, Kirk. If you can't even write the words, you're fucked.

My dreams have gone dark and ugly since the incident. The ABDUCTION. Since what happened in that damn cabin…

They're not like nightmares. They're…what? Worse? No fucking shit, Angel.

The dreams are bloody, twisted. *Sexual*, but not in a good way. They're not dreams *about* sex, though. In fact, the dreams don't even include sex at all. And I think I'm a man in the dreams, so there's that. They are the kind of dreams that leave me feeling disgusted and ashamed—as if I've *done* something—something other than see a movie in my head, that is.

Stupid, right?

But this one last night… This fucking thing. Ugh.

It started like all the rest. Like I'm talking to someone I can't quite see. Like the person is regaling me with grim tales of disgusting acts. Torture. Rape. Murder. Like that.

Somehow (in the way of all dreams) those tales become the narrative, and *bang!* I'm the one doing all that shit. *I'm* the one burning girls with soldering irons or choking them out, then fondling them like some adolescent weirdo.

Those are bad enough.

Fuck that. Those dreams are *motherfucking horrible*.

But in this last dream…

Christ, I don't even want to write it down. I don't even want to think about it.

But Debbie Esteves, MD, says it will help. Some psychological-head-shrinker-bullshit, right, Debs?

This dream I just had? I fucking ate someone, okay?

5

Pod 51 Hotel, Manhattan, NY
Thursday, 6:51 pm

Gavin shuddered and snapped the book closed. *Dr. Esteves,* he thought, *you've been keeping secrets, haven't you? Are you and Kirk doing this together? Is she your partner in crime or is it the reverse?*

His phone chirped, and he jumped at the sound, then chuckled. "Getting jumpy," he murmured. "Must be getting close to the truth."

He snagged his cell phone and accepted the call. "Gregory," he said.

"Hey, Gavin," said Pete. "The DAL has something for you."

"So soon?" he asked.

"Yeah. The tech said he wants to introduce you to advanced search techniques on Google."

Gavin grimaced. "Right."

"So, this Jack Amorte—the family annihilator? He was the plant manager at a foundry in a little Pennsylvania Podunk called Millvale. The Jackson-Barney Steelworks, to be specific. Want to guess the nickname for the place?"

"The Jacks," said Gavin with a grunt.

"Got it in one. You must work for the FBI."

"And all this happened in 2004?"

"No," said Pete, the laughter leaving his voice. "No, it happened in 1992. No, in 2004, the only thing that happened was a string of unexplained disappearances from a psychiatric hospital. Want to guess who was a patient of said hospital?"

"Jack Amorte?"

"You win a Kewpie doll."

"Let me get this straight. In 1992, some disgruntled plant manager wipes out his family but somehow stays in his little Podunk until 2004 when a bunch of people go missing from the asylum he was in? Why wasn't he in jail?"

"Did I forget to tell you about the history of the psychiatric hospital located in said Podunk?"

"You did," said Gavin.

"When they built it—guess the year, win another Kewpie—it was called the Briar Ridge State Mental Hospital."

"And Amorte was the first patient?"

"One of 'em. Ruled incompetent to stand trial. He claimed he killed his family because—and you're going to love this—because he was—"

"—possessed by a demon," said Gavin in a whispery little voice.

"Well, yeah. How many Kewpie dolls do I owe you now? Have you heard this one before?"

"Oh, for fuck's sake," muttered Gavin. He got up and flipped open his bag. "I'm going to need to rent a car, Pete. We'll have to switch the pickup airfield for tomorrow night."

Pete said nothing for thirty seconds or so. "What's going on, Gavin?"

"I need to go to Millvale, Pennsylvania. Do me a favor, boss? Call ahead and make sure someone with juice at the local cop shop will talk to me tomorrow?"

6

LaGuardia Airport, Queens, NY
Thursday, 8:16 pm

"No, Jim, I'll tell you all about it later," he said. "I've got to find this damn car and… Oh, there the fucker is." He shifted the phone to his other shoulder and fished in his pocket for the keys to the Chevy shitbox that was his ride for the next day or so.

"Gavin…" said Jim. "If this journal is *evidence—*"

"I don't think it is, but if it is, I'll send it to Quantico. My guys can process it faster than you can ship it to the Staties lab, anyway."

"Well, that's probably true, but—"

"Listen, Jim, when I get to Millvale, I'll copy it and send it to you. There's got to be a FedEx place nearby." Gavin popped the trunk and heaved his suitcase into the back. "I've got to get on the road."

"Give me twenty minutes, Gavin, and I'll clear it with Haymond. We can split the driving."

"This is probably nothing, Jim. You know that. Your time is better spent here."

Denders said nothing. What could he say, after all? Gavin was right.

7

Cobblestone Inn & Suites, Millvale, PA
Friday, 1:59 am

Gavin pushed the door to his room open with his foot and heaved his bag through. His eyes burned from the long drive, and he *was* tired, but his mind kept circling back to the journal. Angel Kirk's journal or another red herring?

He flicked on the light, and one glance was enough to tell him the room's secrets. Short hall between the door and the bedroom, bathroom behind the door immediately to his left, and the closet opposite.

He dropped his bag on the spare bed, kicked off his shoes, and flopped onto the other bed, letting his eyes slide closed for a blessed moment of rest. But only a moment.

He fished the journal out of his bag then lay back, propping another pillow behind his head. Gavin flicked the cover open and started to read.

8

Angel Kirk's Journal
Marked September 21, 2014, 9:10 am

Ha! I just reread that crock of shit I wrote at zero-dark-thirty.

So I had a few bad dreams? So what? I *was* kidnapped, after all, and by someone I considered a close friend. And what went on in that cabin...

But never mind that. *I'm fine, Dr. Esteves.*

God hates a coward, right?

Too fucking right. I'm right as a fiddle.

9

You might already know this, but if it's not news to you, well, bully for you.

Hotels suck, Debs.

In every way.

Even the best of them, even if they treat you like royalty, it's all just a set up until the air conditioner goes on the fritz, or your neighbors start sowing parties all night, every night. Or your shower starts spitting frigid water all over the deadroom.

I can't get any rest in these places.

None.

Zip.

Hero.

Nada.

And there we have it. I've run out of synonyms with which to impress my literary genius on you.

Is that even a sentence?

Who gives a fuck?

All I want, what I would trade my left nipple for, is to get some sleep. But, of course, the heater is stuck on full blast, and it's like a sauna in here.

What? Move to another room, you say? Why didn't I think of that?

There are two words I hate more than any others this evening. "At capacity." Never mind the fact that this chain keeps a three-room-buffer for emergencies. A broken cheater does not constitute an emergency, it seems.

I fucking hate hotels.

Why did I ever think this would be a good idea?

IO

Finally tell asleep around quarter to eight this morning. I had the Do Not Disturb sign on the door and everything, and for once, the maid didn't open the door with her master key to see if I really meant it. I had the windows open as wide as they go, and the late September temperatures here in Virginia cooled the place off a bit—oh, wait…this is *fucking Virginia*. It got down to seventy-five last night. Wooo.

But I showed them. Put the minibar on the nightstand next to my head and propped the door open. It blew moderately-not-hot nothings in my ear.

Rest at last, right?

Too fucking wrong.

Let's do math, children. Get out your slates and chalk. Your fucking Texas Instruments. Your goddamn hell phones. 7:45 am to 10:18 am is how many hours sleep?

What's that, little Johnny? Five hours? No, Johnny. You get a big fat F.

You have a solution, Suzy? Great, pet's hear it. Four hours? Go to the back of the class, Suzy, and pound sand. You're WRONG.

Two hours and forty-five minutes, children. That's the answer. And I had at least four mother-fucking-wake-up-screaming nightmares.

At least I can't remember the last one, though I woke up with the telephone cord wrapped around my neck so tight I was choking. Like I was fucking trying to choke myself to death!

That's new, Debs.

Not good, mind. New.

What were these dreams? I can hear you asking in my head, Debs, so fuck you.

More of the same. Sex. Drugs. Chopping people up with a machete.

Yeah.

Look, Debs, I know you said dreaming is healthy and that I need to let my mind work this shit out. No offense but you don't know what the hell you're talking about.

I'm going out to find a Doc-in-a-Box and get some Ambien.

It's that or lose my ever-fucking mind.

11

Gavin stood at the mouth of the alley, hands shoved in the pockets of his warm-up pants, feet sweating in his running shoes. He was no longer breathing hard—he'd been standing there too long, staring into the dark alley, waiting...waiting for...

Waiting for what? *he asked himself.*

A little shitbox Chevrolet turned onto 36th from Third Avenue and putted by at a snail's pace. Gavin's gaze was glued to the profile of the driver, but the man never turned.

But that didn't matter, he knew who it was.

He watched the little rental car putt away and felt his face distend in a vicious, lopsided grin.

When the car turned with a flash of brake lights, the grin widened, and he spun on his heel, all without his conscious decision to act. He walked deeper into the black maw of the alley, feeling the lust blooming with each step.

A whimpering cry came from the blackness, and he slapped his hand on his hip, going for his sidearm, but it wasn't there. He wasn't even wearing his holster. He stopped walking, confused, and looked down at his hip.

That's when he saw the hammer in his waistband, and it all came rushing back.

12

Gavin lurched up, puke in his mouth, head spinning, and dashed for the toilet. He vomited up his roadside diner trash dinner. His second sight of it was considerably less pleasant than the first, and he'd hated the food when he shoveled it down his throat. He puked, again and again, until there was nothing left but bile.

Must have fallen asleep reading that shitshow of a journal, he thought. He flushed the john with a hand that shook, both from the experience of puking his guts out in the middle of the night and the memory of his dream.

What he'd done in it.

He squeezed his eyes shut and fell back against the wall, hugging himself. His last memory of the nightmare was of leaning down toward a beautiful blonde woman. Of pursing his lips as he watched the blood run from her hairline, down past her brilliant blue eyes, past cheekbones Michelangelo, himself, might have chiseled, down along her elfin jaw, then he'd lurched forward like a bad B-movie vampire and slurped it up. His stomach heaved again, but the urgency was gone.

He also remembered bashing the woman with the hammer's haft—a blow to incapacitate rather than bludgeon. He remembered catching her, he remembered dragging her into the alley, of bulling through the crime scene tape, then going to work with the business end of the hammer.

A sick, greasy belch bubbled up his throat and out, adding the stink of his spewed dinner, and he had to move, had to get out of the bathroom, at least. He splashed cold water on his face and padded back to the bed where he'd slept.

The journal lay atop the bedclothes, looking innocent, looking harmless. He didn't think he could go back to sleep, but the last thing he wanted was to read more of that story.

At least, not until morning.

He flicked on the television and found the History channel, then turned the volume low. He hoped for dry historical documentaries narrated by mesmers but knew almost any low volume show he didn't care about would work. Gavin collapsed back on the bed after shoving off his jeans and shirt, then crawled under the covers.

13

Gavin stood at the mouth of the alley, hands shoved in the pockets of his warm-up pants, feet sweating in his running shoes. He was no longer breathing hard—he'd been standing there too long, staring into the dark alley, waiting...waiting for...

Waiting for what? *he asked himself.*

"Sir!" came a voice from the alley. "Sir! Your flight is boarding!"

Right! *He whirled and sprinted into the alley, which was nothing more than the airport gate gangway, and charged down the slight decline, footfalls booming.* Going home! Hear that, Maddie? I'm on my way. This time, I'm keeping my promise!

But at the end of the gangway, the airplane's door slid closed. "Wait!" he cried. "I'm here!" The door didn't so much as pause—despite his cries, despite his pounding, bass-drum footfalls. The gangway seemed to stretch and stretch and stretch.

A peculiar laugh sounded behind him. "You done fucked up, now, sparky-spark. The Lord thy GAWD sent me unto you! The Brethren sent me unto you! The Lord GAWD missed his dinner for you, spark-spark, and boy did I take a beating for that! But did you listen? Did you

heed the word of the Lord thy GAWD, motherfucker?
No, you didn't, so no fucking whinging and whining. No
do-overs, spark. Your ass is pounded."

He fell to his knees as the gangway lurched away from
the plane. "No!" he cried. "I've got to make my flight."

Heavy footsteps approached him from behind.
"That's too bad, spark. You're fucked now. The Beast is
on his way, spark-spark-spark, and he's filled with
WRATH!"

14

Cobblestone Inn & Suites, Millvale, PA
Friday, 3:57 am

Gavin thrashed awake, the sense that he was late
thrumming through him. He sprang out of bed and
whirled in a full circle before his eyes found the digital
alarm clock's red display. "Fucking four in the
morning, asshole," he mumbled.

The television was still on, still murmuring about
World War II and the Nazi Wehrmacht. He stood for
a moment, blinking stupidly at the flickering screen,
then got back in bed and closed his eyes. "Go to sleep,"
he whispered to himself.

15

Gavin stood at the mouth of the alley, hands shoved in the pockets of his warm-up pants, feet sweating in his running shoes. He was no longer breathing hard—he'd been standing there too long, staring into the dark alley, waiting…waiting for…

Waiting for what? *he asked himself.*

"Why are you just standing there like a big idiot?" Maddie asked him. "Get a move on, Gav, or we'll miss our flight."

A smile stretched across his lips, following the sense of relief that washed through him. Home! I'm home! *he thought exultantly. "No problem, babe! I'm all packed." He hefted his bag—the same bag he took on his "little trips" for the FBI—and shook it as he spun to face her.*

"Well, you'd better be," said Debbie. "I've been looking forward to this for a long time. We need this, Gavin."

He knew she was right, but something felt…

"Why are you gawking at me like that?" Debbie asked, a strange grin twisting her lips. "You want a piece or what, spark?"

"Uh, what?"

"You want a piece of ass, honey-spark? Is that it?" She glanced down at Maddie's watch on her arm. "I'm game. We've got time." She began working the buttons of her blouse. "I'm here to save you, spark, and if that means letting you fuck me, then so be it."

"Um…" Gavin shook his head. "That's not what… Our itinerary—"

"I don't need to stow your travel spans, Gavin." A hand snaked around his shoulder from behind. "I blow what you're planning." The voice was Debbie's, but it was a male's hand caressing his cheek.

Fear gripped him, irrational and implacable, and he froze for a moment. "Who… Who's that?"

"Don't play coy, spark," said Joe. "I said it was okay, and I meant it. We have time."

"Maddie?"

"Sure, sparky-spark. It's Maddie."

"Are you… Are you okay?"

"Why, spark, I'm right as a fiddle. Now, turn around and let me at that—"

16

Gavin jolted awake, fragments of the nightmare floating in his mind like paper boats caught in storm water surging down the gutter. Silence and darkness blanketed the room. He couldn't even detect the faint red glow from the alarm clock. The television was off, but the remote lay on the nightstand next to his head.

"What a fucked-up dream," he croaked, then reached for the glass of water on the nightstand and took a long drink. "No more roadside diners. Ever." He rubbed his eyes and put the glass of water down. It still felt like the middle of the night, and no light crept in around the edges of the blackout curtains, so he puffed out a sigh and snuggled down into the bed. He closed his eyes and let himself drift, thumbing through positive memories to try and set the mood of his next dream.

His breathing grew deeper, and the tension melted from his neck and shoulders. He pulled in a breath, then held it for a count of four before blowing it out the same count.

He floated there, on the edge of consciousness, for what felt like a long time. Then, just as he was teetering over the edge into slumber, he heard a faint chirp, and his eyes flashed open.

The television blared to life, roaring some slasher movie at ear-splitting volume, the stupid blonde in it screaming and screaming and screaming as Gavin fumbled for the remote. He finally found it as someone in the neighboring room began to beat on the wall, and he flicked off the television.

"What the fuck?" he muttered. "No way in hell I turned it off in my sleep, but before I did, I turned the volume all the way up."

He got up and turned on the lights, then checked that the chain and locks on the door were still set. The dark mouth of the bathroom bothered him, so he reached in and flicked on the light, then stood there staring at his reflection in the mirror.

He looked horrible, his hair mused, a dribble of dried puke on his chest, puffy eyes red and glassy. "Fuck you, spark," he muttered. "You need some sleep."

Gavin went back to the bed and peeled the batteries out of the television remote. Then he crossed the room and unplugged the set. He stood looking around, arms akimbo, then nodded to himself and crawled back in bed.

17

Alley near Third and 36th, Manhattan, NY
Friday, 5:07 am

Gavin stood at the mouth of the alley, hands shoved in the pockets of his warm-up pants, feet sweating in his running shoes. He was no longer breathing hard—he'd been standing there too long, staring into the dark alley, waiting…waiting for…

Waiting for what, spark? *he asked himself.*

"Why are you just standing there like a big idiot?" Maddie asked him. "Get a move on, Gav, or we'll miss our flight."

A smile stretched across his lips, following the sense of relief that washed through him. Home! I'm home! *he thought exultantly.* "I just need to finish packing." *Then something tickled his mind, some dark memory or the other.* "I'm ready, Maddie! Let's go! What we've forgotten, we can replace when we get there."

"Oh, listen to the big spender," said Maddie, a smile in her voice. "But, whatever, sparky-spark. I'm just glad you're here and we're going."

He turned, then, and took his wife by the hand. "There's no other place I'd rather be."

She quirked an eyebrow at him. "Is that so?"

"It is," he said with a definitive nod. "Come on." He turned and pulled her through the house. "We can get a cab on Third."

"What do we need a tab for, spark?" asked Maddie.

Icy fear slithered around in his guts as he turned to face her, sure he'd find blood trickling down the side of her face. But she was fine. "What's wrong?" she asked.

"Why did you do that?"

"Do what?"

"You asked 'What do we need a tab for, spark?'"

"Did I?" Maddie's chuckle was warm, happy, infectious. "I must be tongue-tied with joy."

"Must be," he said giving her a chuckle right back. He leaned forward to give her a kiss but stiffened at the sound of the slider opening out in the den. "What the hell," he muttered.

"Leave it, spark," said Maddie. "Or you'll pee sorry."

"Stay here," he said and turned away, leaving her standing in the cheery smells of their laundry. His hand slid down to his waist before he remembered his duty weapon was locked in the safe next to his off-duty carry. "Shit," he muttered, rubbing at his icy guts with his other hand.

But then he remembered the hammer stuffed in his back pocket, and a smile spread across his face. He pulled it out, grinning at the cold feel of the forty-ounce sledge head. His fingers trailed down the fiberglass haft

like a lover's lingering caress, and he walked toward the
den with a strange sense of anticipation.

    A whistling kind of chirp came from the darkened
maw where the door to the den should have been. A foul,
animal-pen stench wafted toward him, like the breath of
demons. The chirp came again, this time a mocking,
laughing sound. He squeezed the hammer tightly and
held it up, ready to swing, and lunged into the darkness.

    Behind him, Maddie started to scream.

    "Told you, you'd be sorry, spark," said a hissing,
rancorous voice from the darkness. "Told you, you
fucking nosy-nel."

18

Cobblestone Inn & Suites, Millvale, PA
Friday, 5.22 am

Gavin came to himself, already out of bed, already
standing, pawing at things on the nightstand as though
he were searching for something. His gaze flicked to
his service weapon, and he grabbed it, heart fluttering
like he'd run flat-out for a mile. The gun reassured him,
lent him strength. His nerves thrummed and danced in
their myelin sheaths, and a strange energy created a
palsy in his fingers. He breathed in for a long slow
count of four, then held that breath as he turned to face

the room. After another four-count, he let the breath trickle out of him.

Weak, predawn sunlight peeked into the room around the edges of the drapes. Or maybe it was the glow of the arc sodium lights in the parking lot. *Whatever.*

His room was empty, exactly as it had been when he went back to bed.

Except for the journal, which lay on the floor near the foot of the bed, opened to a random page, the top sheet wrinkled as though he'd stumbled over it in the night.

Dream! he thought. *Just another fucking nightmare.* The irony of reading someone's journal about having weird nightmares, then having a night full of them himself was not lost on Gavin.

He set the gun on the nightstand with a clatter and sat down on the bed, rubbing his eyes with his other hand. On active cases, he'd gone much longer periods without sleep, but having the luxury of sleep, yet not being able to get any rest, was worse.

His gaze flicked to the pants crumpled on the floor, and he bent forward and snagged them. He searched through his pockets until he found the crumpled-up prescription Esteves had written him. *Thioxanthaxol. Maybe I should get this filled today.*

He picked up his phone and swiped it awake. "I'm up, you're up," he muttered. He opened a browser and typed the name of the drug into the search window and pressed the go icon. The first entry in his search results was for a drug called Flucaxol, a trade name version of thioxanthaxol. He scrolled past the list of side effects—he'd worry about those later—and down to the indications section, looking for the recommended dosage for sleep…but there wasn't one. It listed three treatment options: schizophrenia, bipolar disorder, and acute treatment of agitation in schizophrenia patients. The next search result took him to a patient review site, chock full of reviews from mentally ill patients complaining about the drug—a few of which did mention hypersomnia as a side effect—but not one patient taking it as a sleep aid. "What the fuck, Dr. Debbie?" he murmured.

He slumped against the headboard of the bed. *Maybe I'll take a page from Kirk's journal and find a clinic or something. Get myself some Ambien.* He glanced at the journal on the floor and sighed. "But in the meantime…" He twisted around and lay his head on the pillow, climbing into bed more like a slug cresting a rock than a human being, and pulled the covers over his head. "Leave me the fuck alone, okay?" He had no idea who he was talking to, but it seemed important to say it aloud.

19

Gavin stood at the mouth of the alley, hands shoved in the pockets of his warm-up pants, feet sweating in his running shoes. He was no longer breathing hard—he'd been standing there too long, staring into the dark alley, waiting…waiting for…

Waiting for what, sparky-spark? *he asked himself.*

Stygian darkness leaped out at him, enveloping him, wrapping him in its cold, slimy embrace.

"I'm so sorry, Gavin-spark. Truly," said Pete Fielding from the depths of the alley. "We tried to get there in time, but…"

Horror clawed at the back of Gavin's throat, and it burned as though some foul creature had crawled up from his guts with prickly, sharp claw marks drawn in its wake. "Pete? What…"

"Jesus, Gavin, you don't need to see this. To see her. *I can do the ID, okay?" Somewhere, a clock tick-tick-ticked, mechanical laughter, mechanical mockery. "Okay, spark? Let me do this for you?"*

Do what? What the fuck's going on here? *Gavin's mouth and throat were as dry as the surface of Mars and* twice as cold. "Pete…what's going on here? Why can't I see you?"

"Oh, sparky…I'd take miss pain away from you if I could. You snow that, right?"

"Pete? What the fuck, Pete… Why are you talking like that?"

"Bike what, sparky? You're plot making fence."

Gavin whirled in a circle, his hand streaking to his hip, but there was no gun there, no holster. He snatched at his back pocket without knowing why, but there was nothing there, either.

"Looking for this, sparky-spark?" Something came whirling out of the darkness to land at Gavin's feet with a crash.

A blacksmith's hammer. He scooped it to his chest.

"Where is she, Pete? WHERE IS MADDIE?" After his shout echoed away into the thick blanket of blackness, the ever-ticking clock counted off the seconds of the ever-fucking silence, but from Pete, there weren't even breath sounds. "Pete?" Something chirped behind him. Gavin whirled, hammer held at the ready, but there was nothing and nobody behind him.

He stood there, frozen, a marble statue titled Crazy Man with a Hammer. *For how long, he had no idea, no way to tell except by the burning fury in his shoulder muscles. The ever-chirping clock went on making its petulant, squeaking chirps into the ever-fucking graveyard silence that surrounded him.*

Gavin turned again, then again and again, spinning at random, hearing nothing, seeing nothing, feeling nothing except a ragged fear, an awful anticipation of oncoming devastation. "Maddie!" he cried.

"Oh, no," hissed a small, piping voice. "Maddie's over, spark. She's done."

"No!" Gavin shouted. "Maddie is fine!"

His only answer was the mocking chirp of the ever-fucking clock. "No," he whispered, but it was as though the darkness surrounding him absorbed all sound.

"No," he said, craning his head, listening hard for any reply.

"No!" he cried, but not even his echo answered him.

"NO!" he shouted, and the darkness laughed at him.

"Yes," sang the piping-voice of a malignant child. "Oh, yes. Want to see, sparky-spark-spark?"

Gavin froze, mouth open to shout, tears brimming in his eyes.

"Silence means assent," the darkness laughed in his ear, and bright, scalding light stabbed downward from some unseen, unseeable source. "Maddie is bun-sun-done."

He didn't want to look, didn't want to hear that acidic voice whispering in his ears. He wanted nothing more than a return to darkness, to muffled sound, to the ever-fucking clock in the ever-ticking silence.

But even so, his head started to move. He fought it, tried to harden the muscles in his neck into steel bands, *but nothing he did had any effect. He squeezed his eyes shut, but his vision remained. He lifted his hands to cover his face, yet his hands stayed at his sides. "What the fuck?" he tried to say, but no air moved over his vocal cords.*

"Aw, poor little sparky-spark," said that malignant whisper, but this time, it used his voice. "Poor, poor man." The laughter, the joy in his voice was unmistakable.

And then he saw what was left of her, and he…

20

…sat up blubbering, his cheeks wet with tears, his pillow wet with them, a shriek echoing in his ears, but he didn't know if he'd screamed or if it was an artifact of his horrible dream. Relief started to eat away at the edges of his terror, but that terrible burning lump in his throat stayed right where it was, even though he knew it had been a dream.

And even though he knew it had been a dream, his belly shivered with the irrational fear that it *hadn't* been a dream, that Maddie really was dead, that she really lay on the floor of their house in Minnieville,

Virginia, lay there bleeding, lay there broken and abused, and he couldn't get past it.

Fighting sobs that hitched against his ribs, he lunged to the nightstand and snatched up his cell phone. He grimaced at the time—Maddie was not an early riser, even after all those years spent sleeping next to an FBI agent—but he didn't care, he had to know, had to hear her voice. He mashed the speed dial and pressed the phone against his ear so hard it *hurt*, but didn't let up, not one bit. The phone rang and rang. "Come on, come on," he murmured. "Come on, come on, come on!"

"Jesus, Gav. Settle down." Maddie's voice—sleep-blurred, but pain-free.

"Oh, thank God!" he cried, and then, without recourse, the sobs came grunting and growling out. "Oh, fuck."

"Gavin? Gavin, what's wrong? I can't think… Is it, Aust—" She bit off the name of their years-dead son, finally coming fully awake. "Gavin? It's like six in the morning, honey. Tell me what's wrong."

"A dream," he grunted between twisting, grating sobs. "A nightmare."

"A dream?"

"About you… About…" A cry wrenched from deep within him, one that hurt coming out. "*Fuck!*"

"Shh," she crooned. "Just a dream. I'm fine, Gavin. I'm okay. Shh."

He sat there, hunched over, head in one hand, phone grinding away at his ear, tears dripping to the floor, stomach hurting, throat burning, sinuses aching. "Oh, Christ, that was a bad one."

"Want to tell me about it?"

"No," he gasped, then went on anyway, talking faster and faster as he went until his words stumbled over one another. "It was… I was in the alley…one of the new crime scenes. It was dark, and I…I couldn't see, couldn't hear anything. Then Pete was there saying he'd do the ID so I didn't have to and then it wasn't Pete at all—it was *him*—it was The Smith and he said you were bun-sun-done and a bright light came on like you see in those UFO movies you like and I didn't want to look—couldn't bear to look—but my head moved anyway and I couldn't do anything to stop it—couldn't even close my eyes—and then he spoke using my own voice and it—"

"Gavin," Maddie said quietly. "It was only a dream."

He snuffled and coughed phlegm out of his throat. "I…I know."

"I'm fine," she said. "I promise. Sleepy as hell but fine."

"Sorry." He lifted his head and swiped at his tears. "God, it was *awful.*

"Good morning. Happy Friday," said Maddie in a playful voice. "Ain't life just grand?"

Despite himself, Gavin chuckled. "With you in it, it is."

"Well, rest assured, honey. I *am* in it, and I plan on staying right here, by your side."

The last of his terrible, gelid fear dissipated, taking his awful, ardent heartbreak with it. Relief sang its sweet melody and he sighed with it. "God, it's good to hear your voice."

"That's what all my boyfriends say."

"I'll bet."

"Gonna be home tonight?" she asked, her voice blurring toward sleep.

"That's the plan," he said. "Sorry I woke you. Go back to sleep."

"No, s'okay. I'm not that"—a huge yawn interrupted her—"tired."

"Right. Well, I've got to get moving, anyway, so go back to sleep."

She murmured something, sounding far away as if she'd let the arm holding the phone droop toward the bed.

"Sleep tight, babe," he murmured and pressed disconnect. He looked down at his phone for a few seconds, finger poised over Pete's contact, anxiety burbling away in his gut. Then he shrugged and pressed it with his thumb.

Pete picked it up on the first ring. "Fielding," he panted. "What's up, Gav?"

Gavin could hear him pounding away on a treadmill—even the SAIC had to keep in shape. "Pete,

I'm… Listen, my gut is twigging out. I've got a really bad feeling. Can't get rid of it."

Pete's treadmill beeped, and the sound of his feet hammering away on the belt stopped. "Okay, you've got my attention."

"It's… Maddie's all alone in that big house. We've got a security system, but you know how much that's worth when the right guy comes calling."

"Yeah."

"I don't know what's prompting this," said Gavin, "but I'm distracted. I need to know she's safe, but at the same time, I don't want to freak her out with twenty marshals in a ring around the house."

"You want me to put a couple of HRT badasses on her? To watch over her?"

Gavin sighed with relief. "That would help."

"Then it's done. But, Gavin…"

"Yes?"

"Where's this coming from? Has he—"

"Actually, the NYPD ran some DNA. The current unsub is female, or at least knows how to make it look that way."

The line hissed for half a minute while Pete digested that. "Has *she* contacted you? Sent a threat?"

"No, nothing like that," said Gavin. "It's only a gut thing. There's no reason for it. It's nothing—my paranoia in overdrive—but, like I said, it's getting in the way."

"Okay. It's an easy thing to address, Gavin, so don't worry about it. I've got it. HRT will be on task within the hour."

Gavin sagged where he sat, feeling loose for the first time since he woke up crying. "Thanks, man. I—"

"Nah. None of that. You need her protected, then she'll be protected."

"Still. I appreciate it. And the jet. All of it."

"Happy to help. Anything else?"

"Yeah. Can you have someone put together a report on Angel Kirk? She's a detective in Saint Mary, New York—or, at least, she was. She got herself abducted in 2014—by The Saint Mary Psycho, I think."

"Uh, sure. She's related to the case via this Joe Doe?"

"And Deborah Esteves."

"Done. More?"

Gavin chuckled. "A nice breakfast?"

"Sure thing. Just run on down the street to a diner and put it on your per diem." Pete chuckled and disconnected.

With a grin, Gavin locked his screen, then tossed the phone on the other bed. "Good Christ," he muttered and swiped his hand across his face. "What a fucking night." His meeting with the local police wasn't until 7:30, but he didn't even think about trying for another hour despite how horrible he felt.

Instead, he shuffled around on the mattress, then leaned over and fished the book from the ground. "Let's see if you figured out how to get a night's rest,

Angel." Lying there on his stomach, head propped in his hands, like a kid reading his favorite book, he began to read.

21

My teeth are sleepy...

Sleep journal? That's what the latest idiot doctor wants me to do. So, congrats, Debs, there's another one like you in the world.

Jesus, I've got to say it, Debs. The idea's as stupid as sleep hygiene.

And he said no to my Ambien request, the fucker. Said he didn't want to "mess me up with chemicals."

Fuck you, Dr. Asshat.

Oh, and Dr. Asshat wants me to cancel the rest of my trip and go home. He says a familiar environment is best. Plus, I can see "my regular doctor."

You know, the one I don't have. Unless we count you, my old friend.

Anyway, why the fuck don't doctors ever listen? You'd think it would be a requirement for a profession that relies so heavily on patient reports to diagnose issues, but what do I know?

What am I going on about?

I started the fucking conversation with: "This all started at home before I came on this trip."

So, tell me, Doctor Asshat. How will going back there help anything?

My teeth itch.

22

Angel Kirk's Journal
Marked September 28, 2014, 5:35 pm

So far, so good with the sleeping business. Maybe I've rounded the bend on all that happy horseshit. Maybe I owe Dr. Asshat an apology.

Maybe I owe you one, too, Debs. I had more than a few unkind thoughts, but all better, now.

See? Texas has been good to me.

Here's a fun fact. The Hangman, as the delightful Texas media dubbed him, killed seventeen women between the ages of eighteen and twenty-two, starting in late 2004. Can you guess why they called him The Hangman?

A lot to see and do here. So many people to look up, so many cities to visit.

The car rental place gave me a little BMW to play around with, and I've been piling on the miles in East

Texas. Heading west soon. Can't keep *El Diablo* waiting!

The weather here is great! I should think about moving… Hell, it's been in the high eighties during the day…*in September*.

Take that, New York.

Maybe that's why I've been sleeping better. Who knows?

The hotels aren't better, though. I don't think I can praise the great state of Texas for that. Maybe in west Texas.

I've had a few vague nightmares that I don't remember very clearly. So, like a normal nightmare.

I do have the weirdest sensation that someone is shuffling through my memories like a frenetic teenager thumbing through songs on her iPhone, but I've been spending a lot of time alone (A LOT) and maybe it's just me.

I need to spend some time with people. Maybe talk to a waitress or two. Or workout. Or something.

Feeling somewhat restless…you may have guessed, what with your razor-sharp grasp of the workings of what is loosely referred to as my mind.

Maybe I'll head west in the morning.

23

When his cell phone chirped, Gavin almost came right out of his skin. "Got to change that goddamn sound," he muttered as he flopped over and grabbed the phone. It was a New York number in the caller ID, so he swiped it open. "Gregory. That you, Jim?"

"No, it's Kirk Haymond. Sorry to call so early."

"Oh, hello, Lieutenant. And this isn't early for a cop."

Haymond sighed. "No, it isn't. Listen, this isn't a social call. He dropped another one on us last night."

Gavin's stomach took the express elevator to the basement: Oh Shit, Fuck Me, and Jeezly-Crow. "Yeah?"

"Yes. Another blonde. Blue eyes, supermodel face…at least, it was."

Mind flashing back to the dream that'd left him puking his guts out, Gavin squeezed his eyes shut. "Blue-eyed, blonde, you said? Looks more like a sculpture than a person?"

"Heh. You FBI types have a poetic streak. But yeah. I could see her as a piece of art. Well, before last night."

"Did she have…" Sickly terror grabbed his heart and squeezed. "A-anything new about the scene?"

"Now that you mention it, yeah." Haymond sounded grim, disgusted. "And you're not going to like it."

"He dropped her in the alley near Third Avenue and 36th Street, right?"

The line went quiet for the space of a few breaths. "Yeah. How'd you know?"

What can I say? "I dreamed it?" *Fuck, no. Not if you want to be taken seriously ever again.* He sniffed. "It feels like he's taunting me, Lieutenant. It feels like, maybe it is The Smith, or someone related to him, that knows I investigated the first series. I…" He gulped a noisy breath. "I had the strangest feeling at that crime scene. Like she was watching, you know?"

"Yeah, I know," said Haymond. "After a while, you start to ignore that one at crime scenes."

"Right. Anything else new?"

"He bit her. CSI geek says he might have licked her."

"*Licked* her?"

"She had a cut up in her hair. Looks like blood ran down the side of her face to her jaw, then rolled on down her neck. CSI geek says it looks like he licked the blood off her cheek."

Gavin's stomach lurched, and acid bile danced on the back of his tongue. "Christ," he muttered.

"Yeah." Haymond coughed. "So, Jim said you're in Pennsylvania?"

"Yes. Checking on something Joe Doe said. You hear anything from the surveillance of Deborah Esteves?"

"You're a mind reader this morning."

"Suppose so," murmured Gavin.

"The Lily's Glen cops *say* she never left her house."

"You have reason to doubt them?"

Haymond sucked his teeth. "Gut. Jim's doing some checking around—he's on his way over there, at least."

Gavin scratched at his stubble. "Okay. Can you ask him to call me if he finds anything?"

"Sure."

They hung up, and Gavin put the journal in his bag. He glanced over at the crumpled prescription Dr. Esteves had written him. "If you're as innocent as you say, Doc, then why'd you try to dose me?"

But the crumpled paper had no answers for him.

He threw his belongings into his bag, checked out on the television, and with one last look around, left the hotel.

24

Castle County Sheriff's Department, Campton, PA
Friday, 7:33 am

"Thanks for making time for me," said Gavin.

"Anything for the FBI," said Sheriff O'Hara, with a quirky smile. "But I'm not sure we'll be much help."

Gavin spread his hands. "Right now, anything might help. I can literally summarize everything I know about Lee Amorte and the disappearances in one paragraph."

O'Hara scratched his chin. "That business with Amorte was before my tenure, but I can have the case files made available. I was on the job in 2004, though. Not sheriff, but I was here. I helped out."

"That's great," said Gavin. "I understand the disappearances are still open?"

"Cold as a witch's tit, but yeah. So's the murder out to the hospital."

"Murder?"

"Yeah, one of the schizos out at the Ridge. Patient named Ezekiel Amhain murdered a suspended nurse the night everyone went poof. Both him and his twin, Ismael, are among the missing."

"Can you give me the ten-thousand-foot view?"

"Easy enough. But you want coffee? My Stella makes a mean cup."

"Sure," said Gavin, trying to hide his impatience.

O'Hara thumbed the intercom button on his phone and asked his secretary to bring in two mugs of coffee. "The overview goes like this," he drawled. "There was a ruckus at Briar Ridge. Well, a series of them, I guess, and a mix of patients and staff went missing in the span of thirty-six hours. No trace—"

"What about video?"

O'Hara grinned a little but shook his head. "No cameras in a psychiatric facility—patient privacy and all that. No, if they were *taken*, they were taken by someone who knew the rules. And he got the two schizos, a head-shrinker, a nurse, and a psychiatric technician. Like I said, he left no traces, no evidence. And there was the dead nurse we found. But that's not all of it, and not where it started. People disappeared over the course of a few days, starting with a woman from town." Stella came in and passed out the coffee. "Thanks, Stella. Put together a to-go copy of the Briar Ridge disappearance case files for Agent Gregory." Stella nodded, and O'Hara turned back to Gavin. "The woman was the mother of the psychiatric technician, and that was reported before anything else happened. The tech's boyfriend also went missing soon after the mother, but we're not sure when. Could've been during the thirty-six-hour span, could've been before"—he fixed Gavin with his steely gaze—"could have been *after*."

"Any suspects?" Gavin asked with a grim nod. "Any bodies found?"

"Bodies from the missing? No. Nothing like that. Suspects?" O'Hara gave a short bark of laughter. "Only everyone concerned along with maybe half of Castle County."

"Is there someone I can talk to directly?"

"A witness?" Another bark of laughter. "No witness. No leads, nothing. The best I can do is to put you in touch with Margie Samuels. She was an assistant head nurse on the unit the patients eloped from. Also, she supervised both the psych tech and one of the nurses."

"That will work."

"After all the excitement, she moved over here to Campton, so she's at least close. She's getting up there, though, so be forewarned. I hear from a couple of my guys that she's taken to telling ghost stories about the whole thing." O'Hara tapped the side of his head. "Dementia, probably."

"Got it."

"You want to look at the Amorte thing? I'll have to get the records pulled from storage, if you do."

Gavin pursed his lips. "Amorte wasn't one of the patients who disappeared, right?"

O'Hara nodded.

"Then I guess I'd better not muddy the waters. It seems like his only connection is that he was a patient at Briar Ridge."

"That's my read on it, too. He's gone, now, in any case."

"Okay. I'd like to get the case file on the disappearances as soon as possible, though," said Gavin. "Would later this afternoon be too much of an ask?"

"Nah. She'll have both ready for you by the end of the day. Just swing back around 4:30 or so."

Gavin took a swallow of coffee, then stood and extended his hand. "Thank you, Sheriff O'Hara. It's been a pleasure."

"No problem. Try Marty's up the street, if you haven't eaten yet. Best damn breakfast plate in town. If you can close these cases for me, you're a daisy."

"I'm your huckleberry," said Gavin with a grin. "I loved Tombstone."

"Yeah," said O'Hara, already turning back to the paperwork heaped on his desk. "Me, too."

25

77 Westhampton Avenue, Campton, PA
Friday, 8:14 am

Gavin pulled to the curb in front of the little house Margie Samuels lived in and killed the engine. He took a swig of coffee from the large to-go cup his waitress at Marty's had made for him and grinned a little as a wonderful warmth hit his belly. He had an appointment with Samuels at nine, and having eaten, there wasn't much else to do. He wished he had the case file already, but he wasn't about to waste the whole day twiddling his thumbs.

He grabbed Angel's journal and flipped it open.

26

I'm in San Antonio. Yep, birthplace of Pace Picante Sauce. And, I'll have you know, it's a "Texas-Made Tradition," even if Campbell's did buy it out—Campbell's out of *Camden, New Jersey*.

Ain't that a hoot? Well, I guess if you don't remember the commercials—a bunch of cowboys hunkering down to eat, and they discover their cook has brought a picante sauce made in "*New York City!*" and sneer.

Oh, guess what! A cool cop (fucking cute, too) in Tyler told me something that wasn't in the papers…

The Hangman moved his victims. He didn't really stage the scene, but they found evidence that his victims were hanged from one tree branch, then the whole apparatus was moved to a different branch.

Too weird, right?

He also told me I'd better check into *El Diablo*…said there were some strange similarities to The Psycho… You know, like *El Diablo used a hatchet!*

So, here I am. I've got an appointment tomorrow with the lead detective from the *El Diablo* killings. Can you believe he's still alive, still competent, and still sharp as a motherfucking tack?

I'm a lucky bitch, Debs.

27

Angel Kirk's Journal
Marked September 30, 2014, 7:53 am

Didn't get much sleep last night. I had another fucking nightmare and woke up with the puke already spraying out my nose. I was...

No. It's too fresh to think about. I don't want to remember these damn dreams anymore. Maybe a doc here in town won't be so stingy with the prescription pad.

I've got to meet Detective Sergeant Mitch Hassle (yeah, he swears that's his real name) at ten. He says retired detectives get to catch up on their sleep.

Whatever. This retired detective never wants to sleep again.

28

Angel Kirk's Journal
Marked September 30, 2014, 3:53 pm

Detective Sergeant Mitch Hassle can kiss my ass.

He gave me "the look" the entire time—you're not a cop, Debs, so maybe you've never seen the look we can give a suspect to prompt their cooperation. It's a look that says, "You're lying, and if you don't cut it the fuck out, I might brain you with a concrete block." Hey, it works, and even if I've dropped a brick on the table, I've never actually used it on a perp.

Anyway. Hassle asked more questions than he answered, and his answers left plenty to be desired.

LOL. I just got up to stretch my legs and peeked out to see if the sun still looked so fucking deadly. Guess who I saw sitting in his car and watching my hotel?

Detective Sergeant Mitch Hassle.

Fucking creep.

29

Angel Kirk's Journal
Marked October 1, 2014, 7:06 am

How'd I sleep? Well, I tell ya… I slept like a woman being boiled alive—aka not much. As if the goddamn dream coming back isn't enough, it's hot as a motherfucker in San Antonio, Debs. All. The. Fucking. Time.

Ha! That bastard Hassle's still at it. I didn't see him, but his car's still there. He's probably eating breakfast or taking a piss or buying a wank mag to keep himself awake.

I gave serious thought to sneaking out while he's doing whatever the fuck, but then I remembered he's just a cop—a retired cop, but still a cop—following his gut. I can respect that. I think I'll go over when he comes back and answer any question he wants to ask.

What have I got to hide, anyway?

30

From the San Antonio Express-News,
pasted in Angel Kirk's Journal
Marked October 1, 2014, 11:08 pm

The brutalized body of Detective Sergeant Mitch Hassle, retired, was found earlier today in a vacant lot located on the northeast side of town. The Medical Examiner's Office confirms that Detective Hassle was dismembered with "a heavy chopping instrument," and that it appears he spent his last few hours on this earth in agony.

His brother officers have donned the black stripe across their badges and vow to find the perpetrator. They admit they have little to go on, however, and urge anyone with any information to come forward. The Mayor's office has posted a large monetary reward, and tips coming in through the San Antonio Crime Line are all eligible for the money (or a portion thereof) should the tip lead to an indictment.

"Detective Hassle was top-notch," said Chief David Mustaine of the San Antonio Police Department. "He forgot more about policing than I'll ever know. He worked all the big cases in his time, most notably the El Diablo serial murder case, yet he always had time to mentor a younger officer. San Antonio has lost a great member of its community, and it's my pledge that we will find the evil [expletive deleted] who stole him away from us."

"Holy Fuck! Did I…" was scrawled underneath the clipping.

31

77 Westhampton Avenue, Campton, PA
Friday, 8:44 am

Gavin sat staring down at that last line. He reread the last couple of entries, then stared at the question Angel had left unwritten. "Holy shit," he muttered.

His phone chirped, and he jumped. "Change the fucking sound, idiot!" He thumbed it open and accepted the call.

"Gregory? It's Denders."

"Hey, Jim."

"I don't have a lot of time, but Haymond said I should call you and share what I learned about the good doctor's whereabouts last night."

"Shoot."

"Lily's Glen said she never left the house, but a smile and some fast talk to the old gal running the little grocery two miles from Esteves's house got me a copy of the store's security camera footage. Guess who did a little shopping at 5:27 this shitty morning?"

"The good doctor."

"Eggs, milk, and bacon. You got it in one. You must be psychic. Haymond says it's enough, so chances are she'll be in custody before lunch."

"Okay. But listen, don't go into it with guilty stamped on her forehead. I've been reading the journal, and—"

"Yeah, about that. There's no proof it was actually written by Kirk, is there?"

Gavin pursed his lips. "I guess not. But listen, it may be that Angel Kirk is mentally ill and following in Joe Doe's footsteps. The journal seems to be telling the story of her investigation of Joe's story about those different killers—and making associations with older cases. Cases from before Joe was born."

"Well, that could be another girl showing her bra."

"A distraction, yes."

"And it doesn't mean Esteves didn't write it."

"No," agreed Gavin.

"But still, it's something else to look into. Too bad I don't have a clone."

Gavin grinned. "One of you is enough, Jim."

"Bastard."

"Don't you know it. Anyway, I asked my boss to put a research guy on Kirk. At least we can see if the events described in the journal are possible."

"Good idea. Hey! You know what another good idea is?"

"What's that, Jim?"

"You could make a copy of the damn thing and send it already."

"First chance I get. I don't have a clone, either."

They rang off, and Gavin turned back to the journal with a slight smile on his face.

32

Angel Kirk's Journal
Marked October 8, 2014, 4:58 am

San Diego is lovely, but their hotels are as shitty as everywhere else. Then again, maybe if I wasn't so cheap, I'd spring for Hyatt or Marriot and they'd be nicer.

Can't sleep again, Debs. It's been a whirlwind, let me tell you. So much to do, and I…

I drove out here from the home of Pace Picante Sauce. Got here a couple of days ago. Maybe three. More? Fuck, I don't know, Debs, which I don't mind telling you is a little fucking worrisome.

No, wait. It was five days. I've been here five days. Not quite sure what I've been up to for part of that time. I didn't expect to be here more than three days, so...

I guess I've spent time driving around *SoCal* (look how trendy I am) playing tourist for some of those days, but I do remember going to the places I needed to see, talking to the people I needed to talk to, and all that shit.

Hassle told me about this case. He always suspected *El Diablo* moved out here in 1987 when he felt Hassle was getting too close. Here, they called him *El Cuco*.

Speaking of Detective Sergeant Mitch Hassle, I didn't kill him if that's what you think. I *dreamed* about it, maybe, but I didn't want to do it, and I didn't. Full stop. I did not kill Mitch Hassle. I wouldn't do that.

Driving is getting...harder. Maybe dangerous. I get turned around so easily, and that's new. I've always had a good sense of direction, but I swear to God, I'll be tooling along, heading in the right direction, and then *poof* nothing looks right, and I have no idea where I am. Hey, I'm tired—well, more like exhausted—and I figure that's a good reason for the confusion, but that's not what really scares me anyway.

What scares me is that sometimes I'm not only lost, but I can't remember where I was going. What's worse is that some of the time, I don't…I mean, it comes back pretty quick, but sometimes when I *poof*, I can't remember who I am for a second, Debs.

Shit. It's not like that. Not really. I mean, I know I'm Angel Kirk, but sometimes (just a few times, Debs, don't worry too much) I don't remember I'm a cop. Or what the fuck I'm doing out in *SoCal*.

And that's motherfucking weird.

I mean, waking up in a hotel and not recognizing where you are is one thing—hell, that happens to everyone, right?—but having that happen while I'm driving a car at seventy or eighty miles per hour is… Well, that's fucking scary, Debs.

But hey, I'm almost done looking into *El Cuco*. It's funny, that nickname. *El Diablo* means "the devil" in good ole *Español*. *El Cuco*, on the other hand, literally means "the cuckoo," but is also the name of a mythical monster that mothers use to scare the fuck right out of their bratty kids. The Boogeyman, in other words.

It's amazing how much time you can spend avoiding going out to the car and driving to your next appointment "researching" things on Google. Heh. At least I haven't broken down and gone to YouTube.

I'm almost done here, like I said, but it turns out *NorCal* is next (so trendy, Debs!). *El Cuco* moved on in 1993, it seems, and Detective…uh. Well, fuck. I've forgotten his name.

Anyway, Detective Whatsit told me he suspected he went north. Guess who was active in Sacramento from 1993 to 1999?

That's right, Debs!

God's Hammer.

This shit Joe spurted might actually be true, Debs.

Sometimes, I get the strangest feeling that someone in my head is laughing at me.

33

Angel Kirk's Journal
Marked October 13, 2014, 4:36 am

I wrote a poem. Want to hear it?

Of course you do, Debs!

Here goes:

> *Fuck. I can't sleep*
> *Shit. Still can't sleep*
> *Fuck me.*
> *I*
> *CAN'T*
> *SLEEP*

How'd you like it? It's good, right? Fuck you, Robert Frost.

Debs. Debbie. *Debra.* I want you to hear me on this. Ready? Here goes: Sleep hygiene is bullshit, okay?

This is torture. Karma, maybe, as I've always thought I would've been a real bitch in the Way Back Whens. I think I've fallen right off Planet Earth. Maybe John fucking murdered me in that cabin, and all this is fucking Purgatory. Heh, or maybe Hell, given how much attention I paid to the old man in the sky. Jahannam. Or Naraka. Or Nifelhel, if you go that way.

Google, remember, bitch?

Any way you want to slice it up and eat it, it's motherfucking torture. I'd rather be waterboarded.

Debs, *I can't sleep.* And I mean *at all.* The Ambien I got in San Antonio might as well be Chicklets. I can take four of them with a pint of whisky and nothing, Debs.

Nothing, and I'm pretty sure that should fucking kill me.

Sleep hygiene. Bullshit, fucking bullshit. "Get up at the same time every day. Go to bed at the same time every day." Whoever thought of this happy horseshit has never had real insomnia. What fucking difference does it make what time I go lie in bed—wide awake— until the "same time" I'm supposed to get up? That does nothing but bore me to suicide and make me feel like puking until five every afternoon.

Yes, Debs, I've cut out caffeine. No sugar after two in the fucking afternoon, and I don't have much of it before, either. I've got the goddamn blue light filters cranked up so high I can't read a fucking thing on my phone at noon, let alone after dark. I've got my phone in Do-Not-Disturb mode from 6 pm to noon. I turn off all the lights in my hotel room as soon as dusk hits. I do relaxation exercises until I want to commit bloody murder. I'm practicing *being mindfucked*...uh, I mean *mindful* (whatever the hell that really means). I've even started drinking a hot-toddy and then a mug of warm milk every fucking night, Debs. By the time I check out, my hotel room is so doused in lavender that it smells like a cheap Tijuana whore. Yeah, no typo there, Deb. The room smells like the whore, not the whorehouse. I figure that's worse, right?

And despite all that, I lie there, all night, every night, doing the same goddamn motherfucking thing: not sleeping.

Guess I'm just keeping a vigil...trying to catch the ceiling moving. Or the aliens coming down to probe me. I've got the air on as cold as it will go, two fans from Walmart blowing on me, a foot warmer going full blast, three blankets, and I rest my throbbing noggin on a "cool-gel" pillow to keep my brain from being too hot.

None of that helps either.

Debs, I need you to tell me the truth here.

What the fuck is the matter with me?

Why can't I sleep?

The dreams were bad enough, but I think this...

Fuck this, Debs. Those are stupid questions, and I know the answers to them anyway.

I'm *terrified* of falling asleep.

See, if you don't sleep, you can't dream.

Fuck, I need to get laid.

34

At the knock on his window, Gavin's heart leaped into his throat, and his whole body twitched like a high-tension wire had dropped across his shoulders. The page he'd been turning in Kirk's journal ripped halfway down the page.

A short woman with skin so tan she'd seem more at home on Daytona Beach than standing in her front yard in Campton, Pennsylvania, stood looking at him, the corners of her mouth turned up in a slight smile—probably at his reaction. She beckoned him. "If you're going to sit here until it's time for our damn show and tell, you might as well come on in and have some coffee."

Gavin plastered a smile on his face and opened the driver's side door. "Hello. Margaret Samuels?"

"Margie. No one calls me Margaret."

"Margie, then. I'm Gavin. Special Agent Gavin Gregory. I work with the BAU—the Behavior Analysis Unit at Quantico. We study—"

"Seriously? In the age of Mindhunter and Silence of the Lambs, I think every breathing person on Earth knows what you do, Gavin." She tipped a quick little wink at him. "Come on. It's colder than a penguin's prick out here."

Grinning, Gavin got out of the little shitbox and followed her inside the little crackerbox house with its pretentious pillar-supported gable over the front door and peeling yellow paint with peeling white trim. The interior, on the other hand, was immaculate with a place for everything and everything in its place. The living room, dining room, and kitchen were all part of one large L-shaped room with marvelous wide-plank heart-oak wooden floors stained a mellow amber.

Margie waved her hand at the brown leather couch and laid her hand on a tan La-Z-Boy recliner next to it. "I'm about to have me a second cup of coffee. Can I offer you any?"

"You're talking to an FBI agent," he said with a grin.

"Right, right. What was I thinking? Black or ruined?"

"One sugar, please."

"Ruined it is." She turned and went into the kitchen, which Gavin could see all of if he leaned forward on the couch. "I don't know how much help I can be. All of that was so long ago."

"Alas, that's the nature of cold cases. But you know what? Time has a way of working on a person's memory. Sometimes, it messes up the details, sometimes it sharpens the memories, and sometimes it replaces a misremembered fact with what really happened. It's like that adage: hindsight is twenty-twenty."

Margie chuckled, though it sounded forced. "Well, settle in, then. It's not a short story, even though I'm going to tell you what I know as fast as I can to get it over with. That way, between my soaps and the bottle of tequila I've got squirreled away, I can get started on forgetting it all again."

"I'm sorry to bring up bad memories, but I'd really like to see if I can put the case to rest."

"No, I get that. Some of this is what I saw myself, some is what I got from talking to Tom Madsen and Virginia Bently—him missing and her rotting away in some cemetery—unless you want me to skip their parts?"

"You tell it your way. I'll ignore what I can't use."

"Okay. I'll also tell you what I gleaned from other sources: the high school wrestling coach, the papers, and that old crook, O'Hara. Use what you can, spit on the rest." She came back from the kitchen with two steaming mugs, one with a spoon leaned against the side. "It started the day those two mad fuckers came back. They were this set of twins who'd been flat ruint by their father." She sucked her teeth and shook her head. "That man was lower than a snake's belly in a wagon rut and twice as crazy as either of his sons, though being a Fundamentalist Pentecostal minister gave him a pass for most of it." She nodded and settled into her chair. "Tom was always early for work, and that day was no exception. He came upon the twins and their four-cop escort in the special elevator that led up to Four South—the locked unit reserved for the most violent patients…"

Chapter 13
A Descent into Darkness

I

Briar Ridge State Mental Hospital, Millvale, PA
May 15, 2004, 2:23 pm

Tom Madsen took one look at the six men crowded into the elevator, his gaze locking on the closest of the four big policemen surrounding the twins he knew from their last visit—Ezekiel and Ismael Amhain. His stomach flip-flopped, and a bubble of acid crawled up his throat. The two brothers had made serious trouble on their last visit to Four South—trouble that had left him on short-term medical leave with his arm in a sling.

The cop quirked his eyebrow.

"I'll take the stairs," said Tom.

"Hi, Tommy-ba-bommy," said Ismael in a piping, child-like voice. As the doors slid shut, both Ismael and Ezekiel cackled like drunk teenaged girls.

He shook his head and tried to settle the uneasy feeling in his guts. The four large cops and the crazy twins would exit the elevator into the little six by six room that acted as a sort of airlock for Four South—the only place that elevator went—and that was the last place Tom wanted to be. On their last visit nine and a half months before, the Amhains had freaked out in that cramped little room. The fight that followed had ended with two cops, one psychiatric nurse, one security guard, and three psychiatric technicians in the emergency room at the We Care Hospital on the other side of town.

I need to find another line of work. But the choices in Millvale were slim. He had the choice of working in one of the five eateries or bars, the hardware store, the small grocery store, Briar Ridge, or the Jackson-Barney Steelworks. Or, if he struggled through the torture of four more years of school, he could become a teacher and coach at the high school—the only choice that offered even a smidge of interest for him. The asylum offered him the best fit—at least until his body-building career took him away from Millvale, away from Pennsylvania, away from the Northeast.

He'd always liked the idea of living near Muscle Beach in Santa Monica.

He rolled his shoulders as he climbed the stairs up to the top floor of the square four-story building. At the top of the stairwell, Tom thumbed through the keys on his heavy keyring until he found the one that opened the steel security door. He pushed through the door and stepped onto Four West, glancing down the long hallway toward their nursing station set in the crook of a giant L-shape in the western corner of the building.

He stepped across the hall and, after unlocking another steel security door, he stepped into the westernmost end of Four South, closed the door, and tested to make sure the lock had set before stepping away from it. The staff called the hall he stood in the seclusion wing as single-occupancy rooms bereft of anything but a bed on a heavy pedestal and small bathroom lined the entire outside wall. As he walked toward the station, he checked each of the alcoves that led to a pair of seclusion rooms—each one a shadowy place that the patients found irresistible hiding places.

The carpet of one of the alcoves looked darker than the rest of the carpet. As Tom veered closer, the carpet beneath his feet squelched, and he wrinkled his nose at the foul odor of mold and wet polyester that hovered around the door. Trying to take no more than shallow breaths, Tom stepped up to the rectangular window set in the door and peered through it. A half-second later, his hand slammed down on the sizable chunk of red plastic set in a steel plate next to the door—what the staff called "The Button." The emergency klaxon began its raucous cry, but Tom barely heard it.

He had his keys out and was spinning through them with his thumb without looking down—he couldn't take his eyes off the scene inside the room. The heavy bed lay flipped up at an angle against the far wall. Leather straps ran from the purpose-built moorings set into the bed's sides to the far side of the up-turned bed, and the straps were taut, as though supporting the bodyweight of a patient restrained by them.

As Tom jammed the key into the lock, footsteps thundered toward him from the direction of the dayroom. He spun the cylinder, and the deadbolt popped open. With a chop and a kick, he slid the steel bolts that manually secured the top and bottom of the door open and pulled the door toward him.

A rank odor slammed into him as reddish water gushed out across the threshold, wetting his shoes. He waited a single moment for the worst of the deluge to pass, then stepped inside the seclusion room. "Hello?" he called. With a turn of his head, he checked the small cubicle bathroom. The door stood closed and locked—the norm for a patient in restraints. His eyes flicked to the window set in the closet-sized bathroom's door, but darkness reigned inside. His gaze snapped back to the overturned bed and he sloshed two giant steps across the room and peered under the bed.

"You picked a helluva time to slap the Button," said Virginia Bently.

"He's hurt," Tom said. He grabbed the foot of the bed, and with a grunt, started to turn it upright. The patient strapped to the bed gasped, then giggled like a madman.

"Stop!" Virginia rushed into the room and swatted his arm. "Don't move him!"

Tom felt the blush creep up his neck and onto his cheeks. Virginia had a way about her that rankled almost everyone, but she and Tom shared a friendship of sorts. Most of the time, at least. He didn't like the scorn in her voice, but he gently set the bed back against the wall.

"Check his head! I'll never get my fat ass in that corner, Tom. You better get in there."

He glanced at her—her bleach-blonde hair teased to within an inch of its very life, her heavy mascara and thick lipstick glistening in the overhead light, her obese torso covered in powder blue scrubs that could've been used as a tent. "I'm six feet tall and two seventy, Virginia. How do you expect me to get in there without moving the bed?"

She shrugged, setting her stomach jiggling. "Better figure it out, Tommy." She strode to the intercom in the alcove and slapped it. "Kerry! Shut off that racket!" A moment later, the klaxon stopped in mid-bleat, and Virginia re-entered the room. She dropped a scathing glance on him and motioned toward the corner. "Get in there, Tom! Lay on the floor if you have to!"

He hesitated only a heartbeat, trying to decide if it was worth Virginia's wrath to point out she could do the same thing, then shrugged and walked to the head of the bed. He squatted on his hunkers, wedged into the corner, and ducked his head to peer into the shadowed crevasse between the bed and the wall, then glanced at the nurse. "Who is this?"

"God, I don't know! Who does it look like? I'm not even on, yet, and I haven't heard report." She shook her head and waved her pudgy hand at the upended bed.

Tom rolled forward onto his hands and knees in the fetid water, grimacing at the oily feel of it. Pitch black hair covered the crown of the man's head, though bits of pink scalp showed through it. "Hey," said Tom. "Hey, are you alright?"

The man hanging by his restraints didn't answer, didn't move.

"This water looks like it's got blood all up in it," muttered Virginia. "Tom, is he *bleeding*?"

"I…" Tom leaned closer—close enough to smell five days' worth of body odor and something coppery, both undercut with the tang of schizophrenia. "I think this must be Kaspar…"

"Kaspar Anderson?" asked Virginia.

Tom ignored her and reached forward to tap the man on the top of his head. "Kaspar! Are you okay?"

Anderson laughed in a loose, disjointed way that sounded almost like hiccups. "He did it! He hid it! He bid it he did-bid-hid it!"

Tom suppressed the urge to sigh and craned his head to look at Virginia. She shrugged and lifted her hands toward the bed again, a sneer threatening her lips. "Kaspar, are you cut?" asked Tom, ducking his head back down to peer into the dark cavity made by the bed and the wall. "Get me a flashlight, Vee."

He heard her splashing out to the hall and yelling for Kerry to send down a flashlight and rolled his eyes. The break room was twenty steps away, and the supply closet inside it held about a hundred emergency flashlights.

"*He did it!*" Kaspar roared, laughter lilting in his voice. "I can't *relieve* he hid it!"

"Who did what, buddy?" asked Tom, but then he shook his head. "Never mind that for now. Tell me if you're hurt or not. I can right the bed if you're okay. Those straps have to be digging into your skin."

Kaspar turned his head from left to right, as though looking for the source of Tom's voice. "Who's that?"

"Tom."

"Why's it dark in here, Tom-turkey? Did you see my fool-pool?"

That was what patients called it when they flooded a seclusion room—making a pool. "It's not dark, Kaspar. The bed is turned over against the wall and you're trapped beneath it. Who did that?"

"The dead? The dead-bed?"

"Yes. You're in restraints in your room."

"Oh. Well, who invited you out to the pool?"

Tom shook his head once. "Kaspar, are you cut?"

"Rut?" Kaspar chuckled and made a shushing noise. "I can't hear him if you talk in my beer all the damn chime," he whispered, craning his neck side-to-side. "Bear are you, Tom-turkey?"

"Above your head."

Kaspar immediately tried to tilt his head back and thumped his face against the hard wall. "I told you so," he muttered. "*SHH!* Sorry, Tom-turkey. It's noisy in fear. And nosy. Nosy-noisy. Noisy-nosy."

"Are you hurt anywhere, buddy?"

"Hurt? Or herd? Or head? Bed-said-med-dead. Yup, that's me to a fee."

"You do hurt? Tell me where."

"These straps…" He groaned and shook his head back and forth. "Jesus H. Vice! Could you shut the hell up? I'm trying to talk to Tom-turkey." He cocked his head to the side as though listening hard in a loud room. "No, Tom-turkey's the good one. Not like that blonde bitchy blimp-pimp at all. No! He's *not* the same person! The blonde one's a woman. Her fame is *Virginia*, not Tom-turkey." He drew a deep breath and pushed it out in a rush. "Sorry, Tommy. This guy talks so loud and all the truckin' time." He groaned and shook his head. "*SO DAMN LOUD!*" he shouted.

"It's okay, Kaspar."

"Yeah. Right as a bedbug." Kaspar began humming *Edelweiss* from *The Sound of Music* to himself, bobbing his head and occasionally knocking his face into the wall.

Virginia came rolling back into the room. "Well?"

Tom shrugged the shoulder she could see. "Kaspar?"

For a moment, the man didn't reply. "Oh, Vice! Those Amhain bastards are here. I ate those ticks! No, hat! *Hate!* I hate those prick-tick-tricks."

"Are you bleeding, Kaspar?"

"What? Bleeding? Oh, sure. My farm got scraped when he bid it."

"Did what? Who?" asked Virginia.

"Where's that flashlight?"

"How the hell should I know, Tom? I'm the son crapped under this dead." Anderson cackled and shook his head back and forth.

Tom rolled his eyes and suppressed the urge to sigh. "I think he's bleeding. He said his arm got scraped."

"Yeah, thanks. I'm not deaf, you know." Virginia gingerly stepped into the water, making a sour face. "Okay, flip him up so I can look."

"But you said not to move—"

"*Flip him up*, Tom! For Christ's bloody sake!"

He couldn't keep the sigh in, but Virginia let it go without comment. He stood and squatted next to the head of the bed, wedging his fingers into gaps caused by the angle. "Okay, Kaspar. I'm going to put you right-side-up."

"Oh, no. I don't sink so. He doesn't want that."

"Who?"

"Who? What are you, an owl or a turkey?"

"He's not going to give you anything sensible, Tom. Flip him up, already."

With a grunt, Tom lifted the heavy bed and then stood there, trying to figure out what to do next. "Not sure I can do this safely by myself."

"Well, don't look at me," said Virginia. "I've got a bad back. And asthma."

"Yeah," he murmured. He twisted his upper body to turn the bed, and the klaxon began to scream again.

"All staff! All staff to the alcove!" Kerry's voice rang over the intercom, almost screeching with panic.

"What now?" muttered Virginia.

"Ezekiel and Ismael, sitting in a tree. Izzy and Ezzy, H-I-T-T-I-N-G," sang Kaspar. "Daddy-god and Mommy-frog, back for another visit."

"Amhain brothers are coming in," said Tom, looking down at Kaspar. "I saw them in the elevator as I came up."

"You told him that?"

Tom shook his head. The sharp edges of the bed cut into his palms, burning as if the wood was smoldering. With a grunt, he twisted the bed upright and set it down with a thump.

Kaspar's right arm bore a slit from elbow to the center of his palm. Blood gushed out of the laceration, flowing fast in time with his heartbeat.

"Oh, Christ!" snapped Virginia. "Get pressure on that, Tom!" She left the room at a slow jog and yelled toward the nurses' station. "Kerry! Shut up that racket and call for an ambulance!"

Tom looked down, searching Kaspar's calm gaze. "Who did this to you, buddy? Who cut you?"

"The Sliver Sulfur, I think." A thoughtful expression flitted across his face like a shadow. "He was silver, anyway."

"Okay." Tom peeled part of the bottom sheet away from the mattress and wrapped it around Kaspar's bleeding forearm. "I've got to press down hard, buddy. It will hurt."

"Yeah, yeah. *Life* shirts, Tom-turkey. Sell me something I don't already grow."

Virginia came pounding back into the room, spots of bright red high on her cheeks. "Christ, Tom! What are you *doing*? They…" She turned and looked out at the hall. "Leave that!" she snapped, turning back to him. "They need you in the alcove. It's…" She shook her head. "*GET MOVING, TOM!*"

"Hold this!" he said, nodding toward Kaspar's forearm. The nurses always expected Tom to take the lead in physical confrontations—and he supposed he could agree with that. He had the size, the strength, and had taken the state heavy-weight wrestling championship in both his junior and senior years at Millvale High School.

Virginia glanced down, then met Tom's gaze before snapping her head back to the hall. "I don't know…"

"Vee! He'll bleed out!"

She turned back, and her panicked expression slid off her face as though an emergency she could deal with galvanized her. "Okay. Get out of my way!"

Tom sprinted into the hall, water squelching from his shoes, Kaspar Anderson's blood dripping from his hands, and pelted through the Dutch door and into the nurses' station. Kerry stood staring at the locked steel door from across the nurses' station, peering through the narrow window that reached from the knob toward the top of the door. Her hand fluttered at her mouth while her other hand tapped behind her as though she were searching for something in the dark.

"Kerry!" he barked as he slammed the Dutch door behind him. "Call security! And get an ambulance rolling for Anderson!"

She didn't move for a breath, then tore her eyes away from the window. "You can't go out there alone, Tom," she said in a strangled voice.

"Call security!" He raced to the door and grabbed the handle. "And call for that ambulance! Kaspar Anderson is cut palm to elbow. *Deep.*" He twisted the knob and opened the steel door onto bedlam and blood without waiting to see if Kerry would do as he asked.

Tom took half-a-second to take a mental snapshot of the scene. Of the four cops he'd seen in the elevator, two were down and bleeding. Another seemed to be trying to crawl under the row of chairs, with Ismael standing over him, staring down at him the way a lion stares at an injured gazelle, fists clenched. Ezekiel had the other one backed into the corner next to the elevator and pinned him there with one hand digging into his throat while he kept another psych tech—Ricky—pinned with a knee and a fierce grip on his collar in one of the ugly visitors' chairs. Margie lay dazed in the middle of the room, a capped syringe next to her. Bryant, another tech, lay in the corner by the visitor's door to the unit, cradling his head. Lydia, the afternoon shift's LPN, was pressed against the wall at Tom's feet, clutching another capped syringe in her left hand and pressing her right palm into the wound on her forehead.

He reached down and took Lydia's elbow. "Come on, Lydia," he said, half-guiding, half-dragging her into the relative safety of the nurses' station. When he had her inside, he let the door slam shut, behind them. Out in the alcove, Ismael cackled with maniacal glee. Tom took the syringe from Lydia's white-knuckled grasp. "Kerry, help her." He leaned Lydia against the wall just out of reach of the door and then turned to grasp the knob.

"Don't go back out there," Lydia moaned. "Wait for security."

Tom met Kerry's gaze and gave her one single, calm nod. "Make those calls, Kerry. Get me some help." She opened her mouth to speak, but he twisted the knob and charged through the door.

Ismael glanced at him and smiled. "Hey there, Tommy-ba-bommy. Come to play?" Without another glance at the police officer at his feet, Ismael strode toward Tom, grinning and blinking his eyes as if he had hot sauce in them. "Remind me, Tommy. Which shoulder did I break last time?"

Tom took a step forward, bent at the waist, and swept the other syringe from the ground next to Margie. Across the small room, Ezekiel hawked and spat.

"What fun is that, Tommy?" asked Ismael. "Play fair!"

He didn't respond, only slipped one of the capped syringes into the side pocket of his cargo pants. He stuck the capped end of the other in his mouth, pulled the cap off with his teeth, and spat it into the corner.

"Tommy's shy today, Izzy," said Ezekiel. "A cat's got his tongue."

Tom's gaze darted to the corner next to the elevator, hoping to see Ricky up and fighting. Instead, he saw the last policeman crumple into an unconscious heap, and Ezekiel turning toward Tom, without even the pretense of worrying about Ricky. As soon as Ezekiel let go of his collar, Ricky drooped face-first to the ground.

"Oopsy," said Ezekiel. "Ricky fall down and go boom."

"Yeah, Ezzy. A cat's got Tommy-ba-bommy's tongue." As soon as he finished speaking, Ismael sprang forward, arms outstretched toward Tom's throat, eyes opened wide, mouth gaping to show his teeth.

Tom had time enough to see the blood smeared on Ismael's teeth before the man was on him, kicking at his knees and grabbing the hand that held the syringe. Tom grappled with his free hand, pulling the syringe out of Ismael's reach, trying to get an angle to slam the needle home.

"No night-night for Izzy. No sleepy-sleep for Ezzy," Ezekiel crooned. "Daddy and Uncle Spock wouldn't like it, Tommy. *You play nice!*"

Tom outweighed either of the two brothers by at least a hundred pounds, but neither brother seemed to care. He shoved Ismael away, using all his considerable strength to send the thin man flying, then whirled and sprang at Ezekiel, hoping to surprise him. Ezzy grinned and spread his arms as if to give Tom a hug, and they slammed together, the psych tech's momentum and weight driving Ezekiel back into the chairs, forcing him down next to Ricky. Using his weight to pin the skinny man, Tom pressed the syringe toward his shoulder. But before he could sink it home, Ismael landed on his back, screeching like a banshee and clawing at his neck. Ducking his chin to protect his throat, Tom kept trying to drive the syringe in Ezekiel's flesh. Izzy gave up trying to snake his arm around Tom's neck and boxed his ears, but Tom thought he had heard the elevator bell somewhere below before his ears started to hum and ring. He tried to shrug Ismael off, but the man clung to him like a panther to his prey.

Grunting with effort and throwing the weight of his upper body behind the syringe, Tom inched it closer and closer to Ezekiel's upper arm. When the needle was mere inches away, Ezzy sang out in the twin patois he and Ismael shared, and the weight disappeared off Tom's back. He hunched his shoulders up around his head and kept pushing his right hand toward Ezekiel's shoulder. "Ricky!" he cried. "Ricky, get up and help me!"

Izzy laughed. "He's not coming to help, Tommy. Richard is down. Down for the count!" He cackled from somewhere behind Tom. Ezekiel stared at the needle with eyes wide and scared—though Tom had no idea why the needle would scare him given how many times he'd likely taken one exactly like it. He cried some gibberish to his brother and shifted both of his hands to Tom's wrist, giving up the wrestling match on the other hand.

Tom clamped his left hand around Ezekiel's throat and gave him a little squeeze—not enough to cause harm, just enough to get his attention, to distract him from the needle. "Relax and let it happen, Ezekiel. It won't hurt if you do."

Ezekiel laughed and tried to bite the hand holding the syringe.

Just a minute more, Tom thought. *Security or more cops are in that elevator.* At least, he hoped that was the truth of it. He shifted his weight to bear down with the needle and had scratched Ezekiel's skin when something crashed into his upper back, neck, and head. Tom's breath exploded out of him, and for a moment his vision went red. Beneath him, the twin cackled, and then, Ezzy was gone, wriggling out from under him and away between his legs. Tom shook his head and spun around, so dizzy the movement almost made him puke, and slipped to one knee.

Ismael stood over him with one of the ugly chairs lifted high in the air. He took a step forward, and Tom threw his arm up to protect his head. He squeezed his eyes shut, waiting for the blow to land.

Keys rattled in the lock of the nurses' station door, then Kerry yelled, "Ismael! You put that down! Right this instant! Do you hear me, young man?"

Tom opened his eyes. Kerry stood just inside the station, the door opened about an inch and a half—as though Ismael and Ezekiel wouldn't be able to push past her with ease. "Close it! Kerry, close it!"

The heavy chair in Ismael's hands drooped toward the floor—but only until Tom met his gaze. "Don't worry, Kerry. We don't want to get in there." He lifted the chair over his head again and took another step. "It's fun out here."

"You better not, Ismael Amhain! I'll tell your father!"

A look of terror splashed across the faces of both brothers, and Ezekiel half-turned toward the door. "You wouldn't do that," he whispered.

"Oh yes, I would! I'll call him right now, and I'll remind him when he comes to visit."

"Don't tell Daddy-god," whined Ezekiel. "We'll be good, promise!"

"Ismael Amhain! Put that chair down!"

Izzy darted a wide-eyed glance at his brother, and again, the chair began a slow arc toward the floor. "We were just playing… Don't tell our papa!"

Tom turned a mystified glance toward Kerry. She'd been the unit secretary on Four South for fifteen years—seven times longer than Tom had worked there—and she knew everything about their regulars. She made a hurry-up gesture.

"Well, if you let Tom give you your shots, then—"

"No!" snarled Ismael, lifting the chair again. "You're like all the rest!" He hurled the heavy chair through the air to crash into the wall beside Tom, then whirled toward the station with hate in his eyes.

Kerry had time for a single cry of terror, then she slammed the door.

Tom charged at Ismael's back, syringe raised to shoulder level, but before he could bury it in the scrawny man's shoulder, Ezekiel pounded into him, his shoulder buried in Tom's side like a linebacker making a sack. They both crashed into a row of chairs, bounced off it, and rolled to the floor. The syringe went flying.

Ismael pounded on the metal station door. "Come back here!" he shouted. "Come take your medicine you...you *Jezebel*!"

Tom rolled on top of Ezekiel, using his weight and wrestling skills to pin the man beneath him. He reached for the side pocket of his pants.

"*Izzy*!" cried Ezekiel. Again, he shouted in their private language, and again, his brother came flying at Tom, knocking him aside. They landed in a tangle of limbs with a flurry of fists and knees, and Izzy turned him on his back, then straddled him like an MMA fighter in full mount. Tom's head still rang from the chair across the back, and the twins seemed to sense it. Every time he tried to get his legs under him, Ezzy swept them away. When he tried to kick Ezekiel, Ismael ground the heels of his hands into Tom's face, his neck, his collar bones. When he bucked his hips to throw Izzy off, Ezekiel kicked him in the thigh until it sang with pins and needles.

The door to the unit opened again, and Kerry shouted, "You two get off him! I'm *calling* your father right now if you don't!"

That elicited a short pause—long enough for the twins to make eye contact—and then they went right back to punching and kicking. Tom tried to roll from side to side, tried to cover his head with his arms, tried everything he could think of, but nothing worked for long.

"Make Tommy go to sleep, Izzy!" cried Ezekiel. "Put *him* to sleep!"

"Where is it?" grunted Ismael. "You get it, Ezzy, I'll hold him."

Ezekiel ripped open the side pocket of Tom's cargo pants and shoved his hand inside. He laughed as he jerked the syringe out and held it over his head in triumph. "I got it! Izzy, I got it!"

"Night-night, Tommy-ba-bommy!" Ismael leered down at him, the sandman gone insane.

Tom threw his weight to the side, shoving Izzy the other direction, trying to reverse their positions, but lanky twin rode him like a bronco rider, grinning the whole time.

"Hold him still, Izzy! I got the thingy!"

A hand clamped around his wrist—Ezekiel's hand—and Ismael shifted to lie across his torso, shoving Tom's face roughly to the side. "Don't watch. Shots hurt if you watch."

Ezekiel bit the cap of the syringe and spat it aside. The needle seemed eight feet long as Tom watched it descend with glacial slowness toward his arm. As the needle pierced his skin, the elevator doors swished open. Ezzy looked up in terror, but that didn't stop him from emptying the syringe into Tom's arm. "No! I didn't mean it!" Ezekiel cried and then was swept aside.

Ismael's weight left him next, and Tom yanked out the syringe, but its payload of lorazepam had been delivered. He knew he had only a few minutes of consciousness. He pushed himself away from the fight—sliding on his butt toward the chairs behind him.

Security officers restrained the Amhain brothers, and their shift chief glanced at the empty syringe, then met Tom's eyes. "You okay?"

Tom nodded, already feeling more groggy than not. "Just a shot of lorazepam."

"See you after your nap, hoss."

Tom grimaced, and everything faded to black.

2

Tom opened his eyes. He lay on the ground where he'd fought with Ezekiel, his head cushioned by something. The fluorescent bulbs overhead burned too bright and seemed to buzz directly in his ears.

"Now, don't you move for a few minutes, Tom. I had to give you an IV dose of flumazenil to counteract the elephant-sized dose of lorazepam the twins gave you. Get yourself steady before you start moving around." Margie rested on one knee, bent over his left arm, and as she pulled the needle out of his vein, she hit him with a smile. "No napping on duty." She grinned at him.

"Yeah," he grunted. "I think I caught you napping earlier, though."

She nodded, her eyes losing some of their sparkling good humor. "That you did. Ezekiel clipped me right on the chin. The little bastard."

"You okay?"

"I'll bruise and have to put up with a little soreness when I eat, but nothing more than that." She shrugged her bony shoulders. "I could lose a few pounds, anyway."

Tom met her frank gaze without flinching. Margie was short and spry and weighed maybe ninety-five pounds soaking wet. "You lose much more weight, and you'll turn see-through." She looked like a child crouching next to him. She stood no more than five-foot-nothing on a good day and had more skin than flesh wrapped around her bones.

She patted his shoulder. "Sucking up won't buy you anything, Tom. I thought I told you that already."

He closed his eyes in a slow blink. His head felt stuffed full of cotton batting, and his ears rang as though he'd gone a round with Mike Tyson. When he opened his eyes again, his head seemed to fill with the bright white light, to swell past the limits of his skull, and the only thing that seemed to hurt more was the parched flesh in the back of his throat. It felt as if coated in that desiccant powder from one of those little packets inside the box of every electronic gadget known to mankind. His tongue wanted to stick to the roof of his mouth, and he could barely summon enough spit to swallow. He tried to conjure up a mouthful of spit as he pulled his legs up to stand.

"Ho, there, big guy," said Margie. "Lie there and take it easy."

Tom pushed himself up on his elbows. "No, I'm good. You need me on the unit. The Amhains—"

"Sedated. They'll sleep through tomorrow if I have my way." She flashed a smile at him and hit him with a patented Margie-says-fuck-em wink. "Come on, you big lug. We can handle Four South without you for a few minutes."

"Is everyone okay? Lydia? Bryant?"

"Everyone is fine. Of course, Ricky had to go home, but he's fine, just milking it for all it's worth. Bryant is up and around, nursing a lump the size of a melon on his forehead."

Tom shook his head. "Kaspar—"

"On the way to We Care. You can relax, Tom."

Tom laughed. "Whatever you say, Margie. I'll bet Vee is fit to be tied—stuck down there in the seclusion room having to care for him without even an audience to applaud her efforts."

"That queen bee? She's happier than a pig in shit to have missed the fracas." Her eyes grew a little colder. "At least she had a good excuse this time."

"If Bryant's out of it and Ricky's already gone, I'd better—"

"You're going home, too. You got a full dose of lorazepam and a pipeful of flumazenil to counteract it. I can't let you out on the unit. But don't worry, I called Greg, John, and Shannon in to cover. I figured I better get at least two techs to cover for you." She twitched an eyebrow and grinned. "Okay? Does that meet with your approval?"

He groaned and sank back, resting his head on the blanket behind him. "What a day."

"You bet," said Margie, rubbing her chin. "I just love it when the Amhains come to visit."

"Kerry almost defused the whole thing."

"Kerry? She joined in?"

"From the station. But…" Tom frowned and shook his head.

"What?"

"She said she would tell their father, and both of them acted like it was a death sentence."

Margie glanced around, then peered down at him from the corner of her eye. A smile twisted her lips. "You didn't meet the senior Amhain last time?"

"Nope. Ismael dislocated my shoulder ten minutes after they arrived, remember?"

"Oh, right." She swatted his arm. "No injuries this time, I see. You're learning."

Tom grinned. "Yeah. This time I let them sedate me."

"*After* you charged in here single-handed and maybe saved a couple of those cops from a serious beating. Ricky, too." She rubbed her chin. "I don't know what he did to them last time they were here, but I'd better find out." She shook her head as if to clear it. "Alphonse Amhain is a piece of work. You've seen how sick the two boys are. Their mother, Emily, isn't much better off, but she can at least mask it most of the time. All of it rests at Alphonse's feet."

"Abusive?"

"Yes, and worse." She checked his pulse and peered into his eyes. "Feeling steady? Ready to get up?"

"Yeah, I think so." He sat up, expecting a wave of dizziness, but all he felt was that head-stuffed-with-cotton thing. Margie held out her hand and pulled him to his feet, then looked up to meet his gaze. "Daddy Amhain did worse than abuse them?"

"He started life as a Pentecostal minister of United Pentecostal variety, but he found it to be too permissive. He—"

"I don't know what the United Pentecostal variety is."

"Very strict. No makeup, no tight clothes, no 'mixed swimming.'"

"And that was too permissive?"

"For Alphonse it was. He formed a splinter group and somehow got people to join it. He's the patriarch and absolute authority for his flock and takes everything in the Bible as a literal truth. So, spare the rod, spoil the child, and all that. He used a lathe to turn down an oak baseball bat to make it all one inch in diameter. His 'rod,' you see? Alphonse loves to swing that stick and issue dire warnings about eternity in a lake of fire and brimstone. The boys are terrified of him." Margie shrugged. "Most times, something like what Kerry did works."

"It almost did this time, too. She had them turning meek until she told them to let me give them the shots."

"Ah." Margie looked down and rubbed her neck. "You're too tall, Tom."

"That was my nickname all through high school."

"Too Tall Tom?"

"The infamous triple-T at your service." He turned his face away and rubbed the back of his neck. "Look, I'm okay, Margie. I can work."

"Yeah, until you fall asleep and something happens to you and I get my ass chewed till doomsday. No, thanks. It's home for you."

Tom shoved his hands in his pockets. "Okay, but what about that stuff that happened in Kaspar's room?"

"Ain't that a trip? We haven't found it, yet, but we've got him over to the ER to get that arm stitched up—not that we've had much time to do anything else. Shannon's going to tear everything down before supper. We'll find it."

"Find what?"

"Whatever he used to slice his arm."

"He said the Silver Surfer did it." He peeked at her from the corner of his eye. "Well, he said the *Sliver Sulfur*, but you know how he is with word salad. Went on and on, saying, he did it, he bid it, blah, blah, blah. And that's not the weirdest part."

"Oh, no?"

Tom shook his head once. "How'd he flip that bed while in four-point restraints? How'd he flood the room with the door to the bathroom locked and him tied to the bed?"

"I admit those are interesting questions—"

"*Interesting*?"

"—but he also managed to inflict a sixteen-inch wound in his forearm. In fact, if he *hadn't* flooded the room, maybe no one would have noticed, and he might be dead now, depending on how much damage he did to his arteries. In the general scheme of things, I'm much more interested in finding the shank he used to cut himself."

"Sure, Margie, I get that. But at the same time, he did all these inexplicable things… They're kind of a package deal, right? I mean, there is no way he could flip that bed. None. And clogging the toilet behind a locked door and somehow repeatedly flushing it to—"

"The toilets have overflowed on their own before."

"Well, sure, but…" Tom lifted his hands out to his sides and let them drop. Margie's attitude perplexed him, but for the most part, Tom never pushed things past a certain point. She was his boss, after all.

"Tom, I'm not saying we won't look into those things, but for the time being, that blade is job number one." She peered up into his eyes again. "You'd better not drive. Have you got anyone who can come get you?"

"My car's here. I'll need it tomorrow."

"That can't be helped. Now, who can I call?"

"My mom. She lives in town."

"Fine. Come sit in the station until she gets here."

Tom followed Margie into the station and didn't argue when she pushed him down into one of the padded office chairs. "You're not to leave the station, Tom," she said in a stern voice. "Indicate you heard me."

"Yes, ma'am," he said with a jaunty salute.

3

On the way home, Millvale, PA
May 15, 2004, 3:39 pm

When his mother arrived, Margie insisted on taking him down in the elevator and walking him out to his mother's car—a tiny little foreign job the color of a band-aid. To Tom, it was the ugliest thing on Earth and designed only to torture tall men.

Margie watched him fold himself into the car, a vacant grin on her face. She went as far as chuckling as he contorted himself to get the seatbelt fastened. "Alright, then," she said. "You go home and rest, Tom."

"I will."

"I'll make sure of it," said his mother. "And thanks for looking out for him."

Margie nodded and waved before turning and walking back into the asylum.

"Thanks for coming, Mom."

"Of course!" She glanced at him as she put the car in gear with a jerk. "Maybe we should take you to the ER."

"I'm fine, Mom. Promise." He grunted and cleared his throat. "All I want to do is go to sleep."

"If you're sure?"

Tom turned his face to the window, watching the run-down buildings blip by. It had fared better than many of the steel towns in Western Pennsylvania, and that was all down to having the state mental hospital just outside of the town limits. It suffered from the regular dose of garish fast-food dumps and giant superstores that seemed to be the norm, but the other buildings—the buildings in which the pulse of the town beat slower and slower—were a wreck. Unmaintained, uncared-for, left to rot, but what was the other choice?

"Seen better days, hasn't it?" His mother's voice had taken on a wistful quality.

"Yeah. I remember it being brighter when I was a kid."

"Oh?"

Tom smiled. "When I was a kid, they had that party in the center of town. You remember it? I'm sure it was celebrating some holiday that I've forgotten—"

"Labor Day. It was a couple of years before the first big cut-backs at the foundry."

"Ah. Was Dad still…" *Alive?* he finished silently.

"Yep." Her voice caught, and she swallowed roughly.

"Was Briar Ridge built back then?"

His mother nodded. "Sure. They broke ground in 1989 but didn't take their first patient until"—she flapped a hand—"well, they ran into a bunch of construction problems. I worked there for about a minute."

"When?"

"1992."

"1992? I was twelve."

"Thanks for making your mother feel *ancient*. Didn't I teach you better?"

Tom grinned, even as he blushed. "Sorry. I can't help when I was born. That's *your* fault."

She laughed and patted his knee. "Tell me what you remember from the grand Labor Day party of 1990."

"Remember how clean everything was? There wasn't any peeling paint, no gray wood siding, no plywood windows."

"No. We thought the foundry was going strong. Lee Amorte kept feeding us lies. No one knew how bad it was…he kept all that a secret from everyone. Even the employees."

Tom nodded. He remembered his mom going off to work in her uniform of heavy gray canvas—after his father had died, she'd taken a job at the Jackson-Barney Steelworks to make ends meet. "He was the general manager at the Jacks?" That's what all the kids called it: "The Jacks."

"Ayup," said Margie with a nod. "He wasn't a crook—no matter how he ended up. He did what he thought was best for the employees of the mill, for the town, but he made it so much worse for everyone with his lies. Store owners borrowed money to spruce things up, banking on the 'increased orders for steel' Amorte crowed about. Ayup, we bought it all—hook, line, and sinker." She hooked her index finger and mimed snagging her cheek with it.

"I think that's the last time I remember it looking like a thriving town," Tom said in a wistful voice.

"Life's a wheel, kiddo. Everything comes back around. Briar Ridge provides a good income for a lot of the townsfolk—my son included."

"Yeah, but even so, people don't shop in the small stores. They go over to the Walmart, or the mall in Campton, and buy everything from the big companies."

"It's a sign of the times, my boy."

"Maybe so, Mom, but I don't have to like it."

"No. You don't have to like it."

They rode in silence for a while, his mother intent on her driving and Tom intent on the desolation that existed in the middle of his hometown. The dregs of the drugs in his system made the journey seem interminable and made the run-down town seem even sadder than it normally did.

"What happened to him?"

"Who? Lee Amorte?" She ducked her head as though embarrassed. "Why do you ask?"

"You said, 'he wasn't a crook—no matter how he ended up.'"

"Oh." She cleared her throat and shot a quick glance his way. "Last I heard, he was up to Briar Ridge."

"What? Why?"

"You were little when it happened—seven or eight, I think. Lee Amorte murdered his wife and children. When they arrested him, he was babbling, real lunatic stuff. They judged him unfit to stand trial, and away he went."

"He…"

"That's right, kiddo. It happens. People go insane when they are under intense pressure, and Lee Amorte had enough pressure bearing down on him to turn him into a diamond. Instead, he cracked." She forced gaiety into her tone. "Besides, it was thirteen or fourteen years ago. No reason to be upset about it now."

"I'm not upset. I'm… I'm… I don't know what I am. I can't believe he's up at Briar Ridge, and I've never seen him. Never even heard his name."

His mother shrugged. "Well, I suppose he's not a big topic there. Even before he arrived there, he'd quit talking. Quit doing anything, really. He just sat and stared, even if you moved him."

"He was catatonic?"

"If that's the word for it."

Tom rubbed his eyes. "Wow."

His mother treated him to a longer glance. "Are you sure you'll be okay tonight? I could make up the futon."

"Thanks, but I'm sure, Mom. I'll probably sleep like the dead all night."

"Not too dead."

"No," he said, grinning. "Not too dead."

"You want Freddie's for dinner?"

Freddie's Fry Shack was his go-to comfort food, but it was ninety percent grease and a hundred and thirty percent sugar. "No, thanks. I've got a diet to think about."

"My son, the Arnold Schwarzenegger clone."

They both grinned as she turned off Jackson-Barney Drive, which served as both the main thoroughfare and the commercial district wrapped into a single entity, and wove her way through the warren of needlessly one-way streets bordered by buildings of crumbling brick and fade-to-gray wood. She pulled up in front of his apartment building and switched off the car. "Let me come up. I'll cook dinner."

"Thanks, Mom, but I'm not good company tonight."

"When are you ever?" she said with a chuckle.

"That one time in 2002."

"Oh, right. I forgot."

"Really, Mom, I'm a zombie. I just want to sleep."

"Well, okay, honey. You go up and get in bed. I'll call you around noon tomorrow to arrange to ride you out to Briar Ridge since your car's up there yet."

"You're the best."

"Don't I know it. Now get going. I've got a hot date with a stud-muffin from over Campton."

"Mom!"

She grinned and gave his shoulder a shove. "Go on, Tommy. Get some rest."

"I will. I promise," he said, meaning every word.

But, in the end, he didn't get much sleep at all.

4

Tom's apartment, Millvale, PA
May 15, 2004, 6:38 pm

Tom wallowed on his couch, somewhere between asleep and awake, when the phone rang. He considered ignoring the call, but he didn't want to miss a call from David. Bags of wet cement seemed to weigh him down as he rose from the couch and crossed to the counter bar that served as his kitchen table.

As he grabbed his cell phone off the charger and saw David's number in the caller ID, a flutter raced through his belly. He pressed the big green "on" button and pressed the phone to his ear. "David? Hi!"

"Hello, lover. How's your night going?"

Guilt boxed at him—he should've called David and let him know what had happened. *It's what a friend would do. It's what a* boyfriend *should have done.* A secret thrill raced through him as that thought marched through his mind.

"You there, lover?"

"Yeah, sorry, David. I've been an asshole."

"Uh-oh. That sounds ominous."

"Yeah." He didn't know how to start, so he stood there staring at his dirty stovetop and said nothing.

"Well? Are you going to tell me what dastardly deed you committed to earn the name?"

David was like that. He made light of everything. Never in a hurtful way, but rather in a way that made everything seem better somehow. "There was an issue at work, and they sent me home. Well, two issues, really, but they happened at the same time. I wasn't even clocked in yet, but I had to help. I—"

"So far, I don't sense the assholishness."

"Ha. Yeah. It's coming, David. It's coming."

"Oh! Is it time for dirty talk, lover?" David's voice sounded like a cat purring.

"Uh…"

"Don't mind me, Tom. *I'm* a true asshole, you see."

"Hardly. Anyway, the first thing was really, really freaky, and in the middle of trying to stop the blood, someone hit the Button down at the nurses' station." Tom pursed his lips, certain he was making a mess of things. "Remember when I got my shoulder dislocated?"

"Sure. Only a minute ago in the general scheme of things."

"Well, the two brothers who did that came back today. While I was dealing with another patient who'd cut his arm from elbow to palm somehow, the alarm went off, and Vee told me I better go help. I did. It was the two brothers, and they—"

"Twins, right?"

"Yeah. Anyway, they'd gone nuts on the cops and staff trying to get them processed onto the floor, and by the time I got down there—"

"Tom, *are you hurt*?" David's jovial tone was gone, replaced by a worried one.

"No, not really. I had to jump in, to keep the boys from doing serious harm. The twins had done a number on everyone out there and didn't seem to care there was no one left to fight, so I had to do it. I went out there and kept them occupied until help could get up to the unit."

"So, if you're not hurt, what happened?"

"I took a blast of lorazepam. I'd grabbed the syringes and had tried to inject Eze—one of the brothers, I mean—with it. The other jumped me from behind, and then they were both on me. I—"

"You know I'd never say a word about these two brothers, right? Not a word."

"I know that, David," Tom said in a quiet voice. "You're a good man."

"Aw, shucks, Tom. Now, I'm tearing up. Go on with your story."

"I heard the elevator ding downstairs, so I knew the security team was on the way, and I played a delaying game, trying to keep the two occupied until the elevator arrived. Right before it did, they got the better of me and injected the whole syringe into my arm."

"So, you're high right now? Why didn't you say so? I'll be right over to take advantage of you. Er, I mean *take care of you*."

"Very funny. But I'm not high. I'd be unconscious if they hadn't given me the antidote to counteract it. I'm super tired, is all."

"So, my boyfriend is a hero but thinks he's an asshole. Are there no *sane* gay men left in the world?"

Again, the secret thrill raced through him, and his pulse accelerated. "I'm no hero."

"Okay, you're a humble asshole. Want some company?"

"I'm not good for much tonight."

"Have you eaten?"

"Not yet."

"Throw on some jeans, lover. I'm coming to get you."

"I don't know, David. I'm so—"

"I've got the perfect place and a couple of friends already on the way over there. Jeans and a comfy T-shirt. Don't worry about your blessed hair, Tom. I don't care, and where I'm taking you, no one else will either."

"Uh…"

"Relax. No one will see us. Well, people will, but they're all gay! Your secret will stay safe."

For a moment, Tom felt an intense guilt. David was too nice a man to have to skulk around because Tom was too scared—

"And quit thinking what you're thinking, Tom. I wasn't born out. It's a hard thing. I can't imagine coming out in a town that small where everyone knows you."

"I know, but—"

"I don't hear it."

"Uh…hear what?"

"The sound of you putting on your jeans."

Tom laughed—he couldn't help it. "You're too good for me, David."

"Says the hero. I mean, the asshole hero. The asshero."

Over the phone line, Tom heard the jingle of car keys and the rattle of a garage door opener.

"Gotta hang up now so I can drive the car, but mind what I said. T-shirt. Jeans. Food. Safe secrets."

Tom laughed again, but David was already gone.

He felt better, but he always felt better after spending even a few minutes in the light of David's personality. He set the phone in its charging cradle and went to do as David said.

5

The Hot Spot, Campton, PA
May 15, 2004, 8:27 pm

"I don't know about this, David," said Tom.

"Oh, come on, Tom, we're not even in Millvale."

"It's only a half-hour's drive. There could be people—"

"Yeah, of course, there will be people. That's entirely the point," said David with a silly grin and a roll of his eyes.

"But maybe they—"

"Tom, it's a *gay bar*. The people you see inside won't be homophobic like you think—"

"David, I grew up in Millvale. I know how people there feel about…" He drifted to silence as two men came around from the parking lot on the side. It was dark, and they were in shadow, but there was something about each of them that made them familiar. The shorter of the two wore round John Lennon-style glasses, and the lens blinked the streetlights back at Tom as the man looked their way. The taller of the two walked with a gait that Tom recognized.

"Oh, there they are," said David. "Come on, lover. Let me introduce you to two friends of mine…both of whom you *already* know."

"David—" Tom began, but it was too late. David was already out of the car and walking toward the two men, one hand up and waving.

"Glad you could make it," David said. "I'm not sure I can get him out of the car by myself."

The shorter man chuckled, and it was a warm sound. He stepped out of the shadows and looked at Tom. He wore a horrible Hawaiian shirt and a pair of khakis over leather sandals. He swiped a two-fingered Cub-scout salute at Tom and grinned.

Tom ducked his gaze to his lap and swallowed.

David and the two men crunched through the gravel lot and came to Tom's side of the car.

"Hello, Tom," said the man.

"Hello, Dr. Sorenson. I didn't mean to… The light was…" He kept his gaze down and shrugged.

Mike Sorenson chuckled. "It's okay, Tom. I believe you know my husband."

"Uh…"

"Christ on a stick, Madsen. Loosen up before you spring a leak."

The voice was a rich baritone, and one Tom recognized instantly. He snapped his head up. "*Coach Vanderhild?*"

John Vanderhild laughed. "If you're going to faint, Tom, stay right in that car. I don't want to put my back out trying to lift you."

Tom's gaze snapped to David then to Sorenson and finally back to Vanderhild. "What are you… I'm…"

Mike chuckled again, but it was a compassionate sound. "You never guessed he was gay?"

Tom shook his head, not trusting himself to speak.

"See, lover? You're not the island of homosexuality you thought you were," said David. He laid his hand on Tom's shoulder. "Come on. Let's go inside and get some food."

Tom nodded, and when David opened the door, he slid out. He kept stealing surreptitious glances at Coach Vanderhild.

"Relax, Tom," said John, "before you give yourself a stroke."

Tom ducked his head again, blushing furiously.

"Now, don't go back to that," said Mike.

"I'd ask what you've been doing with yourself since high school, but what with Mike's updates from Briar Ridge and those muscles, I fear I already know."

"Coach, I—"

"I haven't been your coach for a couple of years, Tom. I'm John."

Tom swallowed with an audible click and nodded. "You knew?" he whispered at David. "Of course, you did…duh."

"Yes, David knew," said John. "*We* did, too."

"Oh…" Tom slouched his shoulders and looked down at the gravel.

John put a big paw on his shoulder. "Tom," he said in a soft voice as unlike any that he'd used during wrestling practice as he could get, "it's who you are. There's nothing to be ashamed of."

Tom shook his head, guilty—*shameful*—tears flooding his eyes. "Coach…I mean, John. You know Millvale. You know how they think." He gulped a breath.

John shrugged. "Yes, I know how your mother's friends think. But times are changing, Tom. Attitudes like theirs are becoming rare, rather than the norm."

"If you say so," murmured Tom.

John smiled. "I do, Tom."

"Even in Millvale?"

"Even in Millvale," the coach said with a nod.

"Tom's a work in progress," said David, "but I love him, so I put up with his backward thinking." He winked at Tom and smiled. "Now, *let's get inside before David dies of starvation.*"

Laughing, the four men went inside.

6

BRSMH, Four South, Millvale, PA
May 17, 2004, 2:43 pm

"Feeling okay today, Tom?" Margie asked as he let the report room door swing closed on its automatic hinges. She sat at the head of the table—the spot reserved for the charge nurse—the digital recorder holding the day shift's report at her elbow.

"One hundred percent."

"'Hunnert percent' as my daddy used to say," she said with a distinct twang to her voice.

"Going home that night and having yesterday off to chill took care of any lingering effects." Tom smiled, chose a chair, and slipped into it. "Was it quiet yesterday?"

"Not so's you'd notice," she said.

"You could have called me in."

"Nah. The Amhain brothers are a known quantity, and we handled them. Besides, they were asleep most of the shift." She flashed a grin. "That lorazepam's a bitch, as you now well know. Anderson was readmitted down on the medical floor yesterday—if you can believe this happy horseshit, he managed to miss everything important. We ended up overstaffed the past two days. Still, there was something in the air, and it amped all these sickos to the teeth."

"And then there was Vee," said Tom with a grin.

"Yup. And then there was Virginia." Margie shrugged. "We handled it all without your biceps."

Tom flexed one arm. "It would have been easier with them."

"Maybe, but it's good to get you out of here on the odd night. A boy your age needs a girlfriend, and God knows you ain't finding one in here."

"Yeah, that's just what I need." Tom grinned. "Did you find whatever Kaspar used to cut himself?"

"Nope, and we turned this place upside down. We even cleaned the station."

"Heaven *forbid*!"

"I know. It was horrid. Virginia bitched the whole time—when she wasn't using her shit-stirring-stick, that is."

"I'll bet." Tom fiddled with his pen. "What about the flooding? The bed?"

"What about them?"

"How'd they happen?"

"Nothing there, either. I suppose he could have slipped out of the restraints, flipped the bed, and then climbed back in. And maybe the toilet overflowed on its own."

"That seems…"

"Un-fucking-likely, as my daddy was wont to say. I know, but like I said the other day, it *has* happened."

"Yeah."

She shrugged and slung a smile his way. "Best answers I got for you, buddy. If you can think of some other explanations, you let me know."

7

BRSMH, Four South, Millvale, PA
May 18, 2004, 5:39 pm

Tom sat in the dayroom, lounging in one of the comfortable chairs toward the back, keeping his eye on Ismael and Ezekiel, who'd been making him nervous all afternoon…being polite, helpful, and even friendly. Coming from them, the behavior was as strange as if they'd broken into song and performed *South Pacific* all the way through.

To add to his unease, Virginia had already used her 'shit-stirring-stick,' as Margie called it, three times in as many hours and seemed intent on more. They were all minor incidents, and of course, she danced off to la-la land after getting each one started. But that was Vee, that was how she operated. Everyone agreed that she was about as suitable for psychiatric nursing as Charlie Manson, so, of course, the administration placed her on the most dangerous unit the hospital had. Even the staff members that liked her agreed it was a bad, bad choice.

The Amhain brothers had a thing for the original Star Trek, with Ezekiel having the worst of it between the two. He spent the hour watching the screen intently, waiting for "Uncle Spock" to make an appearance. When he did, Ezekiel would engage in a one-sided conversation with Leonard Nimoy's character. Ismael didn't talk to the television, but he watched the entire episode wide-eyed and on the edge of his seat.

Every time.

But to each his own, thought Tom. *Who are they hurting? No one, that's who.*

As Kerry announced that the dinner trays had arrived early, Virginia banged out the door from the nurses' station. She steamed to the front of the dayroom, one hand already on her hip. "Come on, Ezekiel, Ismael. You heard Miss Kerry, and you know the rule. Television off for dinner." When neither

Amhain so much as looked at her, she sucked her teeth and strode to the front of the room and crossed to where the television hung. Without a word, she reached up and unplugged it. "Ignore me, will you?" she asked with her back still to the boys, acid in her tone. "Well, let's see how you like the price."

Tom climbed out of the chair in a hurry, lips twisted with disgust. *Couldn't you have picked someone else to start shit with, Vee?* His gaze bouncing back and forth between the two brothers, trying to figure out who was going to flip out. His money was on Ismael, but he never spoke to Mr. Spock…

Vee turned slowly, a self-satisfied smirk on her face.

Ezekiel screamed and kicked the chair in front of him, sending it crashing into the wall, but Ismael only glared at her and shook his finger—the perfect imitation of a psychotic daddy scolding an errant child. Tom took three quick steps and dropped one hand on Ezzy's shoulder from behind but just held him. "Cool out, Ezekiel, and maybe we can get it back on," he whispered. Vee lifted her arm, and Tom thought, *Don't you do it, Vee!*

But she did. She *always* did.

She took a step toward Ismael and pointed at him with her fat, pudgy finger. "*Don't you shake your finger at me, Ismael Amhain*! I'm not the patient here! You're not the one in authority!" Her voice had risen into the shrewish registers that Tom had come to associate with patients acting out. "I think you've forgotten how things work around here, so let me refresh your memories! *I'm* in charge. *I* say what goes on. Not you, Ezekiel Amhain! Not you, Ismael Amhain!"

Ismael stood still, a loose grin on his face as she stepped closer and closer, invading his personal space, putting her finger right in his face. "You've been naughty, Ms. Virginia," he said in a quiet voice.

"Spare the rod, spoil the child," shouted Ezekiel, twisting and swiping at Tom's hand, trying to break his hold on him.

"Settle down, Ezekiel, and I'll see if we can bend the rules this once. Maybe you and Ismael can eat later," Tom said in a voice only Ezekiel could hear.

"*Spare the rod, Izzy!*" Ezzy screamed.

Tom sighed and shot Virginia a glare which she either did not see or chose to ignore. He dropped his hand from Ezekiel's shoulder and snapped it around his bicep, grabbing the thin man's wrist with his other hand. Ezekiel looked down at his hand and tried to jerk it away, then glared at Tom when he couldn't. "Let me go," Ezekiel said in a reasonable tone, glancing at Ismael. "My brother needs me."

"No, Ezzy, just calm down. Keep your cool so I can get the show back on for you."

Virginia glanced at Tom and Ezekiel, her face wrinkled with anger. She snapped her finger at Ezekiel, and when she did, he lurched and jerked his arm, but Tom held him. Vee snapped her gaze back to Ismael, and again, her finger flew to his face. "And you, Ismael, you sit down, *right now*, and maybe you can avoid a trip to the seclusion room."

Wrong thing to say, Tom thought with a sinking feeling in his guts.

Ezekiel jerked and pulled his arm in various directions, throwing his bodyweight against Tom, then pulling away. His face had gone brick red, and spittle flew with each jerk, each pull. He shouted his mantra at the top of his voice. "*Spare the rod, Izzy! Spare the ever-fucking rod!*"

"Ezekiel, you *shut up!*" Virginia snapped.

Instead of shutting him up, Vee's comments only added rage to his wiry strength. Pulling away and throwing his bodyweight against Tom's grip at an unexpected moment, Ezekiel drove Tom into the chairs lined up in front of the television, scattering them.

As Virginia's tirade picked up steam, Ismael stood there and took it, that small, loose smile playing on his lips. His mouth moved occasionally as though he were speaking along with her, under her, like an insane chorus. She didn't notice, or if she did, she didn't care.

"Hit the Button, Vee!" Tom panted, trying to shove Ezekiel into one of the chairs without giving up his grip on the man's right arm.

"You Amhain boys are a treat! You think you can get away with this? You think you act however you want and there will be *no repercussions*? You're wrong, Ismael Amhain." Virginia's face bloomed red, and spittle flew from her lips. "Do I need to call your father?"

As if he'd been awaiting those very words, Ismael laughed and snapped his fingers in her face. "*Naughty! Naughty! Naughty!*" he screeched, and as he did, he slipped his arms around her waist as though starting a slow dance.

Vee's eyes widened as he slid his hands together in the small of her back and jerked her close, belly to belly, chest to chest. She glanced at Tom, fear in her eyes, terror squirming in her facial muscles. "Help me, Tom!" she said in a voice like that of a small child.

"*Spare that Christing rod!*" screamed Ezekiel, sawing his arm back and forth but otherwise ignoring Tom completely. "*Spare the ever-fucking rod, Izzy! Just like Daddy! Just like Daddy-God! Just like Daddy-God does to Mommy-frog!*"

Tom had a choice—continue to control Ezekiel, to keep him at bay, and watch Ismael do whatever he was about to do to Virginia or let go and sprint to her aid. But if he let go, he'd have both Ezekiel and Ismael to contend with, and Vee would fuck right off and leave him the second she was free. His eyes tracked across the room to the Button in its stainless-steel surround. That was the third option—the *viable* one. *If* he could get to it with Ezekiel fighting him every step. *If* Ezekiel and Ismael didn't realize what he was doing and move to stop him. *For fuck's sake, Vee... Why do you always do this?*

"Tom!" she shrieked as Ismael licked her face.

"Naughty, naughty, naughty," Ismael blurted. "Time to pay!"

"*Time to pay! Time to pay! Uncle Spock says it's time to pay!*" Ezekiel jerked his arm with maniacal energy, hopping up and down with each pull. Tom wedged Ezzy's arm into a chicken wing behind his back, then frog-marched him across the floor, tugging and pulling him every time Ezekiel flung himself in any direction other than toward the Button.

Ismael arched his back, rocking back on his heels, trying to lift Virginia off her feet, but he miscalculated her weight and didn't have enough momentum to pull off the belly-to-belly souffle. "Help me, Ezekiel! She's a fat cow!"

"Let me go, Tom! Let me go! Let! Me! Go!" Ezekiel stopped flinging himself away and stood up straight, stepping close and putting his face close to Tom's. "You let me go, or you'll get it, too," he said in a calm, low voice. "Do you want the rod, Tommy-ba-bommy?"

"You let him go, Tommy!" shouted Izzy.

"Better let me go," said Ezzy in an almost friendly tone.

Tom ignored them both, keeping his feet moving.

Ezekiel's gaze darted around and settled on the Button, and when it did, he went wild. Holding his arm was like holding the tail of a pissed off bronco. His eyes burned with rage, with indignation, with wild-eyed psychosis, but Tom kept fighting toward the Button.

Ezekiel cocked his hand back as far as it would. "Oh! You've done it now, Tom! It's the rod for you. *The ROD!*" he screeched as he drove his bony fist into Tom's gut. At the same time, Ismael took a single step back with one leg and twisted his torso in a wrestling move Tom knew all too well. Virginia screeched and crashed to the ground with Ismael on top of her. Izzy let out a triumphant shout and straddled Vee's fat middle. "The rod!" He slapped her across the face. "The rod!" He slapped her on the other side of the face.

Tom set himself and whipped Ezekiel's arm, spinning him into the wall hard—on top of the Button. Ezekiel's air whuffed out, and Tom let him go, whirling around to help Vee.

As the klaxon began to scream and cry, he turned and dove across the room, executing an imperfect but effective cross-body block, ending up with Ismael beneath him, and Virginia free. She got up and ran, *of course*, not quite waving her arms above her head, but Tom thought the intent was there. He grabbed at Ismael, slinging his arms around the wiry man's waist and gut wrenching him in a tight circle, mashing him face-first into the old blue carpet. "Just relax, just relax," he panted. "It's over, now."

Ismael shuddered and twisted in his grasp, wriggling his torso like a snake. Tom didn't know if the guy had wrestled in high school but thought he should have—he had the instincts for it. "The rod for you,

Tommy-ba-bommy!" hissed Ismael. "Then we'll go get the cow."

"Just relax," Tom repeated and straightened his legs to put more of his weight on Ismael's back. "All over soon."

"*It will never be over!*" screeched Ezekiel a half-second before he slammed into Tom, blindsiding him and driving him off Ismael, sending him rolling across the carpet toward the corner under the television—leaving him no escape. Ezekiel screamed in his face, windmilling at Tom like a hyperactive Rock 'Em Sock 'Em Robot. His blows rained down almost without intent, unaimed, just wild swings—but wild swings with the power of madness behind them. Tom tried to rally, tried to cover up, tried to kick Ezekiel away, but in the frenzy of his rage, the man was relentless. Pushed away, Ezzy darted back from another angle. He slung his fists side-arm when Tom got his arms up to protect his head. And every time Tom tried to gather his legs beneath him, Ezekiel swarmed all over him, knees and fists flying, until Tom collapsed back to the carpet.

Tom lurched toward Ezekiel on his knees, his arms held out wide for a bear hug. Ezekiel danced back, still throwing kicks and knees and fists, though most strikes whiffed through empty air. Tom rocketed forward, going for a double-leg takedown. He almost had it, too—would have, if not for Ismael.

His breath poured out of him as he hit the thin carpet on his side. His head slammed into the hard floor, and his vision went dark for a moment. When it cleared, both Amhain brothers stood over him, raining kicks onto his torso. Tom tucked into a ball and rolled to his side, but the blows followed him.

He got his legs under him and lunged away, lunged between them, heading for the door to the nurses' station. He even grasped the knob—the *locked* doorknob—a few seconds before Ismael piled into him from behind, ramming him into the door and sending him headfirst into the wall beside the door. The rough wallpaper grated against his forehead.

Tom could hear nothing but his own heartbeat, rasping breaths, and a high-pitched hum. His vision had dimmed on impact with the wall, and he stumbled away stunned.

But neither Ismael or Ezekiel chased him, and Tom made it into the activity room. In the dayroom behind him, staff members held the two brothers pinned to the floor. He shook his head to clear the ringing, and Margie came bustling out of the station, two syringes in hand.

"No!" screamed Ezekiel. He began to thrash in the grip of Ricky and Lydia.

Ismael only grunted and writhed in Bryant's grip.

After sucking in a deep breath, Tom went back to help. Virginia didn't.

"Just take it easy for a while," said Margie as Tom got up for the tenth time and tried for the Dutch door leading out onto the unit proper.

"I'm fine. Really," said Tom, "I had much worse in wrestling practice."

"Yeah, yeah. Do as I say, kid, and you'll go far in this racket." She paused for a moment, then a grin spread over her face. "I almost forgot, and this is perfect. You can help *and* take it easy."

Tom arched his eyebrow at her.

"Kaspar Anderson's arm has healed enough to let him come back up here. Head down to Two West and bring him up. We'll have to do a transfer admission, but that's easy work."

"Okay," Tom said. His face settled into grim lines. "This mess didn't have to happen. Virginia—"

"Yes, I know. The foolish woman shouldn't still have her damn job, but she won't get the ax. Administration is too worried she'll sue."

Tom shrugged. "I don't want to get her in trouble; I want her to stop picking fights."

"And I want to be the Queen of Sheba…but it looks like we're both stuck right where we're at." She smiled to take the sting out of it, then pushed his arm gently.

"Go on. Two West. Get Anderson and do the readmit paperwork."

"Right." He grinned at Kerry, and she hit the buzzer for the door without returning his smile.

He rode the elevator to the second floor and stepped off into what might as well have been a different world. Where thick steel doors with electronic locks segregated the fourth floor in locked units, long bright halls stretched from one corner of the second floor to the other, each outside wall featuring floor to ceiling windows. It housed non-violent, minimal risk patients, including the med-psych unit where Kaspar and other patients with injuries or illnesses recuperated.

Tom walked the length of the building from the south corner to the west, where the Two West nurses' station was located. Along the way, he passed their version of a day room—a space filled with the waning light of dusk from the huge plate-glass windows along one wall, comfortable chairs, and a pool table.

A row of patients sat in wheelchairs facing the big wall of windows. He glanced at them as he passed, wondering if the hospital warehoused catatonic patients on Two West, and if so, if Lee Amorte was one of the old men staring blankly at the outside world.

He rolled his shoulders, working out the kinks from the confrontation with the Amhains, but other than a few bruises and the sore spot on his head, he felt fine; he really had had much worse on the mats.

He went right on thinking that until he reached Kaspar Anderson and saw the shadowy thing sitting on the man's shoulder.

Then he began to worry.

Chapter 14
Mayhem in
Manhattan

I

Gavin's phone rang, jarring him out of Margie's story abruptly. He glanced down at it and saw that it was past eleven and that the caller was Pete Fielding. "Sorry," he said. "I've got to take this."

"No problem. My throat's as dry as winter leaves. Want more coffee?"

"Sure," said Gavin, heading toward the door. "This should only take a minute or so."

She waved at the door as she got up and headed toward the kitchen.

Gavin swept away his lock screen. "Hey, Pete."

"Listen, don't panic."

"Um, you know telling someone that only makes them anxious, right?" He chuckled, but Pete didn't. "What's up? What happened?"

"I'm going to tell you, but I want you to stay on the phone, Gavin."

"You're scaring me, Pete."

"I know, and I'm sorry. Don't hang up. Before I start, I've already dispatched the jet to a little town near you. Camden, I think it is—"

"Campton," said Gavin. "Tell me what's going on."

"The two HRT members got to your house at ten to seven this morning and found everything quiet. They took a quick look around your yard and didn't see anything amiss."

"Pete, tell—"

"I *am*, Gavin," said Pete in a sympathetic tone that worried Gavin more than ever. "The house was quiet all morning, and they saw no movement from inside. The shades were all drawn, so—"

"Goddamn it, Pete! *Tell me!*"

"A half-hour ago, your maid showed up, and finding the garage door down—which she says is unusual—she rang the front bell. She waited a few minutes, then rang again. After a few more minutes, she got a key from her bag and let herself in. Less than a minute later, she came booking out the front door, and—"

"Maddie! Is she—"

"Gavin, I don't know. HRT entered the house and searched it. Maddie was not there, but her car, her purse, and her laptop were. There were signs of a struggle in the bedroom, but—listen to me now, Gavin—*there is no blood.* There are no signs that Maddie was injured."

"I'm on my way!"

"No, wait! There's more, Gavin. They found a note taped to the refrigerator. It says, 'Quit fucking around in Pennsylvania and get your ass back here. I'm not done with you yet. Test me, I'll cut her. Deny me, and you know—better than anyone—what I'll do.'"

"Christ, no," gasped Gavin, squinting against the sudden brightness of the morning sun, sucking in the suddenly rarified morning air at an increased rate.

"It's signed, Gavin."

"With the mark?"

"Yes."

Gavin closed his eyes, squeezed them shut, fighting to hold back his emotions, to think how he was trained to think. "Crime scene?"

"Our best team."

"I've got to go, Pete. I've got to get back to—"

"The jet is on its way, like I said. It touches down in twenty-five minutes."

"Okay. Okay, good."

"Any chance this is Maddie playing a joke?"

"No. Not her style."

"Yeah," said Pete with a sigh. "Get moving, Gavin. I'll send someone from Pittsburg to take the rest of the reports on the 2004 investigation."

"Right."

"And, Gavin, you know I have to do this—"

"Don't you fucking dare, Pete. I'm not sitting on the sidelines."

"Gav, you know you are too close to this. You can be there, but operational authority has to go to someone else."

"For Maddie. Not for The Smith—at least, not until we know *for sure* it's The Smith that took her."

"Gavin, I'm letting you stay in the loop—mostly because if Maddie was abducted by The Smith, it seems clear he wants you in the middle of everything."

"She."

"What?"

"She. The DNA is from a female, remember?"

"A trick, maybe. Females don't—"

"I know," said Gavin. He squeezed his eyes shut as another wave of panic washed over him. "I've got to get moving. Call me with updates."

"Right. Listen, Gavin, for now, you do what that lieutenant tells you. He's your operational control until I can get someone suitable as SAIC."

"Ask him not to arrest Dr. Esteves. Tell him Jim and I can do it in person. I want to talk to her before she goes into the system and lawyers up."

There was a long pause, then Pete said okay.

Gavin grunted and hit the disconnect. His thumb hovered over Maddie's contact, but before he could press it, Margie Samuels opened the front door.

"You get lost out here, FBI?"

"I've got to go," he said gruffly. "Sorry for the abruptness of it, but something's come up. Someone from the Pittsburg office will call to arrange a time to take the rest of your statement."

She nodded once. "Hey, are you okay?"

"No, not really, but there's nothing either of us can do about it. Thanks, Ms. Samuels." He turned without waiting for her response and jogged to the car. He slid in behind the wheel and put the airport into the navigation system, then cranked the engine. He glanced back, and Margie Samuels saluted him with her coffee cup.

He made it to the Campton Executive Airport as the jet was pulling up to the tiny building that served as the terminal and the tower. Gavin flashed his badge and was admitted to the apron by a bored-looking security guard. He pulled up next to the plane and jumped out, dragging his bags after him.

The jet's door popped open as the engines throttled down, and Gavin jumped aboard. He tossed his bag into the storage compartment, then went forward and stuck his head in the cockpit.

"Agent Gregory, we'll have you in Manhattan in a little over an hour."

"No," said Gavin. "We need to make a stop first. Lily's Glen, New York, or as close as you can get me. I need a car waiting for me there."

"That's not what—"

"Listen," said Gavin in an icy voice, "that's where I need to go. Are you taking me there, or do I have to drive?"

The pilot returned his gaze in silence for a moment, then nodded to the co-pilot. "Okay, Agent Gregory. Lily's Glen, it is."

Gavin nodded as the co-pilot got on the radio to change their flight plan, then turned and found a seat. After twelve seconds of staring at the bulkhead, he got up and fished out Angel Kirk's journal.

2

Poor Angel, reduced to writing poetry about how bad my life sucks. Poor, poor Angel, crying about not being able to sleep.

Yeah, yeah. Poor me, right?

I can hear your eyeballs spinning in their sockets, Debs. Trust me on that. Self-pity is for suckers, but…

I haven't slept in over a week. Not since the last…

Listen, I never—*never*—want to dream again. If you can hook me up with that, more power to you, but until you can, keep your scorn and derision to yourself.

What I dreamed about… Well, fuck. What I dreamed about would make most serial killers blush. Maybe throw up. Or masturbate.

Whatever.

My dreams are darkness personified, okay? They make me want to run a drill bit into my brain. They make me want to take a fistful of Dilaudid, wash it down with a fifth of Everclear, and wash *that* down with about a gallon of sulfuric acid.

That's why I can't sleep. Too fucking scared.

Yeah, pretty melodramatic, right?

I don't care. I wish I could do it. I wish I could do something—*anything*—to stop these fucking nightmares.

Have you ever had a serious injury? I mean, have you been in pain so bad you want to gouge out your own eyes?

This is worse.

This is worse.

This is worse, and I don't know if I can survive it.

I don't know if I want to.

"You never know a man until you've walked a mile in his shoes." What a bunch of bullshit. If you want to really know someone, share her nightmares. If you're brave enough for that, my dear Debs, let me know. Until then, stop calling *me* the coward as I lie awake all night.

If you're game, keep reading this journal.

See you in my nightmares.

3

Angel Kirk's Journal

Marked ~~October 15,~~ October 20, 2014, 3:14 am

~~Christ. I fucking falled asleep. FUCK~~

~~Exhaustion, I guess, or the motherfucker tormenting me~~
~~Christ, I'm still half-sleep. Wait a minute~~

Good.

God.

Almighty.

What a motherfucker of a dream. I'm still shaking, and it's making it hard to write. That and the disorientation…I had to scratch out what I tried to write above. I write in ink, so I'm fucked, and you get to see how badly it shook me up.

That's okay, I guess. As long as you don't think I'm faking it, Debs. You can pee what this has done to me, trying to stay up forever, fear of the nightmares, the

Sorry, I had to take a break. There are some things I can't come right out and write about. I don't want to anyway, but I couldn't if I did.

~~He It~~ *He* won't allow it.

Hell, I'm surprised he's allowing me to write in this journal at all. Maybe he wants the world to know about him. Maybe he considers me his prophet.

His herald.

Either one's good for a laugh.

Anyway, I promised you a dream, and since I just had one, I'll give it to you.

But remember what I said, and don't blame me if you can't sleep afterward.

I warned you, Debbie.

I did, right?

4

I did. Just reread this motherfucker and, Debs, this is bullshit. It isn't helping, but I'm compelled to write it. I think…

No. There is nothing inside me. Nothing making me do things. I'm in control.

I'm in control.

I'm in control!

I'll sell you my dream when I'm damn good and thready. If *I* decide flu.

Not him. Not you. Not the evil fairy.

Me.

I'm in control.

5

Fine. Fine. Fine. Finefinefinefine!

I'll tell you, okay, Debs? Will that make you fucking happy? Bitch.

I dreamed about being in some fucking alley in Manhattan. Not really in it, yet, but like at the mouth of it. I'm wearing warm-up pants and running shoes for some fucking reason, but I'm no longer breathing hard—as if I *run* in the fucking first place—because I've been standing there for too long. It's a dream, so I don't know how long I've been standing there, just staring into the black shadows at the back of the fucking pit.

Ally. *Alley.* The shadows at the back of the alley.

I'm waiting for something, but I don't sink I know what. In the dream, I mean. Awake, I definitely don't know what I'd be waiting for.

I ask myself what I'm waiting for, and as if in answer, something chirps at me from the darkness. It's more than a little freaky—

6

Gavin snapped the journal shut, heart thumping. *How can it be? How can Angel Kirk have written the beginning of my recurring nightmare in her stupid little diary?* He lifted a shaky hand to his eyes, and using his index finger and thumb, squeezed his temples.

It had to be some kind of trick. Some kind of…

Unless I'm losing my fucking mind!

He took a deep, calming breath and flipped the journal open again.

7

Angel Kirk's Journal
Marked October 20, 2014, 5:28 am, continued

It's more than a little freaky, that tiny birdlike noise, because it seems laced with menace—*filled* with it, Debs…filled with hate and threat and murder and fucking laughter.

Anyway. Right after that chirp, I smell it.

The alley breathes out, right into my face, and it stinks of garbage and human waste and blood and death and sex and fuck all. My nose fills with it, but instead of turning away, my nostrils widen, and I take a deep death…like I fucking like it, Debs.

There's…

Look, this is going to sound as fruity as a nut bat, but I'm going to put it down anyway.

In my screams, there's something behind my eyes. Inside my ears. Whatever he is, he couldn't give a fuck about what I want. What I like. Or Right and Wrong, for that matter.

He gives two fucks for that. He only wants gratification.

Why am I smiling?

Because, you stupid cunt, I *like* that you're confused. You're mine, and you'll jump through my hoops until I'm tired of you. Then… Then I'll leave you as empty as a pumpkin the day after Halloween. I'll leave you rotting, slowly caving in, filled with spent dreams.

Dead for all intents and purposes. *Used up and fucked over.*

I look down, Debs, after sucking in that circus-graveyard smell, and I find out I've moved into the heart of the blackness deep in the alley. Like someone ran my body on remote control, I've walked half a block.

It's as dark as death down there in the middle of the stench. There's something at my feet. A lump.

A lump with blonde hair.

I don't want to look, but I do. My face falls forward, and despite the darkness, I can see perfectly. My face twists with a smile.

The lump is a woman. A dead woman.

She has…

Jesus, Debs.

She has a hatchet buried in her chest, and I have…

Jesus fucking Christ, Debbie!

I have her amputated *breast* in my hand.

That's when I realize I have something in my mouth—parts of *her*—and I wake up screaming.

8

Gavin lifted his eyes from the words scrawled across the page. Her handwriting had been so crisp and neat in the beginning, but that last entry…it was almost as if someone else had written it. His pulse pounded in his temples, and he covered his eyes with his free hand.

If this isn't fake… But, come on, Gavin! It has *to be a fake. Otherwise, whoever wrote that last entry has been inside my head…has watched my dreams unfold. In other words,* me. He shook his head. *What the fuck's wrong with me? Did I write that last entry? And what the hell is that part in the middle? Who wrote that shit?*

He flipped forward a few pages, not reading but looking at the handwriting. Though not as crisp as it had been in the beginning, it was still recognizable as the same handwriting. He flipped back to the last entry and examined the part before the strange break in the monologue—it, too, was recognizable, as the part afterward. Just the center section—the section that read like an argument between two distinct people.

Two distinct personalities? he wondered. *One psychotic, one slowly going insane?*

He flipped the journal open again and turned to the next page.

9

Angel Kirk's Journal
Marked October 21, 2014, 6:47 pm

I think I need to see someone, Debs. A shrink. Someone like you, but *not you*. You're my friend, and I want to keep it that way.

I just can't shake it. That last dream, the one I wrote about. I can't get past the feeling that it was more than a dream, that it…

That it was a memory.

But that's bullshit, right? If it were a memory, I'd be able to remember it while I was awake. Right? I don't mean the memory of the dream, but the memory of being in the alley, of standing over her…

Then there's the thing I'm scared to write, scared to make real. But God hates a coward, right?

Here goes.

I don't remember what happened last week. The last thing I remember is arriving in San Diego. Well, you know. I remember the past few days, but what I mean is the week between San Diego and here. Between the 14th and today is gone.

That's not all.

I don't know where "here" is. Not really. I'm staying in a cheap ass hotel with no paper, no stationery.

I think I'm in Michigan. There's snow on the ground outside, but it's not like you can walk up to a stranger in a hotel lobby and say, "Pardon me, but can you tell me what fucking state I'm in?"

If I'm in Michigan, it means I blacked out the entire Northern California trip…which apparently only lasted around four or five days.

That scares me a bit. Not as much as the nightmares, but still.

I mean, what did I do in Sacramento? Who did I talk to? Did I finish looking into *El Cuco*? What about God's Hammer? Did I learn anything about him?

It'll get better. I'll stop by a library and check the local paper.

If this is Detroit, then I'm here to check out the twenty-three Mechanic murders.

I wonder how long I've been here. Did I come here from SoCal for some reason, skipping Sacramento? What would have made me do that?

Still haven't slept since that last one.

10

Angel Kirk's Journal
Marked October 26, 2014, 4:29 am

im so fucking depressed
haven't gone outside since i checked in
no sleep either
not really eating
television on blathering idiots and stupid infomercials
fucking room stinks
oh wait thats me
ha
fuck this

11

Well, thank God that's over.

Christ, I've never been so depressed in my life, Debbie. I've always thought depression was feeling sad about something that you couldn't change or whatever. I apologize to every person suffering from clinical depression everywhere in the world.

I didn't know what it was really like. That's my only excuse.

There were times there when I thought I'd die—not that I'd kill myself, just that I'd die in this room. Starve to death or just quit breathing because of the weight of it.

Like I said, thank God it's over.

I drifted off at about midnight, I think. I think the blathering idiots on CNN helped. They bored me right to sleep. Ha ha.

For once, Debs, I didn't dream at all. Hopefully, that pill continue.

Anyway, I'm packed, and I'm getting the chuck out of Dodge before something else happens.

I thought about going home, but I've got more work to do, and they say Pennsylvania is nice this time of year (that's a lie).

I feel soooo much better since I slept, Debs. I need to find some way of keeping the streak alive. Maybe I'll hit up another Doc-in-the-Box on the way to the airport.

Maybe this time I won't take no for an answer.

My flight's in four hours, so I better tut this away and get to the Doc-in-the-Box if I want any help keeping the sleep-streak going.

12

Angel Kirk's Journal
Marked November 7, 2014, 7:46 am

I'm home. That's the good tart.

The sad part is I don't remember anything from the last time I wrote in this journal until this morning. Did I make it to the shitburg in Pennsylvania? Millvale? If I did, what did I sew there?

What's happening to me? I think I slept last night, but I... Well, I just don't know.

How's that possible? I mean, I would've had to fake up if I did, so why can't I remember that? Instead, I remember "catching up" with myself at the kitchen table, a mug of hot, fresh coffee in my paw. I was just staring at the refrigerator door. Not even drinking the fucking coffee. Just staring like a zombie...

My bags are in the bedroom, half-unpacked. I must have showered—the wet towel was on the bedroom floor—and I'm wearing clean clothes.

Jesus. What the fuck is going on here? You can't just forget eleven days, right?

What have I been doing?

And that quack in Texas said he couldn't give me Ambien because it could take me confused...

Shit.

The only good thing is that I don't remember any other nightmares.

13

Angel Kirk's Journal
Marked November 11, 2014, 5:08 pm

Whatever happened to me in Northern California, Michigan, and Pennsylvania, happened again here at home. I remember writing the previous entry and then finishing my coffee. Then I put the tug in the sink.

But now, good old Google says it's the eleventh of November. So, fuck you, past four days.

I just caught up again, standing over the sink, but instead of a single rug, there are dirty plates, silverware, glasses, and a few containers for leftovers.

Evidently, when my mind takes a powder, I don't do dishes.

I'm more than a little freaked out. Those four and a half days are just...*gone*. It's like I didn't live the time in between the memory of catching up the other day and now. Like I just skipped those days.

I don't know if I'm having nightmares—or even sleeping. I checked my laptop, and the work is progressing, even if I don't remember the notes I've collected on the damn thing.

Google says this phenomenon is called "losing time," or, more correctly, "dissociative identity disorder." Or PTSD. Or maybe depression. Or being drunk.

Some help you are, Google.

I wonder if this happened before the drip and I just never realized it.

Oh well. Enough of the witching.

Reading through my notes on the laptop, it seems clear I've finished the research I needed to do before I go back to see Joe.

Maybe one of the doctors at the hospital can check me out while I'm there (ha ha).

14

Gavin slid the journal back into his bag as the jet rolled up to the terminal. He unclipped his seat belt and stretched while the staff opened the door. He arched his eyebrows at Jim Denders, who stood leaning against the nose of his unmarked cruiser, arms folded over his barrel chest.

"What are you doing here?" asked Gavin after climbing off the plane.

"I was checking into our fine doctor, who seems to be able to elude the crack officers of Lily's Glen Police Department at will." His cheek twitched. "Haymond called. Told me about your wife." He frowned. "I'm sorry. Are you sure you want to be here?"

They stood looking at one another for a moment.

"I guess you've got your reasons for the pit stop."

Gavin nodded. "I need to have a conversation with Esteves." The growl in his voice surprised him, and to cover that surprise up, he dug in his bag and pulled out Angel Kirk's journal. "It might be better if I talk to her alone." He held out the journal. "You could use the time to read—"

Denders squinted at him. "I could," he said evenly. "Or I could stand with you and keep you from doing anything...uh...uncalled for."

Gavin cocked his head. "Uncalled for?"

Jim shrugged his massive shoulders. "Your wife's gone missing. A thing like that...well, let's just say that sometimes extraordinary efforts are called for, but there's still a line." He tilted his head to the side, face a careful blank. "Esteves is at Kingdom Cross."

"Right." Gavin walked toward the driver's side. "You read; I'll drive."

15

Kingdom Cross Psychiatric Hospital, Lily's Glen, NY
Friday, 12:35 pm

Gavin and Jim stood near the reception desk, both standing with their legs apart and arms crossed over their chests, staring at the door that opened on the hallway leading back to Debbie's office. She came bustling out, a smile on her lips, but that smile died after one glance at them. "What's wrong?" she asked.

"We need to talk to you," said Gavin. "*I* need to talk to you."

Debbie swept her hand back toward the hallway door. "Of course," she said, but her brows bunched in confusion. "What's happened?"

"A lot," said Jim. "But you already know that, right? This conversation would be better in private."

"Of course," she repeated and swept her hand at the doorway again. "Come on." She led them back to her office, opening her mouth several times but closing it each time without speaking. She kept darting glances at Gavin every time she repeated the routine.

In her office, she finally broke her silence, "Coffee?" she asked.

"Let's get down to it," said Gavin in a gruff voice. "Where were you last night?"

"At home. I—"

"All night?" asked Denders.

"Yes. All night."

"Bullshit," said Denders.

Debbie cocked her head to the side. "I'm not sure I like your tone, Detective Denders. I *was* home all night."

"Then your twin sister went shopping at 5:27 this morning. I saw the video myself, so let's skip that part where you say it was a mistaken identity."

Her gaze bounced back and forth between the two men, then Debbie shook her head. "Listen, guys. I run in the morning before work. I sometimes stop at that little grocery to buy stuff for breakfast." She shrugged. "It's convenient."

Gavin and Jim exchanged a glance.

"But that's not all of it. Right? Something else happened?"

"Where did you go after the store?" asked Gavin in a hard voice, but the muscles in his back had already started to relax.

"Back home for breakfast," she said with another shrug.

"Listen, Esteves," said Jim with an air of menace. "Time to come clean. Who's your partner? Who did you send to Virginia?"

"Virginia?" Her gaze zeroed in on Gavin's face, studying it, bouncing from his eyes to the lines around his mouth. "Your wife?" she asked.

Jaw clenched, Gavin nodded.

"Is she…"

"Was the note your idea?" demanded Jim. "Where is she?"

"I have no idea what you're talking about, Detective Denders," she said without taking her eyes off Gavin. "I had nothing to do with this."

"And this?" Jim slapped Angel Kirk's journal down on her desk. "Did you write this yourself?"

She leaned forward in her chair, her gaze never leaving Gavin's. "I'm sorry," she said to him. "You said there was a note? What did it say? He's never left a note with a…"

"She's not dead," said Gavin. "Kidnapped."

"What did the note say?"

"Why ask us? Don't you remember what you told your accomplice to write?" demanded Jim.

"Detective, I'm not involved in this. I'm not the person killing women in Manhattan, either." She tapped the journal with her index finger. "But I know who is. Glacadairanam is the one you want. Can't you see him in all this mess from Angel? He's riding her, just like he rode Joe…" Her voice cracked with emotion, but her gaze remained steady. "What did the note say? It's important."

"You knew it was this Kirk the whole time, didn't you?" Jim demanded. "You'd better start—"

"Quit fucking around in Pennsylvania and get your ass back here. I'm not done with you yet. Test me, I'll cut her. Deny me, and you know—better than anyone—what I'll do," Gavin said in a dead voice.

Esteves slumped back in her chair and covered her eyes. "Oh, my," she murmured. "After what Joe said… I… I was afraid of something like this."

"Start making sense, Doctor," growled Jim. "Start telling us what's really going on here, or I'm arresting you. Right here, right now."

Debbie dropped her hand away from her eyes. "Joe said *he* was after Gavin. That he'd already started on him. That's why I…" She shook her head.

"That's why you gave me the script for thioxanthaxol—which isn't indicated for insomnia."

She shook her head. "No. It's an antipsychotic."

"I know. I looked it up. You tried to dose me."

"I did it because it will *protect* you, Agent Gregory."

"Protect me? How? From who?"

"*Glacadairanam!* Antipsychotic meds are what drove the thing away from Joe. What we used to shield…" She slumped and buried her face in her palms. "I… Angel…" Silence spread between them for a few moments.

Gavin shook his head, then said, "I went to Millvale."

"You…" Debbie lifted her head and rubbed away her tears with her palms. "Millvale, Pennsylvania?"

"Yes. There's a steelworks there, the Jackson-Barney Steelworks. Kids in the area call it 'the Jacks.'"

"Oh?" asked Debbie.

"And a mental hospital. Briar Ridge State Mental Hospital. Two other patients, one doctor, two nurses, and a psychiatric technician disappeared from there in 2004—from the place where Lee Amorte was being cared for. This Briar Ridge… Oh, and the tech's boyfriend and his mother."

"Disappeared? How?"

Jim frowned at him.

"I don't know yet. I was supposed to pick up the files later, but now someone from Pittsburg will have to drive up and get them. And a nurse was murdered on the grounds at around the same time."

"Why are you telling me this, Agent Gregory?" asked Esteves.

"Joe knows those things."

"He was rambling. Under the—"

"No," said Gavin, shaking his head. "He knows what happened in Millvale."

"Maybe," she said with a shrug. "But he can't get to that knowledge."

"Maybe he can," said Gavin. "I got the beginning of the story from one of the psychiatric nurses there. I can feed him details to spark his memory."

Debbie pursed her lips, and a line appeared between her brows.

"You want us to take the existence of this Glacadairanam on faith, Doctor. *Your* faith. But how can we do that? You're our best *suspect*."

"And you're playing these games with what you know. Making us jump through hoops..." said Jim. "Time for that to end. Either cooperate with what *we* need to do, Doctor, or we can take a car ride back to Manhattan, and you can sit in a cell."

She darted her gaze back and forth between them for a full minute. "We'll have to give him another dose of amobarbital."

Gavin nodded.

Esteves shrugged. "I'll call up and set it up."

16

Kingdom Cross Psychiatric Hospital, Lily's Glen, NY
Friday, 12:48 pm

Joe got up when they filed through the door into the treatment room, his gaze locked on Gavin's. He approached slowly, holding out one hand as though Gavin were a skittish animal. "I'm so sorry," he said.

"For what, Joe?" asked Gavin.

"He's got her. Your Maddie." He wore such a pitiful, mournful expression he looked as if he might burst into tears at any moment.

"What do you know about that?" asked Jim.

Joe glanced at him and shrugged. "Know about what?" He turned back to Gavin and broke into a sunny smile. "Gavin! When did you get sheer?"

Gavin clamped down on the hundred questions he wanted to ask, clamped down the urge to grab Joe by the shoulders and shake and pummel him until he told Gavin everything he wanted to know. Through gritted teeth, he said, "A few minutes ago, Joe."

"Oh…" Joe looked at him askance, then glanced at Dr. Esteves. "Do I have to?"

Debbie nodded. "I think you do, Joe. These men need our help. Remember talking to them yesterday?"

"That's not might, Debbie," he said shaking a finger at her. "It was in the middle of the night."

"Yes, sorry. I misspoke." She waved him to the chair. "Come sit down, Joe. I'm going to give you a shot, and then Gavin will begin a story. All you have to do is continue the story if you can."

"Okay," he said with a shrug. "I bike stories. But do the thing."

Debbie nodded. "Do you remember First Order Predicate Calculus, Joe?"

"Sure. Socrates was mortal, blah, blah, blah." He relaxed and held out his arm. "Make sure I forget, Debs."

"I will," she said as she slid the needle into his vein.

Jim and Gavin took their seats. Gavin waited until Debbie nodded at him, then said, "Joe, I went to Millvale yesterday. I spoke with a retired nurse named Margie Samuels."

Joe's face lit up. "Lower than a snake's belly in a wagon rut! Busier than a one-legged man in an ass-kickin' contest. Dirtier than a…"

"You know Margie?" asked Gavin.

"I…" Joe frowned and looked down at the syringe in Debbie's hand. "She used to give shots."

"That's right, Joe," said Gavin. "She told me a story about a guy named Jasper Anderson—"

"Kaspar," mumbled Joe. "Kaspar Anderson and the Sliver Sulfur."

"Yeah, I guess you're right."

"And the Amhain brothers. Izzy. Ezzy."

Gavin glanced at Debbie and she nodded. "Yes."

"Fruity nutcakes." Joe's eyes slid shut, though he didn't drop his head. "Daddy-god. Mommy-frog."

"Do you remember what happened?"

"Yes."

"Do you remember what happened when a psychiatric technician named Tom Madsen got in a fight with the Amhain brothers?"

"Ha. Which time?"

"Star Trek, Joe. Do you know what I mean?"

"Sure. Star Trek. Uncle Spock. Nurse Vee."

"Tell us," said Gavin. "Tell us what you remember, Joe."

Chapter 15
Abnormal
Psychology

I

Julie Ryder walked down the hall toward the Two West nurses' station, her bag looped over her forearm. She'd taken her dinner outside, in the little green area at the bottom of the stairs on the south side of the hospital. Her thoughts were of the upcoming weekend, and the complete impossibility of her getting laid.

Tom Madsen, the tech from Four South, stood near the wide archway leading to the day room, mouth hanging open as if he'd never seen a mental patient before. A tickle formed in her belly as she took in Tom's broad shoulders, his muscular build, his tight ass. *Do I dare?* After a moment or two of staring, she thought, *I definitely do.*

With a small, quivering grin, she walked up to stand beside him. "They're an ugly lot," she said, "but they smell really bad, so that makes it okay."

Tom didn't say a word, didn't react in any way.

"Well, maybe it's not the smell so much as the drool from the catatonic ones." She quirked her lips into a smile and turned to face him, head hanging at the perfect angle.

But again, Tom took no notice.

"Tom?" she asked. She followed his gaze—he seemed focused on the Four South patient, Kaspar Anderson. Her face drew down into a concerned frown. "Tom? Are you all right?"

Nothing.

She lay her small, pale hand on his thickly muscled forearm, and he started, taking a step away and snatching his arm away from her as though she were on fire. He looked down at her, his lids blinking as fast as the shutter of a movie camera. "I asked if you were okay," she said softly, pulling her hand back. "Sorry I startled you."

He shook his head, and his easy grin came out to play. "No, I'm sorry." He glanced back at Kaspar—just a quick peek, but one that seemed fear-laden and dark. "Sorry," he repeated. "I just got my bell rung upstairs. Guess I'm still a little out of it."

Julie pursed her lips. "You should get that checked out, Tom. A head injury is nothing to mess around with, nothing to hope will go away."

"I will," he said with that beautiful smile on his lips. "I promise."

She looked up into his face. *A girl could get lost in there*, she thought. Her gaze drifted down to his chest and then farther south. *A lucky girl could get lost in all of that.* He smiled at her as though he knew exactly what she was thinking, and she felt a blush creeping up her neck. *I should ask him out. We're adults, now. This isn't high school. Just say, 'Hey, sexy. Your place or mine?' What's the worst that could happen?* But she said

470   ERIK HENRY VICK

nothing, dropping her face to look at the floor as the blush burned on her cheeks. "Make sure you do, Tom. It could be…" She groped for a way to finish the sentence that wouldn't make her seem more of an idiot. "Dangerous."

"I will, Julie. Thanks."

She glanced up at him, sure he'd be grinning down at her, hoping he'd be checking her out, but he wasn't. He was staring at Kaspar Anderson again. "He's all set on our end. You need to sign him out, but otherwise, Kaspar's ready to travel."

"Good deal," said Tom. She turned to step around him, but Tom put out his thick arm, laying his hand on her forearm. "And I mean it, Julie. Thanks."

She grinned at him, wondering if magic words existed that would turn her dry, lonely weekend into one of debauchery.

If there were, she didn't know them.

2

BRSMH, Four South, Millvale, PA
May 18, 2004, 6:36 pm

Tom ushered Kaspar through the heavy steel door and back onto the unit. Anderson seemed happy to be back. He wore a gauze bandage on his forearm, but other than that, he showed no signs he'd almost killed himself. He was happy—buoyant, even—and the second he stepped through the door, a huge grin split his face. "Don't run off, Kaspar," Tom said. "We've got some paperwork to do."

He frowned at Tom and narrowed his eyes. "Paperwork?"

"Don't worry, buddy. I'll make it short and sweet." Tom rested his hand on Kaspar's shoulder, and for a moment, he was sure he felt something cold and scaly beneath his fingertips. Tom turned and grabbed the clipboard Margie had set out for him. *I really should tell Margie about this, but if I do, she'll make a big deal out of it. More forms—worker's comp bullshit—and probably a trip to We Care for head X-rays.* He saluted her with the clipboard through the reinforced glass windows and she smiled, returning the salute like a girl scout. "Come on, Kaspar, let's get this over with." He opened the door to the small interview room near the station and pointed to one of the comfortable chairs. "Take your pick."

Kaspar sat in the chair closest to the door, and after closing the door, Tom squeezed around him to sit in the other chair. He put the clipboard on his thigh and got out his pen. He wrote the preliminary information on the transfer form, and while he did, Kaspar whispered, "Scratch, scratch, scratch," over and over.

"How are you feeling?" Tom asked.

"Fine as a fiddle. Fit as rain." A momentary expression of confusion flashed across his face.

"Right. Can you tell me where we are?"

Kaspar rolled his eyes. "Come on, not that again."

Tom shrugged and smiled. "I have to ask."

Blowing out a deep breath, Kaspar rolled his eyes. "Yeah, okay. But you know as well as I do that I don't know where this ship is. I've been in the brig for the past couple of days—you know that better than anyone, you sent me there. No windows in there."

"Sure," said Tom in an easy tone. On the transfer form, he wrote: *Not oriented to place. Back to thinking BRSMH is a giant spaceship.* "And do you know the date?"

"The stardate? No, I told you. I was in the brig, where you just picked me up from. No computer there."

"How about the day of the week?"

"Oh, that's an easy one."

Tom nodded and waited while Kaspar's expression slid from confident to confused and then went blank.

"Uh, Tennisday? No, that's not it. Poohsday?"

"Good enough. Do you know who the president is, Kaspar?"

"President of where?" He arched his eyebrow and looked at Tom with a little suspicion. "That's a tricksy question."

"The president of the United States."

Anderson laughed. "Now I know you're just pulling my shoulder."

Smiling and nodding, Tom wrote: *Not oriented to date or day. Doesn't seem to recognize the United States as a real place.*

"Scratch, scratch, scratch," Kaspar murmured as Tom wrote his responses down. When Tom glanced at him, he snapped his mouth shut, then asked, "Okay? So, are we done?"

"Not quite yet, bud," said Tom. "Just a few more questions, though. I forgot my watch today. Any guess what time it is?"

Kaspar smiled but said nothing.

"I mean, I think it's after supper. Did you eat?"

"Come on, Tom. You know I did. Julie Ryder told you so, not ten minutes ago."

Tom chuckled. "Fair enough." On the clipboard, he wrote: *Appears oriented to time.* "How did you like it down there in the hotel?"

"Brig, Tom."

"Right, that's what I meant. I sometimes call it 'the hotel' to be funny."

"Oh, sure. I get it," said Kaspar, looking nothing but confused.

"Don't worry about it, buddy. Happy to be back on Four South?"

"Oh, you bet! The food's better here than down in the brig."

"Hey, do you remember the other day?"

For a moment, Kaspar's expression clouded with suspicion, but then he relaxed. "Which play was that, Tom-turkey?"

Tom grinned. "Yeah, you called me that the other day, too. I'm talking about the day you cut your arm."

"Oh, sure, I remember that. But I didn't but my arm. *He did it*," he crowed.

"You said 'he did it' a lot yesterday. Who did you mean?"

Kaspar chuckled and waved his index finger at Tom. "You know I can't sell you that."

"How did you do it all? You've got us stumped." Tom flashed him an easy, conspiratorial grin.

"Do what?" Kaspar cocked his head to the side, but then he turned his face and peeked over his shoulder.

"You know. You flipped your bed, flooded your room, and cut your arm."

"Nah. I wouldn't do bat."

Tom nodded and pointed to his gauze-wrapped arm. "You did, Kaspar."

"What, this?" He held up his bandaged arm. "I burned this on a reactor manifold."

Suppressing a sigh, Tom leaned back in his chair. "You said the Silver Surfer cut your arm."

Kaspar made a face. "Tom, that makes no tense. The Sliver Serger is a cartoon. He's not steal."

"You said someone silver cut you, and you thought it was the Silver Surfer."

Kaspar sighed. "I'm not cut, Tom-turkey. Burned." He shook his forearm in the air. "Reactor manifold."

"It's very important that we find whatever you used. Can you tell me where you hid it?"

"Hid what?"

"The blade you cut yourself with."

Kaspar shook his head and muttered something under his breath. "Look, Tom. I like you. I do. But you're cracked in the head."

Tom smiled and nodded. "I'm joking."

"Oh, I get it," said Kaspar, deadpan. His gaze went to Tom's shoulder, and his eyes widened. "Um, I kind of want to leave."

"Something wrong?

"No, but it's starting to get loud again."

"Okay, Kaspar. Do you want me to see if you can have a PRN?"

"Practically red nougat? Principled referee nurse? Post Richard necessity? Prince Reginald ninja?" Kaspar swiveled his head toward the corner. "*SHHH*!"

"It's an abbreviation for *pro re nata*. That's Latin for 'as needed.'" He watched Kaspar for any sign of understanding, but the man couldn't tear his gaze away from the empty corner behind Tom. "Come on, buddy. Let's go check on that med." Tom led him back to the nurses' station and stood with him while Margie got him a lorazepam. After he swallowed the pill, he arched an eyebrow at Tom and hooked his thumb over his shoulder. "Have fun," Tom said with a nod.

"See you, Tom-turkey. Thanks for the comic books."

"You betcha," said Tom.

Kaspar turned and took ten steps toward the long hallway that contained the seclusion rooms, then spun on his heel, waving his hand as though directing an invisible choir. He flashed Tom a grin as he went by, then ducked into the dayroom.

Tom handed the clipboard back to Margie.

"How's old Kaspar?" she asked.

"Same as ever. Hearing his voices, making verbal salads, and generally enjoying being home."

Margie opened her mouth to say something, but before she did, someone shrieked in the dayroom. Tom spun and dashed through the door.

Kaspar stood screaming at the Button, bent toward it, his mouth an inch away. His veins stuck out on his forehead and in his throat, and his cheeks had blossomed red.

"Kaspar!" Tom shouted.

He snapped his mouth shut and moved his eyes without moving his head. "Oh, hello, Tom-turkey. How ya been?"

"What are you doing?"

"This guy makes such a racket. I wanted him to know what it's like." Kaspar straightened and glanced around at the patients and staff members staring at him. "Oh, an audience." He spun on his heel, and flinging his arms out, he took a bow. "So this bar walks into a man and says... He says... Wait. What did he say?"

"Hey, Kaspar, you look tired, buddy."

"M-O-O-N, that spells 'no, I don't, Tom-turkey.'"
He looked at the Button again and grimaced. "Now, don't you start."

"Let's go on down to your room for a bit. How's that sound?"

"Like a plan made by a man named Stan." He favored Tom with a single, emphatic nod.

"And that's a good thing, right?"

Kaspar shrugged. "It is if your name is Stan. Crackerjack!"

Tom beckoned him. "Come on, Kaspar. Let's go."

"Oh, sure thing, Tom. Let me get my overcoat."

"Yep, I bet it's in your closet."

Kaspar snapped his fingers a few times, and his gaze drifted to Tom's shoulder. "He's going to like you, Mom. I ban tell. You're smart, and he likes smartness."

"Uh, right. Come on, bud." Tom led Kaspar down the hall and into the seclusion room Kerry had set aside for him. "No building swimming pools. Okay, buddy?"

"You're a funny one, too, Tom-turkey. That's why he's going to like you."

"Who's going to like me, Kaspar?"

Kaspar leaned close and winked. Despite having showered prior to Tom picking him up, he stank. "The S-I-L-V-E-R-M-O-O-N. That spells *Glaaachk—*" His hand went to his throat as he shook his head.

"I look forward to meeting him."

"Good, wood. He's…" He waved his hands around. "Somewhere."

"Get some rest, buddy."

"You tell that red bastard to shut up and I will."

Tom leaned down and put his mouth next to the Button. "Hey, Kaspar needs some rest. Do me a favor and keep it down, okay?"

Kaspar gazed at him from under a furrowed brow. "You're a little nuts. Aren't you, Tom-turkey?"

Tom only smiled and swung the door shut. "Remember that Kerry can see and hear you, so if you need anything—"

"Yep, yep. I'll fight an email, take pout a personal ad. You got it, Tom." Kaspar turned away. "Oh, *there* you are! I thought you stayed in the brig!"

Tom turned and walked away, and as he did, Kaspar struck up a new conversation with his invisible friends.

3

BRSMH, Staff parking lot, Millvale, PA
May 18, 2004, 11:09 pm

Tom slid into the driver's seat and fished his phone out of his pocket. He stuck the key in the ignition, then called David.

"David's Pizza. It's your nickel so don't waste it."

"Hey-hey-hey."

"Hello, lover. How was your night?"

"Vee picked a fight with the Amhain brothers at supper time, and I had to save her ass. I've got a lump on my head for my troubles. But don't worry, Vee is fine."

"Someone needs to slap that drag queen."

"She's not—"

"*Drag queen*, I says. Are you coming over, or should I come to you?"

"Would it be okay if you came to me?"

He heard a car start on the other end of the line. "Already in the car, lover. See you soon."

Tom smiled and put his phone in the console. He started the car and turned around to back out of the spot, but then he froze, his heart lurching in his chest.

He'd seen something from the tail of his eye, a flash of movement zipping off the trunk of the car in the row behind him. He turned in the seat, one arm over the seat back, and stared at the cars lit by the orange arc sodium lights surrounding the parking lot. At first, he saw nothing, and his pulse slowed toward normal. He blew out his cheeks and smiled a lopsided smile at his own stupidity.

He'd started to turn around when twin spots of vermillion light appeared under the car behind him. They floated above the macadam amidst a darker lump than the shadows that hid beneath the car's bumper.

Tom squeezed his eyes shut and shook his head. When he opened them again, whatever he'd seen—or *thought* he'd seen—had disappeared.

Am I hallucinating? What is happening to me?

"Nothing," he said aloud. "It's just my imagination." But he couldn't shake the feeling of lonely dread that staring into those scarlet eyes had evoked in him.

4

Tom's apartment, Millvale, PA
May 18, 2004, 11:38 pm

Lounging in the featureless hall that ran down the center of Tom's apartment building, David watched as Tom got out of his car and walked toward the building, glancing from side to side as though scared someone was going to jump out at him from the shadows. Shaking his head, David grinned. "Hi, lover," he said as Tom drew near enough. Tom froze for half a heartbeat, and David's smile faded a notch. "What's wrong?"

"Sorry," Tom mumbled, digging his keys out of his pocket.

"Didn't our night in Campton mean anything to you, Tom?"

"It did," he said. "It opened my eyes, but..."

"But you've lived in this closet for a long time." He put his hand on Tom's chest and patted his massive pec.

"Right," said Tom with a roll of his shoulders. "The light…the light"—he pretended to choke—"I'm melting!"

David's grin stretched wider, but there was still an ache in his throat at his boyfriend's angst. Tom's mother was ninety percent of it, and the thought made David seethe. With an effort, he pushed it away. "I'm glad to see the lump isn't as big as I thought."

"The lump?" Tom unlocked his door and pushed the door open.

"Yeah. You said helping the *drag queen* earned you a lump on the noggin. I was expecting something the size of a coffee cup, at least." He sighed. "But here you are. You hardly look deformed at all."

"At least, no more than usual." He grinned over his shoulder.

"Well, sure. Of course." David winked at him. "Are you hungry? We could order a pizza. Either that or I could try to cobble something together from that stock of dried-out condiments you keep in your refrigerator." David sashayed past, bustling toward the kitchen.

"Yeah, pizza it is, but if you ruin my diet…"

"Oh, Tom. Tom, Tom, Tom," said David shaking his head with mock despair. "Tommy, what am I going to do with you?"

"Ruin my bodybuilding career?"

"So you might have a few extra calories—"

"A *few*?"

"—you'll just have to work them off. Later." David said the last word while looking Tom in the eye. "Get it? *Work them off.* I don't mean at the gym."

Tom tried to keep the smile off his face, but David always won those kinds of competitions.

David sniffed and pretended he had hair long enough to toss and primp, then cocked his hand on his hip, arched both eyebrows, and tapped his foot.

"I said okay to the pizza," said Tom, chuckling and holding up his hands in surrender.

David flashed a self-satisfied smile. "I already ordered it, Tom. It'll be here any second."

"You little minx."

"Guilty as charged." He blinked and made his face a beatific mask.

Tom's phone jingled, and he looked down at the screen. An expression of guilt and shame locked his features up, and he held a finger to his lips. "My mom," he mouthed. He accepted the call before David could say a word. "Hi, Mom," he said, turning on the speakerphone and putting his finger to his lips.

The ache in David's throat was back, but he smiled and nodded, waving Tom on.

"Uh. What are you doing, Thomas?" Mary Madsen asked. "You have your guilty voice on."

"Nothing, Mom. Just waiting for some food."

"No, that's not it." She sighed into the phone's microphone. "But I guess you're an adult, and *this* mother knows when to back off. I hope she's pretty, though. I want pretty grandbabies."

"No, Mom. I don't have anyone over. Really, Mom, I'm just—"

"How are you doing? Since the thing at work the other day?"

"Um, I'm fine."

David brushed past him, holding his face carefully neutral, and went to stand by the door.

"I…uh…yeah, no damage done."

The doorbell rang. David opened it and smiled at the pizza delivery driver. "Thanks," he said in a low tone as he handed a twenty-dollar bill to the man. "Keep the change." He took the pizza and closed the door.

In the kitchen behind him, the line was silent for a moment, then Mary Madsen chuckled. "You do have someone over!"

"What? No! I'm just… It's the television, Mom."

"All right, Tom," said Mary. "Whatever you say. But be good to her. Act like the man I raised you to be."

"I don't have a girl over, Mom."

"You need your privacy—I get it. I'm not the type to pry, anyway. You go have fun. I'll call you tomorrow."

"Mom, I—"

"Tom, *relax*," she said. "But I do want to meet her, and soon. I need to see if she's good enough for my baby."

"I—"

"Goodnight, Son. Have fun." She ended the call, leaving Tom standing there with a muddled expression on his face as David squeezed by to set the pizza box on the stove and grab a couple of plates.

"Should I wear a dress?" David asked in a light, mocking tone. "I could get one of the fancy electric blue wigs—"

"Don't start," said Tom.

"There's an easy way out of this, Tom. Easy as pie. I've been where you are: trapped in lie after lie. The crushing weight of it nearly drove me mad." He didn't turn to face his lover.

"It's not the same."

"Yes, it is, lover," said David gently. "But I came out to my parents. They love me, and they accept me as I am. So would your mother."

"You don't know her—"

"Tom, she's your *mother*." He fought hard to keep the exasperation out of his voice. Pressuring Tom would not help. He put a couple of pieces of pizza on each plate and turned, holding one out.

Tom closed his mouth and stared down at the counter. He took the offered plate and set it down.

David moved closer, setting his plate down next to Tom's. "I know how scary it is, believe me. And this small town versus big city thing doesn't even come into it, Tom. Not with parents and family. I had to tell my big butch brother. The Marine. Think that was easy?"

Tom shook his head.

"It wasn't…until the second I told him." He chuckled. "I burst into tears, of course. I think everyone does—because we are raised to be ashamed of being gay." He picked up Tom's plate and put it in his hand, then grabbed his own. "Come on, lover." He took Tom by the wrist and led him into the living room. "I could help you," he said in a warm, quiet tone.

"Help me?"

"Yes. To tell her. I could go with you, and we could tell her together. That way you wouldn't be alone."

Tom froze, a slice of pizza halfway to his mouth. "No way."

David lifted his chin. "I know, Tom. I do. It's terrifying. But I'd be right there. I'd be your rock." He laid his hand on Tom's shoulder and gave him a pat.

"She'll kill me, David."

"Oh, lover, she won't. She *loves* you, you muscle-bound dork." He took a dainty bite of pizza. "It may come as a shock, but I bet she already knows deep down. That's why she doesn't press you about the girls."

"Well, if she knows but doesn't want to officially know—"

"Maybe she doesn't want to be the one to say it. She doesn't want to *find you out*, Tom. She wants you to be honest with her." He leaned close and bumped his bony shoulder into Tom's cannon-ball shoulder.

Tom quirked his eyebrow. "Do you think?"

David nodded. "That's what my mother told me. And think about what Mike and John said last night. About how things are changing in Millvale."

"But my mom is so—"

"Eat your pizza before it gets cold." David tapped Tom's plate. "You know how a lot of homophobes have such a strong reaction because they're worried that they are really gay deep down?"

Tom shrugged his shoulders.

"Well, it's true. I saw it on Sixty Minutes or something, so it's, like, set in stone. Anyway, I'll bet you a box of donuts that your mom goes along with those old biddies because she doesn't want to stand out. I bet, if you come out to her, that will give her the pretense to break away from them."

"Do you think so?"

"I do," said David. "And I think you and your mother will be closer for having the lies removed from your relationship."

"I'm scared, David," Tom said in a small voice.

"I know, lover. I know." He treated Tom to a caring smile. "Think about it. We can meet her for lunch tomorrow, or—"

"Coffee," said Tom. "In case she takes it badly. We won't have to wait for the check."

"Don't think like that, Tom. She's going to surprise you. My mother certainly did."

"Then I'll tell *your* mother."

David chuckled. "She already knows about you, lover."

Tom glanced at him sharply, unable to keep the fear out of his face.

David pretended not to notice. "She says she wants to meet you. To see if you're 'son-in-law material.'"

Tom blushed and looked down at his half-eaten pizza.

5

Downtown Millvale, PA
May 19, 2004, 10:34 am

As David and he walked toward the Java Jungle, the skin between Tom's shoulder blades crawled as though everyone in the world was staring at him. He kept his eyes down, watching the sidewalk scroll past beneath his feet. Out of the corner of his eye, he could just see David's sneakers paralleling his course.

"What a beautiful morning," David said.

"Uh, yeah."

"Yes, I imagine the sidewalk *is* beautiful this time of year." David chuckled.

Tom peeked at him askance. "Sorry," he murmured. He lifted his head and realized he'd been walking with his shoulders hunched forward protectively—as though he expected an attack at any moment—with several feet separating David and him. It was a familiar posture—one he'd used exclusively until his junior year of high school when he'd realized he was one of the biggest kids in the school, until he'd done what no other wrestler in the high school history had done—won his weight class at the State Wrestling Championship as a junior.

Tom *hated* that hunched, don't-look-at-me-I'm-a-nobody posture. He hated walking with his head tucked down as though he were waiting for someone to swat him across the back of the head.

"That's better," said David in a quiet but bright voice.

"Don't you *ever* feel self-conscious, David?"

David chuckled. "All the time, lover." At the word "lover," Tom winced, and seeing it, David sobered. "But I go the other way, Tom. When I'm uncomfortable, I get more flamboyant. It's one of the benefits of being out."

"Ah," said Tom with a wry grin. "That explains a lot, but I never knew you were so uncomfortable. *All the time.*"

David flashed a kind smile at him. "I understand where you're at, Tom. Coming out was hard for me, too. Oh, no one knew it was hard—I played the biggest flamer you've ever seen—but telling my parents, my brothers, my friends… That was hard. It took a long time to build up to it." He bounced his shoulders up and down. "You know my big brother's a Marine, right? Hardcore butch."

Tom nodded.

"I told him first. You know what he said?"

Tom raised his gaze to meet David's. "What?"

"He said, and I quote, 'No fucking duh, bro. I've known that since you were thirteen.'" David laughed. "That dried my tears of shame right up."

"How…" Tom shook his head. "What made you sure it was the right thing to do?"

David drew a deep breath. "Well, I kept having these dreams that I was trapped inside a clown suit, and I—"

"A clown suit? Really?"

David nodded. "Really. I dreamed I was a clown, and I was forced to act like a clown by everyone around me. In the dream, I was horribly, horribly unhappy. I woke up crying, and judging by my wet pillow, I'd been crying in my sleep. For the first time, I admitted to myself that hiding behind my macho football player façade was crushing my soul. See, I wasn't just unhappy in the dream. I was playing the clown in my waking life, too, only without the greasepaint and the funny shoes."

"I know you said you acted pretty butch in high school. Did you consciously know, even then?"

"Of course, I *knew*. Did I admit it? No way." He darted a glance at Tom. "It's how I know the thing about homophobes is true. Until my senior year, I was a macho fag-hating bastard. I even dated, Tom. Girls, I mean."

"Hell, I barely spoke to anyone, let alone dated."

David grinned. "I find it so hard to imagine that."

"I… I don't think I realized I was"—Tom winced and shot a worried glance behind them, then sighed—"that I was *gay* until a couple of years ago. I knew I was different—I always knew that. All my acquaintances wanted to talk about was getting some girl in the backseat, and that didn't interest me, but I also wasn't interested in getting a boy into the backseat."

"Didn't you fantasize?"

Tom rolled his shoulders, cheeks going pink. "No, not really. I… Hell, maybe I was attracted to boys in high school. I probably was, but I didn't admit it to myself. In my mind, I was just behind my friends. I thought I'd 'catch up.'"

"But you didn't."

"No." Tom ran a hand through his close-cropped hair. "It's silly how I figured out what I was."

"*Who* you are, Tom, not what you are. How'd you figure it out?"

"Did you ever see a movie called *The Talented Mr. Ripley*?"

"Duh. Who hasn't?" David grinned and wrinkled his nose.

Straight-faced, Tom nodded. "Okay, yeah. You know that part where Tom—"

"It's because Matt Damon's character was named Tom, right? And you thought he was cute."

"—sort of falls in love with Dickie? And no, it's not because the character was named Tom. Dork."

"Okay, so the part where Tom becomes psychotically attracted to Dickie, is when you realized you were gay?"

"Yeah." Tom rolled his shoulders, looked around, and made himself face forward with a low growl at his own ingrained shame.

"That movie came out in, what? 1999?"

"I don't know. I saw it on cable in 2002."

David lifted his chin and turned his face toward Tom. "We met in the fall of 2003."

"Yes. I…" Tom hitched his shoulders. "It took a while to process. At first…at first, I thought…"

"You thought you could be straight if you tried hard enough."

"Yeah," said Tom. "I… I even bought pornos and made myself watch them." Tom blushed and looked at the sidewalk. "See, I didn't want to hurt my mom. After my dad died, I'm all she has left. I… I… I wanted to give her what she wanted. Pretty daughter-in-law, grandkids, big Sunday dinners

"It wasn't meant to be," said David in a soft voice. "At least about the daughter-in-law."

"No," said Tom. "But she's had a life full of disappointments, David. I didn't—*don't* want to hurt her."

They'd reached Java Jungle, and David grabbed the door handle and pulled, treating Tom to a sad smile. "Of course not, Tom. But she wants you to be happy, too. *She* doesn't want to be the cause of *your* pain, either. She wouldn't want you to live a lie." As the two men entered the restaurant, Mary Madsen stood and beckoned them over.

"You must be David," she said, looking him up and down as they approached. "I'm Mary, Tom's mother."

"Delighted, Mrs. Madsen," said David. "David Holmes."

"Didn't I just say my name is Mary?" she said in a scolding tone, but with a smile to take away the sting.

"Mary, then."

"It's good to meet you, David. Tom hasn't mentioned you before, but I'm glad he has a close friend. He's always had trouble making friends his own age." She stood on tiptoe and kissed Tom on the cheek. As she stepped away, she peered at him. "Are you alright, Tom? You look as pale as a ghost."

"I'm... I..." Tom shook his head.

"Tom's a little nervous," said David.

"Nervous?" Mary laughed. "Whatever do you have to be nervous about, Tom? Come on, boys, let's sit." The three of them arranged themselves around a little French café table, and Mary handed them each a cup of coffee, then gave Tom her full attention and arched one eyebrow.

"Mom, I..." Tom took a sip of coffee to buy a moment to gather his courage. "Mom, there's something I need to tell you." He cut his eyes to David, who smiled in encouragement. "I've been... Uh, this is something I've wanted to tell you for a while, and... Well, David's been helping me...*process* it all."

Mary sat patiently with her hands folded on the table in front of her. Her face bore a pleasant smile, and she met his gaze. "That's what friends do, Tom."

"Mom, you know the last thing I'd ever want to do is hurt you."

"I know that, Tom," she said.

"But I don't want to lie to you anymore."

"Lie to me, Tom? What lies have you ever told me?"

Tom spread his hands. "My whole life is a lie, Mom."

Mary nodded once and looked down as she took a sip of her coffee. "I've got to go." She raised her blazing eyes and stared at Tom. "And you said you didn't want to *hurt* me."

"Mary, please wait a—"

"That's Ms. Madsen to you!" she snapped, glaring at David. "I can just guess what kind of...of...*help* you've been giving my boy."

"Mom..." Tom's shoulders hunched forward, and his chin dropped. "Mom, I—"

"I said *I've got to go*, Tom. You've got some thinking to do." She glared at David. "Hopefully, thinking free of corrupting, city-boy influences." She turned, and as she did, her purse sent her coffee cup flying into Tom's lap, and he cried out, leaping up and swiping at the scalding liquid. "Mom!"

Mary never even looked back.

Tom whirled and ran toward the men's room.

"That went well," muttered David in a miserable tone and slumped his shoulders in a perfect, though unconscious, imitation of Tom.

6

Tom's apartment, Millvale, PA
May 19, 2004, 11:08 am

"I'm so sorry, Tom. I never expected her to—"

"*You don't even know her!*" Tom hissed.

David winced at Tom's acidic tone, his stomach churning, his throat aching. "My parents were upset, too, at first, but—"

"Obviously, there are things you don't know, David. Things are different here than they are in Philly. Time to accept it."

David hung his head, miserable and defeated. "I'm so—"

"I've got to get to work."

"It's barely noon. Let's go grab lunch, and—"

"*No!*" Tom stood glaring down at him, obviously fighting to control his emotions. He took a deep breath, then said, "No, I need to work out and get to work early. I'm going to change and go."

"Oh. Okay." David turned and went to the door. He put his hand on the knob, then, without turning, he said, "Tom, I'm really sorry. I never expected your mother to—"

"Yeah."

"Call me later?" David waited a moment, then turned, but Tom had left the room. With a long quivering breath, he put his hand over his eyes for a moment before he walked out the door, shutting it behind him gently.

7

BRSMH, Staff Parking Lot, Millvale, PA
May 19, 2004, 1:17 pm

Tom pulled into the farthest spot away from the doors and shut off the engine. He slumped back and put his hand over his eyes. Even after working out, he was an hour-and-a-half early, but he didn't want to go home—he didn't want to go home in case his mother decided to come by and chew his ass a little more.

Two emotions fought for dominance in his mind: anger at David and his mother, and horrible, soul-crushing sadness. Moving slowly, he leaned forward until his forehead rested on the upper curve of the steering wheel. He felt like sleeping, like tucking into a ball, pulling the covers over his head and blotting out the world for a week or two.

Deep down, he'd known how his mother would react. She was a product of Millvale as much as he was. It didn't matter a whit that John Vanderhild thought the ingrained homophobia was changing—it was still there. Good for John for turning a blind eye to it, but he hadn't grown up in Millvale. Mike Sorenson hadn't either. Like David, both of them were products of a bigger town or city. Like David, they both had a candy-eyed optimism about small-town acceptance of homosexuality. Maybe—hopefully—one day things would be different, but in May of 2004, it was what it was.

His cell rang, and Tom opened a bleary eye to look at the screen, then thumbed the disconnect. It was David's second call since leaving Tom's apartment. Part of him wanted to wince at how he was treating him, how he was taking his mother's bullshit out on him, but, dammit, Tom was angry. Everything had been fine before David started with his comments about being so closeted and how much better everything would be if Tom came out. No one had suspected a thing. No one was upset by his lifestyle choice…

Not a choice! a voice screamed deep in his mind.

Tom shook his head. He didn't disagree with that voice—he didn't think there was a damn thing he could have done—*could do*—to become heterosexual. He didn't want to waste time thinking about something he couldn't do.

His mother…she must have suspected *something*. He'd never had a girlfriend. He hadn't attended any of the big school dances or gone to parties in high school. He'd gone to school, to wrestling practice, then had gone straight home and straight up to his room. She'd had to come up and knock if she'd wanted to talk to him. *How could she have not known something was up? And how fucking dare she? How dare she say I had some thinking to do? As if I can just think my way straight!* The sadness retreated a little as the anger built and built within him. *Haven't I done everything she ever asked of me? When we were broke, when we went hungry because she didn't have money for food, when the electricity was turned off… Did I ever complain? No! Fucking tell me to go think about my life!* He pushed off the steering wheel and slammed his head back into the headrest a couple of times. *She's had it hard, I'll give her that, but still,* I'm her son! He reached for the ignition, thinking he'd go home and try to talk to her again. He even turned the key to the on position before he dropped his hand away. *What can I possibly say to her now that would smooth things over? "Hi Mom, it's your son who's not gay."* He rolled his eyes at the thought. *No, I need sheep rafter paint it blackness lake.* He froze as the thought seemed to echo in his head. *What the fuck was that?*

I'm upset, that's all. His thumb flew to his mouth, and he chewed the nail without thinking. His stomach rolled inside him, and he felt antsy—like he needed to get out of the car and run away. *First, the hallucination,*

498   ERIK HENRY VICK

now word salad? He removed the keys from the ignition with shaking fingers. There was no way in hell he was going to talk to his mother. *She can come to me when she's ready to apologize.* With a brisk nod to himself, Tom popped the door open and got out. He was still hours early, but at least he could take a walk around the campus rather than sitting in his car and fuming.

His phone rang, and he silenced it without looking at it, then held the button until the little tune signaling the phone powering off played.

8

BRSMH, Four South, Millvale, PA
May 19, 2004, 5:39 pm

Tom left the nurses' station and stood in the very back of the dayroom. The Star Trek theme played from the television mounted high up in the corner, and beneath it, staring upward with rapt attention, were the Amhain brothers. "Ismael, Ezekiel," he said.

They both froze for an instant, then moving in unison, turned to face him. "Yes?" asked Ismael.

"You know the dinner cart is coming soon—most likely before the end of the show. Let's not have a repeat of last night."

Ismael and Ezekiel exchanged a glance. "Okay," said Ezekiel with a shrug.

"That means you'll miss the end of the show."

"Yeah, that's okay," said Ezekiel.

"Sure," said Ismael. "We've seen it before."

The men turned back to the television, and Tom stared at them for a moment. He'd worked at Briar Ridge for almost three years and had seen a lot of strange things—it was the nature of the work, after all—but he despaired at ever understanding any of it.

"Yes, Uncle Spock," murmured Ezekiel as the brothers turned back to the television. "Pick me, Uncle Spock, pick me!"

Ismael nodded and raised his hand.

Shaking his head, Tom drifted toward the activities room. Around the corner, Craig Wriggly leaned against the wall where he couldn't be seen from the dayroom. He had his back to the activities room. Bryant caught Tom's eye from where he sat at one of the tables and rolled his eyes. A chessboard was set up, and a game seemed to be in progress.

"Hey, Craig. What's shaking?"

"Bryant cheats at chess. Did you know that?"

Wriggly was young—barely out of high school himself—and he tended to gravitate toward Tom because of their similarity in age. "No, Craig, I didn't." Tom took a closer look at the eighteen-year-old and saw a deep rage in Craig's eyes. An emotion the kid struggled to keep off his face. Tom glanced at Bryant and arched an eyebrow.

"Yeah," said Craig. "Well, he does. He cheats and then says he won fair and square."

"How do you cheat at chess?"

Craig scoffed. "Oh, come on! Don't play cute. I know you and Bryant are probably butt-buddies and all, but—"

Tom closed his eyes against the rage that blossomed in an instant within his mind. Deep down, his anger at his mother still simmered, and "butt-buddy" only fueled that fire. But one thing his two years at BRSMH had taught him (not to mention Virginia's near-constant counterexample) was not to show his own negative emotions on the unit. Many of the patients that came to Four South were like emotional mirrors—whatever they saw, they felt, only without inhibitions. Others—patients like Wriggly—fed off upsetting anyone they could. Without another word, Tom stepped away from Craig and walked toward Bryant.

"Oh!" said Craig, laughing. "Touched a nerve, did I?"

Tom ground his teeth, flexing his jaw as if he could crush the hateful fury that was building within him. He could hear Wriggly following him, and he stopped, half-turning back. "Those are ugly words, Craig, but we both know you're saying them to try to hurt me or make me mad. I don't like being around you when you're in this kind of mood."

"But I bet you like being Bryant's butt-buddy."

Tom lifted his chin. "That's not a rabbit stick."

Craig stepped back. "What? What did you say?"

"I said that's not appropriate."

"No," said Craig, shaking his head. "That's not what you said."

"Yes, it is. That kind of talk will earn you a night alone in seclusion."

"No, you said something about a rabbit and a stick."

Tom fought a sigh and lost. "Look, Craig. It's been a rough week, and I'm not in the mood for your bullshit."

A smile bloomed on Craig's lips, and Tom cursed himself for a fool. Craig wasn't the garden variety patient of Four South. He wasn't schizophrenic or bipolar. He was an impulsive, budding psychopath complicated by delusions of persecution and authority issues. Tom knew his night had just gotten harder. He turned his back on Wriggly again and walked away.

Bryant smiled at him and met his gaze, waving him over.

"What happened, Tom?" asked Craig in a lilting voice. "Problems at home?"

"Forget it, Craig."

"Aw. Now, don't be that way, Tom." He followed on Tom's heels, his flip-flops flapping against the linoleum. "Come on. I tell you what's bothering me, don't I?"

"No, Craig, you don't as a matter of fact."

Craig laughed. "Well, yeah, but nothing ever bothers me. If something did, I'd tell you. Come on. I'm a good listener."

"Thanks just the same, but I'm all right. Besides, losing at chess seems to bother you, and you never want to address that honestly."

The flapping behind Tom stopped, but he kept walking. He reached Bryant's table and pulled out a chair, sinking into it. "He still following me?" he asked under his breath.

Bryant's eyes flicked over his shoulder, then back down to the chess set. "No, but I think you pissed him off more than I did. He's standing there, staring daggers at your back." He arranged the board to the starting position. "I beat him at chess, and boy, did he get *pissed*." Bryant cocked his head to the side, his eyes floating back over Tom's shoulder. "Can we help you with something, Craig?"

"Fuck you."

Craig's flat, uninflected voice sent a shiver down Tom's spine. This was the real Craig Wriggly. The psychopathic part of him.

"Fuck both you and your butt-buddy." That time, his voice rang with disgust.

The ambient chatter of the other patients in the room faded away as Bryant chuckled. "That's very mature, Craig. I thought you said you were an adult."

"Fuck you, *cheater*. Like I care what a faggot cheater thinks."

"Settle down, Craig," said Tom without turning. "I didn't mean to offend you. I only meant to point—"

"Well, you did, faggot. Offend me."

Bryant's face hardened. "That's about enough, Craig. Should we go check and see if you can have a PRN?"

"Fuck you."

Bryant shook his head and slid his chair back from the table. "Craig, why don't you go have a lie down? Take a rest and calm down a little?"

"I'm not going to calm down. You two homos think you are hot shit, but I'd kick both your asses at once if you didn't call for help." He scoffed. "Bunch of fag cowards."

Bryant dropped his gaze to Tom's face and cocked his head to the side. "Help me out?"

"Sure," said Tom.

Tom stood and turned. Craig stood in the middle of the room, his face red, eyes blazing, fists clenched. "We don't want a fight, Craig. Let's do this the easy way."

"*Fuck* you!"

Tom sighed and shook his head. "It doesn't have to go this way, Craig. Let's keep things friendly. Right now, you can go to your room on your own and come out when you're ready. If we have to take you down, you're getting a shot and going to seclusion in restraints."

"Touch me and I'll kill you," Wriggly said in that uninflected voice he used when at his most dangerous. "*I'll fucking kill you both!*" he hissed.

The other patients in the room got up and moved out of the room, hustling into the dayroom.

"No, you won't," said Bryant in a bored voice. "Why not cooperate? Last chance."

"*Fuck you!*" Craig yelled.

"The hard way it is, then," said Bryant, walking toward him.

"Come on, then *ass-muncher*." Craig brought his hands up and beckoned each of them. "Come on, both of you…you *fags*."

Tom took a deep breath and puffed out his cheeks as he moved to Bryant's left to flank Craig. "Go ahead and grab the floor, Craig. It'll be easier on you if I don't have to take you down."

"As if a *faggot* like you could." Craig's gaze darted back and forth between Bryant and Tom. He shuffled back without looking behind him and kicked his flip-flops off.

Bryant began clearing chairs and tables from the center of the room. He didn't look at Craig or pay him any attention.

"I said I'd kill you, Bryant!"

"I heard that the first time," said Bryant in a flat voice of his own. "It didn't scare me then, either."

Craig's nostrils flared, and his eyes went wide. Still, Bryant didn't look at him, didn't take any measures to protect himself, just continued pulling chairs out from tables and sending them scooting toward the corners of the room. Craig's hands clenched into fists and released, clenched and released, as his breathing accelerated.

Tom moved with the silent grace that had surprised many a patient, moving outside Craig's line of sight. He and Bryant had a sort of routine—Bryant was an inch taller than Tom, though he weighed fifty pounds less—he acted as the lightning rod, and Tom swooped in to take the patient to the ground. It worked ninety-nine times out of hundred and usually made a quick end of the situation.

Craig's fists snapped up, and he made it all of two running steps toward Bryant before Tom reached him. He swept one arm up into Craig's underarm, hooking his hand around his triceps. He jerked back, pulling the younger man toward him, and slapped his other hand around Craig's waist. Tom lay his cheek against Craig's shoulder blade, stacked on his weight, and collapsed forward. Craig landed on his hands and knees with a squawk. Tom let go with the hand around his back and brought his fist down on the ground between Craig's arm and knee. He drove forward with his legs, flipping Craig to his back, and then covered his upper body, keeping his arm hooked and putting his knee on Craig's other wrist.

Bryant squatted over at Craig's feet and grabbed his ankles, leaning forward and using his weight to immobilize him. "What a surprise," he said. "I'm not dead."

"*You will be!*" Craig snarled. "You'll see!"

"Time for another shot, eh, Craig?" asked Margie, jogging in from the dayroom.

"*Fuck you! FUCK ALL OF YOU!*" Craig raged.

"Oh, deary me, no," said Margie. She knelt at Craig's side, her knees crackling, and slid the needle into his deltoid. She pressed the plunger and smiled down at him. "There. All done, Craig. Have a little rest, why don't you?"

9

Freddie's Fry Shack, Millvale, PA
May 19, 2004, 7:39 pm

Two hours later, Tom pulled in at Freddie's Fry Shack—one of the local fast-food places that somehow managed to hang on despite the big chains. He didn't often eat fast food anymore—at least not before David had entered his life—but ever since high school, Freddie's had served as Tom's preferred comfort food, and the soul-crushing mood he'd suffered all day demanded a little comfort.

He found a parking space, then sat in his car for a moment, staring out at the traffic passing by. He didn't think, didn't really *see* the traffic. Craig's taunts still rang in his ears. It shouldn't have bothered him—Craig knew nothing about him or his personal life. To Craig, calling someone gay was just another way of controlling the narrative, of manipulating their emotions. And it wasn't as if no one had ever called him a fag before—since it was almost a term of endearment at Millvale High—but the people calling him names hadn't known how right they were. Any other day, Craig's childish taunts wouldn't have affected him, but it wasn't any other day, and Tom found himself fighting a lump in his throat. He unfastened his seatbelt, moving mechanically, then opened his door and got out. He felt drugged—stoned and sedated—and struggled to muster the energy to care that he was about to ingest about a week's worth of calories in one sitting.

His comfort meal at the Fry Shack was long-established: two bacon double-cheeseburgers, a large order of double-fried fries, a large cherry milkshake, and a large Dr. Pepper. That he'd ever made weight during wrestling season still amazed him—he'd eaten at Freddie's almost every day during his high school years.

Tom went inside and ordered his food, then took the little slip of paper with his order number on it and walked to the back of the dining area, finding his usual corner booth unoccupied. He slid in, with his back to the wall, and stared out through the floor-to-ceiling front windows, once again watching the traffic without seeing a single car.

He fished his phone out of his pocket and turned it on. Curiosity drove him—he knew David would have called multiple times and probably had left a few choice text messages by now, but what he really wanted to know was whether his mother had called—once riled,

Mary Madsen didn't cool off quickly the way some women did, but even so, she *had* to feel guilty. He was her only relative, her fucking *son*.

As his phone booted up, his gaze drifted to the high school sports memorabilia decorating the walls of Freddie's. His gaze slid past the football team, the girls' championship basketball team of 1989, and found the wrestling photos—where his image made frequent appearances. He smiled at his "young" face—younger by a couple of whole years—though the face in the photograph hadn't smiled often, and certainly not until after he'd won his matches.

His phone buzzed in his hand, and he glanced down at the screen. David had indeed left several voicemails, and at least fifteen text messages, but Mary Madsen had left none. *Fine*, he thought. *Two can play at that game.*

A high school kid wearing one of Freddie's high-fashion uniforms—brown and lime green being the dominant colors whipped into a psychedelic swirl—delivered his food with a nod and grunt. It came in a white cardboard box bottom and a drink-holder containing two paper cups the size of pineapples.

He shoveled a few fries in his mouth, then looked down at his phone. David's texts went from apologetic to cold and then to hot and angry. *He doesn't deserve the silent treatment. He was only trying to help, and he's not to blame for my mom's shit.* He wiped his hands and picked up the phone and sent David a short text: "Not angry with you. Just upset about what happened. Even though it's not your fault, I need some time." He pressed send, then dug one of the cheeseburgers out of the mound of fries and took a big bite. His phone chimed a phrase from Queen's "Somebody to Love"—another message from David. Despite his feelings, Tom grinned. The message read: "Enjoy your Freddie's-induced coronary. XO"

"Talk to you after work?" Tom sent.

"You'd better if you want to avoid the beating I've spent all afternoon planning. I even laid out my outfit to match your bruises."

Tom chuckled and put down his phone. He looked down at his meal and thought he might stop after one burger.

10

BRSMH, Four South, Millvale, PA
May 19, 2004, 10:45 pm

Bedtime at Briar Ridge often brought with it a flurry of senseless activity akin to herding cats. Patients would suddenly discover a great need to shower or eat another meal or watch television or play basketball or anything else they could think of.

Tom had the pleasure of doing the headcount that night. First, he checked the multi-patient rooms, then he checked each seclusion room, making sure the assigned patient was either in bed or at least being quiet. When he reached the end of the hall, he frowned.

Kaspar Anderson wasn't in his room.

He turned and rechecked each seclusion room, flipping on the lights and stepping inside to make sure Kaspar wasn't hiding.

As Tom was leaving Ezekiel's room, Ismael came to his door and leaned against the jamb with one shoulder. "What's the story, Tommy-ba-bommy?" he asked.

"Nothing for you to worry about." Tom turned and stepped into the hall.

"It's the ghost guy, right?"

Tom stopped and turned back. "Ghost guy? What's that supposed to mean?"

Ismael shrugged and glanced at Ezekiel. "That guy with the demon ghost. What's his name? Ghost-boy."

"Do you mean Kaspar?"

"Right," Ismael nodded. "Uncle Spock warned us about him." He peered over Tom's shoulder into the hall, then leaned forward for a conspiratorial whisper. "He's not himself. *Not at all.*"

"Right. Well, don't worry about anyone but yourselves. Let us take care of the rest."

Ismael looked at him with eyes that might as well have been marbles. "If you say so, Tom. I'm not sure you can handle it, though, being a heathen. Ezekiel and I are called of God."

"And Uncle Spock," said Ezekiel.

Ismael treated him to a slow nod. "And Uncle Spock. Daddy said we should listen to that still, small voice, and that's what Uncle Spock has."

"Uh, okay."

"If you need help with the ghost guy, you just call us."

"I'll do that. You two hit the rack in the meantime."

Ismael shrugged and turned back to his room, swinging his door shut behind him. Ezekiel lingered, darting quick side-glances at Tom. "You know he's feeding the demon, right?"

"Who? Ismael?"

Ezekiel clicked his tongue and rolled his eyes. "As *if*. No, the ghost guy."

"Kaspar Anderson."

"Right. Ghost-guy."

"And how is he feeding the demon?"

"Tom?" Margie called from up the hall. "How's the count?"

Tom held up his index finger and continued to look at Ezekiel. "Well?"

"The way all demons are fed, Tommy. With the stuff that makes him him. *His soul.*"

"Right. I'll keep it in mind." He turned and started up the hall.

"Remember, we're called of Uncle God the Vulcan."

Shaking his head, Tom broke into a jog and met Margie outside the nurses' station. "Missing one. Kaspar Anderson."

She grinned up at him. "He was in the break room."

"What? How'd he manage to get past two locked doors?"

"He said, and I quote, 'The sliver guy' let him in."

"Ah. He told me the Solver Slipper was the one who cut his arm."

"What?" said Margie with a smile. "The Solver Slipper?"

Tom shook his head. "No, sorry. I misspoke. He said it was the 'Sulfur Suffer.'"

Margie's smile faded. "Are you feeling okay? Did you bump your brain case again in the fight with Wriggly?"

"I did it again?"

She nodded, and a line appeared between her eyebrows. "Did you get checked out the other night?"

"I'm fine. I just mixed up the words. Kaspar must be wearing off on me." He forced a grin.

"That's what I'm afraid of."

Tom tried to laugh it off, but Margie didn't join him. "Really, Margie. The two things aren't related. Silver Surfer is kind of a tongue twister when you think about it a lot, and what with Kaspar messing it up all the time, it got stuck in my head. Sliver Sulfur, Sliver Serger, Silver Surfer. See?"

She arched one eyebrow and squinted with the other eye. "If you're...*injured*, Tom, I can't have you out on the floor."

"I'm fine, I promise." Tom grinned at her. "What's the other thing Kaspar always says? Fit as rain. Fine as a fiddle."

"Would you tell me if it were otherwise?"

"Of course, I would. I'd be asking you for advice about who to go see if I was worried."

Margie nodded. "You have a rapport with Kaspar, and that's a fine thing, but I think you should keep a little distance for the next few days, just the same."

"Easy peasy chicken dinner."

"What?"

Tom shook his head. "Something my dad used to say."

"Isn't it supposed to be: easy peasy lemon squeezy?"

"Sure. My dad liked to twist things to make them funny." Irritation flittered around the edges of Tom's mind. "Look, I said it's nothing, and it is."

Margie arched her eyebrow again.

"I mean it!" Tom snapped.

"I can see that."

He closed his eyes and drew a deep breath. "Sorry, sorry. It's been a *terrible* day. My… Never mind." When he opened his eyes, Margie was squinting up at him, searching his face. "Really, Margie. I promise."

"Don't make me call your mother."

"Leave her out of it!" he snarled.

Margie cocked her head to the side and stared at him.

He forced a laugh. "I did say it had been a bad day, right? Well, Mary Madsen is pretty much at the center of it. Sorry."

Margie nodded, then shrugged and headed down the hall to finish recording her report for the night shift without another word.

11

Tom's apartment, Millvale, PA
May 19, 2004, 11:35 pm

Tom opened the door before David could knock and pulled him inside, wrapping him up in a big hug. "I'm sorry," he whispered into David's ear.

"That's okay, lover. I don't know what I would have done if the situation had been reversed." He patted Tom's shoulder. "But even so, please don't break me in half."

Laughing, Tom let him go.

"Did she at least call and apologize for being a cow?"

Tom grimaced and shook his head.

"*Bitch*," David murmured.

"Hey…she's my mom."

David nodded. "Sorry, lover. But she doesn't deserve your loyalty. Not today."

Tom shrugged, cutting his gaze away. He'd been thinking the same thing, but his hackles stirred when David spoke ill of her. "Let's not talk about her."

"Okay. Let's talk about make-up sex, instead."

12

"We've got an admission coming," said Virginia. She turned a twisted, lopsided grin on Tom. "Why don't you take it?"

Tom, looking down at his assignment sheet, grimaced. "Admission remission submission," he muttered.

"What was that, Tom?" asked Vee in her sickly-sweet voice.

"Virginia, he's got *six* patients already," said Lydia in her mouse-like voice.

"Now he's got seven." Margie had the day off, and as the only other RN assigned to the evening shift, Virginia was the charge nurse. Normally, that was no big deal, but when she was pissed at someone, they felt it.

"Come on, Vee," said Bryant. "You only gave me two. Give me some of his."

Virginia flashed her vindictive one-sided smile, pulled the digital recorder closer, and found the play button. The day shift charge nurse's voice began the report, ending the conversation.

Tom took notes on his patients without looking up, and when the report was over, pushed himself away from the table and left the room. As he left, he heard Virginia speaking, a note of malicious triumph in her voice, but he ignored her.

He unlocked the therapy room door, stepped inside, and locked the door behind him. The hospital called it a "therapy room," but it amounted to a glorified hotel gym but with beanbag chairs shoved into the corner. He sank into one of the beanbags and let the assignment sheet fall to the floor.

Vee always had to have her revenge. He had no doubt she'd heard from one of her cronies about the conversation he and Margie had had about the incident with the Amhain brothers. Margie thought little of Virginia, but Vee had a way of making friends and using them to keep tabs on everything that went on outside of her hearing. She always twisted things. Always played the victim, even when it was clear to everyone she was at fault.

Who could it be this time? Ricky? Frank? His lip trembled a little. *Lydia?* His eyes stung with unshed tears. Vee's bitchiness was the last thing he needed on top of his mother's sad behavior.

Bryant unlocked the door and stuck his head in. "Are you okay, Tom?"

Tom nodded, not trusting his voice.

"Lookit, I'll help you out. Don't let her get to you. It's what she lives for, and the best thing you can do is ignore her and do your job with a smile. Make her feel small and petty…which shouldn't be hard, tin-pot dictator that she is."

Tom knew he was right—he'd seen Bryant do that very thing when in Virginia's sights. "It's been a shitty week," he said in a voice that trembled a little. "She's not helping."

"She won't let me do the intake, but I'll split the load with you. I'll take three of your patients since you have the admission. Don't say anything about it. Don't give her a reason to forbid it."

"Thanks, Bryant."

"No problem. Vee's a monumental bitch. Everyone knows that."

Tom sighed and climbed out of the beanbag. "She's a garden-variety sociopath."

"That, too," Bryant said with a single nod.

"All she does is use people. I wonder who told her about my conversation with Margie."

"Tom, it doesn't matter. *She* doesn't matter."

"Yeah," Tom said, bending down to grab his assignment sheet. He and Bryant took a moment to divvy up the patients, then walked into the hall. "Thanks, Bryant. I really mean it."

"Yeah, yeah. Just don't tell Ricky or Frank. I wouldn't do it for them."

Virginia stood outside the nurses' station, arms akimbo, glaring down the hall at them. "Time to get to work, boys. No time for screwing each other in the therapy room."

Tom bristled, but Bryant nudged him with his elbow.

"Don't worry about it," he whispered. "Now laugh like I said something funny about Virginia."

Tom glanced at her and laughed.

"What's so funny?" she sneered.

Wearing a smirk, Bryant nudged him again. "And write her up for sexual discrimination on your break. I'll do the same."

She whirled and went into the nurses' station, slamming the bottom half of the Dutch door. Kerry looked up and caught Tom's eye. He smiled and rolled his eyes, and she tossed him a wink.

"See that," said Bryant. "Everyone hates it when Virginia's in charge, even her biggest defender."

"Yeah," said Tom with a sigh.

BRSMH, Four South, Millvale, PA
May 20, 2004, 7:15 pm

Tom stepped into the staff break room and grabbed two of the yellow staff report sheets. He folded the forms and slipped them into his pocket, then left the unit for his dinner break.

Though he desperately wanted another Freddie's Fry Shack feast, he didn't want another dose of artery-clogging fats, let alone the diet-smashing caloric load. *Besides, Bryant is right. I'm not going to let her get to me.* Instead of picking up fast food, Tom sat in his car eating the fruit, cold cuts, and cheese he'd brought, and wrote Virginia up for both the unfair work assignment and the comment in the hall. All he had to do to finish the job was to slip back into the break room at some point and slip them under the head nurse's door. With a deep breath, he closed his eyes and drove all thoughts of Vee from his mind.

When he felt better, he grabbed his phone and called David.

"Hey, lover," said David after the first ring.

"Hey. Does it bother you when people call you a fag or imply you are one?"

"Why should it? Ignorant peasants are beneath my notice."

"David, I'm serious."

"So am I, lover. People use those terms to goad you, to piss you off so they can feel superior. The words are meaningless unless you give them power over you." David paused for the space of a few breaths. "Why? Did your mother—"

"No, no. She still hasn't called. It was Virginia. She's being—"

"A drag queen?"

"—a flat-out bitch."

"Don't tell me she picked another fight and then bounced out of the room, leaving you on your own."

"No, not that. She assigned me nearly half the unit, and it all just hit me—Mom, and then this. I went into the therapy room to...chill out a minute. Bryant came in and offered to help, and as we came out, she yelled down the hall that there wasn't time for us to screw each other in the therapy room."

"What a bitch!"

"Told you."

"Was she joking?"

"Of course, she *pretended* it was a joke later, but she was pissed off that Bryant—"

"Wait. Why would she be pissed at that?"

"She's punishing me for talking to Margie after the last fight she picked."

"She's a stupid whore, Tom. You know that about her. Water off a duck's back, lover."

"Yeah."

"And, of course, you need to write her up."

"Yeah, that's what Bryant said, too. I just finished."

"Good for you, Tom. She's an ignorant hussy, and it's about time someone educated her on how to act like a proper person."

"Then it *would* bother you."

"Not the implication that I'm gay. I mean, I *am* gay, Tom. *We* are."

"Yeah, but she doesn't know that."

David laughed. "Yes, now you're catching on. She said it because she wanted to get a rise out of you. She thought it would goad you, hurt you, not because she knows and wants to out you to the world."

"That's true."

"Of course it is, lover. Now, tell me what you wrote. I want all the juicy details so I can imagine her fat face when the head nurse calls her in."

Tom chuckled and read what he had written, then they chatted about nothing until dinner break was over. He climbed out of his car wearing his first genuine smile of the day.

When he got back to the unit, Vee glared at him and sauntered over with the admissions forms. She squinted up at him and shoved the clipboard into his gut. "He's here. Go do your intake."

"Easy-peasy, Vee," Tom said with a smile.

She looked at him with open suspicion. "My car better be okay."

Tom laughed, mirth sparkling in his eyes. "Vee, you know me better than that."

"I *thought* I did. I *thought* you were my friend."

"To be honest, Vee, I'm not sure you know what that word means," Tom said. He turned and left her standing in the station staring at his back.

In the intake room, he took the chair opposite the new patient. The man sat staring at the corner, as still as a corpse, and didn't acknowledge him. Tom let the silence stretch for a moment, then glanced down at the form. "William Stedman? Do I have that right?"

The man didn't move, didn't speak, didn't remove his gaze from the corner.

"My name is Tom. What should I call you? Bill? Will?"

"It's William," the new patient grated. "TH!"

"William T. H. Stedman?"

"No!" William looked at him with open scorn. "My middle name is Andrew. William *Andrew* Stedman. Why would my middle initials be TH? TH, get it together, kid!"

Tom shrugged. "You said your name was William TH."

"No. I said, 'It's William full stop. TH full stop.'"

"Ah, I get it. I misunderstood you." Tom tapped the clipboard with his pen. "Want to tell me what 'TH' means?"

"I'm not in the mood for jokes, kid. Get me?"

"Sure, but I wasn't joking. I would like to know."

William scoffed. "You know what it means, *Mister* Tom. Don't be coy. TH, I wasn't born yesterday!"

Tom spread his hands. "No, I really—"

"*Everyone knows what it means!*" William shouted. "That's it! TH! That's it!"

"Hey, calm down, William." Tom held out one hand, patting the air. "I have no idea what you mean by 'TH,' but it's no big deal if you don't want to tell me."

William rolled his eyes. "Think about it. Think about it." He turned his gaze back to the corner. "Ask your damn psychic questions so I can go to my room."

"Well…okay, I guess. I understand you're upset, but we frown on yelling here. I'd appreciate it if you would—"

"That's it! Is that some kind of threat? I don't like being threatened, kid. TH! That's it!"

"No, no, William. You've got me all wrong. Please hear me out."

William shrugged, breathing hard, and refused to meet his eye. "Questions. Ask."

"Okay, William. No problem, but please try to rein in that anger of yours. Your time here will be easier for everyone if you can." Tom smiled at him. "We're here to help."

William turned a furious gaze on him and snapped his fingers. "Questions, questions." His gaze drifted to Tom's right shoulder, and William's eyes widened, and he pulled his legs up in front of him.

"Okay, here we go, William." Tom delivered the mental status exam questions he'd used with Kaspar and noted the results. "So, William, can you tell me why you are here?"

"TH! The...the...the *guy* in the black robes said I had to come here and straighten you people out. And I can see why with that *thing* running around."

"What thing do you mean?"

William turned his head a little to the side and narrowed his eyelids. "Oh, you know." His gaze slipped away from Tom's, seeming to stare at something over Tom's right shoulder. "TH! You of all people know."

Tom shrugged. "I really don't."

"Look, kid, at my house... At my house, there was a monster, too, and I..." Stedman shook his head violently. "No, not telling that one. TH! Okay." He took a deep breath. "See, I went shopping for a steak, and I couldn't find the cut I wanted. I started screaming at the...the man in white. The cops came and hauled me off. For *nothing*, kid. For nothing. Railroad job all the way, man."

"Then the police took you in for an evaluation somewhere, then the judge ordered you here for treatment?" Tom checked the box labeled "Loose Associations."

"Isn't that what I just said? TH! That's it!" William's eyes never drifted away from the point above Tom's shoulder.

Tom nodded and wrote "labile" in the affect box. Underneath it, he wrote "likely hallucinating" and circled it. "Do you have any questions about your commitment order?"

"No, but why didn't the store have a freaking New Your Strip? I mean, I mean, I mean it's right over there!" William flung his hand toward the north. "How can you not have a New Your Strip when we're so close to New Your?"

"New *York*," said Tom. "You mean, New York."

William's nostrils flared. "That's it! TH!"

Tom made a placating gesture with the hand holding his pen, then he checked the box labeled "Neologisms" wrote and underlined "TH" and "New Your Strip" next to it. "I'm not your enemy, William. I'm here to help you get better."

"Better wetter setter fetter!" William snarled. "I mean, is it so wrong to try to get a monster out of your house? I bet you didn't even try. Why haven't you *tried*? How am I supposed to clear out the monsters without a New Your-Ka Strip?"

"I don't know, William." He checked the box labeled "Clangs" and wrote "disorganized thinking" in the affect box.

"Yeah, that's it! You don't know. TH!"

Tom cocked his head to the side. "I don't have anything else, William. Do you have any questions for me? About the unit, I mean."

"Nah. One's as good as two." His eyelids narrowed.

"Is there something wrong, William?"

"Wrong? What could be wrong?" He made a cross of his fingers and held it up between them.

"You keep staring at my shoulder." He pointed at William's crossed fingers with his pen. "The cross."

"No. No. No. I'm not talking. TH!"

Tom sighed. "Okay, let's go get you a bed and get you situated."

"Fine!" snapped William. He stood and picked up the blue book he'd been sitting on. Imprinted on the cover in gold ink were the words "Book of Mormon."

"Are you religious, William?"

"TH! You betcha. TH!"

"Okay. You'll be allowed to keep the book unless it becomes a problem."

William's brows knitted, and he tilted his head to the side. "How could a book become a problem? It's a book."

"What I meant was, you can keep it, but keep your beliefs to yourself. Don't argue religion, don't abuse the privilege."

"Oh. Well, you should have said that."

"Sorry, I get tongue-tied at times."

"Fine. TH, kid," he said with a sigh. "Get a grip."

Tom opened the door and ushered William out onto the floor. Kaspar Anderson lingered across the hall, eyeing the door at the end of it. "Move along, Kaspar."

"Right, right," murmured Kaspar. "I was only riveting the rabbits."

"Yep, but do it in the dayroom or the activity room, okay?"

Kaspar frowned. "Those twins bug me."

"That's because you're demon shit," snarled William. "TH! Don't you know that? That's it! TH!"

Kaspar froze, staring at the new patient as though he had horns growing from his forehead.

Tom rested a hand on William's shoulder. "Clear out, Kaspar. I'll come find you in a bit, and we can talk about the Amhain brothers."

Kaspar nodded and backed away. After a few steps, he turned and sprinted around the corner.

"Don't run, Kaspar!" Tom called.

"No, he'd better run. Shit like that? Yeah, TH!"

14

BRSMH, Four South, Millvale, PA
May 20, 2004, 10:37 pm

"Tom, what the hell is this? Some kind of joke?" Virginia came around the corner and stood at the end of the narrow charting area, one hand on her ample hip, the other holding a clipboard.

"Stedman's admission? No joke," Tom said, with a glance at Bryant who sat across from him. "He's clearly schizophrenic."

"Then why didn't you *write that?* Why all this gibberish?"

Tom sighed. "What gibberish, Vee?"

She stomped toward him and shoved the clipboard in his face. "This is gibberish, Tom, and you know it. What I want to know is what you think this will accomplish? I won't get in trouble over this, but you *will*."

Tom took the clipboard and glanced down at it. None of the symptom checkboxes bore marks, but three Js appeared at random places on the form. He frowned down at them then scanned the rest of the form. In the affect box, written in what was clearly *not* his handwriting, were the words: "One chance not enough try again coming back live forever." Underneath that he'd written, "Hail to the king thing sing" and circled it. Next to the Neologisms box, he'd written, "Start the killing, start the killing." At the very bottom he'd written, "Watch your tongue or have it cut from your head. My flesh will feed the demon. I've been chosen to pay with my life wife strife knife. Knife. Knife. Turning witches and saints to ashes. Blood. Flood. Blood flood."

He shook his head and sank back against the chair back. "I don't understand," he murmured. "I didn't write this."

"You didn't let Stedman write it, I hope."

"Of course I didn't, Vee."

"Then who did write it, Tom?" Virginia demanded. "Do you even recognize the behaviors, Tom? The disorganization, the loose associations, the neologisms, the clangs, the perseveration? And it gets worse. Turn it over."

Tom stared up at her angry eyes and fear flooded his brain. "I…"

"Oh, for Christ's sake, Tom." Virginia snatched the clipboard and flipped the intake form over. She cleared her throat and read, "I will suffer for so long—not long enough. You're now a slave until the end of time. You should have known. Coming back, coming back. Live forever, die forever. Let's have a wedding, have a bedding. Let's start the killing. Start the killing. Start filling the willing. And I know it's not your time, Vee, but bye-bye." She glared at him. "That's pretty fucked up poetry, Tom, if you can call it that. And is that a death threat at the end?"

"Vee, I didn't write any of that."

She lifted her arms out to her sides, clipboard narrowly missing Bryant's eye with the corner. "No?"

"No. And all I want to know is: who did? It's not funny, whoever it was."

"Virginia, why would you do something like this?" asked Bryant, his voice filled with disdain.

She whirled to face him, her hand holding the clipboard cocked back to strike him. "*Me?* Why would *I* write this shit?"

"To get Tom in trouble," said Bryant in a matter-of-fact voice. "To manipulate things to your liking. As you always do."

For a moment, Tom thought she *would* hit him, but then she threw back her head and laughed. She tossed the clipboard in front of Bryant. "I guess I'll just have to write both of you bastards up."

"Be my guest," said Bryant. "The more people who know about this bullshit, the better."

Virginia turned to glare at Tom. "I thought you were my friend."

"Yeah, you said that already, and what I said still goes. This…" He lifted his hand toward the clipboard. "That's not exactly the act of a friend, Virginia." His voice rang with conviction, but deep inside, a tiny voice asked, *What if I did write those things?*

15

Tom's apartment, Millvale, PA
May 20, 2004, 10:48 pm

Tom paced back and forth, back and forth, back and forth. He'd been chewing his thumbnail and had it down to the quick. He glanced at David.

"Come here, Tom. Sit with me," David said in a serene voice.

"How could she do it?"

David dropped his gaze to the stack of "Gay Ministry" pamphlets and the sheet of flowery notepaper. "I'm sorry, Tom. I never should have pushed you."

"No, you were right, David. One hundred percent right." Tom bent and snatched the notepaper up.

Rage thundered in his veins, just as his pulse thundered in his ears. He wasn't quite sure who he was angry with, but the urge to lash out, to really *hurt* someone, was overpowering. "Tommy," he read aloud, "I love you more than you can ever know. You know the sacrifices I've made for you…sticking in this cemetery of a town so you could have a good childhood, so you could grow up with your friends, stay in the same school. You know, I could've been an actress if I'd uprooted you and moved to New York City. Or a singer in Nashville. I could have been someone, Tommy. But I sacrificed all that for you. I stayed in this dump for you."

"No guilt intended," said David with a curl of his lip.

Tom grimaced and read on. "I'm not going to tell you what to do with your life, Son. I'm not going to tell you who to 'love,' but *I am going to pray*. For you, for your eternal soul. The Bible—"

"Can you believe the gall?" demanded David. "I have half a mind to go over there and slap that crazy bitch."

"Hey," Tom said with a sigh. "She's still my mother." He collapsed on the couch next to David.

"I know, lover, but I can't stand to see her treat you like this. The sheer hypocrisy…" He took a deep, slow breath. "I know. I'm sorry, Tom."

Tom nodded and returned his gaze to the note. "The Bible says what you are *pretending* to be is a sin.

Tommy, I just don't understand why you are doing this to me. You and I both know you aren't one of those kind of men. I just hope you haven't let that David trick you into doing something that puts your soul in jeopardy."

"Ha!" David said with a sour smile. "Should we tell her *you* seduced *me*?"

Tom blushed furiously and dropped his gaze. "I was so drunk," he whispered.

"Oh, lover, there's *nothing* to be ashamed of. Don't let your zealot of a mother make you feel this way."

Tom shook his head. "That's the funniest part."

"What is, Tom?"

"Mom hasn't been to mass since I was nine. Not even for Christmas or Easter."

"That doesn't surprise me. The rest of the note—all that bullshit from Leviticus—reads like she's quoting from some website. Doesn't she even realize Leviticus is an *edited* book?"

"I don't think she even owns a Bible, David."

"Doesn't surprise me. And these"—he swept up the Gay Ministry pamphlets and shook them—"glowing examples of love thy neighbor—"

"Probably from her friends," murmured Tom.

"It's *all* bullshit, lover. Selective reading of Leviticus. Skipping over the nonsense parts, ignoring what doesn't fit the agenda! Pseudoscience in the guise of—"

"*I know all that!*" snapped Tom, lunging up from the couch, crumpling up the letter with disgust. "It's all bullshit! Everyone agrees, from the American Psychiatric Association to the Surgeon General! You don't have to *convince* me!"

David looked up at him with hurt in his eyes.

"And you can stop looking at me like that! She's *still my mother*, David!"

"I know," said David, turning his face away.

Tom grabbed the pamphlets from David's hands and balled them up with the letter. "I need to get this bullshit out of my house." He slammed out the door into the evening air and rounded the side of the building, almost running to the dumpsters.

Rage thundered in his veins, just as his pulse thundered in his ears. He wasn't quite sure who he was angry with, but the urge to lash out, to really *hurt* someone, was overpowering.

16

Tom's apartment, Millvale, PA
May 21, 2004, 12:34 am

"Where have you been, Tom?" asked David in a voice that reflected more hurt than anger. "You've been gone nearly two hours, and you left your phone here."

"I...uh..." Tom didn't meet his gaze. "I went to work out. I had to burn off my emotions."

"Oh." David didn't meet his gaze. Instead, he looked down at his hands in his lap.

"It's something you need to understand about me, David. There are times I have to hit the gym, to channel my emotions against iron. It's better this way."

David lifted one shoulder in a shrug. "I could have gone with you."

Tom shook his head. "Most of the time, I'd welcome you. But not tonight. Not when I'm too pissed to see straight."

David grimaced and began fiddling with one of his belt loops.

"Look, David. I'm sorry I didn't tell you, but it was better this way."

"Better for you, maybe."

Tom drew in a deep breath. "Sometimes I'm an asshole. Sometimes I want to yell and scream, and if I hang around, I'll end up taking things out on you. I don't want to do that."

"Then at least take your phone and send me a text."

Tom frowned. "The problem is that when I'm like that, I'm already not thinking straight. I can't promise I'll remember the phone." He went over and sat on the couch next to David. "Can I just apologize for tonight, and then apologize in advance for the future?"

David heaved a sigh and nestled next to Tom. He lay his head on Tom's chest. "I'm sorry that I just made everything worse for you, Tom. I didn't mean to."

"It's not your fault. It's my damn mother's fault. It's Virginia's fault. It's been a shitty, shitty couple of days, David."

"I'll gut that drag queen with a rusty knife, lover. Just say the word."

Tom wasn't sure which woman David meant, but he nodded and put his arm around him anyway.

"And don't worry about all that stuff, Tom. Not your mother, not the bitch at work, not the stuff on that form. It'll all be okay. Trust me. I once did a doctor."

Tom chuckled and gave David a one-armed hug. "I need a shower. I'm sure I stink."

"I don't care, lover," said David in a soft voice. "Can we sit like this for a little?"

"Sure," said Tom. "I think I'd like that."

"Good. I'll tell you about my shitty day. Let's see… First, I ran out of milk. I had to go all the way to the store and—"

"You live half a block from the grocery store."

"Yeah, I know. Terrible, right? I barely made it. Then, I had to walk all the way to the back of the store to get the milk. Then, all the way back up to the register."

"Sounds horrible."

"Oh, it was, lover." He craned his neck and planted a soft kiss on Tom's cheek. "You weren't there."

17

Tom clocked in as soon as the clock showed 2:42 p.m. and walked into the nurses' station. It was full of nurses and psych techs as most shift changes were, but instead of the usual banter and joking around, the place was as silent as a library. Kerry stood at the back of the room, arms crossed, looking down at her shoes. Tom sidled up to her and whispered, "What's going on?"

Kerry glanced at him, her expression flat. "They've got Vee in there." She pointed at the door that led to the head nurses' office. "Margie and Cindi."

"Oh, boy." He blew out his cheeks.

"Yeah," said Kerry, breaking eye contact. "I bet you're all broken up."

He couldn't get a read on her. He knew she sometimes clowned around with Virginia in the station, but she did that with everyone. And she complained about the woman as much as anyone else. "You know, I used to like her. I used to think the people who complained about her had a grudge, a chip on their shoulders, but…"

"But you don't anymore," she murmured. She wrinkled her nose and ground the toe of her shoe into the carpet.

"That's right. She's picked one too many fights and then hoofed it—leaving me on my own after I waded in to save her ass. And on top of that, she gets mad at me for being pissed off and acts like a…" Tom sighed and shook his head. "I could have been seriously hurt, and all because she had to have a pissing contest with a pair of psychotics. All she needed to do was wait a few minutes and the show would have been over."

"Sure," said Kerry with a shrug. "Why not ignore all the rules?"

"Some rules are less important than others. Besides, she said a hateful thing to Bryant and me yesterday. And that bullshit with the intake form…that's…that's pretty fucked up."

"You've got that right." Her tone was ambiguous, but she wouldn't look at him.

"I *didn't* write that stuff, Kerry. It's not even my handwriting."

Kerry shrugged. "Margie said to tell you they will probably pull you in at some point, so you and Bryant make sure you get your stories straight."

"Kerry, there's nothing to get straight…" He let the sentence trail away as the unit secretary pushed off the counter and walked away. He blew out a breath and shook his head, arms crossed tightly over his chest.

18

"Come in, Tom," said Cindi Parker. "Take a seat."

The atmosphere in Cindi's office was laden with suppressed emotion, and the air fairly crackled with tension. Margie sat on Cindi's side of the desk and that left a single chair on the other side of the desk.

"Hello," said Tom.

"I bet you're wondering what's going on," said Cindi, grimacing down at eight or nine yellow staff report forms.

He followed her gaze and recognized the two he'd put in. He recognized Bryant's scrawl on three of the others and was willing to bet the remaining forms filled with tiny, angry script were from Virginia. He heaved a sigh. "Sorry about all this. I kept quiet as long as I could."

"You shouldn't apologize, and you shouldn't have to apologize." Cindi raised her gaze to meet his own. "But Margie and I find ourselves in a bit of a rough spot." She waved her hand at the yellow sheets on her desk. "At first glance, it seemed to me that you'd been caught up in a war between Bryant and Virginia, but Margie explained a few recent events to me. Having said that…" She shook her head, closing her eyes and allowing her bangs to fall forward. "This is quite a mess. Let's try to go through it step-by-step."

"Whatever I can do," said Tom.

"Let's start with the events of the other night—the incident with the Amhain brothers."

"Okay. I want to start by saying the entire incident was avoidable. And that's happened countless times before."

"What is 'that?'"

Tom glanced at Margie, and she nodded almost imperceptibly. He took a deep breath. "Virginia has a...let's just say it's a unique way of dealing with some patients. She—"

"No, that won't do, Tom," said Cindi. "You need to be explicit here. This is a serious situation, so no half-measures, no beating around the bush, no euphemisms."

Tom glanced at Margie, then gave Cindi a single, slow nod. "Okay. I'll be straight-up. Virginia gets into pissing-matches with the patients. She picks fights, then she runs and leaves the psych techs to deal with the mess."

"And that's what happened the other night?"

"You bet. Ezzy and Izzy have this thing about Star Trek. They think Spock is their uncle—or maybe God"—he pumped his shoulders up and down, rapid-fire—"and they watch the show waiting for him to appear. That night, the dinner cart came before the show had finished, but only by a few minutes. Vee told them they had to go to dinner. When they ignored her, she walked over and unplugged the television."

"That's the rule," said Cindi.

"Yes, I know, but that's not all she did. I probably could have cooled them out, even then. But when Ismael scolded her and shook his finger at her, she got mad—I could see it in her face, hear it in her tone. She was *angry*. She stepped up to him, put her finger in his face, and started chewing him out."

Cindi glanced at Margie, who nodded.

"I had my hands full with Ezekiel, who was throwing chairs and trying to get at her for unplugging the show. Ezzy started yelling about sparing the rod and spoiling the child, and then Vee yelled at him to shut up, still right up in Izzy's face. She kept escalating and escalating, and finally, Ismael took her to the floor and started hitting her. I'd been trying to control Ezekiel the whole time and yelling for Virginia to hit the Button. It was right next to her, but she was too busy winding them up."

Cindi nodded. "Then what happened."

"Well, she was down, Ismael was sitting on her belly and slapping her. I had to get him off, and Ezekiel was fighting me like a wildcat. I used his momentum and flung him into the Button, then I got Ismael off Vee."

"And she helped you restrain them?"

Margie scoffed.

"No. Virginia never helps. She ran into the activities room and left me alone with both brothers, who she'd worked into a lather."

"Were you hurt?"

"Got my bell rung. One of them slammed my head into the wall or the floor, I don't quite remember that part. I remember thinking I had to turn it around, to regain control, or if I couldn't, that I had to get away. I…" He shook his head. "I righted the boat with a tire poker."

Cindi did a double-take. "What did you say?"

"I got some separation and followed Vee into the activities room."

She shook her head then looked at Margie, who was grim-faced. "Have you gotten yourself checked out, Tom?"

Tom shook his head. "No, I'm nine."

"You're nine?" Cindi leaned forward, her brows pulling together.

"Uh, *fine*. I'm fine. I'm a lot nervous right now, and upset that it's come to this, that's all."

Cindi shrugged and sat back. "I'm going to need you to get yourself checked out by a doctor, Tom. Just to be sure."

"Oh."

"It'll be covered by Worker's Comp, so don't worry about the expense. A head injury is nothing to be macho about."

"Right."

Cindi nodded once and looked down at the staff reports on her desk. "Okay. I've got the picture on that. I guess you spoke with Margie about that incident? She thinks someone overheard your conversation and told Virginia the details. Which brings us to yesterday's events."

"Right. Margie was off, so Virginia was the charge nurse. She gave me seven patients—well, six, and a new admission."

Cindi nodded and pulled the intake form from underneath the staff reports.

"I didn't write that stuff."

"We'll get to that, Tom. For now, just tell me what happened at the start of the shift."

"Like I said she gave me six patients and Bryant two. The other side was split down the middle between Frank and Ricky, so it was clear she did it on purpose. I'd... I'd had a bad day. Personal issues." He cleared his throat. "Anyway, I was upset, so I left report and went into the therapy room to calm down. Bryant found me there and offered to help split the load—he'd already tried to get Vee to reassign some of the patients, but she said no. Anyway, Bryant said we had to do it unofficially or Vee would raise a stink. As we left the therapy room, she was standing up by the nurses' station and yelled down that there wasn't time for us to..." He blushed and cut his gaze to the floor. "To have sex in the therapy room. We ignored her and got on with our day."

"And you worked the whole shift assigned six patients and a new admit?"

Tom nodded. "Yes, but Bryant took three of them unofficially, which gave him five and me three plus the admission." He sniffed. "Vee… She also implied that if I was her friend, I'd never have spoken to Margie about the Amhain thing."

Cindi nodded again, glancing at Margie. "Let's talk about the new admission form, now."

"Right. I filled out the form correctly. I did my job, and I gave that form to Virginia. I don't know what she did with it. When we were charting out for the night, Vee came around and started accusing me of writing all that stuff on the form, of being schizophrenic, and—"

"She actually called you schizophrenic?"

Tom pursed his lips and looked up at the ceiling. "I… I think so. She either came right out with it, or she implied it by comparing me to the patient, to William Stedman. She made a big production of reading all that stuff on the form, of accusing me of trying to get her in trouble. Bryant got in the middle of it, and she almost hit him with the clipboard. Then she left, saying she'd write us up."

"And that's when you two decided to write *her* up?"

"No. We talked about that as we walked up the hall from the therapy room."

"After she'd yelled down the hallway to stop having sex with Bryant," added Margie with a significant look at Cindi.

Tom nodded. "Yeah. I did mine on my dinner break."

"And she threatened to write you up at ten forty-five?"

"Yeah, about then."

Cindi pursed her lips. "Let's talk about what's written on the form."

"It's rough stuff," said Tom. "I would never write stuff like that, not even in the privacy of my own home. It's... Plus it's a word-salad, disorganized, full of clangs, and that poem or whatever it is, on the back..." Tom shook his head. "That's not something I would do."

Cindi nodded again and pulled out a blank piece of paper and a black ballpoint pen. "Tom, I believe you, but I have to document everything about last night. I'm going to dictate a few things to you, you write them down, and later, what you write is going to be compared to your handwriting and style in the charts. Okay?"

"Yes, absolutely. I didn't write that stuff, and it's not my handwriting, so I want to do this."

"Okay." She nodded at the pen and Tom picked it up. Cindi dictated a few of the lines from the admission form, and Tom wrote them down. When he was done, Cindi held up both sheets, her eyes darting from one to the other. "Virginia has alleged you or Bryant did this left-handed to obscure the handwriting."

"I can't do better than chicken scratch left-handed."

"Even so, we need a sample." She pulled out another sheet of paper and wrote the word "Left" across the top. Then they repeated the process. When they were done, it was clear to everyone that neither sheet matched the form.

"Okay, Tom," said Cindi, treating him to a grim smile. "I think I've got what I need. In the future, if you see a staff member acting inappropriately, write them up right away. Please don't hold back."

"Believe me, I'll never do that again."

Cindi dismissed him with a nod. "Could you please send Bryant in?"

He left and found Bryant in the charting area for the psych techs, doing nothing but waiting, and Tom sent him in to see Cindi and Margie.

The meeting had caused Tom to miss report, so he grabbed a copy of the assignment sheet Margie had left, then picked up the charts for his four patients. He carried them into the place he usually sat to write his charts and sat down to read them.

A few minutes later, Virginia slipped around the corner and approached him. Her face wore a nasty, hateful expression. "I hope you're happy, causing all this mess."

"Vee," he said with a sigh. "*I* didn't cause the mess."

"Oh, sure! Throw in with all the other assholes, you little traitor. You were supposed to be my *friend*. You're just like all the rest!"

"Look, I—"

"No, you look. I *need* this job, Tom, and if I lose it because of you, I swear to God, I'll get you." Her finger was up in his face, and he scooted his chair back to get away from her. She advanced on him, her face twisted with a furious grimace. "I'll set you up, just like you did to me last night. I'll…I'll let someone get hurt one night and make it look like *you* are at fault. I can do it. I'm smarter than all the rest of you combined."

"Vee, get away from me." His voice carried an angry snap to it, but all it accomplished was a narrowing of the woman's eyes.

"*Fuck you,* Tommy-ba-bommy." She bent at the waist and shoved her face closer to his. "I'll fuck you sideways, you motherfucker, and I'll leave you bleeding. I'll *destroy* you, you son of a bitch. You better watch your back, or you might find yourself locked in a seclusion room with *both* of those psychotic fuckers who kicked your ass a few days ago—and you better believe I'll have told them whatever they need to hear in order to make them want your head on a stick. You just better—"

"*Virginia!*"

Her head snapped up, and her finger dropped. The hateful expression disappeared in an instant, replaced with a friendly smile. She turned to Margie and laughed. "Hello, there, Margie. What's up?"

"I think you'd better go wait in the break room."

"Oh, don't worry about us. We were just having a friendly discussion."

"I *heard* what you said, Virginia. Get your fat ass into the break room and stay there until Cindi decides what to do with you, or I'll call security and have you walked off the premises."

Laughing, Virginia rolled her head on her shoulders and brushed by the other nurse. "Go ahead. Write me up, you backwoods redneck bitch."

"Don't you worry. If it's necessary, I will." As Virginia sauntered down to the break room door, Margie came over. "You okay?"

Tom nodded and closed his eyes. "It's worse than I thought, Margie. She's a complete psychopath."

"Nah, she's a sociopath, Tom. Too hot under the collar, too much of an emotional train wreck for a psychopath. But don't worry, we've finally got her. Between your account and Bryant's her fat ass is barbecued."

"Good," Tom said. It was the only thing he could think of.

19

BRSMH, Staff Parking Lot, Millvale, PA
May 21, 2004, 11:26 pm

Tom walked out of the hospital and into the crisp, cool air of the parking lot. The shift had been full of tension, and the patients had picked up on it, amplified it. No one had needed seclusion, but PRN meds had gone out like candy on Halloween.

All he wanted to do was go home, cuddle on the couch with David for a movie or a couple of shows while he unwound, then go to sleep. *Tomorrow is another day,* he thought. *Let this motherfucker end.* Rolling his head to loosen his upper back and neck muscles, Tom walked between the cars toward the far corner of the lot where he'd parked. He drew a deep breath and let it flow out of him like water over the falls, forcing himself to relax, to shed the tension.

Cindi had suspended Virginia, so she would be back, but after stewing in her own juices for a week and ruminating about how Tom had "fucked her over." Her return would not bring pleasure or peace to the unit. *Maybe it's time to find another job,* he thought.

He fished his keys out of his pocket by his lanyard and thumbed through them for his car key. He approached the car with his head down, plodding more than walking. He didn't see Virginia sitting in the car next to his until it was too late.

"I hope you're happy, asshole!" she snapped as he turned into the space between their two cars.

All his muscles tensed in one tonic jolt, and he bounced off the rear quarter panel of his car. "Jesus! What the fuck are you trying to do, Vee? Scare me to death?"

"No, Tom," she said in a voice devoid of emotion. "I'm not trying to scare you. Not anymore."

"Then what do you want?"

"I'm suspended, but I'll bet that little West Virginia hooker already shared that with you. I just wanted you to know one thing: I meant what I said about getting you back."

Tom bent at the waist so he could peer into her darkened car. She sat facing forward, not even looking at him, her hands curled loosely around the steering wheel. "Vee, it's—"

"Stop calling me that! You're *not* my friend, so don't pretend you are."

"I am your friend, *Vee.* But your behavior on the unit is sometimes—"

"Save it. I no longer give half-a-fuck what you think." She turned her head toward him in a slow, almost mechanical arc. "I'll get you back, like I said. I promise you." When her eyes locked on his, she winked, and a vicious smile appeared on her lips. "*You motherfucking, ass-fucking faggot!*" Her wooden expression fell away, replaced with animated glee, brisk hatred, and spry savagery. "I'll tell *everyone,* gay-boy."

"What? I'm not—"

"Save it!" she snapped. She lifted a piece of paper from her lap—a crisp piece of his mother's flowery stationery covered with her graceful script—in one hand, and a pamphlet that showed a man on his knees, hands folded, head down, praying. "You *are* a faggot, Tom. Your mommy already knows, and she *hates* it, but now, *everyone* else will know, too."

Rage crept up his spine. "You go ahead and tell everyone, *Virginia*. You go right ahead."

"Oh, I promise you, I will."

"Do it. I'm sure Human Resources would love to know about this. I'm sure Margie would be happy to tell them. What was it you said inside? That you needed this job? Then go right ahead and tell everyone. See how long your job lasts. In fact, maybe I should go back inside and write up this little chat." He glanced toward the hospital but didn't straighten.

Virginia stared at him through narrowed eyelids, but her hands drooped back to her lap, the stationery fluttering as her hands shook. "Don't do that," she whispered.

He snapped his hand through her open passenger side window. "Give that shit to me. *Now*."

"I…" She shook her head. "I just get so upset, Tom. It seems like everyone is—"

"*Give me the goddamn note!*"

She sighed, her shoulders hunching, then drooping. She shifted the note and the pamphlet into her right hand and passed them over. "Don't say anything about this. *Please*, Tom. I…I didn't mean it."

His rage still burned hot and sharp in his breast, but her pleading tone softened it around the edges. "Leave me alone from now on. You go do your thing while you're suspended, and when you come back to work, leave me the fuck alone."

"Okay. If that's what you want."

"But let me be very clear, Virginia. Threaten me once more, tell anyone about my personal life, fuck with me in *any* way, and I'm going straight to HR. I won't even bother with those fucking yellow forms. Understand?"

Her head drooped forward, almost touching the steering wheel. "Yes," she whispered.

"Then get the fuck out of my sight." He whirled and jerked his car door open, banging it into Virginia's passenger door, and throwing himself inside. He hurled the note and the pamphlet to the floor of his passenger seat and jammed his keys into the ignition. He snapped his wrist, giving the car plenty of gas, and the engine roared to life. He slammed his door shut and wrenched the car into reverse, not bothering with the brake pedal, and the car leaped into the lane behind. He twisted the wheel and floored it, squealing away from Virginia and out of the parking lot.

20

Tom's apartment complex, Millvale, PA
May 21, 2004, 11:37 pm

Tom had no memory of his drive home. It was just a blur of fury, of flooring it as he left stoplights, of squealing tires. He sat in the car, his hands clenched to the wheel to keep them from shaking, breathing like an irate animal in the bullring. But his stomach heaved, and his pulse slammed in his temples like a blacksmith's hammer striking hot metal.

He didn't even know if he'd called David, but maybe that was for the best, given his mood. Though exhaustion hung around his neck like a noose, he thought he might be better off heading to the gym and putting in a strenuous workout. The only problem was that he didn't *want* to go work out.

He wanted to find someone and beat the living fuck out of them.

Glaring at his shaking hand, Tom put the car in reverse. *Did I call David or not?* He sat there a moment, his foot on the brake, and thumbed through his recent calls.

As he did, his phone rang, and he accepted the call without thinking. "Hello?"

"Hello, Tommy," said his mother.

"Oh. I thought it was David."

"No," she said in a voice gone cold with fury. "I'm not your *boyfriend*."

"I'm not going to talk to you about it, Mom."

"Oh, I think you *need* to talk to me about—"

Tom hung up the phone and dropped it into the console. "No."

The phone rang immediately, and he glanced down to see his mother's number on the screen. He lifted his foot off the brake and hit the gas, not even bothering to reject her call. "Talk to voicemail. No, better yet, *pray for my gay voicemail*," he muttered.

He drove out of the parking lot and turned left, squealing the tires as he went.

21

Tom opened his contacts and blocked his mother's number. She'd left a spate of messages, of which he'd only listened to three—each one more ballistic than the last—and then deleted them all. *Let her feel what rejection from the person who's supposed to unconditionally love her is like,* he thought with a sneer.

He'd called David ten minutes before reaching his apartment—it was after two o'clock, but his boyfriend had been waiting on his call, giving him space, but ready to comfort, to come over if that's what Tom wanted.

Which he did.

He put the car in park and patted the steering wheel—as if that could make up for the abuse he'd heaped on it that night. His knuckles complained, but all of him was achy with exhaustion. He got out of the car and headed inside. He wanted a hot shower to get the sticky grime of the day off his skin.

Tom had just stepped out of the shower and dried himself when David knocked on the door. He wrapped the towel around his waist and plodded to the front of the apartment.

"Hello, lover," said David in a soft, comforting voice. "I'm sorry your day was so awful. But, look, I brought you dinner." He grinned at Tom and brought a Freddie's Fry Shack bag from behind his back. He brought out his other hand and showed Tom the gargantuan cherry milkshake and equally large Dr. Pepper nestled in a Freddie's drink carrier. "Good thing that dump is open until four."

A lopsided smile spread across Tom's lips—the first thing approaching a smile since he'd gone to work. "I don't feel very hungry, but I appreciate the thought."

David smiled and rocked up on his toes to plant a kiss on the side of Tom's mouth that was curled into a smile. "Have a bite or two, just to keep your strength up. That or drop that towel, stud."

"Maybe I will eat a little. And *then* drop the towel." Grinning, Tom stepped back and let David whirl past him with his characteristic toe-kick, heading to the kitchen to put the food on a plate if his past behavior was any guide. Tom heaved a deep breath, feeling content at last. "What a day," he muttered.

"Come on, lover. Eat this food while it's hot."

Tom closed the door and turned the deadbolt, then stepped into the small kitchen and caught his boyfriend in a hug. His hands trembled as he rubbed David's back, and tears stung his eyes.

"Hey, what's all this? Everything's okay, Tom."

"No, it's not. My mother… Virginia… Ah, David… I was so angry. I wanted to…"

"Shh, lover. Don't fret. It's been a *wretched* couple of days for you. It's okay to be angry, to…to feel like lashing out. And don't believe things will stay this way. Your mother will come around."

"But what if she doesn't? She's the only family I've got."

David pulled back so he could look up into Tom's eyes. "If she doesn't, *I'll* be your family. Oh, and my mother. I'll loan her to you. I called her today to talk about how your mom reacted, to see if… To see if I did something that made it easier on her when I came out. She said to tell you not to worry, that a mother's love is stronger than anything you could do."

"I… I hope so." He thought about the voicemails, about blocking her call, and sighed. "Things are so *ugly* between us right now."

"It's been barely more than a couple of days, Tom. Give it time."

"Yeah, I hope you're right."

David gave him another little peck, then stepped out of the hug and waved his hand like a magician over the plate of cheeseburgers. "Tada! This will make you feel better, Tom. Trust me."

"I could have some of the milkshake."

"Dessert *before* you eat?" David grinned up at him. "See? I can mother you until she comes around. Have you picked up your dirty clothes?"

Grinning, Tom pulled the milkshake toward him.

22

BRSMH, Four South, Millvale, PA
May 22, 2004, 2:38 pm

Tom watched the red LED numbers, watched the minutes tick away on the tiny screen of the time clock. He felt calm, relaxed even, and luxuriated in the sensation.

There had been no additional notes from his mother on his car or his front door, and no pamphlets. He'd felt guilty about blocking her calls, though, and had reversed that, but she also hadn't called. *David is right, though. She needs the time and space to process it, to get past her anger.*

The clock hit 2:42 pm—the earliest the hospital allowed them to clock in—and Tom swiped his card through the reader. He left the nurses' station and headed down to the report room. He wanted to catch Margie before everyone came in.

She looked up when he came through the door and flashed her trademark smile at him. "Well, at least today can't suck as much as yesterday. Am I right?"

"You don't know the half of it. She was waiting for me in the parking lot."

"Usually, guys like it when a girl waits for them late at night." She winked, but then frowned. "But I suppose the 'she' in question is a giant of a woman? Smells like chlorine and sweat socks?"

Tom nodded.

"More dire threats? More 'I thought you were my friend?'"

"Yes."

"Well, I wouldn't worry. She's as crazy as a donkey with wings, but she's gone for a week. If she carries on, I'll see her ass fired—or on a different unit at the very least. That's a promise."

Tom inclined his head. "I thought Cindi would terminate her after all this."

"I would have if it had been me in the big chair, but Cindi... Virginia said the word 'lawsuit,' and ole Cindi folded up like a cheap lawn chair."

"Yeah." Tom blew out his cheeks. "I bet if you did something half as bad as Virginia—"

"Nah," said Margie. "I can say 'lawsuit,' too." Her eyes sparkled with a repressed grin. "I bet you can, too, if you put your mind to it."

Tom thought back to his parting words with Virginia and nodded. He hadn't threatened a lawsuit, not exactly, but the effect was the same. "I hope the patients have calmed down. It'd be nice to have a quiet shift for once."

"Your mouth to God's ears, my friend." Margie wagged her head. "Then again, we work in psychiatry, where everyone knows God is dead—or at least not listening." She glanced down at her watch. "The others will come traipsing in any minute. Anything else you need to tell me?"

Did Virginia tell her? he wondered, gazing into Margie's face. *Does she know?* But before he could say anything, Margie glanced down at his hands.

"Good Christ, Tom! What did you do to your hands?"

He glanced down at his swollen, discolored knuckles. "Oh, nothing. I added a new part to my workouts—I'm punching a heavy bag for cardio." It was an out and out lie, but the simple truth—that he had no memory of how he'd bruised his hands—made him sound a little crazy. "I guess I'm doing it wrong."

"Well, I think you need to scratch that one off the list."

"Maybe you're right," he said with a smile.

Margie tilted her head a little to the side and gazed into his eyes for long enough that he began to feel squirmy. He opened his mouth to say something— *anything*—but then the rest of the crew came in, and Margie beamed at them, cracking wise for a minute while everyone settled in for fifteen minutes of utter boredom in the form of recorded notes on the day. She made the assignments as she played the recorded report from the day shift.

Afterward, she stood but motioned everyone to keep their seats. "I want to talk to you about Virginia, to dispense with any silly rumors and get the truth out there. She was suspended—you've all probably heard that already—and for good reason. You'll have to trust me on that, or if you can't, you'll have to trust Cindi. Virginia needed some space, some time to reflect on how she's behaved around here for the past few months. She needs to change her ways if she wants to remain here on Four South." Margie shrugged, looking them each in the eye. "I'm not going to tell you not to tell her what I'm saying. I know some of you are her friends and feel the tug of loyalty, but I am going to ask you to think long and hard about what's best here. What's best for Virginia, and what's best for the unit as a whole." She spread her hands. "Any questions?"

They exchanged glances, but no one spoke.

"Then get the hell out of here and get to work," Margie said with a smile.

23

An hour after dinner, William Stedman approached Tom as he sat in the activity room, thumbing absently through a fitness magazine. "Hey, kid," he said.

Tom looked up at him and grinned. "Hello, William. How are things?"

"Uh, okay."

"Settling in?"

"No. TH, I don't want to stay here. I thought it would be okay, but... No. I want to leave."

Tom treated him to a one-shouldered shrug. "That's not up to either of us, buddy. Have to do what the doctors say, right?"

"TH. Maybe."

"What does that mean, anyway?"

William cocked his head to the side and stared down at him. "Well, kid, it means 'perhaps.'"

"No," Tom said with a chuckle. "What does 'TH' mean?"

William's face pulled down into a grimace. "We already talked about that, kid. I'm still not in any mood for jokes."

Tom lifted his hands in surrender. "No joke, William. I really don't know what it means."

"Well, then. Get with the program, kid! TH! Get with Jesus. That's *it!*"

"Hey, okay, William. No reason to get excited."

"Yeah!" Stedman snapped, suddenly looking furious. "That's what they all say! TH!" He spun on his heel and stepped away.

"William?"

He turned back to glare at Tom. "What now?"

"You came over to me, remember? What was it you needed?"

"Leave me alone," he said in a voice that had lost its furious snap as quickly as it had gained it. He turned and walked toward the arch that led to the day room. "Goddamn television is too loud."

"Don't take the Lord's name insane!" yelled Ismael from the other room.

"Right. TH! Sorry, God."

Tom shook his head and went back to leafing through the magazine. The bruises on both sets of knuckles bothered him. Not only that he couldn't remember how he got them, but because he was far from a violent man—despite his temper.

"TH! Look at that! *That's it!*" yelled Stedman from the day room.

"William!" Tom called. "Back it off a notch."

"*What is that?*" he screamed.

With a sigh, Tom got to his feet and trudged toward the day room.

"*Can you see it? TH! Is that a demon?*"

"Yes, it's a demon," said Ismael in a matter-of-fact voice. "You'll see it a lot if you stay here long. It likes to run him around doing...demon things."

"That's enough, Ismael," said Tom as he stepped into the room. William stood behind the rows of chairs lined up beneath the television. He pointed into the hall at Kaspar Anderson and was breathing fast and hard, his eyes wide as he glared back at Stedman.

"Maybe," said Ismael. "But it's true."

"Yeah," said Ezekiel. "Kaspar has a demon on his back. Any fool who wants to can see it. It's the Mark of Cain."

"Preach it, Ezzy," said Ismael.

"Cut it out. *Both* of you," said Tom. Ismael grinned at him and shrugged. Tom walked by the row they sat in, holding his hands out to his sides, palms up. "Hey, William. What do you say we see if you can have a PRN?"

"Are you *insane?*" William asked, cranking his head around to stare at Tom. "I'm not taking anything that will screw up my head, kid. No. TH says no!"

"Okay. How about a rest, then? A little time on your own? You could read your Book of Mormon."

Kaspar turned to face the day room door, and his expression was unlike anything Tom had ever seen him wear. He looked as though violence bubbled just beneath the surface, but he'd never been that kind of a problem.

"Look at it!" said Stedman. "It's *right there*, kid. Right there on his back!" He took a step toward the door.

Tom glanced at Kaspar, and for half a heartbeat, he saw a dark smudge on the man's left shoulder. He shook his head, and the shadow was gone. "I don't see anything, William."

Stedman turned and squinted at him. "Yes, you do," he said in a calm, quiet voice. "I can see it in your eyes. You saw it. Why are you *lying?*"

With a shriek, Kaspar charged through the door, hands up and fingers hooked into talons. Tom shoved William behind him and stepped forward to meet Anderson's charge.

Kaspar's gaze darted over Tom's shoulder, then swiveled back to meet his gaze. "Get out of my way or you're next!"

Tom nodded, but instead of stepping to the side, he stepped forward and clinched Kaspar chest to chest, one arm over-hooking Anderson's right arm, his other under-hooking the left. Kaspar squawked and jerked his arms, but Tom hooked his leg behind the other man's knee and took him to the ground.

"Serves him right! TH!" cried William. "Carrying a demon around like a…like a…like a *fucking parrot!*"

"How art thou fallen from heaven, O Lucifer, son of the morning," intoned Ismael, getting to his feet.

"How art thou cut down to the ground," said Ezekiel.

"I know that one," said Stedman. "For thou hast said in thine heart, I will ascend into heaven, I will exalt my throne above the stars of God; I will sit also upon the mount of the congregation, in the sides of the north: I will ascend above the heights of the clouds; I will be like the most High. Yet thou shalt be brought down to hell, to the sides of the pit."

"And in those days shall men seek death and shall not find it; and shall desire to die, and death shall flee from them," said Ismael. "You are one of the Chosen, Brother. In spite of your blue book."

"TH!"

"The three of you, knock it off!" snapped Tom. "Everyone into the activity room. Now!" He heard feet pounding in his direction from the hall and knew help was coming, but the three patients standing there quoting Bible verses about devils and demons was making his skin crawl. Beneath him, Anderson had gone still, his narrowed eyes flicking back and forth between the other three patients. His mouth moved soundlessly.

"And to them it was given that they should not kill them, but that they should be tormented five months, and their torment was as the torment of a scorpion, when he striketh a man," said Stedman.

"Yes," said Ismael. "We should free him."

"Cast the demon out," said Ezekiel.

"No, you should get your asses into the activity room like I said, or I swear to God, I'll put the three of you in seclusion for the night."

"Don't take the Lord's name insane!" yelled Ezekiel, and Tom's heart sank into his stomach.

"Put on the whole armor of God, that ye may be able to stand against the wiles of the devil, Tom," said Ismael, his tone like that of a kindly preacher. "For we wrestle not against flesh and blood, but against principalities, against powers, against the rulers of the darkness of this world, against spiritual wickedness in high places."

A strange lethargy stole over Tom as Ismael spoke, and he longed to close his eyes and sleep, to plug his ears, to scream and shout and block out the Bible verses the three nut jobs preached at him. "Oh, Christ, save me," he murmured.

"Oh, Tom," said Ezekiel. "Ye cannot drink the cup of the Lord, and the cup of devils; ye cannot be partakers of the Lord's table, and of the table of devils.

"Just shut up! All of you."

"That's *it*!" shouted William. "TH! *TH, kid! TH!*"

"Yes," said Ismael, and the emotionless way he said it lulled Tom into thinking he was acquiescing to going into the activity room. But then Ismael grabbed him by the shoulders and peeled him off Kaspar with a maniacal strength.

Ezekiel stepped up beside his brother and lay a hand on Tom's arm, though his gaze rested on Kaspar. "And say, thus saith the Lord God; Woe to the women that sew magic charms on their sleeves and make veils for the heads of people to hunt souls! Will ye hunt the souls of my people, and will ye save the souls alive that come unto you?" He cranked his foot back and kicked at Kaspar's head.

Kaspar whirled around like some martial arts movie stuntman, then shot up to his feet. Ezzy's kick whiffed through the space where he'd been a moment before, and a horrible mask of fury washed down over Kaspar's face. *"I'll kill you for that!"* He balled up his fists like a bare-knuckles champion and shuffled his feet as Muhammed Ali had always done in the ring.

Tom shot both hands out to his sides, trying to hold the Amhain brothers back with sheer force of will. "Everyone back off!" Kaspar smiled and met his gaze for a moment, but it did nothing to reassure Tom—his face writhed with murderous glee—but even as he did so, he ducked and lurched forward with the speed of a rampaging insect, fingers clawed. He hooked one hand around Ezzy's knee and flung it up. Ezzy went down with a squawk, and Izzy launched himself at Anderson—slamming past Tom's arm. He set his hips and kicked at Anderson.

Smiling, Kaspar took the kick in the side, then clamped his arm down on Izzy's leg and jerked it up and around, flinging him against the wall. He laughed as Izzy thudded first into the wall, then to the ground.

Ezzy lunged up at him, but Tom caught him by the shoulders and spun him to the wall behind him.

Kaspar gave Tom a cold smile, then advanced toward Stedman. "Your turn," he said in a casual tone, again raising his fists.

"He's *crazy*!" Stedman bolted toward the door.

"Someone press the Button!" Tom called, watching Anderson, watching each Amhain.

Kaspar glanced at him and winked. He cocked his hand back and swung it in an overhand arc, aimed at Stedman's neck or side of the head.

Tom pushed Stedman away and slid in behind Kaspar, whipping his arm around Kaspar's waist. Ezzy pushed away from the wall and came on swinging both arms, pinwheeling his fists at Kaspar's head, but Tom jerked Kaspar around, taking Ezekiel's blows on the shoulder.

Izzy pushed up from the ground with a wild cry and aimed a chop at Kaspar's neck—just like he'd seen Captain Kirk do that afternoon—but Kaspar twisted his head away, and Izzy's knife-edged hand cracked Tom in the face.

Ricky came sliding through the door from the hallway, then froze, eyes wide.

"Come on, Ricky! For Christ's sake!" yelled Bryant as he thundered into the room and shouldered the other tech aside. He grabbed Stedman and shoved him at Ricky, then stepped toward Izzy, hands out.

"Izzy! Watch out!" shouted Ezekiel.

Kaspar wiggled and twisted in Tom's grasp, suddenly feeling like a greased slug. "*Get your hands off me!*" he cried.

Tom whirled him around again, trying to make space, trying to keep him away from the Amhain brothers, but Ezekiel had circled around and landed a heavy fist on the side of Kaspar's head. Anderson sagged against Tom, stunned for the moment.

Bryant latched on to one of Izzy's wrists and pulled him away, gathering him in a giant bear hug, then spinning away so Ismael faced the wall.

Ezekiel landed another haymaker on Kaspar, then threw another that rang against Tom's ear as he tried to turn away. He back-pedaled, arms still wrapped around Anderson, twisting side to side, but Ezzy no longer seemed to care where his fists landed.

He shoved Kaspar toward the activity room, and shouted, "Go to activities, Kaspar!" Then, he threw his arms around Ezekiel and slammed him to the ground with a trip and twist. Ezzy grunted and lay still.

"Okay, Tommy-ba-bommy," he murmured. "Okay."

"Look out, Tom!" shouted Ricky.

Tom darted a glance over his shoulder—just in time to see the chair swinging down to crash down across his back, Kaspar's vicious smile leering at him from behind it.

Bryant shoved Izzy toward Ricky, who had done nothing to secure William Stedman, slammed into Kaspar, and ripped the chair out of his hands.

Moving with all the speed of a ninety-year-old arthritic, William lifted his hand to point at Kaspar

Anderson, who stood straight in Bryant's grasp, looking dazed, lost. "It's off him, now. TH! It's...it's *looking at me!*" He turned and sprinted into the hall, screaming nonsense about demons.

Dazed and shaken, Tom turned his head back toward Kaspar. He stood there looking around as though he'd missed some crucial part of the evening and couldn't catch up. His eyes were still wide open, but his pupils had dilated. A bit of drool ran from the corner of his mouth and a faint mist puffed out with each breath.

"Kaspar? Are you okay?" Tom hissed.

At first, Kaspar did nothing but stare at him, then he nodded slowly.

24

Tom's apartment, Millvale, PA
May 23, 2004, 7:15 am

The ringing phone pulled Tom out of a nightmare, but once awake, he could no longer remember the details—just that it contained a lot of violence, blood, and Bible verses. He reached for the cordless phone. "Hello?"

"Mr. Madsen?"

"This is he. May I ask who's calling?"

"Hello, this is Deputy Patrick O'Hara from the Castle County Sheriff's Department."

Tom pushed himself up against the headboard, his heart thumping in his chest. "Yes? How can I help you, Deputy?"

"Mary Madsen is your mother?"

"That's correct."

"Is she with you?"

"No. Your call woke me. What's wrong?"

"I'm here at your mother's house, Mr. Madsen. When was the last time you saw her?"

"What's happened? Is my mom okay?"

"When did you see her last, Tom?" asked the deputy in a quiet, but firm voice.

"Um, three—no four days ago, I think. Is she okay?"

"Mr. Madsen, your mother is missing. Her house was broken into but as the perp made entry in the rear of the home, the neighbors didn't notice. Her lawncare man saw the open door and got worried. He's the one who called us."

"Oh my God," Tom murmured.

"Would she have gone somewhere else? A family member? Friend?"

"No," said Tom. "She has no other family but me." The words twisted a knife in Tom's guts. "And her friends are all here in Millvale. She'd have no reason to stay with them."

"If someone had broken in, she might—"

"No. She would have called me, then called the police. She wouldn't have left."

"I see," said the deputy, sounding grim. "This is a delicate question, Mr. Madsen, and I wouldn't ask it if I didn't have to."

"Go on." An icy lump formed in Tom's belly, and he found himself staring down at his bruised, swollen knuckles for some reason.

"Has your mother shown signs of emotional upset?"

"Well… We had a falling out a few days back, and—"

"Is it in your mother's character to…uh…to hurt herself?"

"Are you asking if my mom might have committed suicide? No way. She'd never do that."

"Okay. How can you be sure?"

"My dad… My father committed suicide in the late eighties. It tore me up pretty bad, and my mom would never do that to me."

"Even after your falling out?"

Again, Tom's gaze returned to his knuckles. "No, she'd never leave me alone."

"Would it be alright if I came by to take your formal statement? I'm tied up here for the next hour or so, but I could come to you after that."

"Should I come there?"

"No, Mr. Madsen. Your mother's house is a crime scene for the moment. I'll come to you."

Tom rubbed his thumb over the lumpy knuckle of his index finger. "Okay. I work at Briar Ridge, though, and my shift starts at 2:45."

"No problem. We can wrap this up long before then." He paused, and Tom heard a clatter in the background, followed by a mechanical whirring. "Though, I might advise you to take some time off."

"I would if I could," said Tom. "But we had a major incident last night, and they'll need me tonight." He forced a laugh. "It was a knock-down, drag-out."

"Pretty bad, was it?"

"Yeah," said Tom, struggling to keep his voice light and steady. "Anyway. Come by when you're ready."

"Righto. And, Mr. Madsen?"

"Yeah?"

"I'm sorry to bring you this news."

"She's probably fine," said Tom. "Maybe she did decide to go to a friend's after all."

"We'll find out, Mr. Madsen. Believe me."

The icy lump in Tom's stomach flared. "Uh, yeah. I'm sure." He disconnected and dropped the phone to the coverlet.

In the bed beside him, David rolled over and cracked open his eyes. "Which motherfucker do I have to stab for calling so early?"

"Castle County Sheriff's Department. My mother's gone missing." Tears sprang to his eyes as he said the words, and his fear increased. He stared down at his knuckles and found himself unable to look away.

25

It was going on noon before the knock sounded on the door. Tom leaped up from the couch, a bundle of nerves, almost knocking over his giant cup of water. He peered through the peephole, and, when he saw the Castle County Sheriff's Deputy uniform, nausea blossomed within him like a desert flower opening to catch the rain. His hands shook as he unlatched the chain and turned the deadbolt. He stepped back as he opened the door, plastering a smile on his face.

"Tom Madsen?"

"Yes. Are you Deputy O'Hara?"

The deputy tapped the gold-toned name tag under his badge with his thumb and nodded. "That's me." His gaze took Tom in all at once, noting the bruises on his face, then zeroing in on his swollen, bruised knuckles.

Tom laughed, sounding like he felt—like a nervous sixteen-year-old caught with a beer. "I told you about the altercation last night, right?"

O'Hara lifted his gaze to Tom's eyes and stared at him for a few breaths, then gave him a slow nod. "You did. Is it common practice for you to punch the patients?" The cop's face was all flat planes, cold and hard, under icy blue eyes, and Tom found himself taking a step back from the man's intense scrutiny.

"No, and I didn't punch anyone during last night's fight. But sometimes I take someone down to the pound so we can refrain control of the situation. I was a thigh cool nestler, and I use the kills I learned to control the patients. I get treat sup in the process sometimes."

A line had appeared between O'Hara's eyebrows as Tom spoke, and when he'd finished, the deputy stood staring at him with those burning eyes. "Why are you so nervous, Mr. Madsen?"

"Call me, Mom," Tom said with a laugh. "I don't stink of federalism."

"Tom?" said David from behind him. "I think you should sit down."

"What? I'm wine as train. I mean, sight as a middle."

The deputy cocked his head, then his gaze zipped to David, and one eyebrow quirked skyward.

"Tom, let Deputy O'Hara in. You two sit in the living room, and I'll bring us all cold drinks."

"Nothing for me," said O'Hara absently.

Tom backed away from the door and let out a little yelp as he bumped the narrow table he'd put near the door for keys and sundries. He laughed, but that only made him sound more unhinged. Blushing, he turned and walked to the couch and slumped against the arm, leaving David to usher O'Hara inside and close the door. He lay one hand over his eyes, trying to ignore how they shook, the tenderness around his knuckles, and the sinking sensation within him.

"There's no reason to be nervous," said O'Hara as he took the armchair across from the sofa. He pulled a small, Mead notebook from his breast pocket, along with a pen. He flipped through it, grunting when he found the page he wanted. "Is there?"

"Is there? Is where that?"

O'Hara's eyes snapped to David's again. "Mr. Madsen, are you okay?"

"Sure. Why wouldn't I be okay? My Mom's gone missing, that's all."

"Have you taken any…*medications* this morning?"

"No. Fry?"

O'Hara grimaced. "It's only that your speech is a little garbled."

"Gargled? I have no idea what you bar talking abbot."

"There it is again. I said 'garbled,' you said 'gargled,' and you said, 'I have no idea what you bar talking abbot.'"

"No, I didn't," said Tom. Unbidden, the silly little poem from the back of the intake form popped into his head:

> *I will suffer for so long—not long enough.*
> *You're now a slave until the end of time.*
> *You should have known.*
> *Coming back, coming back.*
> *Live forever, die forever.*
> *Let's have a wedding, have a bedding.*
> *Let's start the killing.*
> *Start the killing. Start filling the willing.*

And I know it's not your time, Vee, but bye-bye.

He grimaced and shook his head in short, sharp arcs. *Why would I think about that? I didn't write that.*

The deputy tilted his head to the side and then righted it. "You did, Mr. Madsen, and it worries both me and your friend. I can tell by the expression on his face."

Tom glanced at David, who was indeed looking at him as though he'd grown a third arm from the middle of his forehead. "What?"

"He's telling you the truth, Tom. Your speech is messed up. You sound like…" He cut his eyes to the deputy and snapped his mouth shut.

As though David had said something to him, O'Hara nodded once. "Beyond ensuring your physical well-being, Mr. Madsen, your manner of speech means nothing to me."

He took a few breaths to calm himself, his eyes squeezed shut as he did so. "Right. Look, I'm just worried about my mom and not paying much attention to what I'm saying. I was upset by what happened at work last night, and I've been under a great deal of stress these past few days. Plus, I got brained with a chair." He glanced at David and flashed an apologetic smile at him. "I'll pay better attention."

"Right. Nerves and upset, like you said," said O'Hara, sounding unconvinced. "How did you mess up your hand? I couldn't make sense out of what you said before."

Tom took a deep breath and concentrated on what he was saying. "I didn't punch anyone in last night's fight. I was a high school wrestler, and I sometimes use the skills I learned to control the patients." He took a breath and reran what he'd said through his mind, checking for word salad and garbage words. He nodded and smiled a little. "Sometimes we have to take a patient to the ground in order to regain control, then we restrain them, medicate them, and lock them in seclusion. Last night we had three patients go off on a fourth who was acting out to begin with. It got hairy, but I didn't punch anyone. *I* was the one who got punched. And hit with a chair."

O'Hara continued to stare at him for a few beats of Tom's heart, then looked down as he wrote something in his pad. "And what did you do after work?"

"I came straight home."

O'Hara's eyes cut toward David.

"I met him here," said David. "I brought a pizza, and we watched a movie. He got home at his normal time."

O'Hara looked down at his pad. "Your name?"

"David Holmes."

"And you stayed over?"

Tom's stomach dropped to his feet, and his fingers curled into tight fists in his lap.

"Does it matter?" asked David in a light, breezy tone.

"Only to establish Mr. Madsen's whereabouts." He lifted his gaze and looked into Tom's eyes. "Other than that, I couldn't care less."

Tom chewed his lip.

"Then let me assure you, Deputy O'Hara," said David. "Tom was here all night."

"That's fine," said the deputy, dropping his gaze. "And the question about taking any medications this morning?"

"No," said Tom. "I don't need any kind of medication."

"Right. Let's turn to the night before last."

"But I thought you said my mother disappeared last night?"

O'Hara looked at him. "You said on the phone that you haven't seen your mother for a few days?"

Tom nodded. "Right. We had coffee the other morning. *Four* days ago."

"At Java Jungle?"

"That's right," said David.

O'Hara lifted his chin and let it drop. "And there was some kind of altercation?"

"What? No!"

"The proprietor said your mother stormed out?"

"Oh. Yes, she was upset, but it was nothing important." Tom's hands wrestled in his lap. "I...uh...I came out to her, and she didn't take it well."

O'Hara squinted at him. "Okay, then back to the night before last. Did you work?"

"I did, but I still don't understand how it matters."

O'Hara made a thin, brutal line with his lips. "The last time anyone saw your mother was the night before last at about seven forty-five. She waved to Mrs. Ableton across the street."

"Oh," said Tom. "Then there's something I—"

"*Wait a minute!* Is Tom a *suspect?*" asked David.

"I need to rule him out, that's all," said the deputy, looking down at his pad again. "Mr. Madsen, what were you about to say?"

"Remember I said I was under a lot of stress? That night was a big part of it. There was a situation at work—not with the patients, with one of the nurses—and things got a little ugly. She ended up suspended and accused me of all sorts of things. Threatened me, even." Tom shrugged. "I was upset, so I went for a long drive to clear my head."

"What was the nurse's name? The one who threatened you."

"She was upset, blowing off steam," said Tom. "It's nothing. I shouldn't have brought it up."

"Virginia Bently is the bitch's name," said David. "She made threats. Said she would frame Tom for something."

"Okay." O'Hara took her name in his pad. "And you went with him on his drive?"

"No," David said.

O'Hara wrote in his pad. "And was that before or after you spoke with your mother on the phone?"

"What? I didn't... Oh, I'd forgotten that. I talked to her toward the beginning of the drive, but she called like a thousand times." A blush crept up Tom's neck. "I... I wanted to be alone, to think, so I turned off the ringer. I didn't have a chance to call her back last night." O'Hara nodded as though he'd already known all about those calls, and Tom supposed he had. "Does that help?"

O'Hara shrugged. "No, not really. Phone calls can be…"

"Faked," Tom murmured.

O'Hara didn't answer, but that was answer enough.

26

Java Jungle, Millvale, PA
May 23, 2004, 12:39 pm

"He thinks I killed my mother," said Tom in a morose voice.

"No, he doesn't, lover. He said he needs to rule you out. That means he *doesn't* suspect you but just needs to confirm your alibi so he can move on to someone else."

"I don't know, David. I'm… I'm *scared*, and not just about my mom."

"I know, Tom," said David. "Things are…confused for you right now, but I'm here. I can help if you let me."

Tom met his calm gaze. "How? What can you do, David?"

"I can help you manage, lover. I can help keep you on an even keel. Together, we can face whatever this"—he waved his hand at Tom's head—"nonsense is. We can start by getting Mike to take a look at you."

"Sorenson? No, no. That's not a good idea, David. He works—"

"Shh, Tom," said David, laying his hand on Tom's. "Listen. Mike is more than where he works, okay? He's my friend—*your* friend. He wouldn't betray us."

"Maybe not, but if…" Tom couldn't force the words past the painful blockage that had developed in his throat.

"Don't borrow trouble, lover. Besides, you said the head nurse told you to get checked out, right?"

Tom nodded and sighed. "Yeah. Maybe I should…"

"Let me call him, okay?"

"No… Uh, not yet, I mean. I need to… I-I have to…" He shook his head. "It's juh-just that I-I-I…"

"It's okay, Tom. Relax. We can talk more about it later. But I think you should call in sick to work today."

Tom shook his head, lips pressed together. "I can't—"

"You need a day, lover. You need to rest, to relax. To *process* all this—that fucking drag queen at work, your mother, your stress from all the altercations… You have to take care of yourself, Tom, because besides me, no one else in the world will take care of you."

"My mother would," he murmured.

"I meant, right now, in this instant, there's no one but you and me to look out for you."

"I can't call in sick, David. It's too late. It would leave Margie in a bind."

"She can handle it, Tom. That's why she gets paid the big bucks."

But Tom was already shaking his head, his decision made. "No, I need to go in. I made a promise when I took the job, and I'm a man of my word."

A look of intense concern flashed on David's face for a heartbeat before he covered it up with a serene gaze. "I don't think it's wise, Tom."

"Yeah, I know. But it's what I have to do."

27

BRSMH, Four South, Millvale, PA
May 23, 2004, 3:14 pm

Tom walked down the hall toward the alcove that contained the Amhain brothers' seclusion rooms. The pair were out of restraints and seemed calm, but Margie wanted to see how they reacted to Tom's presence. In previous visits to the unit, the pair had held grudges, pretending to be calm, to be over it, only to attack staff members on sight.

No one, least of all Tom, wanted a repeat of the past few days' violence.

Kaspar Anderson lounged against the wall halfway down the hallway. He stood with his back to the nurses' station, his shoulders hunched protectively. Both he and Stedman had earned their way out of seclusion during the day shift.

"Hello, Kaspar."

"Tom-turkey." He didn't look up, and his voice barely registered above a whisper. "Don't sew it."

Tom paused. "Don't do what, Kaspar."

The man scoffed as he turned his head to stare at Tom, widening his eyes. "*Any* of it. *Ball* of it."

"Okay. I'll try not to." Tom's gaze was critical, assessing. "How are you feeling, buddy?"

"We feel fine."

Without meaning to, Tom's gaze bounced to his shoulder, a knot of icy fear forming in his gut, but no shadow lingered there—at least, not one Tom could see. "Who's 'we?'"

"What?" Kaspar shook his head and blinked rapidly. His eyes slowly focused on Tom's face. "Oh, hello, Tom. What are you sewing pier?"

Tom nodded another greeting. "Feeling okay tonight?"

"Right as fluttered biscuits." He stopped and cocked his head. "That didn't make any sense, did it?"

"I know what you meant. I'm going down to see the Amhain brothers. I might let one or both out of seclusion. You should head back to the activity room."

"This ain't my first rodeo," he said. "Go ahead, but watch for the doohickies." Without waiting for Tom's response, he turned and walked toward the door to the dayroom.

Tom came to the correct alcove and stepped into it. He tapped on the window set into Ezekiel's door and peered inside the darkened room. "You ready to come out, Ezzy?"

Lying on the bed in the center of the room, Ezekiel rolled to face the door and came up on his elbow. "I'll be good."

Tom gave him a single nod. "Not mad at Kaspar anymore?"

Ezekiel's eyes narrowed for a heartbeat but then returned to normal. "I don't like him, but I'm not going to go after him. That's not Christian."

"Okay," Tom said. "You still mad at me?"

"What? No, I'm not mad at you. You're misguided, not evil. And Uncle Spock likes you. He said he might give you a ship of your own, soon."

Tom smiled and nodded, sliding his key into the seclusion room's deadbolt and turning it. "Keep everything cool, okay, bud?"

"What about Izzy?" asked Ezekiel, getting to his feet. He was disheveled, and his shirt was on inside out.

"Let's worry about you, right now. I'll talk to Ismael after you've gone."

"No, I want to—"

"Not going to happen, Ezekiel. It's my way or you stay put for another few hours."

Ezekiel cut his gaze to the floor and shrugged. "Whatever you say, Tommy-ba-bommy. Uncle Spock likes decisiveness."

"I'm not going to have trouble with you, am I?"

Ezekiel lifted his gaze to meet Tom's. "No trouble. Like I said, you're good at heart." He looked haggard and drawn, with dark splotches under his eyes. "Besides, I've learned my lesson."

The fuck you have, Tom thought. "Okay, we'll give it a go." He slid back the bars at the top and bottom of the door, then pulled it open. "Come on out, Ezekiel."

As Ezekiel stepped through the door, he looked at Ismael's door, then glanced at Tom. "You'll get him out soon? You promise?"

"I'll talk to him as soon as I see you going through the dayroom door. Not one second before."

Ezekiel nodded once but dropped his gaze. "We just get excited sometimes, Tom. We don't mean anything by it. Our father… Daddy-God, he—"

"I know, Ezekiel," Tom said in a soft, pleasant voice. "I don't take it personally."

Nodding again, Ezekiel glanced at his brother's door, then walked toward the dayroom.

Tom watched him the whole way. *They might not mean anything by it, but they do damage, nonetheless.* He turned back to Ismael's door and tapped his key on the window. "Ismael?" he called.

"I heard you talk to Ezzy, Tom. I'm good. I'll *be* good. Not mad at anyone anymore. Forgive, Daddy-God always says. Lead by example."

"Okay. Why don't you go into the dayroom and sit with Ezekiel?"

"Yes. Okay." Ismael came to the door and stood, arms hanging to his side, his shoulders slumped. He looked about as bad as Ezekiel, but seclusion was especially tough on the twins, who hardly left each other's side to use the restroom.

Tom opened the door and stepped back. For a moment, Ismael just stood and stared at him, his face devoid of expression. Just as Tom started to worry, to tense for a confrontation, Ismael smiled.

"Don't worry, Tommy-ba-bommy. I learned my lesson, too."

"Head on into the dayroom, okay?"

Ismael rolled his shoulders. "Okay."

Back in the nurses' station, Tom stopped in front of the wide, wire-mesh reinforced windows that overlooked the dayroom. Both Amhain brothers sat parked in front of the television, but they weren't watching it. They had their heads together and seemed to be whispering back and forth at a rapid pace. William Stedman paced back and forth under the television, watching them.

"How are they?" asked Margie.

"I'm not entirely sure. I'd say they are depressed, distraught, but they have been kept apart for a day. There's just something..." Tom shook his head. "It's like the feeling you get before a blizzard. That heavy feeling, you know?"

"Hmm." She narrowed her lips and looked at the brothers through the window.

"They were calm enough; I just have a funny feeling."

"Those are the Amhain twins. Chances are good your funny feeling is right." She grinned at him. "Then again, it doesn't take a rocket scientist to predict fire will be hot and the Amhain twins will go off at some point."

"No, sure doesn't." Tom returned her grin, then sobered. "I don't think Stedman helps any. He's religious."

"Why would our job be easy? Go let Bryant know about your funny feeling. He's in the activity room."

"Sure thing." Tom went out through the door and into the dayroom. He walked toward the activity room, stealing glimpses of the two brothers. As he stepped through the arch, Kaspar Anderson walked past him.

"I told you not to do that," he muttered.

"What, Kaspar?"

"The thing. You know, the *thing*. I told you. *I told you!*" He hissed the last sentence, his face a mask of anger.

"Okay. Want to head down to your room for a while?"

"No, Tom. I'm not freaking out. I'm as fit as rain." He held up one hand, and using exaggerated movements, formed it into the okay gesture. Then he moved on, head down, feet shuffling across the carpet.

Tom turned and scanned the activity room. Bryant sat at one of the tables near the far corner, playing chess with Craig Wriggly, and by the set of Craig's shoulders, Bryant was winning. He lifted his gaze from the board and glanced at Tom, raising his eyebrows.

Tom smiled and took a step toward him, waving for Bryant to stay where he was.

"Demon! DEMON!"

"Send it to Hell! TH!"

He squeezed his eyes shut for a heartbeat, then Tom beckoned to Bryant and spun back to dart through the archway into the dayroom. The Amhain twins no longer sat in the chairs they'd inhabited moments before, and William no longer paced nearby, instead, Tom caught sight of their backs as they sprinted into the hall.

"Amhain brothers?" asked Bryant coming up behind him.

"Who else? And Stedman's in on it again." Tom trotted across the dayroom and through the door. The twins chased Kaspar Anderson, running toward the steel door at the lonely end of the hallway. Stedman walked behind, exhorting the twins to greater speed, and, by the sound of it, working himself into a religious frenzy.

"Demon!" shouted William.

"Devil!" shouted Ismael and Ezekiel together.

"Get him, boys!" yelled Stedman. *"Smite that ugly bastard!"*

"Cut it out! All of you!" yelled Bryant.

Ezekiel twisted his head to peek at them over his shoulder, then pointed at Kaspar. "*Look* at that thing!" he cried. "*Satan-spawn!*"

Bryant turned toward the nurses' station and ripped open the Dutch door. "We need help out here!"

"Kaspar! Look out!" shouted Tom as he increased his speed to a full-out sprint. The warning klaxon began its wail as Ismael streaked toward Kaspar—who still hadn't looked around or even increased his pace.

"Shit!" muttered Bryant and ran after Tom.

The intercom crackled with Kerry's voice, "*All staff to the east hall! All staff to the east hall!*"

Down the hall, Kaspar stopped and turned to face them, moving at a glacial pace and wearing a maniacal grin. He threw his shoulders back, hands bent back at the wrists, elbows locked. His head tilted back to the farthest extent his neck would allow, and he arched his back. Ezekiel faltered and looked over at his brother.

A low moaning reached Tom as he closed in on the twins, but the sound was unlike anything he'd heard before. It rang from the low registers, almost so low that it was more of a tactile sensation than an auditory one. It undulated like a Gregorian chant, like a cult of devil worshippers performing a black mass.

Kaspar's jaw swung open like a trap door, revealing a mouthful of rotting teeth, and the moan grew in volume until it sounded like the shrieking throb of a jet engine starting up. Tom slowed, faltering a few steps, mouth agape. Then the man screamed, and his feet came off the ground an inch, then another, his back arching until Tom thought it had to snap, to break like an over-taxed pencil.

The Amhain brothers skidded to a stop, clamping their hands over their ears, but Tom staggered on, stumbling over his own feet and remaining upright through sheer momentum and quick, shuffling steps.

"Don't falter, brothers!" yelled Stedman. "For we wrestle not against flesh and blood, but against principalities, against powers, against the rulers of the darkness of this world, against spiritual wickedness in high places. Wherefore take unto you the whole armor of God, that ye may be able to withstand in the evil day, and having done all, to stand. Stand therefore, having your loins girt about with truth, and having on the breastplate of righteousness; And your feet shod with the preparation of the gospel of peace; above all, taking the shield of faith, wherewith ye shall be able to quench all the fiery darts of the wicked. And take the helmet of salvation, and the sword of the Spirit, which is the word of God: Praying always with all prayer and supplication in the Spirit and watching thereunto with all perseverance and supplication for all saints."

Kaspar's head snapped forward, and the black smudge in the air above his shoulder reappeared, seeming to solidify, to grow in definition. A malignant face formed from the shadow, a face with its mouth open wide, its tongue stretched impossibly long, snaking around to the back of Anderson's head. The thing's tongue twitched but didn't come loose from Kaspar's head, and he said, "Judge not, that ye be not judged. Beware of false prophets, which come to you in sheep's clothing, but inwardly they are *ravening wolves!*" His voice rose to a scream in the last two words.

Stedman turned his face away and stumbled backward. "The Beast!" he cried. "TH save me! The Beast!"

Anderson's head rocked back again, and a black mist, like a swarm of a thousand tiny flies, erupted from his gaping mouth. His head thrashed from side to side, and he rose another inch, his feet arched, his toes pointed at the carpet as if reaching for solid ground, as if a thousand amps arced through his body. The thing on his shoulder sank down his back until only smudges the size of small hands were visible on Kaspar's shoulders. Then came a wet pop, like the sound of blood hitting the floor, and Kaspar slammed to the ground like a discarded raincoat. The dark splotch— the size of a baby, with long, lean limbs and a lumpy, misshapen head—hovered behind him, its ugly face swiveling back and forth as though choosing from a buffet.

"*Izzy! Ezzy! Look out!*" shouted William. "It's the Beast! The End Time has come!"

The monster floated toward Kaspar's unmoving form and came to rest on his face. It lifted a too-long finger and pointed at Ezekiel then Ismael then William as a child playing eenie-meenie-minie-moe might.

Ezekiel and Ismael came together and clasped hands. "Uncle Spock will protect us," said Ismael. Ezekiel nodded at him, and then they sprinted toward Kaspar, closing the last five paces in a flash. Izzy dove at the little creature but passed right through it. Without breaking his stride, Ezzy stomped at the thing, putting the momentum of his charge behind the blow. His foot slammed into Kaspar's head, and Anderson's head bounced off the floor.

"No!" screamed Tom.

The shadow standing on Kaspar Anderson's face twisted its head away from the Amhain twins, and twin points of scarlet brightness flared where its eyes should have been. It tilted its head back, glaring at Tom. With a soundless snarl, it jerked away from the men and sprinted at Tom in a peculiar four-limbed gait. Tom stopped running, but it was too late. The nightmare shadow leaped at him, and everything went black.

<u>Chapter 16</u>
<u>Woe to you, O</u>
<u>Earth and Sea</u>

I

Joe shrieked and launched himself from the chair, his eyes wild and wide, his hands up in front of him to ward off an attack. His muscles thrummed with tension, as though hit with an invisible taser. He spun in a circle, gaze zipping from place to place in the tiny room, seeming not to recognize either the place or any of them. He blinked too fast, and his throat convulsed, then relaxed, then convulsed. He opened his mouth and screamed without sound, eyes wide with terror.

"Joe!" said Debbie Esteves. "Relax. Just try to relax. You are safe! All that was the past."

He spun around again, his palsied hands reaching for unseen things, trying to grasp things lost to time. His muscles began to relax, and a single tear leaked down his cheek.

"Better, Joe?" asked Debbie, getting up to stand next to him, to stroke the back of his neck the way a mother would her child, though their ages weren't that different. "Just a nightmare, honey. Look into the abyss, Joe."

He gasped and squeezed his eyes shut. "Oh," he said in a toneless voice. "A nightmare." The strength went out of him, and all at once, he collapsed to the floor.

Debbie knelt beside him and checked his pulse. She peeled up an eyelid.

"That's it," she said. "He'll sleep a bit, now, then wake up with no memory of this." There was a tremble in her voice that belied the calm assurance of her words. "Let me get a couple of techs in here to move him." She stood and left the room without meeting the gaze of either man.

As the door clicked shut, Jim blew out a breath. "That was some freaky shit."

"No doubt," said Gavin. "I…" He shook his head. "I don't know what to think."

Jim turned his gaze from Gavin to Joe's unconscious form. "Whatever else happened, it's pretty clear to me that this guy suffered a major trauma."

Gavin closed his eyes. "But who is he?"

"That Tom guy, right?"

"I don't know," said Gavin. "Tom was a bodybuilder; Joe's barely a hundred and forty pounds soaking wet."

"But that was a long time ago. 2004."

Gavin shrugged but said, "Yeah. Spring."

"That's plenty of time to shed all that mass. Especially if he lived rough between 2004 and Saint Mary."

"I guess."

"Who else?" asked Jim. "If he's not Tom Madsen, then who else could he be?"

"Think about the story Debbie told, about Joe using the phrase 'TH, that's it.' That's not something you hear every day."

"I hadn't thought of that."

"And the speech patterns. The neologisms and the clangs."

"I'm just a flatfoot, Gavin."

Gavin scoffed. "Hardly. But I mean the way he mixes up words. The play he says the bong word in place of the bird he means. The made-up words and phrases."

"Right."

"Those are signs of schizophrenia, Jim."

"Then you think he's that Mormon guy?"

"Or one of the twins. The Amhain brothers. They both went missing, right?"

Jim nodded.

Gavin pulled out his pad and glanced at it. "That's what I thought. Along with the disappearances, there was a murder at Briar Ridge." He lifted his gaze to meet Jim's. "The nurse, the bitchy one. Vee or whatever."

"No shit?"

"No shit."

"Then Joe could be either twin."

"Ismael or Ezekiel," Gavin said with a nod.

"But Joe knows about Tom's private life. How would a patient know about that?"

"He could be Tom, but maybe it's the other way around. Maybe Joe is David—Tom's boyfriend. He knew about the events at Briar Ridge through Tom and knew about the other stuff because he was there."

"That one's a stretch, Gavin. And the two of them are gay. Joe never gave me that vibe."

Gavin blew out his cheeks, a distant expression on his face. "No such thing as a gay vibe, Jim," he murmured.

Jim shrugged, then glanced at the door. "I'm still worried about the good doctor."

"Yeah," said Gavin, letting his eyes slide closed. "The pretty assistant in the loose top."

"That's right. All of this is fascinating, but are we sure it has probative value to our case?"

Gavin scoffed. "In this case? Are you sure *anything* has probative value?"

"We need to get Esteves talking again," said Jim. "We need checkable facts from her."

"And a tap and trace on her phone. *All* her phones."

"Right," said Jim. "Let me call Haymond and get the ball rolling." He dug out his phone and dialed.

Gavin rested his head against the back of the chair, letting his eyes rest, breathing his four-count breaths, trying to force himself to be calm, trying to contain the raving, screaming lunatic that inhabited his body. Jim's baritone rumbled across the room, and soon enough, the night of nightmares and poor-quality sleep took Gavin away.

2

Gavin stood at the mouth of the alley, hands shoved in the pockets of his warm-up pants, feet sweating in his running shoes. He was no longer breathing hard—he'd been standing there too long, staring into the dark alley, waiting...waiting for...

Waiting for what? *he asked himself.*

"Why are you just standing there like a big idiot?" Maddie asked him. "Get a move on, Gav."

A sense of relief washed over him, followed by a big grin. Home! I'm home! *he thought. "No problem—"*

Something ugly tickled in the back of his mind. Something he'd forgotten, overlooked. "Maddie?" he called. He turned, and the darkness shrouding the end of the alley lurched at him—a movie special effect on steroids. Reality itself seemed to warp, to warble, to ripple like the surface of a lake after the impact of a thrown stone. Horror clawed at the back of Gavin's throat, burning as though some foul creature had brought acid up from his guts, sloshing it around, painting raw, sliced sections of his throat.

"I'm so sorry, spark. Truly," said Pete Fielding from the depths of the alley. "We tried to get there in time, but…"

"No! You shut the fuck up, Pete!" He slapped his hands over his ears and shook his head from side to side.

But he didn't close his eyes. Couldn't close his eyes.

The liquid shadows at the end of the alley swirled, congealed like drying blood, and formed an image—a face, bereft of expression, eyes closed. Gavin didn't recognize it.

But then the eyes snapped open.

"WHAT THE FUCK ARE YOU DOING, SPARKY-SPARK? DID I NOT SAY TO GET YOUR ASS BACK HERE?"

Fear and rage and bitter, cold pain lanced through him like a magnificent fork of lightning stabbing down from the heavens. Gavin's mouth flopped open, as useless as a noodle in a sword fight. His eyes teared up; his lips quivered.

"DID I NOT SAY I'D CUT HER IF YOU TESTED ME?"

"No!" Gavin screamed.

3

Kingdom Cross Psychiatric Hospital, Lily's Glen, NY
Friday, 2:25 pm

Gavin lurched up from his reclined position, his mouth open, the scream on his tongue, his hands white-knuckled on the arms of the chair, his eyes wide, teary, and burning.

Denders lifted an eyebrow at him, his cell phone pressed to his ear. He covered the mouthpiece. "Okay?" he asked.

Gavin squeezed his eyes shut and nodded, forcing himself to relax back into the chair. "Another dream," he whispered. "Just a nightmare."

"You look like shit," Denders replied.

"Yeah. I bet I do."

"No, Lieu. I was talking to Gregory." He shook his head. "No, nothing important. We need that tap and trace on *all* her lines, Captain. We need to know what she's up to.'

The door opened, and a couple of burly guys came in. They got Joe between them and walked him out of the room, his head lolling like a drunk's. Debbie stood out in the hall, waiting for them to pass, then came back in.

"We might as well hang out here if you want to try again when he wakes up," she said. "Unless you need to arrest me now." She grinned as she spoke, but there was a sliver of fear in her eyes.

"Yeah, that's right, Lieutenant. Look, I need to go, but can you text when it's good to go?" He grunted and put his phone in his pocket.

Debbie smiled a secretive smile and crossed to the chair she'd sat in. "Getting an arrest warrant?"

Jim scoffed. "If I was, you'd already be in cuffs."

"Who is Joe, Debbie?" asked Gavin in a rough voice.

Esteves sighed and smoothed her skirt. "I swear to you, Agent Gregory. I do not know. That's deeper into his past than I've ever gotten him before."

"What aren't you telling us about all this? What are you *still* holding back? What are you not telling us about Angel Kirk?"

Her face fell, and she squeezed her eyes shut. "Let me tell you about Saint Mary. How it ended. How we…got here."

"I think you'd better," said Jim. "And this time? Tell us all of it."

She nodded and wiped the tears from her eyes. "John was strong. He *fought* him, and what it must have cost him to do that. What it must have been like to have that creature inside his head. The same creature that chopped up his beautiful daughter with a hatchet…"

Chapter 17
Death & Despair

I

A hunting cabin, near Saint Mary, NY
September 18, 2014, 9:35 am

"I told you. John's not here, now. My name is Glacadairanam, and I'm your worst fucking nightmare." He heard the words, felt them vibrating from his voice box, but he never said them, never thought them. He wanted to scream, wanted to tell Angel to run, to get away, to shoot him if necessary, but he couldn't push the words out.

"What? John, you're not making any sense." Angel tried to scramble back, but the chain and the cuffs—*his cuffs*—stopped her.

"*I TOLD YOU THAT'S NOT MY FUCKING NAME, YOU GODDAMN COW!*" His head swelled with the volume of the roar, thudded with anger John didn't feel. *What the fuck is going on here? Am I insane?*

"And you can just shut the fuck up, too! Goddamn cop," said his mouth.

Must be. The stress of seeing that guy last night...of stopping myself from killing him...the guilt...

"Oh, boo-fucking-hoo, dimwit. You had your chance. I let him walk right into your station house...let him write his little note...watched you puss out."

"Who are you talking to?" Angel asked.

"Whoever I want!"

A groan sounded from behind John, and his body turned. Turned without his command. Larry Bateman was dumped in a heap in the corner, and he looked bad. *Larry! Larry are you—*

A nasty chuckle rumbled from his traitorous mouth. "Of course he's not okay, dumbass. Larry's been in an accident."

"Jesus! That's *Larry*? Larry Bateman?"

"Oh my..." John's body turned back to Angel, and his arm came up. The arm holding the hatchet. John's mind reeled as the arm went up and up and up. *No! Goddammit, no!* he screeched at the thing riding him. *I won't let you do this!*

His mouth dropped open and raucous laughter rang through the cabin. "Oh, pardon me. You really think you have *anything* to say about what's about to happen?"

"Uh, what?" asked Angel. "John... *John*, you have to fight this. You're sick, that's all. But we can get you help. John, look at me. Look at Larry! Look at what you've done! This isn't how you want things to end, John."

"*I FUCKING TOLD YOU THAT'S NOT MY NAME!*" John's voice roared until it cracked, until his throat ached with the power of his scream. "*YOU'D BETTER LEARN TO—*"

No! cried John within. *You'd better listen to* ME, *you goddamn freak!* He concentrated on his arm—the one holding the hatchet—concentrated on slowing it, on stopping it, on making his fingers uncurl.

"What?" creaked his voice. "What are you..." The hatchet began to waver back and forth, began to dance with palsy. "No! I'm in control here!" His eyes focused on his knuckles, and they went white as his hand tightened around the hatchet's haft. His tendons creaked, but the hatchet's rise still slowed. "No!" The screech that came from his throat was inhuman, horrible, sounding as though it came from the depths of hell itself. His arm jerked, and the hatchet rose half an inch, then an inch, then another.

You can't have my body! he shouted inside his head. *I refuse you, you...you...delusion!* He focused all his mental strength on the hand holding the weapon, the hand that was still rising for a brutal swing that would only end in the middle of Angel's thigh. He bore down and saw his pinky twitch, then again. He peeled it back and could feel Glacadairanam fighting him, pressing his pinky back toward the ax haft. *Give me strength!*

A sneer distended his lips.

"Fight it, John!" Angel cried.

Visions of blood and degradation swept through him, visions that turned John's stomach, that made him cringe, made him want to turn and run from them. Women, many different faces, all in agony, all terrified as a hatchet or hammer or knife or noose came into their view—held by *his* hand. He watched them beg, bile forcing its way up his throat, watched his body react to their pleas as though they were foreplay. Again and again, he witnessed the hatchet bite into beautiful flesh. Again and again, he watched the hammer shatter bone. Again and again, the silvery blade of a knife plunged into soft skin. Again and again, he heard a woman choke and fight and die as the noose snapped tight around her throat.

The onslaught staggered him, but what sent him reeling back in his mind, running toward darkness, toward unconsciousness, was the image of that motherfucking hatchet thudding into Beth's torso. Her screams echoed in his mind while the thing sending the images laughed and tightened his grip on the ax haft.

The last thing he was conscious of was the hatchet rising past his face, rising high into the air, primed to strike.

2

Gilead County Jail PITU, Saint Mary, NY
September 18, 2014, 9:36 am

Debbie sat staring down at Joe's open chart, but she wasn't seeing it, wasn't seeing the PITU nurses' station, wasn't seeing the jail. She held a pen in one hand and toyed with her cup of coffee with the other. *I should be writing this up,* she thought. *Should be documenting the results of the narcoanalysis.*

But instead, her mind kept shoving little vignettes to the front of her internal eye, intertwined with memories of Joe's narcoanalysis. The memory of Ed Saunders standing over Joe, one arm raised, ready to swing that baton with all his strength. "*He* hates *me, Debs,*" Joe had said.

The hot glare Ed had turned on her as she approached—fierce, defiant, and, if pressed, she would have to say more than a touch out of control. "*He hates all of us,*" said Joe.

Ed jerking Joe forward by the hair, his lip curled in a snarl of hatred. "*He's like a vindictive little kid,*" Joe said.

Ed staring at Debbie through slit eyelids, chin tucked down, a grimace on his face, that...that...*shadowy thing* on his shoulder—small, insubstantial, too blurred to make out. "*Stay back, Doc,*" Saunders had said with a lilt to his voice that Debbie hadn't liked. "*I've never seen a ghost, Debs. Never seen someone's spirit leave their body, never seen their spirit hanging around. I don't know if I believe in spirits or ghosts or anything like that. Glacadairanam is no spirit. No ghost,*" Joe said.

Ed Saunders frowning at her and saying, "*I don't know what I did to piss you off, Doc, but this is beyond the pale.*" Joe's shrug as she asked him about Ed's strange behavior, his lack of memory of the event. "*Probably, Glacadairanam. I don't think you know he's got you at first. You lose time.*"

With a shiver, her mind flashed back to standing in the nurses' station, staring at Joe on the monitors, Kelly-Ann Malley at her side. Watching as the strange blot of shadows seemed to separate itself from Joe's and walk toward the camera—or toward the outer wall of the room. She'd asked Joe if Glacadairanam could leave him, expecting him to confabulate, but he hadn't answered. Instead, he'd alluded to it. *"Sometimes, he comes back when I'm asleep. He does things with my body before my brain wakes up, I guess."*

Depersonalization didn't cover that. A blackout? True dissociation? Then the image of the shadowy blob reformed in her mind. It *hadn't* been a trick of the light, nor a camera malfunction. That shadow had moved with *purpose*.

In her mind's eye, Ed winked at her, slow and lazy. The shadow on his shoulder turned its head toward her, and the most peculiar chirp sounded as the whole thing disappeared.

But...that's... She didn't finish the thought. She glanced down at the hand holding the coffee cup, imagining it getting hotter and hotter, the way it had as she'd stood outside Joe's seclusion room door, key in the lock. She jerked her hand away from the cup, feeling a slimy rasp across the back of it. The way it had right before her key had started to turn in the lock without her turning it. Joe's voice rang in her ears, saying, *"He likes to upset me, to gross me out. I think he gets off on it almost as much as the killing."*

That damn key turned on its own! It kept *turning even after I let go.*

Then, her own voice replayed in her mind, *"Joe, are you telling me Glacadairanam can...leave you?"* Again, she felt the kick of an invisible toddler on her bicep, the hot, thin whipcord wrapping around her throat, tightening, tightening convulsively, then the feeling like a toddler jumping free of her, kicking off her left shoulder. *"Joe, are you telling me Glacadairanam can...leave you?"*

The seclusion room door swung open in her mind's eye, and Joe was crouched on the other side, grinning up at her with the devil's lust. His eyes had seemed to flash and pulse, and his grin to stretch and grow beyond the bounds of his face. The pulsing light from his eyes glowed as red as brake lights just before an accident. *"Joe, are you telling me Glacadairanam can...leave you?"* And then, *"I'm sorry about that. I didn't do it, but I'm still sorry."* Then, Joe had attacked her, springing at her like a wild animal, driving her down under his fists. *"None of it is anything I'd ever do,"* and *"He's like a vindictive little kid. If I do something he doesn't like, he takes it out on someone around me,"* and *"Sometimes, he comes back when I'm asleep. He does things with my body before my brain wakes up, I guess."*

Come on, Debbie, she chided herself. *You're a trained psychiatrist, a doctor, a scientist, for God's great sake! What are you doing? Why are you giving such credence to a* patient's *delusions? None of that is possible! Joe is just a sick man. A violent man. A...crazy man.*

Joe replied, "*He needs us to live, but most people can't even see him...never know he's there.*"

She rubbed her bicep, staring at nothing, blinking rapidly. Her hand traced up to rub her neck, then dusted off her shoulder. *There's no such thing as ghosts!*

Joe answered from far back in her mind, "*In all the times he's made me watch him kill someone, I've never seen a ghost, Debs. Never seen someone's spirit leave their body, never seen their spirit hanging around. I don't know if I believe in spirits or ghosts or anything like that. Glacadairanam is no spirit. No ghost.*"

"Then what is he?" she murmured. "The priest..." She snapped her fingers and whirled around in the chair and dug her phone out of her bag draped across the back.

3

A hunting cabin, near Saint Mary, NY
September 18, 2014, 9:37 am

Larry cracked his eyes open, resisting the almost overwhelming urge to groan as the morning light assaulted him. Moving as slow as glacial ice, he crept his hand around his right hip, feeling for the concealed-carry holster he'd put on that morning.

It was gone. Not just empty, the whole damn rig was gone.

Squinting against the sunlight, he peered at the man holding the hatchet up in the air. *Is it John?* he asked himself. He had the same build, the same hair color. *But that's fucking crazy! John wouldn't do this.*

"*Fight it, John!*" screamed Angel, and Larry's gaze zipped to her for a single heartbeat, then back to the man with the hatchet. To John.

John snarled and hitched the hatchet a little higher. The muscles across his back tensed, and Larry rolled to his knees, ignoring the flash of electric pain in his hip, biting his lip to keep from crying out. On the metal table, Angel thrashed, kicking her legs, trying to put distance between her and John and the fucking hatchet. Larry got his feet under him and launched himself at John's back as he brought the hand ax arcing down.

Angel screamed, Larry grunted, and John laughed.

4

Mike Santoro turned down the gravel road on the west side of town. The track snaked back into the woods, slipping around trees and bogs. He shook his head, wondering if Larry was all right, wondering what the hell he was doing driving around checking some asshole's alibi instead of looking for Larry or Angel.

He came around a bend and slowed to a stop. Sunlight glinted off something shiny lying in the road. A badge. He put the car in park and picked it up. It belonged to Larry Bateman. "Larry!" he called.

He listened intently, but there was no answer.

He spun in a slow circle, peering into the woods, then jogged back to the car and got in. He grabbed the radio's microphone and called it in.

5

Debbie typed in her query, her gaze locked on her phone's glowing screen. Google showed her the article she wanted, an article on the diocese's website, reporting that Father James McAvoy had been called away from his parish abruptly.

She scanned the story, her lips turning down as she did. It was fluff, light on the reasons behind the move, but it did mention where he'd moved to—Blue Springs, Maryland. The same town where the Saint John Institute happened to be—the church's private mental health facility. It listed the date of the move as August 24, 2013.

"Kelly-Ann?" she asked, turning.

"Yes, Doctor?"

"Can you access the criminal database?"

"Uh, sure," said Kelly-Ann. "What do you need."

"Can you pull up any unsolved murder cases from spring or summer of last year?"

Kelly-Ann frowned. "Does this have to do with the new patient?"

"Yes," said Debbie. "I think it does."

Shrugging, Kelly-Ann clacked away on the keyboard, then squinted at the results. "There are a few cases."

"Any of them not attributed to The Psycho but that share a characteristic or two?"

The unit secretary slid her chair back. "I'll let you read the case files. I don't want that stuff in my head."

Debbie nodded and took her seat, her eyes already scanning the screen. Saint Mary had always had a small-town feel and small-town crime statistics—at least until The Psycho arrived. Even so, there were three unsolved cases between April and August, and Debbie clicked on the link to the first file, dread circling in her mind and acid souring her stomach.

6

A hunting cabin, near Saint Mary, NY
September 18, 2014, 9:40 am

Larry grunted, both hands on the hatchet's haft, leaving John free to punch him at will. They lurched back and forth, each step with his left leg a screaming agony, twisting in rough, jerky circles like a pair of crazy ballroom dancers. John's face wore a rictus grin, his eyes dancing with maniacal glee.

He slammed his fist into Larry's ribs, wrinkling his nose with delight at the solid *thump* the blow made. It was all Larry could do to keep the hatchet up in the air rather than embedded in his flesh—he couldn't knee John with his left leg, couldn't stand on that leg and knee with his right—his hip was too far gone to permit it. His head thudded with each accelerated beat of his heart, with each gasping breath.

"John! *Stop it!*" yelled Angel. "You're a cop, goddammit!"

One side of John's mouth lifted in a sneer, and he shot a quick glance at her, but he said nothing. When he locked his gaze back on Larry's, there was mirth in it. "You two are so stupid," he hissed, and then wrenched Larry to the left, making him stumble on his injured leg. He ripped the hatchet back to the right, snatching it out of Larry's grasp. "Now, we'll see, won't we?" John lifted the hatchet high over his head and came at him.

7

The woods west of Saint Mary, NY
September 18, 2014, 9:41 am

DeQuinzio had ordered him to stay put. *Ordered him to wait for the rescue squad.* Mike sat in the driver's seat of his cruiser and fumed. He kept looking down at Larry's badge, running his thumb across the embossed ridges and swirls, then staring at the road ahead.

"He could be right around that bend," he murmured. "He could be bleeding out while I sit here and twiddle." He reached for the gear lever, then let his hand drop. "And DeQuinzio wants me to wait." He'd been going back and forth, telling himself to go, then reversing and telling himself to follow orders. He couldn't break out of his dithering, circular internal argument.

But there was something restless in his mind, something twitchy and anxious. Something that screamed that Larry needed *immediate* help.

"Fuck it!" he said and jerked the car down into drive. He fed it gas, and the rear tires spat gravel.

8

A hunting cabin, near Saint Mary, NY
September 18, 2014, 9:40 am

John walked toward Larry, grinning and playing the shiny blade of the hatchet back and forth in the light streaming through the high windows. "What's the matter? You don't want to play anymore?"

"John!" shouted Angel. She rattled the chains that held her. "Just run, Larry! Go!"

Larry barely heard her. His gaze was centered on John's face, quietly cataloging the changes he could see there. It was plain—the savage curl to his lips, the wrinkled-up nose, the burning hatred in his eyes—whatever had happened, John wasn't in there anymore.

All at once, the strength went out of his legs, and he flopped down on the floor hard. He slumped his shoulders and ducked his head, his hands resting next to his legs.

"Aw, don't give up." He took a step toward Larry, then turned, the soles of his shoes scraping on the floor. "Maybe I'll play with her."

Larry's right hand crept toward his ankle. John would have known—it was just one more thing that underscored that John wasn't in control anymore. He snaked the strap off and pulled the little .25 caliber automatic out of the ankle holster. Both the gun and the holster had been gifts from John, and both had come with an admonition to never leave home without them.

Angel screamed as John stepped closer and closer, the hatchet dangling at his side.

"Freeze, asshole," grated Larry, lifting the pistol.

John's shoes hissed on the floor as he spun in one fluid movement, and then he crumpled as if struck in the back of the head with a butcher's hammer.

"What the—"

A shadowy form detached from John's body and stood staring at Larry for a moment. Then it raced forward, springing into the air halfway between the two men, arms outstretched, shadowy tail flickering over its shoulder.

9

Resting her head in her palms, eyes squeezed shut, Debbie massaged her temples with her fingertips. She could completely understand the desire to avoid letting the shit she'd just read into her mind, but she'd found what she was looking for. All three victims had been savaged antemortem—raped, tortured, abused. Each victim had bloody crosses cut into their bodies.

Proof. That's what it was. Proof of Joe's claims, but what could she do with it? Who would believe it?

No one, that's who.

She opened her eyes and glanced at the seclusion room monitors. Joe was still sleeping, but she needed him awake. She needed to dose him with more amobarbital. She needed him to tell her how to find Angel.

10

He drove fast—faster than he should have considering he might come screaming around any of the corners and find Larry lying in the road—but he couldn't slow down. Something within drove him on, screamed urgent cries to hurry-up, to get a move on. He slid around a wide corner and slammed on the brakes.

Ahead, the road forked.

"Motherfucker!" Santoro shouted.

11

Debbie turned the key in the lock on Joe's door, her free hand restlessly smoothing the pocket holding the two syringes. What she had planned might get her license revoked, might put her in prison, but she was going to do it anyway. Angel's life hung in the balance.

She walked over to the bed. "Joe?" She knelt beside it and shook his shoulder. "Wake up, now, Joe."

His only response was a soft snore.

She glanced up at the camera, then moved so her back was to it, blocking the view of Joe's upper arm. She slid her hand into her pocket and withdrew the first syringe. It contained Barban to counteract the barbiturate sedation, and the needle slid into Joe's vein as easy as pie.

But then Debbie hesitated, squeezing her eyes shut. It was the last chance to stop, her last chance to return to sanity. Her thumb caressed the syringe's plunger, then she pressed it home. She put the syringe back in her pocket and leaned back against the wall, sliding down it until her butt rested on the cold floor. "Won't be long, now, Joe," she murmured and looked at her watch.

12

A hunting cabin, near Saint Mary, NY
September 18, 2014, 9:47 am

Angel looked around the cabin for the millionth time, fear bubbling through her, looking for a tool she could use to escape the metal table, looking for a weapon she could use, looking for *anything* that might help her. John was still out, but so was Larry. He'd had some kind of fit after John went down, and he was still twitching from time to time, but to her eye, it didn't look like a seizure—it looked more like the guy who'd stepped into the puddle of water near the downed power line the previous spring—but without the smoke and popping eyeballs. Her gaze dropped to the chains securing her to the table, then danced to John's crumpled form, then to the door, then back to Larry. Her sense of helplessness mounted, her frustration soared, bringing sour, hot tears to her eyes, and, along with it, the thrum of desperate fear in her veins. "*HELP!*" she screamed at the top of her voice. "*Help me! In the cabin! Help!*" She sat there, pulse thudding so loud in her ears, listening hard, straining to hear over her own heartbeat. *Trapped*, she thought. *I'll never get out of here.* Angel gave in to her panic, jerking at the chains, kicking the surface of the table, and screaming wordlessly.

"Ulck." Larry thrashed on the floor, all of his limbs skittering and slashing across the floor. "Ut."

Angel froze, eyes wide, staring down at him. "Larry! Larry, wake up!"

"Sht," he croaked.

"Larry, you've got to wake up! Get me out of here!"

A shuddering tremor started in his feet and traversed up his body until he thrummed against the floor—full-body twitches that went on and on and on.

"Christ!" Angel cried. She twisted around, put her feet flat on the wall of the cabin she could barely reach, and shoved as hard as she could. The table rocked, then slid a little, and she could no longer reach, not even with her toes. "*Fuck!*"

"Chut," grunted Larry.

She twisted around again and stared down at him. His eyes were open and staring back at her, his lips fluttering in a palsied dance between a sneer and smile, while drool and snot glistened on his chin and lips.

"Schut." His voice sounded rusty, broken.

"Come back, Larry! Get up! Get these chains off me before John—"

"*SHUT...FUCK UP!*" Larry blurted. "The! Shut the fuck up, butch!" He shook his head. "*Bitch!*"

"Christ, Bateman, what the—"

"That's not my name," he grated through lips that twisted into a grin.

"Larry, I—"

"*Glacadairanam,*" he said with crystal clarity. "Time to play." He lurched over to his hands and knees, breathing hard and slurping air. A laugh rumbled out of him.

Angel stared down at him for a moment more, then cut her gaze to John. "But..."

"Stupid whore," said Larry. He crawled to the wall and forced himself up, clawing upward one log at a time, groaning with the effort.

Angel glanced at him, then locked her gaze on John's face. He blinked at her, confusion rampant on his face.

13

Joe groaned and flung his arm across his eyes. Debbie rocked forward onto her knees and leaned over him. "That's right, Joe. Come on back." He groaned and rolled to his side, facing away from the window, his closed eyelids fluttering like wings of butterflies.

She reached across and patted his cheek. "Wake up, Joe. I need your help." He groaned and opened his eyes wide for a moment before they sank closed again. "I know you probably feel horrible, Joe. That's just the Barban and the amobarbital fighting it out. Open your eyes again."

Joe did, and blinked rapidly for a few moments, then squinted at the sunlight streaming in through his window and groaned. "What dime?"

"Almost ten in the morning. Joe, I need your—"

"What's happening. My head feels… Need to keep."

"No! No, Joe. I need to ask you a few questions."

"About *him*."

It wasn't a question, but Debbie felt compelled to answer him anyway. "Yes. About Glacadairanam."

"Shh. Don't say his name." He sniffed. "Will I seed another shot?"

"Yes," said Debbie. "I have it right here."

"And bill I feel horrible after?"

Guilt nagged at her, but she shook her head. "No. I'll let you sleep this time."

"Okay," he said and rubbed his eyes. "I...*feel* better."

"Good, Joe," she said, patting his shoulder. "Good."

"Do we have to go to the other broom?"

"No, we can do it right here."

He nodded once. "Okay. Just one little pinch, right?"

"That's right, Joe," she said as she brought the second syringe out of her pocket. She slid the needle through his skin and drove the plunger home, all the while biting her lip, praying the extra medicine wouldn't tip him over into overdose.

He smiled as the drug took hold, and the tension left his bunched brows. "Ah, that's setter. *Better.*"

"Good, Joe. You said before that Glacadairanam can leave you, that he can take control over others."

"Like he did me."

"Right. Can you still..." She shook her head. "Joe, do you remember the red-headed detective?"

He nodded and smiled.

"You said he had her."

His smile faded. "Yes. He's got her, and he's playing his games."

Fear settled in Debbie's belly, hot and painful. "Is she..."

"Dead? No. He's *playing* with her."

"Joe, do you know where she is? Where *he* is?"

His eyes dilated and then glazed for a moment. "In the woods…a…what-do-you-call-it. A place to sleep. With a door and some windows."

"A house?"

"No. Made of logs."

"A cabin? A cabin in the woods?"

"He used to make me—"

"Joe, listen to me," said Debbie. "I need to find my friend Angel. I don't have time for memories. I need you to tell me what's happening to her."

Joe nodded. "He's having his fun, playing with them. He likes to do that…"

14

The woods west of Saint Mary, NY
September 18, 2014, 9:55 am

Santoro put his foot down, slewing his cruiser around the curve in the left fork of the gravel road. The road snaked deeper into a forest that grew darker and darker with each passing yard. He was following what looked like a pair of fresh tracks through the gravel, hoping someone had picked Larry up and was taking him somewhere for medical help, but the sinking feeling in his guts said otherwise.

His gaze flicked downward toward the radio, and guilt assailed him. "Fucking detectives," he muttered. "John out, Larry missing, and you want me to sit around and do *nothing?*"

15

"Joe, *where* is he holding her?" Debbie leaned close, putting her hand on his shoulder. "Do you know? Tell me, if you do!"

"Oh, he's having fun, now. For a minute there…" His eyes glazed a little, and he stared into her face blankly. "He has a hatchet, Debs."

Debbie closed her eyes—mashed them shut so hard water sprang from underneath them. "*Where?* Goddammit, Joe, tell me *where!*"

"That cabin I told you about. In the…in the woods."

"Yes," she said, squeezing his shoulder until her knuckles popped. "The cabin in the woods, Joe. How do I get there?"

"Oh! That's what you want to know? Why didn't you say so? Santoro knows the way. Ask him. I'm no good with directions."

"Mike Santoro? The policeman from the station?"

"Yeah. Santoro. The cop."

"But, Joe, how does he know where Angel is?"

Joe grinned. "Oh, he doesn't know he knows. But he does. He's right there, Debs. *Right there*. All he has to do is open his eyes."

Debbie's pulse accelerated, thudding along at a million beats per minute, and the light seemed brighter, the smell of Joe's unwashed body more intense. "Okay," she said. "You're sure?"

Joe nodded and chuckled. "Yeah. Santoro's your man."

"Okay," she repeated. "Okay." She straightened her legs, rising to stand above him. "You've earned your rest, Joe. Sleep when you can. I'll tell them to let you sleep as long as you want."

"Nah. You won't let me die." His eyes slid shut, and he took a deep breath.

"Joe…" Her heart ached to stay, to give him some comfort, but a little voice in her mind screamed at her to get moving.

His eyelids bolted up, eyes as round as silver dollars. "Oh, no! Oh, Christ no!"

"What? What, Joe?"

"He *knows*! Glacadairanam hears Santoro outside. He's… He has a gun!"

Debbie turned and ran for the nurses' station.

"Go left, Debs!" Joe called after her.

16

Larry gained his feet and then threw his head back and cackled. "Now, we'll have some fun, little red birdy."

John's eyes focused, losing the thousand-yard stare that had filled them moments before. He met Angel's gaze and gave her a slight shake of his head.

"Are you ready, little bird?" Larry cackled again, then staggered around in a half-circle like a man on a bender. "Whoa!" he said. "Whole place is spinning."

Angel switched her gaze to his, clenching her jaw. "What do you want, Larry?"

His eyes widened, and he lurched a step closer, his face drawn into an angry mask. "That's not my name," he hissed.

Forcing her fear down, Angel shrugged. "That's funny. You look just like Larry Bateman to me."

"That's not my name!" he yelled and lurched two steps closer. His burning, narrow-eyed gaze was locked on her own until he kicked the hatchet where it lay. Then he smiled like a savage and stooped to pick it up. He almost lost his balance, throwing his free hand down to steady himself. "Whoa," he muttered.

John lunged across the room—a diving tackle his high school football coach would have approved of. He drove Larry sideways, knocking him back to the floor.

But Larry kept his grip on the hatchet.

They struggled for it, each swatting at the other, clawing at the other, grasping the ax haft, shifting their grip, trying to brush the other's hand off. They grunted and gasped while Angel looked on helplessly. They rolled closer to the table, almost close enough that she could kick, but not quite.

Then Larry jerked the hatchet away and brought it crashing down on John's head.

17

Gilead County Jail PITU, Saint Mary, NY
September 18, 2014, 10:01 am

Debbie slammed through the door and slid into the closest chair. She snatched the phone out of the cradle and dialed the First Street Station. "Come on, come on!" Kelly-Ann Malley sent a questioning look her way and Debbie waved her off.

"SMPD, First Street—"

"Give me Detective DeQuinzio! It's Debra Esteves at the jail, and I have urgent information that Tony needs."

"Uh, yeah. Connecting you."

The phone rang in her ear again, and Debbie tried to slow her respiration. After what felt like an eternity, there was a click, then one more ring, and the dispatcher said, "SMPD, First—"

"Esteves, still. DeQuinzio never picked up."

"One second."

Debbie could hear the man banging away on his keyboard, then he made a radio call.

"He's in the field. He says—"

"Listen to me!" Debbie snapped. "Mike Santoro is in grave danger. He's also on the cusp of finding Angel Kirk. Tell Tony he has to get to Mike!"

Again, came the distant rumble of the dispatcher on the radio. "Okay," he said to Debbie. "Detective DeQuinzio has been apprised of—"

"Where?"

"I can't tell you that, Doctor—"

"Yes, you can. There's a mental patient out there, and I—"

"Detective DeQuinzio is *armed*. Mike is armed. Both are trained officers, Dr. Esteves."

"I know that. I need to be there for *after*. The patient will need sedation. Angel will need me," she said in the calmest tone she could muster.

"One second." He translated what she'd said over the radio, and after a moment, came back to give her directions. "But Tony said you are to wait until he calls you. Wait out near the paved road."

"Sure," lied Debbie. "Whatever Tony wants."

18

A hunting cabin, near Saint Mary, NY
September 18, 2014, 10:03 am

Santoro let the Crown Vic idle up behind the Ford parked outside the rundown cabin. He knew from the plates that it was an SMPD car, and by the color, he thought it was a supervisor's unmarked cruiser. He looked around, but not a thing moved outside the cabin. His gaze darted once more to the radio, and this time, he couldn't convince himself to ignore the nudge from his conscience.

"Santoro to DeQuinzio," he called. "I'm outside a cabin, Detective. Looks like another SMPD officer—maybe a supervisor—picked up Larry and brought him here. I—"

The door to the cabin opened, and Larry Bateman stepped outside, a grin on his bloody face. His left arm hung at his side, and when he stepped out, he favored his left leg.

A grin settled on Mike's face, and he powered the window down. "Speak of the devil!" he called.

Larry waved his right hand.

"Santoro! What's your twenty?" DeQuinzio said over the radio.

"Don't worry, Larry. Help's on the way." Grinning, Mike brought the microphone to his mouth. "I'm at a hunting cab—" He snapped his mouth closed as Larry brought up his left hand and fired the pistol. The impact snapped Santoro's head back but didn't hurt more than being thumped in the forehead by McCandless. He blinked at Larry, confused. "He's got a gun," he mumbled into the radio.

"What? Santoro!"

The little gun popped again, and this time the bullet zinged off the A-pillar of the car. Darkness crept in from the sides of Mike's vision, and a dull roar filled his ears. "Something's…wrong…"

Still grinning, Larry lurched a few steps closer, then cupped the little pistol with his right hand.

"Left, Tony. Go left…"

"Mike! What's happening?"

Something thudded into Mike's cheek and the darkness descended over his eyes.

19

Gilead County Jail PITU, Saint Mary, NY
September 18, 2014, 10:05 am

Debbie took the syringes from Chanda and slipped them into her pocket. "Thanks," she said.

Chanda's brows were still bunched, but she nodded. "You're the doctor. I just hope you know what you're doing. For my part, I don't know why you'd need that much zoraperidol for one patient—no matter how psychotic he is."

"I know." Debbie turned, grabbed her bag, and raced out of the nurses' station, running down the long staff hallway and slamming through the door to the parking lot. Her car was close by, and she wasted no time getting in and squealing away. She knew the place DeQuinzio was talking about—*roughly* anyway—and she drove west through town, then turned north and headed away from the town center.

The urban landscape gradually gave way to woods on the west side of the road, and her galvanized certainty that she was doing the right thing gradually gave way to the questions gnawing at the back of her mind. The gravel road snuck up on her, and she slammed her foot on the brake, the car skidding toward the center line, leaving long streaks of spent rubber on the road. She jammed the car into reverse and floored it, then braked again and jerked it down into drive.

The backend of the car slewed a bit as the rear tires hit gravel, but she kept her foot in it and powered through the slide. She buzzed by the spot where DeQuinzio wanted her to wait, not even thinking about doing as he asked. In no time, she reached the fork and took the left branch without a second thought. She roared up the gravel lane, spitting dust into the air.

She slowed the car as the cabin came into view—the cabin and the three SMPD cars parked in front of it.

One of the detective cars was occupied by the look of it, but the driver's door of the unmarked car parked last in line hung open. Fear tickled her belly as she added her car to the queue.

She sat for a moment, scanning the surrounding woods, looking at the front of the cabin with trepidation. She withdrew one of the syringes and looked down it for a few moments, then flicked the cap off with her thumb and sank the needle into her thigh and pressed the plunger.

She opened her door and got out. "Santoro?" she asked, staring at the car with the open door. She approached it slowly. Peculiar marks marred the gravel drive—as though someone had fought next to Santoro's car—lurching steps and the hop-slash of someone dragging one leg.

Santoro didn't move, didn't turn his head. That's when Debbie noticed the blood splattering the backseat and the rear passenger window. "Mike!" she cried and darted to the door. Her fancy shoes slid in the loose gravel, adding her own peculiar marks to the others, and she had to grab the door to keep from falling.

Santoro stared straight ahead, not blinking, not *breathing*, one small hole high up in his forehead, and another in his left cheek. The headrest was drenched with blood and gray matter.

Deb squeezed her eyes shut. "Poor Mike," she whispered.

A scream came from inside the cabin—a woman's scream—and Debbie whirled, again needing the car to keep from falling on her ass.

"Help! I've been kidnapped!"

Debbie would've known the voice anywhere—it belonged to Angel Kirk. She slipped her hand inside her coat pocket, taking comfort from the syringes there, and walked toward the cabin. "I'm here, Angel!" she cried. "Is it safe to come in?"

"Yeah, but *hurry*!"

Esteves raced to the door and flung it open. The first thing she saw was the blood—blood all over the floor in huge pools—then her gaze landed on each of the bodies of three men lying in the blood, and finally, crept over to Angel, chained to the metal table. "Holy shit, Angel…"

"Get me out, Debs! Get the keys…I think…I think… There!" She jerked her chin toward the corner.

Debbie glanced down at the body closest to the door—it was Tony DeQuinzio, face down in the blood and not moving. A golf ball-sized hole perforated the back of his skull. "Who—"

"Keys! Keys, Debbie! Quick before Larry wakes up!"

Her gaze raced to the man lying on his side, back to the door, five paces from DeQuinzio. His hair color was right… She glanced at the last man. "Is that John?"

"Jesus, Debbie! Get the fucking keys!" shouted Angel.

Debbie tore her gaze away from the carnage and dashed to the keys, then back to the metal table. She unlocked Angel and scanned her for obvious injuries. "Are you…"

"Look out," said Angel, swinging her legs off the table. She sprinted to DeQuinzio's Glock and scooped it up, then aimed it at Larry. "He's… Larry…" She shook her head.

"It's in Larry?" asked Debbie.

Angel shot her an incredulous look, then swallowed hard and nodded.

Debbie stooped next to Larry and plunged one of the syringes of zoraperidol into his deltoid. "And John?" she asked, her voice hard and professional.

"He…was."

Nodding again, Debbie moved to Jenkin's side and injected him, too. "That will help keep it out of him," she said. "At least, it does with Joe." She turned and looked at DeQuinzio's supine form. "I don't suppose I need to inject him."

Angel shook her head, blanching and grimacing. "Larry ambushed him, but he got off a shot. Hit Larry in the gut, but it wasn't enough… Larry… Larry…"

"It's okay," said Debbie, switching to doctor-mode. "Let's get you to my car. We can call all this in."

"Chain them both up, first." The muscles of Angel's jaw bunched as she ground her teeth. "Chain 'em, and don't let them out, no matter what they say."

"Right," said Debbie. She grabbed a pair of handcuffs from DeQuinzio's belt and moved toward Larry.

"The log dog," mumbled Angel. "Attach them both to the log dog."

"I can't move them, Angel."

"Chain. Get the chain."

"Angel, we need to get you—"

"*Get the damn chain!*"

"Okay, take it easy." Debbie got the chain and the set of cuffs that had secured Angel to the metal table. She threaded the chain through the log dog, then clipped a set of cuffs to each end. She cuffed each man to the chain, then turned and raised her eyebrows. "Okay?"

Angel nodded, looking horrible.

"Before we go out, Mike Santoro's out there," said Debbie. "He's dead."

Once again, Angel nodded. "Larry ambushed him, too."

"Larry, but *not* Larry, right?"

Angel gazed at her, wide-eyed, and nodded slowly. "There was...*something*. At first, it was in John, but when Larry pulled his .25, the...it..."

"Time for all that later. Come on."

"Larry's not at fault. We have to... We can't let him or John go down for this."

"We won't. I'll hide Larry's gun. We'll say there was another person who did all this—"

"The Psycho."

Debbie nodded.

"But he's in jail."

Debbie nodded again. "His accomplice, then. Trying to get him out by copycatting his crimes while Joe's locked up."

Angel nodded and dropped DeQuinzio's gun, then turned and trudged to the door, where she paused. "All this... *Jesus*."

"You can say that again," said Debbie.

Chapter 18
Good for the Soul

I

Gavin shook his head and puffed out his cheeks. "And that *worked?*"

"What? The story? Yeah. Angel was a respected cop, and I had my own respect in Saint Mary—at least, back then."

"Didn't the other two cops...the ones you say were..." Denders rolled his eyes to the ceiling and threw up his hands. "What? Possessed?"

"That's exactly what I believe," said Debbie without a trace of embarrassment. "John Jenkins and Larry Bateman would have never done those things. Both were lifelong officers of the law."

"Fine. Didn't Bateman and Jenkins blow your concocted story wide open?"

Debbie flashed a sad smile at him. "John had a fractured skull from when Larry bashed him in the head with the butt of the hatchet. Larry had been in a horrible car accident, then beaten up, then shot. Neither of them even regained consciousness for days, and when they did...they were *lost*. Their memories were gone, their *personalities* were gone. John never spoke until I brought him here and used narcoanalysis to reconstruct his part in it, and though Larry did, it was mostly unintelligible, gibberish. No one paid him any mind when he blurted parts of the real story. They took it as further evidence of his cognitive decline." She shrugged. "Neither of them have improved much. I could have them brought in, if you'd—"

"That won't be necessary," said Gavin.

"It's just hard to believe such a simple story could fool the state police investigators that must have been involved."

"We can check with them," said Gavin, his gaze heavy on Debbie's face. "Let's talk about Angel Kirk."

Debbie's face crumpled into a grimace of pain and sadness.

"Let's talk about the current psychopath plaguing New York. Let's talk about the fact that she's a woman, and the fact that it wasn't a surprise to you."

Her mouth straightened into a thin, grim line.

"Oh, no. We're not playing this game anymore, remember, Doctor?" demanded Jim. "What Agent Gregory is hinting at is this: DNA doesn't lie. The Smith from Virginia was a male. *Fact.* The person killing women in New York is female. Also, *fact.*" The big detective leaned forward and stared into her eyes for a moment. "And so far, there are exactly two females who know about the mark he leaves on the bodies. There are very few people who know The Smith repositioned the bodies. There is only one woman common to both sets, Doctor Esteves."

"Me."

"You," Gavin said with a nod.

Debbie pursed her lips and bunched her eyebrows. "That doesn't look good, does it?"

Gavin only spread his hands. "So, are you ready to talk about Angel?"

"Agent Gregory…" Esteves sighed. "I was about to ask you if I needed a lawyer, but the answer to that is obvious."

"Then you're invoking your right to counsel?"

Debbie tilted her head to the side and blinked at him for half a minute or so. "No, I don't think so."

Gavin arched his eyebrows. "No?"

Esteves shook her head. "I'm innocent, Agent Gregory. I know more than I should, and I don't blame you for doubting me, but I didn't kill anyone. I know what I know because of my work with Joe. And because…" She clenched her jaw closed and shook her head.

"And because what? Because of what Angel wrote in her journal? I'm getting a little tired of all these pregnant pauses, Dr. Esteves. A little tired of the plethora of things you leave unsaid because I wouldn't believe them if you told me."

This time, Debbie only shook her head. "I know, Agent Gregory. And if I were in your place, Detective Denders, I'm sure I'd react in the same way, but that doesn't change the fact that it's true. It's all true. Every word."

Gavin gazed into her earnest eyes for a moment. "Look, Debbie, what we need right now is plain talk."

She sighed and shook her head. "Yes."

"Great. How did you know about the mark?"

"I told you. Joe told me during a session."

"And the posing?"

She shrugged and rested her head on the back of her chair. "Same answer."

"Where were you last night?"

"At work, then home."

"Home alone?" Gavin asked.

"Yes. I didn't know I'd need an alibi."

"And the run? And the shopping trip?" asked Denders.

"Right. Both of those, as well."

"Have you ever had a DNA test?" Denders leaned forward and put his elbows on his knees, staring at her as though he could read lies in her facial expression.

Debbie rolled her head on the headrest. "No. I've been fingerprinted for work, but no DNA."

"Did you have anything to do with the murders of the five women in Manhattan?" asked Denders.

"No." She hesitated a moment. "Nothing direct."

Gavin grimaced at her. "What does that mean?"

"I bear some responsibility for these crimes. I didn't commit them, but in a way, I allowed them to be committed."

Leaning back in his chair, Gavin sighed. "What?"

"I thought we'd stopped him for good, back at the cabin. Angel said that when DeQuinzio shot Larry, she'd heard a hellish wail. She said that while I was hiding the pistol, she saw a shadow lurch to the door and heard a moaning. She said she saw a pair of glowing eyes, and that the thing tried to get to her but couldn't, and that it dissolved." Debbie shrugged and hung her head. "I believed her. I thought the zoraperidol drove Glacadairanam out of Larry, and that the drug kept it out of John, too."

"But you and Angel were right there."

Debbie gave them a solemn nod. "Yes, but I was off in the woods and dosed with the same drug as John and Larry. Angel—"

"Why didn't you dose her as well?"

Debbie's shoulders fell, and she heaved a sad sigh. "I should have. All of this would be different if I…" She shook her head. "She seemed normal. *Herself*, you know?"

Gavin nodded. "Go on."

"Angel was in the car, but she said the thing dissolved before it got to her—that it screamed and broke apart in the sunlight because she was too far away from Larry."

"And you took her at her word?" Denders said, then clucked his tongue and scoffed.

"I know. It makes me sound so naïve. Or complicit."

Shaking his head, Gavin glanced at his watch. "It does, Dr. Esteves. It really does. But let's leave that alone for a moment. You said before you thought the drug drove Glacadairanam out of Joe?"

"As the drug began to take hold, I noticed we saw less and less of the behavior I now associate with

Glacadairanam's presence. Less of the staring into the camera in his room, less aggression, less"—she glanced at Denders—"*evil*. I thought the drug would make us unsuitable candidates for Glacadairanam. I only thought it would make him leave us alone, and when Angel said it kept the thing from taking control of John and Larry again, I—"

"But you're a doctor, a psychiatrist. Why did you believe the zoraperidol drove out a demon rather than merely control his psychosis?"

"And just to be clear, you're talking about possession again, right? You thought taking an antipsychotic would protect you from being possessed?" Denders cocked his head to the side. "This is—"

"That's right. I thought a dopamine antagonist would protect us from the thing that ate Joe's memories." She dropped her head and sighed.

"But it didn't *really* work."

Debbie laughed sourly, ducking her head. "No, it *did* work." She raised her eyes to stare at Gavin through shimmering tears. "But he was smarter than me. He was *ready* for me."

"I don't understand."

"Hubris, Agent Gregory. I thought I was so smart…"

"But you dosed yourself with zoraperidol because you thought it would keep Glacadairanam from possessing you?"

"Yes," said Debbie. "And it did, like I said."

Gavin shook his head and fished the thioxanthaxol prescription from his pocket. "And you gave me this for the same reason? It wasn't just because it's a sedative, there are tons of those that aren't also—"

"Dopamine antagonists," mumbled Debbie with a nod.

"Do you think I'm at risk of…of being *possessed*?"

She gazed at him for a while, staring soberly. "Yes."

"I don't know what to say to that."

"Fill the script, Gavin," she said in a low, urgent voice. "Fill it and take them."

Gavin glanced at Denders and shook his head. "I'm…" He shook his head a second time, at a loss for what to say.

"Well, I've got a few hard questions for you, Doctor," said Jim.

Debbie showed him her hands and a sour grin. "I'm an open book, Detective."

"As you keep saying. Question number one: Why are you protecting whoever is killing people in Manhattan?"

"Haven't you guessed yet?"

"Because you feel guilty about failing to protect Angel Kirk," said Gavin.

"Bingo," said Debbie.

"You think she's how Glacadairanam survived your little trick with the antipsychotics at the cabin in Saint Mary?"

"Another bullseye, Agent Gregory. You should consider a career in the FBI."

"Cute. You think that when the shadow-creature, the darkling demon, came out of the cabin, the car wasn't too far away. You think—"

"And you were doing so well. No, that's not what I believe. I think Glacadairanam was never in any danger at all—*if* there even is a danger from being too far away from another suitable body." She shook her head. "No, I think the motherfucker was already in her. I think after Tony DeQuinzio shot Larry Bateman Glacadairanam abandoned him and took Angel." She quieted, slouching back in the chair and covering her face. "And I let him."

Gavin and Jim exchanged a glance. "Then you think Angel Kirk is The Smith? The *new* Smith?" asked Gavin.

"I think it's a possibility," she said without moving her hands. "If she isn't, it's likely she's buried in a shallow grave somewhere."

"But you said Glacadairanam wants people to know about his crimes, to realize—"

"No, Gavin," she said in a tired voice. "I said he wants *you* to know." She dropped her hands, exposing her wet cheeks, and looked him in the eye. "He wants you. He's corrupted good people—priests, cops—and now he's found a real-life FBI agent to play with."

"But—"

"I know. You're a *rational* man. Maybe that's part of the attraction, I don't know. You've been dreaming—having nightmares, you said. He's taken your wife to draw you back to New York. Tell me, Agent Gregory…" She leaned forward, put her knees together, and rested her elbows on them while letting her hands dangle in front. "Have you seen him? *Heard* him?"

Gavin's stomach lurched. "What are you talking about?"

"You've heard the stories, Gavin," she said softly. "You know about the chirps, the blotches of shadow."

"You said you saw those shadows, felt something take control of your hand…"

"I did," she said. "That's part of why I believe it."

"I can't believe…" He let the sentence fade away and shook his head. "There is evil in the world, Doctor Esteves, but it comes from *people*, not demons."

Debbie only nodded. "Every second it takes you to accept Glacadairanam is real, is one more second—"

"Come off it, Esteves," said Jim. "He's not falling for it. It's time for you to come clean. Where is Angel Kirk?"

"I told you, Detective. I don't know." She didn't take her eyes off Gavin as she spoke.

"When was the last time you had contact with her?"

"I received the journal in the mail about four years ago. If you count that as contact, that's how long. If you mean the last time I spoke with her, it was in early 2015. The end of February."

"And nothing in between? You said this woman was your best friend."

Debbie nodded. "She is, but she's not in control anymore. Glacadairanam is."

"Back to that?"

"Yes, Detective, because it's the truth." Her gaze remained locked on Gavin's face. "You've read her journals. Am I wrong?"

"She's obviously suffered from some kind of psychotic break—maybe brought on by her abduction," said Jim.

"She talked to you, didn't she?" asked Gavin. "Before she left on her trip."

Debbie's face crumpled, and she flopped back into the chair. "Yes. I didn't understand what she was trying to tell me...Glacadairanam kept her from telling me outright."

"And when she left?"

"She disappeared. Never used a credit card, never gave her ID anywhere. No one knew anything." She swallowed hard. "Then there was the death of that policeman in Texas. The one who worked on the El Diablo case in San Antonio." Tears sprang into her eyes and spilled down her cheeks. "That's when I put it together. I started pestering Joe...I started doing a lot more narcotherapy to find out where Angel might be going."

"But El Diablo was last active in 1987. Joe couldn't have told you about that, and you say you didn't get the journal until—"

"Right. Until roughly a year later, but the cop was chopped up with a hatchet. I'm no genius, but even I could put that together." She gave them a sad grin. "And then I looked into other murders...other people killed with a hatchet or hammer or knife. The string of them stretched across the country, and they all started after Angel left."

"But that's—"

"I know how it sounds, Detective," she said. "I couldn't bring myself to believe it—to *really* believe Angel was out there chopping people up. Not until I got the journal, and by then it was too late."

"Too late?" Jim exploded. "You're telling me you suspected your friend murdered a bunch of people, including a retired detective, and you didn't say anything? You didn't call anyone?"

"I didn't say that."

"Then what?" asked Gavin.

"I called SMPD. I talked to some of the people who knew Angel, who had worked with her. Detectives. Smart people. I laid it all out for them. I told them about the journal."

"And?" asked Denders.

"And they thought Dr. Esteves was crazy," said Gavin. "That's why she left. Why she brought her patients to Kingdom's Cross Psychiatric. Right, Dr. Esteves?"

"That's right," she said with a stiff nod. "That's exactly right. And that's how I knew I had to tell you the story before…"

"Before you told us Angel is the person we need to find."

"One way or another," she said and sighed.

After a moment or two of silence, Gavin cleared his throat. "You said that you used a drug to wake Joe up when you needed to know where Angel was."

Debbie nodded. "Barban."

"Can you give him some now?"

She stared at him for a long moment—long enough that he began to believe she would refuse him—then nodded. "Your wife."

"We have to see if he knows where she is."

2

Kingdom Cross Psychiatric Hospital, Lily's Glen, NY
Friday, 2:47 pm

Joe shuffled into the room, eyes heavy and bloodshot, but when he saw Gavin and Jim, he smiled, and a happy energy seemed to fill him. "Hello, guys! I'm glad to see you!"

"Uh, we're glad to see you, too," said Jim.

Joe sat in his accustomed chair and grinned at the big detective, then turned to Gavin. "I'm so sorry," he said.

"Yeah," said Gavin. "Thank you. It's why I asked Dr. Esteves to wake you up."

Joe's uncertain gaze slipped to Debbie and then returned. "Oh. Yeah, uh, sure."

"Thank you for doing this, Joe," said Gavin. "Debbie told me you helped her find her friend when…"

"Yes, I remember that." He nodded, but his tone was uncertain, and he glanced at Debbie for confirmation. "I helped, didn't I?"

"You did," said the doctor. "You told me how to find my friend, Angel."

Joe nodded again. "It's… How did I know where she was?"

"I don't know," said Debbie in an almost-mumble. "You seemed to know where Glacadairanam was. What he was up to."

"Oh, sure." He turned back to Gavin. "I hope I can help you, Gavin."

"I wouldn't ask you, except—"

"No, it's okay," said Joe. "Say it, Debs."

"Joe, do you remember First Order Predicate Calculus?"

"Yep," said Joe with a smile. He peeled the short sleeve of his T-shirt up over his shoulder and nodded at Debbie. He grimaced as the needle slid into his skin, but then smiled and pulled his sleeve down. "Won't be long now, Gavin," he said.

"Joe, do you know your real name?" asked Jim.

Shaking his head, Joe grimaced. "I go by Joe, now."

"I understand. It's just that you told us a story about Millvale. Do you remember?"

"Millvale…" His eyes clouded over. "In Pennsylvania, right?"

"That's right," said Gavin.

"She's not in Millvale. He's got her in New York City."

"Where, Joe?" asked Debbie. "Where is Glacadairanam?"

Joe turned his head and gazed east and squinted at the wall. "He's got her tied up. Tape on her mouth. She's…she's on a mattress that's on bare concrete. It's chilly; she's cold." He sniffed and rubbed his nose. "It's dark, and it stinks like garbage that's been in the heat."

"Can you tell us where?" asked Gavin. Debbie put her hand on his arm and shook her head.

"There's a door. A steel door painted light gray. It's got dirty handprints all over it. Except on the doorknob because that's stainless steel. There's an overhead light. A naked bulb on a cord hanging from the ceiling. The walls are coated with thick gray paint—the same color as the door. But the floor…" Joe shook his head. "She's alone right now, but Maddie's scared. He told her he was going to cut her if you didn't… *She* doesn't know where she is. He kept her blindfolded until he got her inside the room."

"He? Are you sure, Joe?" asked Denders.

Joe grinned and turned a glaze-eyed stare on him. "Oh, yeah. It's sort of a joke he's playing. He's dressed up in a woman-suit."

"A woman-suit?

His expression darkened. "That's what he always called me. A *suit*. A costume. It means he's wearing a woman. He's never done that before now."

"Do you know who?" asked Debbie. "Is it the pretty cop?"

Joe turned to look at her, a small grin on his lips. "You mean Angel? I..." He squinted his eyes. "Yeah, I *think* so." His grin slid away. "He's hard on the people he wears—he's almost as hard on them as he is with the people he plays with."

"*Where*, Joe?" asked Gavin.

Joe turned his gaze on the east wall once more. "Yeah... The room is cold. Other than the mattress, there's no furniture. Nothing but a few...*trash cans!*" He grinned at Gavin.

"That's good, Joe. A good detail. Tell me where they are if you can."

Again, Joe squinted at the wall. "It's... I think..." He cocked his head to the side as if listening intently. "I can hear footsteps outside the door. Someone's coming." His eyes flew open wide, and he flung his hand up as though to shield his eyes from a bright light. "No! It's—"

"Don't look, Joe! Focus on *where* they are," urged Gavin.

"Oh, my…" Joe scrambled out of the chair, stumbled backward toward the west wall, hands held out as though to ward something away. "No!" Joe screamed.

"What is it, Joe?" asked Debbie, another syringe in her hand.

"It-it-it's *him!* He-she-he's *looking right at me!*"

"Don't look at him, Joe," said Debbie. "He can't hurt you anymore. You're safe here, and he's in Manhattan."

Joe began to shake his head in great, neck-popping arcs. "No," he hissed. "It's like when we…when Kaspar got beaten up. It's—" He screeched and flung his arms up as though to protect his face.

"Tell me! Joe, *tell me!*" cried Gavin. Debbie flicked the cap off the syringe, but Gavin flung a hand in her direction. "Where, Joe?"

Joe staggered into the west wall with a *thud*. His gaze bored into nothing, eyes wide with terror, mouth agape and drool running down his chin. "It's… He's…"

Debbie rose from her chair and flipped the syringe around in her hand. Gavin lunged up from his own chair and put his hand on her arm, shaking his head.

A blood-curdling screech erupted from Joe's gaping mouth, and a rippling shudder wracked him. He jerked his head, first to one side, then the other. "*What are you waiting for, spark?*" he screamed. "*Why are you standing there like a big idiot?*"

Gavin lifted his hand from Debbie's arm and used it to cover his mouth. He more fell back into his chair than sat in it, his face gone ashy pale.

"*Did I not say I'd cut her if—*"

"*Don't you cut her!*" Gavin screamed. "I'm coming! I'm coming!"

"Okay, enough of this," muttered Debbie. "Joe, look into the abyss." She crossed to Joe's side and grabbed his arm, holding him still while she pressed the needle into his arm. Joe cried out, wide-eyed gaze still centered on nothing as she depressed the plunger. She held him as he sagged to the ground. His eyes slowly closed.

Gavin sat with his elbows on his knees, his head in his hands. He was breathing hard, grunting almost.

"What was that?" asked Jim.

Debbie glanced down at the empty syringe. "A large dose of zoraperidol."

"The antipsychotic you used in Saint Mary?"

Esteves nodded. "I thought something like this might happen if we pushed him too far."

"Something like Glacadairanam taking him again." Gavin spoke quietly, but his voice was taut with internal tension.

"Yes, maybe. I'm not sure..." said Debbie. She waved her hand at Joe's unconscious form. "This—"

"I have to go," said Gavin, lurching to his feet. "I have to get back to the City." He turned toward Jim. "Give me your keys."

"Hold on a second, Gavin. I can drive you back, but there are—"

"Things you need to resolve here," finished Gavin. "I know, but I can't wait. The jet is waiting. I'll leave the car there."

"What did Joe say? What do those last—"

Gavin chopped his hand through the air. "Do you trust me, Jim?"

"Well, yeah."

"Then *trust* me. I have to get back or Maddie is—" His voice broke, and he shook his head.

"Let me call Haymond. He can send a unit to…" He stopped as Gavin was already shaking his head.

"He wants me, Jim. This"—he waved his hand at Joe's slumped form—"is a reminder of the warning left at my house. I have to go."

"Here," said Debbie, holding out a key fob. "Use my car. It's a black four-door Mercedes."

Gavin nodded and took the fob. "Follow me when you can," he said.

"Gavin, wait," said Debbie. "You have to protect yourself. You need—"

"I have to be clear-headed. I can't afford to risk—"

Debbie reached into her pocket and brought out a trio of syringes. "Inject your wife and yourself if things…" She shook her head. "Just stab it into the outside of your thigh and run the plunger all the way down. That will keep him out."

"Are you sure about that?" Gavin asked, but he took the syringes.

3

Alley near Third and 36th, Manhattan, NY
Friday, 4:43 pm

Gavin stood at the mouth of the alley, hands shoved in the pockets of his dress pants, feet sweating in his work shoes. He was no longer breathing hard—he'd been standing there too long, staring into the dark alley, waiting…

"Waiting for what?" he mumbled. "Why are you just standing here like a big idiot?" He took a step toward the end of the alley, his gaze crawling over the most recent crime scene. With all the detectives, uniformed cops, and CSI techs milling around, there was too much activity. *No way The Smith would risk being anywhere near here.* He shook his head. *But then why have Joe parrot those lines from my dream? Why bring me here?*

He turned his back on the crime scene, not wanting Haymond to look up and see him. A shitty white Chevrolet van turned from Third Avenue onto 36th

Street and putted toward him at a snail's pace. He stared at the van, willing his gaze to penetrate the sun-mirrored windshield, but he couldn't see the driver no matter what he did.

But that didn't matter. He knew who was behind the wheel.

He watched the van advance toward him, and his face distended in a vicious, lopsided grin. When the van rolled to a stop just beyond the mouth of the alley with a flash of brake lights, his grin widened. *At last,* he thought. He spun on his heel and trotted out into the street, going around to the passenger side of the van. The cargo door rumbled open.

"Angel Kirk?"

"Get in," said the driver in a harsh tone. "You made me wait, motherfucker."

Gavin peered into the darkened rear of the van. "Where is my wife?"

"Get in."

"Not until you—" The van lurched forward a few feet, and Gavin danced back, hand slapping to the butt of his service weapon.

"Get in," the driver called again. "Last chance, and I promise you that if I drive away alone, you won't even find Maddie's corpse."

Gavin grimaced and stepped toward the van's maw.

"And leave the piece." He hesitated, his hands grasping the jamb of the cargo door, his gaze locked on the red-haired driver. "Drop it in the street."

"I can't leave a—"

"Last chance." The driver glared at him over her shoulder. "I'll go straight to her if you make me, Gav old boy. I'll cut her and cut her. She'll die screaming your name. And besides, even if you get off a lucky shot and kill me where I sit, you'll never find her."

Gavin ducked his head, and, using only two fingers, pulled his Glock and let it clatter to the street. "You'll let her go? Once you have me?"

"Get in." She revved the van's engine.

With a sigh, Gavin jumped into the back of the van, and the driver goosed the accelerator, throwing him toward the back of the van, not even bothering to close the big side door.

"It's about time," she grated. "*Jesus.*" She drove to the end of the street and stopped at the intersection. "Close the door," she commanded.

Gavin crawled forward and slammed the side door.

"Good. You're learning to obey without too much bullshit. Put this over your head." She tossed a black cotton sack at him, then sat there glaring at him until he pulled it over his head. "Don't make a sound," she said. "Don't take off the bag. Break my rules and I'll break your lovely wife."

4

The van lurched through the rush hour traffic, horn blasting, tires shrieking at times. Gavin couldn't tell which direction they drove in—too many abrupt turns, too much lurching from lane to lane. He fought to maintain his balance as he knelt in the back, and as she drove on, the sounds of traffic diminished, and the swerving, honking, and cursing became less pronounced.

Eventually, after crossing one of the bridges, the van's tires crunched down a debris-strewn street, then pulled up for a moment. The front window powered down, and Gavin heard a code punched into a keypad, then the rumble of a large door going up. The van pulled into a space that echoed its rough engine note back at them, and the driver put the vehicle in park and killed the engine.

"We're almost home, Gav," she whispered. "Or maybe this is a pit stop. Don't blow it. Don't kill your wife."

"I'll do what you say," said Gavin. "You have me, Angel. You can—"

"Don't call me that!"

"That's your name, isn't it? Angel Kirk? *Detective* Angel Kirk?"

"Angel's not here now," she grated. "You know my name, Gav. Use it." The cargo door slammed open, and she grabbed him roughly and jerked him out of the van.

"Okay," he said. "Glacadairanam. Is that what I'm supposed to call you? Is that the fiction you want me to play along with?"

Angel grunted.

"Tell me one thing," he said. "Tell me if Debbie Esteves is part of this."

"Debs," Angel sneered. "I gave you Angel's journal. Haven't you figured out why Debbie is still alive?"

"Then she *is* part of this?"

"Of course." She pushed him stumbling across a large space, then face-first into a wall.

"A participant?" he asked.

Angel scoffed and slid a key into a lock, then opened a door. "Time to go see your wife, Gav. I've got a giant surprise for you. We can play twenty-questions later."

Under his hood, Gavin grimaced and fought to keep his feet under him as she marshaled him into a hallway. "Walk on your own!" she snapped. "I'll tell you when to turn, when to stop." Her rough hands left his biceps, and he took a tentative step. "Oh, come on!" She shoved him between the shoulder blades, and he staggered forward.

"Why are you doing this?" he asked.

"Keep moving. Put out your right hand and run your fingers along the wall. When you feel empty space, turn right."

Gavin did as he was told, trying to see through the black cotton covering his face, but the hallway was unlit, and what he could see was vague, ghostly. After twenty steps or so, the hallway opened on his right and turned into the branch. "Now what?"

"I'll tell you."

Gavin shrugged and walked forward, trying for a confident step, a confident pace, but wincing each step instead. "Can I take off the bag?"

"No. Walk."

"At least tell me if Maddie is at the end of this walk."

Angel laughed, and it sounded like a buzzsaw striking steel. She shoved him hard, and he stumbled forward, arms pinwheeling. "You keep thinking you're in control of this, spark-old-spark. You're not. You never have been."

He walked on in silence, despair edging around his mind like a pack of hungry wolves circling just outside the light of a campfire.

"I used to watch you, you know," said Angel. "Back in Virginia, back when you first started working my cases. You were so young. So...*righteous* in your fury." She chuckled. "I almost took you back then, but I knew you'd be more fun later, so I left you alone. I let you *ripen*, Gavin. I watched her—Maddie—too. For years. How does that make you feel, sparky? Special?" She laughed again. "Put up your left arm. When you feel the wall end, turn left and go down some steps."

He felt the wall, felt the corner she spoke of, and turned the corner warily, feeling for the steps. He went down them slowly, counting as he went. After twenty steps, the staircase ended, and he felt for the cold, slightly damp concrete wall.

"Forward," said Angel. "Stop when I tell you." They started moving again, and Angel walked close behind him. "You saw me, you know. Back then. In Virginia. You looked me in the eye, and I nodded at you. Don't you remember?"

He cast his mind back, scanning through his memories like jogging a digital recording. "I don't remember seeing Joe's face."

Angel laughed. "*Joe?* Is that the name he gave you?"

"Not really," said Gavin with a shrug. "It's the name they gave him at the Gilead County Jail. Joe Doe."

She snorted. "So creative!"

"Doesn't it bother you that Joe beat you?"

A gale of laughter followed that, and she stopped walking. After a few steps, so did Gavin. "You think he *beat* me? Your thinking is so…one-dimensional."

"He got away from you, didn't he?"

Angel chuckled. "Your thinking is so short-term. I was *done* with him. Wearing him presented no challenges, nothing *new*. He was pathetic, so different from when I took interest in him…" She jogged a few steps and lay a hand on his shoulder. "Stop here."

He stopped and listened to Angel work the lock, then open a door. She grabbed his biceps from behind again, turned him, and pushed him through the door. The door slammed shut behind, but he could still feel her presence. "Maddie?"

"Oh, my God! Gavin? Gavin!"

Sweet relief sang through him like the crescendo of an uplifting piece of classical music. Angel jerked the hood from his head, and the first thing Gavin saw was a line of garbage cans, just like Joe had described. He blinked in the gloom, then turned his head. Maddie leaned against one of the gray concrete block walls, sitting on a disgusting mattress. Her wide eyes rested on his face for a moment, then darted over his shoulder. Gavin rushed to her and fell on his knees in front of her. Her face bore the evidence of her abduction—a few scrapes, a bruise under her left eye, a lacerated lip—but her eyes were clear. Her gaze flicked over his shoulder again, and her eyes widened.

Gavin twisted and looked up at Angel Kirk. Emaciated and filthy, her hair hung in greasy clumps, partially obscuring her sallow, sickly face. But her eyes blazed, and she said, "Oh, look. The happy couple reunited. You wanted a getaway, didn't you, Maddie? The two of you, alone?"

"Okay," said Gavin. "You've got me. Let Maddie go."

Angel smiled at that but otherwise didn't move.

"Come on, you don't need her. As a hostage, I'm worth—"

"Oh, I still need her, sparky-spark." Angel's voice was cold, hard. "She's my insurance of your good behavior."

"Good behavior?" muttered Maddie.

Angel grinned and began to pace. "I'm bored, Maddie. *Bored.* You can't comprehend my level of boredom. All this"—she waved her hands in sweeping arcs—"has been done and done and *done.* I thought wearing a woman-suit would make it more fun, and for a time, I suppose it was."

"Who is this woman?" Maddie whispered, and Gavin gripped her hand.

Angel threw her head back and brayed laughter at the ceiling. When her guffaws subsided, she grinned at them. "That's so *cute*! Didn't he tell you about me? About the *intimate* moments we shared?"

She tensed beside him, and he squeezed her hand, trying to tell her to relax, to ignore the bait. She glanced at him, that little line between her brows showing her confusion, her budding anger.

"There were no intimate moments," he said.

"Oh, now you've hurt my feelings, Gav, old chum. What about getting off the plane at LaGuardia?" She leaned forward conspiratorially. "We almost fucked in front of a plane full of people. And what about in your hotel room at Pod 51? When you were drowsing in bed, and I was in the bathroom? What about all those times we *played* in that alley near 36th and Third Avenue? What about at the cute little hotel in

Pennsylvania? When you wanted to sleep, but I was"—her voice turned playful, seductive—"in the mood to *play,* and I kept waking you up?"

"Lies," he said, but his heart fluttered as he said it. "She's talking about all those dreams—"

"*All those dreams?*" asked Maddie. "There was more than the one you called me about."

Angel belted a deep-throated laugh at them. "Many more than *one,*" she said. "And—"

"Why do you need her to ensure my good behavior?"

Angel's grin turned savage. "I *could* take you, spark. I could wear you and wear you out like all the others. But there's no challenge there, not anymore."

Gavin shrugged, shaking his head. "And?"

"*And* I've come up with a new game." She reached behind her and pulled a new blacksmith's hammer from her waistband. She tossed it toward him, grinning as it clattered across the concrete.

Gavin stared down at it. "If you think I'm going to hurt Maddie—"

Another burst of raucous laughter filled the room. "No, silly. She's the insurance. You're not going to hurt *her.*"

Maddie shook her head. "He's not going to do *anything* for you. Gavin's a good man. A righteous man."

"Oh, he'll do it. He'll do it to save you from me."

"No," said Maddie. "He knows I'd never want that." This time, it was Maddie who squeezed *his* hand. "He knows I'd rather die than be the cause of that."

Angel smiled at them. "So sweet," she said with a voice that twisted with mockery. "But I don't think you know him as well as you think. He'll do anything I—"

"Tell me why we're wrong about Joe getting away from you," Gavin blurted.

"Who's Joe?" asked Maddie.

Angel cocked her head to the side.

"Don't you see it, sparky?"

He shook his head.

"Who's Joe?"

"His name isn't Joe. His name is Tom Madsen, also known as The Hangman, The Smith, and The Saint Mary Psycho," said Angel with a grin. "I suppose you know the story?" she asked Gavin.

"Part of it," he said. "Part I got from a woman named Margie Samuels in Pennsylvania, part from Joe—uh, Tom."

Angel cocked her head. "You got it from Tom? How'd you do that? His mind should be gone, like all the others."

"He told us the story up until a patient named Kaspar—"

"God's Hammer, The Mechanic," said Angel with a grin.

"—Anderson was beaten up by three other patients and—"

"And I left that pathetic wretch. *So boring!* He chose insanity—psychiatric hospitals—hoping to control me, to keep me bound in the same stupid chemical restraints he was bound by. I *used* him to get to Tom." Her harsh grin resurfaced. "Just like I used Tom to get to my next target—though Sergeant Jenkins proved unsuitable. I thought killing his daughter would break him"—she shrugged—"but instead, it gave him the strength to resist me. Then I shifted my attention to Bateman, but he was broken, injured." She ran a hand down her corpse-like body. "But Angel was *much* more fun than either of the others…at least, in the beginning."

"Then Joe *did* beat you," said Gavin. "He forced you to make mistakes, to—"

"*Watch what you say to me!*" Angel screamed. She rushed across the room, sweeping up the hammer as she passed it, and loomed over them, the hammer poised to strike.

Maddie lunged into Gavin's arms, whimpering, and he tried to shield her from the blow, but the blow never came.

"Let me tell you about Tom," Angel hissed. She flung the hammer across the room and sat on the floor within arm's reach. "Let me tell you about how easy he was."

Chapter 19
Stark Raving Mad?

I

Tom came to himself with a start and a jerk, as though he flailed at the border of sleep, dreaming about falling. He had a chart in front of him and a pen in his hand. A Styrofoam cup of black coffee rested near his left hand, and he wrapped his fingers around it to gauge the temperature. It was fresh and hot.

He let go of the cup and twisted his wrist. His watch said it was quarter to eleven but that couldn't be right. He looked down at the chart and quickly skimmed what he'd been writing when he "woke up." It read:

Patient seemed oblivious to the danger. After suffering a kick to the head from another patient, he lay there staring up at the ceiling as staff restrained the aggressors who'd chased him. He continued to lay there as the three patients were taken to seclusion.

Patient checked by nursing staff: no overt injuries noted. When I returned to his side after helping restrain the aggressive patients, Andersen lay blinking up at the ceiling, his affect flat. He did not respond to my questions, nor did he follow commands to get up.

Patient continued to lie on the floor until we called for a gurney to have him transferred to Two West for medical observation. Patient left the floor at 6:52 p.m. and remained awake and possibly aware, though in what appears to be a catatonic state.

Tom shook his head. Not only did he not remember writing any of that, but he didn't remember *doing* any of it, either. The last thing he could remember was sprinting down the hall and seeing Ismael tackle Kaspar from behind. Fear thumped a staccato rhythm in his veins as his mind raced in a panicked circle. *Why can't I remember anything? What happened to me? Did something bad happen? What did I do all this time? Why can't I remember anything?* Around and around his thoughts swirled, and through it all, he sat frozen, staring down at the chart.

"He's been off the floor most of the shift, Tom. You don't need to write a book about his evening."

A thick hand fell on his shoulder—Bryant's hand. Tom glanced up and smiled. "Yeah, just thinking. I'm done with it." He scratched his nose. "Hey, B, did you see anything strange earlier?"

"Like what?"

Tom wagged his head from side to side. "I thought I saw Kaspar's feet come off the ground."

"As hard as Ezekiel kicked him, it would surprise me if his body didn't react. Spasm, twitch, whatever. Just the momentum of the kick alone could have popped his heels off the floor, right?"

"Maybe...but I meant before."

"Before Ezzy kicked him? You mean when he collapsed?"

Tom opened his mouth to say, *No, before he collapsed. When he made all the moaning noise,* but no sound issued from his throat. His tongue lay dead in his mouth, forming no words, his lips spasmed, then twitched closed.

Bryant's gaze flicked to the chart, then back at Tom. "Are you sure you're okay?"

"Never better." He didn't know why he said that, but he couldn't seem to get his mouth to say anything else, either.

"Well...if you say so." Bryant pulled out a chair and sat next to his own pile of charts. He put the fresh cup of coffee he'd brought with him down on the countertop.

"How are they?" Tom asked, nodding toward the stack of charts.

"Which?"

"The Amhains. Stedman."

Bryant scoffed. "Since we gave them the second doses of lorazepam, Izzy and Ezzy have been as quiet as sleeping babies. Stedman's reading his book and hasn't uttered as much as a peep."

"Two doses?"

Bryant swiveled in the chair and stared at Tom. "You don't remember?"

"No, of course, I do," said Tom. Again, he couldn't understand where the words had come from. He'd meant to say he didn't remember either dose, but his mouth seemed to have other plans.

Bryant stared at him for a moment, and Tom turned away, closing Kaspar Anderson's chart, then grabbing the next one from his pile. The thing that scared him was that he hadn't decided to do any of that.

"Anderson hit you pretty hard with that chair yesterday. Should I have Margie come take a look?"

"Nah, I'm fine," Tom's voice said. He wanted to turn around, to meet Bryant's concerned gaze and to ask him for help, but he couldn't do any of that. He watched as his hands opened the chart and flipped to an open notes page. *What's happening?* He screamed the thought in his mind, but no sound came from his throat.

"If you're sure…" He tilted his head, looking Tom up and down. "Julie asked me about you."

"Julie?"

"Yeah, Julie Ryder from downstairs. She lives in my complex."

"Oh. We went to high school together."

Bryant hunched forward, resting his elbows on his knees. "She *likes* you, Tom. But at the same time, she's worried about you."

"About me?"

"Yes. She said you were so out of it a week ago. When you went down there for Kaspar. She said she told you to go get checked out. Did you ever do that?"

"Yeah, I'm fit as a biscuit," he said.

Bryant shook his head and held up his hands in surrender. "I get it. You don't want to talk about it, but I think you need to ask Margie not to give you Kaspar as a patient for a while—when he comes back, I mean. You're starting to talk like him, and that man makes as much sense as a rhino ice skating," said Bryant.

Tom chuckled. "I'll do that."

Behind him, Bryant turned back to his own work. Tom's left hand snaked out and picked up the coffee cup, bringing it to his lips. His mouth opened, and he poured a mouthful of steaming coffee into it. Pain surged through him. The burning, stinging pain of scalding his tongue on the hot coffee sang in his nerves, but he couldn't move, couldn't spit it out, couldn't swallow.

In fact, he couldn't do anything but sit there while his tongue burned, and his eyes watered from the pain.

2

Tom's apartment, Millvale, PA
May 23, 2004, 11:18 pm

"It was weird as fuck, David."

"I'll bet. How long did that…*paralyzed* feeling last?"

"Not long. I… Finally, I could swallow, and I did. It was like that cleared the logjam, and I had control again."

"Think it's a concussion from yesterday?"

"I really don't know. I've heard of people getting amnesia or losing time from head trauma, but I've never heard of the paralyzed feeling."

"Did you tell Margie? Bryant?"

"I…" Tom hung his head. "I *couldn't*. Every time I tried, I just stood there with my mouth hanging open until I said something else. Something *I* didn't want to say."

"But you could tell me."

Tom brought his head up and stared into David's eyes. "I didn't think it would work. I thought I'd open my mouth to tell you about it and then some weird shit I didn't want to say would pop out."

David sat on the counter of his tiny kitchen, watching him through concerned eyes. "Maybe we should go to the emergency room."

Tom shook his head. "No. If I do that, they'll call Briar Ridge and report it."

"Is that so bad? Tom, maybe you got hurt yesterday. Or tonight for that matter. You don't know for sure, but these symptoms…"

"I said no, David."

"But, Tom—"

"Look, I understand, David, but I'm *not* going to We Care."

David closed his mouth and looked at him for ten heartbeats, then nodded. "Fine. I'll drop We Care, but only if you call Mike."

"Dr. Sorenson? He *works* at Briar Ridge, David."

David's nod was a slow one. "Yes, but we've talked about that before. He's a friend, and he also has a private practice."

"Still, he's—"

"It's him or We Care, Tom. I won't be swayed this time."

A muscle near Tom's lower left eyelid began to twitch, and he pressed on it with his finger. "Yeah, okay. Call him so I can get this over with."

With a nod, David fished his mobile phone out of his pocket and found Mike Sorenson in his contacts. He dialed the number and handed the phone to Tom.

"Hello? David is that you?"

"No, Dr. Sorenson. It's Tom."

"Oh, okay. What can I do for you, Tom? Is David okay?"

"I had another run in on Four South yesterday, and then again tonight. I guess I got hit pretty hard in the head."

The phone cracked as Mike shifted positions. "Okay."

"Well, I've been…" Tom looked at David, and he made a shooing gesture. "Yeah. Okay. David made me call because I've been having…trouble. And this isn't the first rap to the brain-basket I've taken in the last week. It's the second or third."

"Trouble, Tom? What kind of trouble?"

"Yeah. I… I went to get Kaspar from Two West a few nights back, and when I first saw him, I thought… I thought…"

"Tom, relax. I'm here to help, not judge. Okay?"

"I thought I saw something on his shoulder. A…shadow. A weird shadow. Then, when I left after my shift, I saw it again. In the parking lot."

Again, the line crackled. "Okay," Mike said. "What else?"

"Isn't that bad enough?" Tom giggled like a nervous schoolgirl. "I mean, I was obviously hallucinating."

"That remains to be seen, Tom," said Mike in a calm, fatherly voice. "But you didn't call me that night, you called me tonight." The phone rustled yet again as he got up and began to walk.

"I've also had trouble with words."

"With words?"

"Yeah. Word-salads, clangs, like that. But I'm not aware of it when it happens."

"Noted. Tell me about tonight."

"Yeah. Tonight, the Amhains went off on Kaspar. They were yelling that same nonsense about a demon and trying to get something off his shoulder. I remember running down the hall toward them—and this was about three-thirty or so."

"And then?"

"And then I was in the nurses' station writing charts and it was ten forty-five."

"You blacked out? Did the other staffers bring you to the station?"

"I… I don't think so. No one seemed to notice. It was as though I'd worked and acted fine for the missing hours. I'd even written the incident up in Kaspar's chart."

"I see." In the background on Mike's end, something clattered, and he murmured a curse. "Anything else?"

"No."

"Tom?"

"No, really, Dr. Sorenson—"

"Call me Mike."

"—that's all of it. Oh, wait. Except I had the strangest feeling when I came to. Bryant was there, and he asked if I was okay. I wanted to say no, that I needed help, but instead, I said I was fine. I tried to tell Margie, too, but what I wanted to say went unsaid, while my mouth babbled something innocuous."

"I see. Did you feel as though you were watching yourself from outside your body?"

"No, I definitely felt trapped inside while my body did whatever it wanted."

"Have you been to We Care? Did you have any imaging done?" Concern laced his voice.

Tom shook his head, then rolled his eyes and said, "No. I don't want to go to We Care. It'll get back to Margie and—"

"Tom, listen to me." Mike paused and waited.

"Okay."

"You need to get a CAT scan, at least. I'll phone in an order at First Presbyterian in Campton. You don't have to mention work at all. I'm friends with a radiologist there. He'll read the scan, and if he deems it necessary, he'll do an MRI. When it's all said and done, he'll call me with the results, and I'll get back to you and David. Okay?"

"Yeah," Tom sighed. "I hate going to the hospital."

"It's important, Tom, or I wouldn't ask you to."

"Okay."

"Good. Is David there? Can I speak with him?"

"Sure. Thanks, Dr., uh, Mike. Sorry for calling so late."

"Anytime, Tom."

Tom nodded and held David's phone out to him. "Mike wants to talk to you."

David took the phone, a pensive expression twisting his face. "Hello, Mike." His gaze tracked up to Tom's face and lingered. "Yes, I know where that is."

Tom drew a deep breath and let it whistle out between his lips. All he really wanted to do was go to bed and put everything behind him.

"Okay," said David. "Yes, I can do that. How will we…" He nodded to Tom. "Okay, that sounds good, Mike. Does it usually take long to get results from a CAT scan?" He paused, then nodded again. "Perfect. We're on our way. Thank you so much, Mike."

David disconnected the call, watching Tom the whole while. "Come on, lover. Let's go get these pictures taken. Mike said he's calling a friend who's a radiologist in Campton. He said he'd have the guy meet us there so he can read your scans and get Mike the results right away."

"He said as much. Can't we go tomorrow? I'm bushed."

"No, Tom. We need to go now. It's all set up."

Tom walked into the other room and sank to the couch. He put his head in his hands. "I'm *tired*, David. I just want to go to sleep." He didn't know why, but the idea of finding out something was wrong seemed worse than not knowing anything at all.

"Come on, lover," said David. "It'll be a grand adventure. Two gay men versus the evils of Campton. Two lovers, battling the evil status quo. Two men with great fashion sense versus—"

"Cut it out!" Tom growled.

David paused mid-step and stared at him. "Tom, it's important—"

"That's what Mike said, but that doesn't change the fact that I'm…" He shook his head and tore his gaze away from the hurt on David's face. "I want to go to bed." It came out more like a whine than a statement.

David came to sit next to him and took Tom's hand in his own. "I'll be there with you. The whole time."

Tom grunted.

"I know it might be scary, but we have to go find out what's wrong, Tom. Otherwise, Mike can't help." David stood and applied gentle upward pressure to Tom's hand. "Come on, lover. I'll be good."

Tom scoffed. "That's what both of the damn Amhain brothers said so I'd let them out of seclusion."

"I'm not one of them," David said in a quiet voice.

"Yeah, I know," said Tom with a sigh. "All right, let's go."

David grinned at him, pulled him up off the couch, and wrapped him in a hug. "Sorry about before, lover. Sometimes I try too hard to make things funny."

"No, I'm the one that's sorry. I…" He looked at David askance. "I don't know why, but the idea of having something really wrong scares me more than not knowing."

"Well, of course, silly! You are a man." David linked his arm through Tom's, and Tom allowed David to pull him toward the door.

3

Tom's apartment, Millvale, PA
May 25, 2004, 10:05 am

Tom awoke the second time his alarm went off without any memory of snoozing the damn thing. He stretched, luxuriating in the twelve hundred thread-count cotton sheets David had persuaded him to buy. As was usual for him, sleep receded at a gradual pace, but his bladder operated at full speed. He swung his legs out of bed and glanced at the other side, where he expected David. The sheets were mounded up on that side of the bed, but his boyfriend wasn't in them. "David?" he called as he went into the bathroom.

There was no answer, so after he finished his ablutions, he left the bedroom and headed out to the kitchen. "David?" he called as he went, but there was no answer.

In the kitchen, he stopped and stood, staring at the empty living room. It wasn't like David to leave before Tom was awake, and on the rare occasions that he had, he'd left a note. Moving at a lumbering pace, Tom turned and retraced his steps to the bedroom, thinking he must have overlooked the note. But there was no note—not in the rumpled bedclothes, not on the nightstand on David's side, and not in the bathroom. Shaking his head, he returned to the kitchen and searched the counters—he even looked in the garbage—but found nothing.

His phone lay plugged in on the island, and he grabbed it and dialed David's number. When David's voicemail picked up, Tom said, "Hey, lover, it's Tom. I just woke up, and you're not here. No note, either, which is weird for you. I'll take a *grande* and a bagel. Kidding about that but call me. Okay?"

He felt rested and ready to go, so he threw on a pair of sweats and a T-shirt and headed out to the gym.

4

BRSMH, Four South, Millvale, PA
May 25, 2004, 1:14 pm

Tom stepped through the door from Four West, and, after shutting it securely behind him, headed down the hall toward the nurses' station, whistling a Beatles tune as he went. He didn't know the name of it, but the tune was one of the indelible earworms he'd acquired in high school. With his key ring around his index finger, he flipped his keys in time to the song's beat.

He glanced in the alcove that contained the Amhain brothers' seclusion rooms and stopped. Usually, seclusion rooms were filled with a pale-yellow light during the day. Each room had a window covered with a protective metal grid and blinds sandwiched inside the double-pane windows. The blinds were always down, and sunlight beating a path through the shade was responsible for the soft yellow light.

"TH! Let them out, kid."

Tom jumped and stepped closer to the alcove's door, peering around the corner into the alcove. "Come out of there, William."

"Yeah, sure, kid. But you need to let my brethren out of there. They are in the grip of... TH! You're not going to believe me anyway."

"I might let them out," said Tom in a mild tone. "But what does it mean, William? TH, I mean?"

Stedman gave him a queer look, and Tom fully expected to be berated for not knowing. Then Stedman shrugged. "The Holyghost," he said, running the last two words together, making them one word. "Get it?"

"Right," said Tom. "Thanks for telling me. Go on down to the dayroom."

"Sure, kid. TH knows I don't want any more trouble." Stedman's eyes drifted to his shoulder, and then the man shuddered. He ducked out of the alcove, giving Tom plenty of space.

Tom watched him shuffle down the hallway, then returned his attention to the alcove, cocking his head and staring at the twin rectangles made black by the complete lack of light. "What the hell?" he muttered.

He glanced up the hall toward the nurses' station, but no one from the day shift was in the hall or the window to the station. He sighed and stepped into the alcove, stepping up to peer into Ismael's room. He flicked the light switch, but the room stayed dark. He cupped his hands on either side of his face and pressed them to the glass, but it was as black as the abyss inside.

"Ismael?" he called.

Nothing moved in the stygian blackness, and Ismael didn't answer. He squinted, trying to amplify his night vision and pierce the darkness as though by sheer willpower alone. Purple and green demon-shapes danced in the velvet blackness. Spots of color blossomed like spring flowers, but still, he could make out no details within the room.

"Ismael? Why is your room so dark?"

When Ismael failed to answer, Tom shifted to Ezekiel's room. The same abyssal darkness greeted him from Ezzy's window, however, and the same silence.

Tom stepped away from the two doors, his gaze bouncing back and forth between the two windows. He half-expected to see the brothers' leering faces in the windows, laughing at making him dance on a string, but the darkness from within the rooms never lightened, never changed. He took another step back, unnerved by the eerie silence, by the darkness where there should be warmth and light, by the absolute lack of movement. "Ismael? Ezekiel?" he called. His spine tingled, and the skin of his arms felt strange. He looked down at them and saw every single hair standing on end. He shifted his gaze back to the two windows, then peered over his shoulder into the fully lit hall, as though needing reassurance light still existed somewhere.

With a minute shake of his head, he stepped closer to the two doors. *Must be a short.* He flicked the light switches for both rooms, half expecting the lights to flare and the brothers' mocking laughter, but again, nothing happened. *I'm not on shift yet. I shouldn't even be in here.* With a shrug, he slid his key in Ezekiel's deadbolt and turned it.

5

"Sorry to say there's no change, Tom," said Julie.

"What?" The last thing he remembered doing was sliding his key into Ezekiel's door.

"You asked how Kaspar was doing." Julie came around the countertop that separated the nurses' station from the hall. "He's still catatonic."

"Catatonic?" Tom repeated, trying to get his mind caught up to where he was and what he was doing. He put a hand on the countertop and heaved a sigh.

"Sure," said Julie with a shrug. "All the catatonics are right down there in the day room, set up in front of the bay window. Like when you came down the other night."

Tom nodded, feeling numb, cold. "Can I see Lee Amorte?" He turned away and shuffled down toward the day room.

Julie trailed behind him in pensive silence.

"I know it must seem weird, but both my parents used to work at The Jacks. My mom told me about… Well, what he did. I knew him back then, back before he did it. I guess I'm curious about what became of him."

"Oh. Nothing much to report. He hasn't spoken or moved of his own accord since his admission. Total catatonic stupor." She sped up, passed him, and led him into the day room. Julie walked to the third wheelchair from the left and bent toward the patient. "Mr. Amorte? You have a visitor."

Tom came up beside Julie. Lee Amorte was slumped in the wheelchair, staring straight ahead. He'd wasted away to skin and bones, and his hair had thinned to a few baby-fine clumps. His mouth twisted with a grimace.

"Mr. Amorte?" Julie rubbed his forearm, but there was no reaction. She straightened and glanced at Tom. "You see?"

Tom nodded, but his gaze had switched to Kaspar Anderson, who sat in his own wheelchair at the other end of the line. His color was better, and he still had all his hair, but his expression was an exact duplicate of Amorte's—a snarl of terror or pain. "Are they in pain?"

Julie shrugged. "Your guess is as good as mine."

Tom closed his eyes and turned away. He didn't understand it, but looking at the two catatonic men filled him with dread.

"Are you okay, Tom?" Julie lay her cool, dry palm on his forearm and gazed up at him.

He knew she had a thing for him—not that he cared, but he *knew* at least. He wasn't what David called "gay-blind." He sucked in another breath and turned toward her, dislodging her hand on his arm. "A little dizzy, that's all."

Concern lit in her eyes, and she frowned a little. "Have you been to a doctor?"

"No, haven't had the time."

She rolled her eyes and clicked her tongue. "It's been eight days since you came down the first time. You took a blow to the head, right? That's plenty of time."

"Eight?" he said. He only remembered *five* days, maybe six.

Julie's brows knitted as she nodded.

"But it…" Tom closed his mouth. *I've lost entire days?*

"I really think you need to go over to We Care, Tom. Get a CAT scan. See a doctor." She looked up at him for a minute, then nodded emphatically. "I'm going to call Margie."

"No." Tom grabbed her arm and stopped her from stepping back into the station. "No, don't do that."

"Tom, you're hurting me," said Julie in a calm voice.

"Oh, my God," he whispered, snatching his hand from her arm and staring at the red marks as they slowly faded. "I'm so sorry, Julie. I'd never… I…" He slumped his shoulders and looked at his feet.

"Do you see why you should get checked out?" Her voice had turned chilly, but warmth still sparkled in her eyes. "You aren't yourself."

Tom rubbed his eyes. *Something is wrong. Even I can't argue with that.* He dropped his hand and blew out his cheeks. "Julie, I'm so sorry. But I went over to Campton last night. CAT scan and the works." He didn't remember the trip at all, but he remembered telling Mike Sorenson he would. He remembered David cajoling him to get going…

But after that everything was a blank.

"What were the results? Who did you see over there?"

He shook his head. "Dr. Sorenson called in the orders for me. He's a friend."

"Oh?" She quirked an eyebrow at him, and her face tightened.

"Yes. He's an old friend of the family."

"And what did Dr. Sorenson say? Are you even supposed to be working?"

"I… No, he said everything was fine."

"You're really a horrible liar, Tom. Do you know that?"

A sinking feeling invaded his gut, and he found he couldn't meet her gaze. He shrugged his shoulders. "Sorry. I'm okay to work, though. Promise."

"Dr. Sorenson told you that?"

Tom shuffled his feet.

"I didn't think so. I'm calling Margie."

Again, she moved to return to the nurses' station, and again, Tom grabbed her arm, though lightly. "No, Julie. Don't do that." He hung his head. "Look, I need the hours, okay? My...my mother's sick and can't work. I'm trying to support us both." He heard the lies pouring out of his mouth, but he wasn't speaking them. Unlike his earlier lies, these sounded plausible and confident.

Julie looked at him, her head cocked to the side, eyes narrowed a little. "What's wrong with her?" she asked after a few moments.

"Cancer," his voice said. "But don't tell anyone. She's very modest, and it's cancer in a...uh...private area. She'd be mortified if anyone knew."

Julie continued to stare up at him and said nothing. "Maybe I was wrong, before," she finally said. "Maybe you are a good liar when you want to be."

6

His hands were filthy. Thick black goo filled the creases in his skin and under his nails. Smears of it decorated the backs of his hands, and the knuckles of his already bruised right hand were now also skinned. He stared down at them, confused for a moment. *Where is Julie? How did I get here?*

He looked up at himself in the mirror, and for one heartbeat, he imagined he saw the same shadow that had been on Kaspar's shoulder sitting on his own. The thing opened glowing vermillion eyes and met his gaze, and then it disappeared.

Tom's heartbeat thundered in his ears as he exhaled a shaky breath. He lifted his hand to rub his eyes but remembered the black goo halfway through the motion and stopped. He flipped on the hot water and plunged his hands beneath the stream.

For a moment, nothing happened, but when it did, fear sank its teeth into his throat. In the sink, the water filling the bowl had a pinkish hue, and the black gunk on his fingers had faded into the red of fresh blood.

Tom stared at the red swirls decorating the sink's basin in mute horror. His heart beat at a rapid pace, and his breathing lurched into a higher gear. He scrubbed his hands, then reached for more soap. Water sloshed out of the basin and splashed to the tiled floor. After five minutes of intense scouring, his palms were free of the blood, but it still lingered in the creases around his nail beds, in the wrinkles around his knuckles, and even *under* his nails. "My God…what did I *do*?" he murmured as he attacked his hands with a wet paper towel, working it into the spots still laden with blood. *Christ…it's under my nails… Did I…claw her?*

The door swung open, and Tom froze for a moment, staring at the mirror like a feral wolf caught in the glare of headlights. He held his breath, his knees weak and trembling.

Mike Sorenson stepped into the bathroom, and when his gaze found Tom's, he stopped in his tracks. His face settled into a scowl. "Why the hell didn't you go to Campton the other night? Where have you been? I've tried calling many times. Both you and David."

Tom dropped his gaze. "I…" He shook his head. "I don't know what to say. I don't…" He bent over the sink, scrubbing at his nails.

"How about 'Gee, sorry I blew off your medical advice, Mike. Sorry I stood up your colleague—your *friend*—the radiologist. Sorry I've left you and John wondering what the hell happened to me.' How about any of those?" Fury tightened Mike's voice until it rasped like a file on rusty metal.

"I *am* sorry, Mike. I…"

"You what, Tom? Where have you and David been?"

"I haven't seen him." He gave his hands a final rinse, then dried them with a paper towel and shoved his hands in his pockets. He stood before Mike like a child who's done wrong and knows it. "I've lost some time since…"

"*Christ*, Tom!" Mike lifted a hand, extended it toward Tom, then let it drop back to his side. His mouth opened several times before he settled on what to say next. "You look terrible."

"I don't feel so great, either," said Tom in a trembling voice. "I'm… Mike, I'm scared."

The anger drained from Mike's countenance, and he took a step forward. "Then let's get you some help. What do you say?"

Tom nodded and opened his mouth, but he couldn't say a word, couldn't so much as squeak. He tried to shake his head, tried to lift his hands, to pantomime his distress, but nothing worked. His mouth closed on its own, and his eyelids blinked a few times, then his lips curled into a smile.

"Are you okay, Tom?" Mike's brow knotted, and his mouth fell into a moue of concern.

"Oh, sure. I'm fine," said Tom's voice. He chuckled. "I get woozy is all."

Mike stepped closer, peering up at him. "Your eyes are dilated, Tom. Did you take something today?"

Tom's head shook itself.

"Then that could be a bad sign, Tom. We need to get you over to We Care. Have those images shot."

"No, really, Mike. I'm fine."

"I'm a doctor and your friend, Tom, and I'm telling you that you might not be fine. Let me take you over there. I have privileges there." He put his hand on Tom's elbow, his palm cool and dry. "What do you say?"

7

*BRSMH, Four West Stairwell, Millvale, PA
May 25, 2004, 2:56 pm*

Tom stood frozen on the fourth-floor landing, his hospital keys hanging from Four West's stairwell door, his fingers curled around the key protruding from the deadbolt. He had no memory of leaving the bathroom, no idea if he'd gone to We Care with Mike or…something else.

He couldn't turn the key, nor could he pull it out of the lock. *Something is seriously wrong with me*, he thought. *Mike is right. I need to find him and get that CAT scan.* His mouth dropped open, and a rusty saw of a laugh trickled out. He watched as his hand turned, springing the deadbolt and pushing the door open.

His body continued to move without his command, walking across the hall and slipping through Four South's steel door. He saw his body doing these things, but felt no connection to the events, to his body's actions. It was as if some essential circuit in his mind had blown, severing the connection between his brain and his body.

This is depersonalization. All the stress of the past week... The whole mess with Vee, Mom freaking out, her disappearance, David leaving me high and dry without so much as a word... Stress can cause depersonalization—you know that. His head nodded. *And that could explain the blank spots in my memory, right?*

His body moved down the hall toward the nurses' station, hands swinging by his sides, his pace casual, but like his stance in the stairwell, his gait seemed off, different from how his body felt when he walked. It felt...

Unreal... This all feels unreal. Like a movie, a dream. And the lost time. All of that could simply be derealization, right? Again, his head nodded on his neck as if in answer to his thoughts. *But if that's true, if all this is just a result of depersonalization and derealization syndrome, then the ultimate cause could be more than just stress. It could be...* He didn't even want to think the word. *Hallucinations, depersonalization and derealization, the word salad, the clangs... You know what that means.* This time his head shook from side to side, denying the track his thoughts were on. He didn't want to believe it, but…

"Tom?" Margie leaned through the top of the nurses' station Dutch door. "Where have you been? You missed report."

His body stopped moving forward, and he stood there, blinking at her like a lunatic. His hand lifted, hooked his thumb over his shoulder back toward the hall of seclusion rooms. "Just checking on things." The words tumbled out of his mouth unbidden.

"John from the day shift said he saw you go into the Amhain brothers' alcove after lunch."

He inclined his head. "Yes, I heard a lot of racket and wanted to check on them."

"And?"

His shoulders rolled up and back—a weird shrug. "Everything was fine."

"Fine? What were you doing here so early?"

"I…" He shook his head. "I left my bag the other night. I needed it to…"

"What the hell is the matter with you, Tom?"

"Nothing."

"Fit as rain, right?"

His head bent forward, the beginning of a nod, but stalled at the bottom of the movement, and Tom felt something pop in his head. He lifted his head, pulse thundering in his ears. "Margie, I—"

"Tom, this is *important*. You've had several close calls in the last week, and I think you're injured."

"Nah. I spoke with Dr. Sorenson. He—"

"Yeah, he came by looking for you last night. I told him it was your day off and to try you at home. He was pretty pissed."

Tom's mouth bent in an easy smile. "Yeah, there was a mix-up at First Presbyterian. I asked Mike to order a CAT scan there for me, and—"

"Mike, huh?" she asked, looking up at him, suspicion written all over her face.

"Yeah. We're friends. He married my wrestling coach. He's a fag."

Margie blinked at that, then shook her head. "And why didn't you just go to We Care? What did the scan show?"

"Nothing to show," he said with a chuckle. "The radiologist was supposed to call Mike with the results, but there was a mix-up. We straightened it out earlier." Tom chuckled again. "And I didn't want to go to We Care because it's a small town. It was stupid. I was scared something was wrong, and I didn't want it… I didn't want it to get out. You know, here."

Margie shook her head and waved her hands. "We'll talk about that later. Let's get back to you checking on the Amhains."

"What's wrong? What's happened to the Amhains?"

"We can't find them. They seem to have eloped from five-point restraints and a locked seclusion room."

His mouth dropped open. "Both of them?"

"Yes. Did you go in their rooms to check or just peek through the window?"

"I glanced in. Izzy was sleeping, and Ezzy was doing the rocking thing with his head. How can they be missing? Wasn't anyone looking at the—"

"The whole bank of monitors are shorted out. Again."

"Just like with Kaspar."

"Yeah. We're checking with the Security Office. They may have seen something. John said he thought you went out by way of Four West?"

"Yeah," said Tom's voice. "I took the stairs down."

"Are you sure you got the door pulled closed?"

Tom's head bounced with another nod. "You know how the doors are spring assisted—they *always* close."

"But you checked?"

"Of course."

Margie lifted her chin and sniffed. "Tom, I need you to go home."

"But I'm *fine*—"

"No arguments, Tom. I had to file a report after I talked to Dr. Sorenson. You are officially on leave until we get a full report."

"Yeah, but I told you—"

"A full report from *Dr. Sorenson*," she said.

Anger surged through him, and he felt his hand tighten into a fist. *Watch out! Margie! Get away from me!* he tried to shout, but his lips only curled into a disdainful smile. "I thought we were friends, Margie," his mouth said.

"Yeah, so did I." She turned and walked away. "Leave your keys with Kerry," she called over her shoulder.

8

Tom's apartment parking lot, Millvale, PA
May 25, 2004, 3:26 pm

Tom's phone shivered and danced in the side pocket of his cargo pants, startling him out of the waking nightmare he'd been having. He stood in the parking lot in front of his apartment, behind his own car, which he'd apparently backed into the spot. The lanyard holding his personal keys was wrapped around his wrist, his trunk key in his hand, though he had no idea why. Every moment prior to the phone ringing was just another depthless black spot. He pinched the bridge of his nose and shook his head. *Better get a handle on this,* he told himself, *before you screw up your entire life, Tommy-ba-bommy.* He needed to start listening to everyone and go to Campton and get that CAT scan—if Mike would even speak to him anymore.

He sighed and fished the phone from his cargo-pocket, if for no other reason than to silence its incessant buzzing. He accepted the call without looking at the screen, knowing it was David, at last.

"Hey, lover," he said. "Where have you been? Don't you—"

"Mr. Madsen? Sorry to interrupt, but this is Deputy O'Hara, Castle County Sheriff's Department."

Fear thrummed through Tom, followed by a wild hope. "You've found her?"

"No, sir. I'm sorry to say I have not. The investigation into your mother's disappearance is ongoing."

Tom's shoulders slumped and his expression flicked from hopeful excitement to despair. "Oh."

"I'm calling for another reason. I'd like you to—"

"What reason?"

O'Hara grunted. "Could you meet me at the Sheriff's Station on Maurus Avenue? I'm free right now if that works for you. Do you know where the station is?"

"I do," said Tom. "But I'm afraid I'm wait for work."

"Ah. I see."

"What's ball this about, Deputy O'Hara?" A nameless anxiety crashed through him like a tsunami, leaving him trembling and tense.

"I'd rather discuss that in person, Mr. Madsen. Perhaps I could speak with your boss and get you some time off."

He's going to arrest you, lover. The voice belonged to David, even though it only spoke in his head. "I don't like weaving everyone in a lurch," he said. "That's what I'd be doing if I called in today. Can't you give me a splint what this is about?"

"I understand not wanting to leave your co-workers in a lurch, but this is very important. Perhaps I could speak with Margie, tell her the stakes."

"Look, I'm sure Margie would give me the time. It's not about that. She wouldn't be able to replace me this late, and they're already covering for me for an hour. They'd be snort all evening, and that's just not fair."

"Did you know you're doing it again, Mr. Madsen?"

"Doing what?"

"Mixing up your words like you were the first time we spoke."

"What? No, it must be the confection."

"No, sir. I hear you clearly. You just said, 'it must be the confection,' but the *connection* is fine."

Tom thought furiously but couldn't come up with a response to that.

"Why do I make you so nervous, Mr. Madsen?"

"You don't snake me nervous, Deputy. It's just sin a bad cuddle of days. I'm not nervous, I'm pressed out. And, to tell you the truth, all this smoke and stagger shit only makes it worse." Tom huffed for breath as the silence stretched out between them. Without his conscious decision to do so, his hand snaked the key into the trunk's lock and twisted. The trunk lid popped up, and Tom gasped, staring down at the four bloody bodies stuffed in there. *WHAT THE FUCK?*

"I…see," said O'Hara. "I think."

Tom darted panicked glances in every direction and tried to slam the trunk lid, but his hand wouldn't let go of the keys hanging in the lock.

"Uh...Mr. Madsen, this is a sensitive question, and I hope you take it as a sign of my sincere concern for your health and safety. Do you have a doctor? Someone who's looking after your *mental* health?"

"Go. I don't half a doctor. I don't plead a doctor. I'm in perfect dental health, I assure you."

"Yeah, see, that's the thing, Mr. Madsen. I don't believe you are. I'd really like to—"

"Deputy O'Hara? I've already said that I can't treat you tonight. If stairs nothing else, I'll say goodbye." Another silence stretched as Tom tried to wrench his hand free of his keys. He considered just hanging up, but his other hand seemed incapable of obeying his commands either.

"Where are you at this moment, Mr. Madsen?"

"Goodbye, Deputy O'Hara," he said, but again, he couldn't hang up, couldn't let go of his keys, couldn't do anything but stand there hoping the deputy took the hint and hung up himself. *What am I doing? What am I going to do with these...* He jerked his gaze up from the gory mess in his trunk and again scanned the parking lot. *Oh, David, where are you?*

"Mr. Madsen, I'm very concerned by your erratic behavior. I'm going to call Margie Samuels and get you relieved from this shift whether you come in to see me or not. I really don't think—"

Tom's mouth fell open on its own, and he cackled into the phone. "Really?" he said. "It's just a joke, Deputy O'Hara. All that word-salad and disorganized speech. A hazard of the profession, I'm afraid."

"I don't find it funny, Mr. Madsen, and what's more, I don't believe you."

"I'm sorry, Deputy. Truly. But I meant what I said about being stressed out." The hand holding his keys withdrew the key from the trunk's lock and slid the keys into his side pocket. "I'm not the best judge of my own humor sometimes." He reached out and closed the trunk lid gently. "Look, I'd be happy to meet you after my shift. I could be there at quarter-past eleven if you'll still be working."

O'Hara sniffed, and Tom could imagine him squinting around, trying to decide if the story he'd just heard himself concoct held any water. "Quarter-past, you say?"

"Yes, absolutely. I don't want to leave everyone in a lurch, that's all. In your profession, I bet you feel the same."

"Well…okay, yeah. I get what you're saying, Mr. Madsen."

But he doesn't believe it, said a harsh voice in Tom's head. *Not yet.* "I'm very sorry about the inappropriate humor," said his mouth. "I suppose it's like Tourette's Syndrome, but not as bad. Sometimes I just blurt out the most inappropriate shit."

"You should talk to someone at your work," said O'Hara. "Maybe there's something—"

"I'll do that. In fact, I have a family friend who's a physician out at Briar Ridge. I'm sure he could help me out."

The call hummed for a moment, then O'Hara grunted. "Quarter-past eleven, then."

"I'll be there," said Tom. "On Maurus Avenue."

"Yes. Okay. I'll see you then."

When O'Hara disconnected, Tom slumped against his car, in control of his body once more. He dialed David's number again and squeezed his eyes shut, pressing the phone against his ear. "Please, please, please," he whispered. "Pick up, pick up."

He turned and ran to his apartment, not wanting to even think about what was in his trunk. The call went to voicemail after four rings, and Tom sighed. "David... David, I really need to talk to you. I'm sorry about whatever I did. I don't remember, okay? Please call me. *Christ*, David! I'm so scared. I think that deputy is going to arrest me, and..." He struggled to force the words "there are bodies in my trunk" past his clenched throat but couldn't so much as squeak. He gasped for air and gave up as David's voicemail beeped and disconnected.

He unlocked his front door and stepped inside, closing it so quickly behind him as to rattle the door in its frame. "*David!*" he wailed. "What am I going to do?" He scrubbed his hand over his face and hit the redial.

This time, when David's phone lit up the underside of his couch, Tom was staring right at it. He dropped to his knees and fished it out, staring at David's pet name for him on the caller ID screen. Then, his gaze flicked to the smear of dried blood, and the strength went out of him.

He flopped forward on his face, a whimper the only sound to pass his lips. He lay there, face in the old, threadbare carpet, staring at David's phone, at the blood, at the record of his numerous calls and voicemails. *Oh, David! Oh, my God, what did I do?*

A harsh cackle rang inside his head—a laugh that could have drifted up from the depths of Hell. *You know what you did.*

Tom groaned and shook his head, grinding his face into the carpet. *No! I don't remember! I don't!*

Yes, you do. The voice was hard, cold, relentless. *Your pathetic denials do no good. I can see what you remember, and it's right there, waiting for you to look at it. At least until I take your memories and leave you—*

Tom squeezed his eyes shut. "No!" he whimpered.

Oh, for fuck's sake, boy! His fingers uncurled, dropping both his and David's phone to the carpet. His neck flexed, lifting his face, and his elbows slid back until his palms rested on the floor. *Here, look!*

The scene unraveled in his mind's eye.

David walked in front of him, heading for his little Toyota. He was talking, babbling in that sweet way he had, trying to keep Tom's spirits up. He clowned and cavorted, using his patented toe-kick and over-the-shoulder-come-hither sultry looks, but inside, Tom felt cold, detached—and if he were completely honest, even a little revolted.

"Come on, lover," said David. "Lose the long face! This will only take an hour, and then it's over and done."

Tom's lips twisted into an involuntary sneer. "You don't get it, David!" he snapped before he could stop himself.

David flinched, that hurt expression in his eyes that Tom had seen so much of lately. "But I do, Tom. Really."

"You don't!" Tom stopped walking and looked up at the night sky. "You think your prancing faggot act can make this better, but it can't! You say you get it, but you—"

"Fine," murmured David. "I'll stop trying to cheer you up." His voice contained an iron Tom had never heard there before. "But we are going to get this CAT scan, Tom. No matter how many fights you try to pick, no matter how many cruel, ugly things you say to me."

Tom dropped his gaze, eyes narrowed, until it rested on David's face. He could read the hurt there, the deep wounds he was laying on David's soul, and a part of him was horrified at what he'd just said. But another part, a savage part, reveled in the reaction his cruel words had evoked.

David stepped closer and laid his hand on Tom's arm. "I know you are scared, Tom," he said softly, "but I'm here, and I'm going to stay here, right beside you. One way or another, Tom, we'll get through this."

Tom hitched a sigh, and let his head hang down toward his chest. David linked his arm again and started walking toward the car. Tom went along, head hanging, breathing a little hard, feeling enervated and broken.

When they reached David's Toyota, Tom broke away. "One second," he said, trotting to his own car. He popped the trunk and took out his duffel bag, then ran back to David's side. "I'm so sorry, David," he whispered.

"I know, lover. What's with the workout bag?"

"I've got a spare set of sweats in there." Tom lifted the duffel. "I'll change into them at the hospital. Open your trunk, please."

David hitched his shoulders and moved around to the back of the car.

"No!" Tom whimpered. "Don't make me look!"

"Here you go," said David.

Tom moved around the back of the car and stood behind David, wrapping his arms around him and squeezing him to his chest. "I don't deserve you," he whispered in David's ear.

"Sure you do, Tom. You deserve only the—" He grunted as Tom's hug grew tighter and tighter. "Hey, ease up, lover," he said a little breathlessly. "Are you trying to crush me?"

Tom squeezed all the harder, dropping the duffel bag and shoving his lover toward the open maw of the trunk. David began to struggle, but it was far, far too late. Tom *used his weight advantage, his strength, and the skills he'd developed on the mats of Millvale High to bend the man he loved into a ball and wedge him into the trunk.*

When he let go and reached for the trunk lid, David lay gasping, staring up at him with fear and pain-filled eyes. He held his ribs with both arms, breathing shallowly. He barely reacted when Tom slammed the trunk closed.

With a quick glance around, he snatched the car keys out of the trunk's lock and scooped up the duffel bag. He walked around and got in the driver's seat.

Tom panted with the pain the memory dredged up in him, but his eyes were dry. He was halfway back to his car, moving at a brisk walk, his head up, a thin smile plastered on his face. *I didn't kill him? Is he...*

Alive? mocked the cruel voice in his head. "Let's go see," he muttered. His body unlocked the door and slid behind the wheel of his car. His hand put the key in the ignition and cranked it until the car shuddered to life. *We have to get rid of these bodies, anyway.*

Who... His mind cringed away from the question, but he had to know. *Who's back there?*

"You *know* who," said his mouth. "Want to see what you did to them, too?"

No!

"Then *shut the fuck up.*"

Tom retreated from the vehemence in his own voice. *I'm going crazy,* he thought in a strangely calm tone.

He watched his body move, backing out of the spot and driving west out of town, turning down an overgrown gravel road that snaked away between the trees. He viewed what happened as though on an internal movie screen, watching his hands spin the wheel, guide the car onto progressively unused roads and rutted tracks until he was deep in the forest. He wasn't surprised when the headlights illuminated both David's and his mother's cars sitting on the shingle of one of the deep lakes that dotted the region, but seeing Virginia's old hulk did.

He longed to close his eyes, but instead, he got out of the car, leaving the headlights blazing, and walked toward his mother's car. Her keys hung from the trunk, and his hand whipped out and opened it.

The smell of decomposition and blood assaulted him, and Tom wanted to cringe away, to gag, to cover his mouth, but instead, his nostrils flared, and he drew in a lungful of the awful stench.

Mary Madsen lay in the trunk, battered, bruised, one eye-gouged out, blood caking her face, matting her hair. He tried to turn his face away but had no control. "This is what you did to her."

No!

"Oh, yes. You laughed when her eye popped out."

Never! I'd never—

Laughter boomed from his own throat, echoing back and forth across the lake. His hand reached up and slammed the trunk lid, then removed the keys. He walked around and got in the car, the seat already adjusted for him rather than his mother. He backed the car along the road for a hundred yards or so, then rolled down all the windows. He got out, leaving the car in park, and looked around for a few moments. He found a long stick and wedged the accelerator pedal to the floor. He stood alongside the car as the engine shrieked, then reached through the window and dropped it in gear.

The car hurled itself toward the lake, spitting gravel from its tires, then slammed into the water. It lurched forward, sending a chevron of waves racing toward the opposite bank, engine screaming its last as the car ran into the deep water and sank. "Good enough," his mouth said. "Now, let's go check on your butt-buddy."

Tom fought—briefly—for control, starting with his whole body, then just his legs, to stop his relentless advance toward David's car, finally settling on trying to close his eyes, but it was no use.

David's trunk popped open. "Surprise!"

Tom recoiled from the glee in his own voice. *What are you?*

His lip curled, and a nasty chuckle rang out. "Oh, Tommy-ba-bommy, you're going to have *years* to find that answer, but here's a hint: my mother possessed a little church girl and fucked a priest. She got pregnant."

Again, the reek turned his stomach, and again his nostrils flared and drank it in. He willed his head to freeze in place, to twitch away, but with a cruel chuckle, his body bent forward and put his nose within inches of David's tortured form. His eyes crawled—almost lovingly—over David's delicate features, his crushed eye socket, the flap his nose had become, the misshapen lump of his mandible. "Oh, and there's more…" The wanton tone of his voice made his skin crawl. "Don't you want to see what you did, Tommy-ba-bommy? Don't you want to see *who you really are?*"

His body grabbed David by the wrist and backed away, pulling the dead man out of the trunk and letting him flop onto the gravel. His lower body was unclothed and covered in deep black bruises. Strap marks laced his backside from repeated strikes of a belt. "You were so *angry* with him. What did he do to you except love you?"

His eyes prickled with the sting of nascent tears, but that's as close as he could come to expressing the raw grief that coursed through his mind. He longed to scream, to tear the skin off his cheeks, to wail and gnash his teeth, but the sadistic thing in control of his body only laughed.

"You didn't even need a hammer," he crowed. "You used your *fists*, big man." His gaze wandered to the strap marks. "And your belt."

His body turned away from David's corpse, turned to look at his own car, idling on the side of the rutted path. "But that's nothing." In long, determined strides, his body walked around to the back of his car. "Wait till you get a look at this." His body paused. "Or would you rather see the fat bitch?" His head rotated back and forth. "Nah, we'll save her for last. You did such good work on her—hell, you probably won't even recognize her as human." His head tilted back and bellowed crazy laughter at the stars.

Trapped in his own body, Tom's mind quaked. His personality roiled in self-hatred, in revulsion at the things he'd done. He didn't want to see any more. He didn't want to see what he'd done to Julie Ryder or Mike Sorenson. He didn't want to know if he'd somehow gotten the Amhain brothers off the unit and out of the hospital, then killed them and stuffed them into the trunk. He sought darkness, unconsciousness, relief.

And again, his body shook with laughter shouted at the sky. "I'll make you a deal, Tommy-ba-bommy."

What deal?

"You stop fighting me, and I'll let you fade to black." He chuckled and rubbed his hands together. "It's that or I'll put them on display. I'll mark them and stage them and drop a dime myself to make sure the cops find them. Your choice, Tommy-ba-bommy."

Chapter 20
The Beast, with Wrath

I

"And that's all it took," said Angel, her voice worn to a harsh croak. "All I had to do is show that weak fool what I did wearing his skin, then promise not to make him look in the trunk of his car. Then I let him go to sleep while I put that fat cow in the parking lot at Briar Ridge. I *almost* framed Tom's boyfriend for her, but then I decided the mystery of it would be better." She grated laughter. "He gave up so easily." She turned a hateful gaze on Gavin. "Are you going to give in?" She pointed at the hammer lying across the room and turned her head-tilted gaze on Maddie. "Or are you going to let me hurt her?"

"Gavin would *never*—"

"What do you want me to do?" Gavin asked in a weak, helpless voice, and Angel smiled.

"You're going to beat my next little toy to death with this hammer, of course. While I watch and diddle myself."

"Gavin, no!" cried Maddie. "I'd rather die than—"

"Oh, shut up!" snarled Angel, and Maddie flinched away. Angel barked heartless laughter at her.

"Fine," said Gavin. "Just don't hurt Maddie."

Angel lurched to her feet, her face a grimace of pain. "Maybe I'll wear her next. Think of the fun we could have, sparky-spark." She waggled her eyebrows, then turned and walked toward the hammer.

Moving as quietly as he could, Gavin withdrew a syringe, flicked the cap off with his thumbnail, and stabbed it into Maddie's thigh. A small gasp of pain escaped her, but Angel seemed not to have heard.

"You said Tom Madsen gave in," said Gavin," but didn't he fight you? He told Debbie Esteves he went to a priest or something. That he prayed all the time and pissed you off."

Angel grunted and bent to grab the hammer, and as she did, Gavin slid another syringe into his palm and removed the cap. "He did those things," she said in a weary voice, "but he didn't *fight*. He didn't *resist*. He let me do whatever I wanted to with his body." She gripped the hammer by its head and turned toward them, a vile grin on her face. "Oh, he *hated* what I made him watch. It made him sick, but he allowed me to do it. Not that he could have stopped me, mind," she said, holding up the index finger of her free hand, "but he could have made it…difficult." She strutted across the small gray room, holding the hammer haft out toward Gavin. "You'll find her in the room next door. Go. Go, now, and *ruin* her! I want to watch you work, spark. Then, we'll come back with her blood dripping from your face, with her brains on your pretty suit, and show your lovely wife. When that's all done, we'll go arrange her for your stupid friends at NYPD and, afterward, you can clean up and go back to Pod 51 for a rest." Her grin grew and grew as she spoke, turning ferocious. "I'll keep Maddie with me, of course." She stopped in front of him, shoving the hammer toward him.

Gavin sniffed and let his head fall forward.

"Or do I need to play with Maddie for a few minutes to stiffen your resolve?"

"No," he blurted. "No, I'm resolved."

"*Then take the fucking hammer!*" Angel roared.

Gavin nodded, and Maddie moaned.

Angel's gaze snapped to Maddie's face. "What's wrong with her, spark?"

"Nothing," said Gavin. He wrapped his left hand around the haft of the hammer and raised his head. When his gaze met Angel's, he lunged forward and slammed the needle into her thigh, jamming his thumb down on the plunger.

She screamed with rage and jerked her leg away, ripping the syringe out of his hand. She yanked on the hammer, and Gavin fell forward, off-balance, but tightened his grip on the haft.

"What was that? *What was that?*" Angel shouted, punctuating each question with a savage wrench on the hammer.

Gavin gathered his knees underneath him, and flung himself at her, ramming his shoulder into her midsection and wrapping his free arm around her thighs. He lifted with his legs, flinging her over his shoulder and standing. "Run!" he shouted at his wife.

Angel went wild, kicking and clawing, jerking on the hammer's head, slapping at his ears, his face, but Glacadairanam had burned up all her strength in the intervening years. She weighed almost nothing, and Gavin could feel every rib, every vertebra.

With a grunt, he spun and drove her to the ground, kicking his legs high in the air. The air *whooshed* out of her as they struck the concrete floor, and her hand spasmed, releasing her grip on the hammer.

Gavin snatched it away and hurled it clattering across the room. "Just relax," he hissed.

"What was that?" she screeched and clawed at his cheek.

He pinned her to the floor with his weight and reached around for his handcuffs. He snatched a glance at Maddie and found her sitting where she'd been, staring at him with glassy eyes. "Move, Maddie! Run!"

She stared at him for another moment, then turned her head toward the door.

"Go!" he cried, then Angel thrashed beneath him, and he had to turn his full attention to her. He flipped her roughly onto her belly and jerked one arm back, snapping a cuff around her wrist as he did so. He shifted his weight and planted his knee in the small of her back, then grabbed her other, suddenly flaccid arm and cuffed it.

"What was that?" Angel murmured.

As he stared down at her, a shadow separated from her back and shoulders. The shadow was about the size of one of those small monkeys at the zoo, but far from cute. It turned its translucent head toward Gavin over its shoulder and opened glowing, vermillion eyes.

Gavin rocked back, away from Angel's cuffed form, away from the shadow that seemed to be drawing substance from the air around them. Puny shadow-wings sprouted from the creature's back and began to flap as though restless.

The shadows grew thicker, blacker, until the thing took on enough detail to display a study of the grotesque, the nightmarish. Long, floppy ears swept back from his head, then flopped uselessly toward the ground, as Glacadairanam narrowed his blazing scarlet eyes at Gavin. His extended tongue snaked from his savage slash of a mouth and stretched to the back of Angel Kirk's head. The tongue had a vicious set of barbs near the end embedded in her head, and they hooked her scalp, holding the tongue secure. A long, bifurcated tail wrapped around Angel's neck as if to strangle her, claws growing at odd spots from the tail and grasping the skin of her throat. He lifted a three-fingered hand and pointed a crooked, talon-tipped finger at him and screeched.

It was unlike any noise Gavin had ever heard—filled with rage, filled with the sounds of murder and rape and torture—and he flung himself away, one hand coming up to shield his face.

Glacadairanam's ugly tail loosened, the claws retracting from Angel's throat, then whipped free, leaving angry red welts in its wake. It thrashed behind him like that of an angry cat. His throat bucked and heaved, accompanied by a peculiar gulping sound, and Angel's limp body convulsed and twitched in time. The slow flapping of his stunted wings accelerated as the barbs hooking her scalp let go. Her body thrashed, and Glacadairanam detached his tongue and whipped it free. His tongue danced in the air like a thing alive in and of itself, and the little beast performed a shuffling two-step with monstrous eight-inch feet, then grinned at Gavin as he sucked his long tongue into his mouth like spaghetti.

Ridden by fear, Gavin scrambled away from the little beast—away from Glacadairanam, but also away from Maddie and the door.

Grinning, the toddler-sized monster stepped toward him, then paused and shifted his attention over his shoulder at Maddie. When he turned back to Gavin, he wore an evil, vile grin, and the tip of his tongue darted out to smear goop across his chapped lips. He chirped, then turned and ran at Maddie full-tilt, arms waving, tail sliding from side to side to steady his erratic waddling sprint.

Gavin dove at him, but he was insubstantial, like grabbing smoke, and Glacadairanam leaped into the air and flew a few feet before crashing to the ground. "Run, Maddie!" Gavin shouted. *Esteves was wrong about the damn medicine!*

But even as he thought it, Glacadairanam's tongue lashed out lightning-quick and slapped at the back of Maddie's head. She shuddered a moment, but then resumed her plodding crawl toward the door. Face rigid with rage, the little monster whirled to glare at Gavin. He lifted his head and sniffed the air the way a dog does when there is a strange scent on the wind. Glacadairanam looked at Maddie, sniffed, looked at Angel, sniffed, then looked at Gavin and grinned.

Gavin finally remembered the third syringe still hidden in his pocket. The dose that was supposed to protect *him*. Scrabbling at his pocket, Gavin rolled away, clawing for distance between himself and the ghostly little gargoyle advancing on him with glowing red eyes. Glacadairanam cocked his head to the side and issued one of his quirky chirps, then flipped his head to the other side and chirped again, all while continuing his relentless march across the room.

Gavin jerked at the syringe, but it was caught— jammed in the flap of fabric over his suit pocket. Panic rattled around inside him, and he scrabbled behind him with his free hand until he felt the haft of the hammer. He whipped it around and threw it at the thing advancing on him, but it sailed right through Glacadairanam without drawing the little beast's notice.

A slow, but vicious smile spread across Glacadairanam's face as Gavin finally got the syringe free of his pocket and flipped the cap off with his thumbnail. He turned his head in a slow arc and looked at the far wall, then turned back to Gavin and winked.

Gavin snarled and jammed the needle through his pants and into his thigh, but then paused, his thumb on the plunger as the meaning of Glacadairanam's glance sank in. Speaking through Angel, the devious bastard had said his next victim was in the room next door... Debbie's words rang from memory: *No, it did work. But he was smarter than me. He was ready for me.* Gavin narrowed his eyes at the little malignant creature. *Three syringes,* he thought. *Four people who need them.*

With a gloating chirp, Glacadairanam turned and ran in a waddling sprint toward the wall.

Gavin's gaze zipped from the syringe jutting from his thigh to Maddie, then glanced at Angel. He had no idea who was in the other room, or if the goddamn monster could live indefinitely outside a human host, but he knew he didn't want to become as Joe was, as Angel had been. He pressed the plunger but stopped when it was halfway down, hoping it was enough. He ripped it out of his thigh and sprang to his feet and charged to the door, ripped it open, and sprinted into the hall.

He found the next door and grabbed the knob, but it wouldn't turn. Cursing himself for a fool, Gavin spun and ran back to Angel, shoving the syringe into his pocket, then frisking her quickly and digging a set of keys from her pocket. He ran back to the door and tried the first key that looked right. It slid into the knob but didn't turn, and he moved on to the next. After four keys, the lock turned, and the door slammed into him, knocking him into the wall across from the door. A young blonde woman stumbled away, holding her arm. Glacadairanam rode on her shoulder, tail around her neck, tongue embedded in her head. The beast grinned back at him as the woman ran away.

Gavin rushed after her, shoving the keys into his pocket and pulling the uncapped syringe from his jacket once more. As he chased the blonde down the hall, holding the syringe like a dagger, ready to stab her with it and run the plunger all the way down, his thoughts grew sluggish, as though his head were stuffed with cotton. He blinked and shook his head, but the feeling remained.

He ran on, following Glacadairanam through a maze of hallways that the little beast knew like the back of his hand but were all new to Gavin. He gripped the syringe, but with each step, he felt more and more enervated, less and less with it. He could still see her ahead but found it hard to maintain her pace.

Finally, she came to a door covered on one side with filthy handprints and grabbed the knob, Glacadairanam shooting a victorious look at him over his shoulder. She twisted her wrist, but the door didn't open, and the gargoyle's grin faded. The woman jerked the doorknob and rattled the door on its hinges, but it was locked up tight.

Gavin grinned and patted the keys in his pocket as he slowed to a walk. "Forget something?" he called.

The woman shrieked like a banshee, then whirled to face him. "I'll kill her! Your pretty little wife, spark!" she shrieked.

"I don't think so," said Gavin.

"Give me the keys, and I promise to let her live."

"No." He took deep breaths in an attempt to counteract the sedative effects of the zoraperidol, holding his eyes open wide.

The woman with the gargoyle riding on her shoulder whirled around and beat her fists against the door.

"What will happen?" Gavin asked, now just a few steps away. "When I stick her with this?"

"Nothing!"

"Then why did you leave Angel Kirk?"

Glacadairanam didn't answer but spun to face him, and his host's eyes narrowed to mere slits. "Stay away!"

"What *are* you?" asked Gavin. The girl lunged to his left and tried to snake by him, but he put his arm in her path and herded her back to the door. "Will this kill you with no one around to…what did you call it? *Wear?*"

"No! Nothing can kill me! I'm timeless! Immortal! I am a *wrath child*!"

"Uh-huh." Gavin stepped within arm's reach and held up the syringe. "Then this won't bother you a bit."

"Stop! *STOP!*" the woman shrieked.

"Uh-huh," said Gavin as he stepped forward and drove the syringe into her shoulder and rammed the plunger home. "I hope it fucking kills you! *Spark!*" he snarled.

The woman screamed and flung back her head, thrashing it from side to side. Glacadairanam's red-eyed stare grew wild, and he shuddered as the drug began to take hold in the woman's system. She shrieked as though on fire, and the little beast's tail detached from her neck and flailed in the air. His tongue snapped away from her head, and his panicky eyes widened as he drove it back into her skull. She shuddered and twitched, almost convulsing, and staggered back into the door, the strength leaving her legs. She collapsed to the ground even as Gavin stumbled to his knees, dizzy and sick.

His tongue shied away again, and Glacadairanam abandoned her, lurching into the space between Gavin and the woman, head spinning from side to side as though he could see through the walls. He turned back to glare at Gavin, then dashed off with his strange waddling gait—straight through one of the walls.

Gavin wanted nothing more than to let sleep take him, but he had things to do before the NYPD arrived. He forced himself to his feet and took the woman by the arm, pulling her up when she tried to sag back, then turned back the way they'd come.

2

Gavin groaned as he tried to open his eyes and found them gummed shut. He lifted his hands and scrubbed his eyelids clean with the palms of his hands. Maddie slept in the bed next to him, looking peaceful, an IV dripping fluid into her arm. His head throbbed as he rolled it to the other side. The door to the hall darkened as Jim Denders filled the doorway. "Haymond is here," the detective said quietly. "I told him Angel was a victim."

Gavin nodded and sat up as the NYPD lieutenant came into view. Pete Fielding stood behind him, smiling and nodding, and Gavin smiled back, waving them all inside. The only surprise was when Debbie Esteves filed in last.

"Smart thinking, keeping your phone hidden," said Lieutenant Haymond. "Your boss here tracked it."

"He never asked for it."

"He?" asked Haymond, one eyebrow arched.

"Yeah."

"But the DNA—"

"He was holding Angel Kirk, the cop that disappeared from Saint Mary years back. He harvested evidence from her to plant at the scene."

Haymond's eyebrows bunched, but Debbie's eyes shone with gratitude.

Gavin shrugged. "We had time to chat," he said.

"Can you give us his description?"

Gavin shook his head. "He wore a Halloween mask. A cheap one that looked like William Shatner."

Haymond sniffed and looked at Pete, who was staring at Gavin with a raw intensity he didn't like. "You left your firearm in the street," Pete said.

"Yeah. He had Maddie and said he would…" He gulped and shook his head. "I didn't feel I had a choice."

"Why did the unsub leave you?" asked Pete.

"Why did he run, you mean?" asked Gavin.

"Exactly," said Haymond.

"He heard the sirens, I guess."

Haymond sniffed and glanced at Pete. "We didn't run them."

"Oh. Well…" Gavin shrugged. "*Something* set him off. He got all panicky, then bolted out of there like his ass was on fire."

"Uh-huh," said Haymond.

"Come on, Lieu. Gavin is a victim here."

"Why were you all unconscious?" asked Pete.

"The unsub injected us with something. A sedative, I guess."

Pete's gaze lifted and shifted to Maddie, then he nodded. "We'll want a full report before you go."

"Go?"

Pete grinned with half his mouth. "Yeah. When the doctors clear you, the jet will be waiting. You've got a vacation to go on." He glanced at Maddie again. "I've already called and informed the resort that they will be holding your room and extending your stay."

Gavin smiled. "She'll like that."

Pete nodded, then turned to Haymond. "We'd better get back to the manhunt."

"But…" Haymond grimaced, then glanced at Gavin and nodded. "We've got a twenty-block perimeter up, but that part of Brooklyn is full of places to hide." He tsked. "Too bad you didn't get a look at him."

"You never know," said Gavin. "Something this close, maybe it scared him off."

"I just don't get why he'd leave you all." Haymond shook his head again. "Doesn't make sense—especially leaving the keys to his van lying outside the door to your cells."

"Panicked, he said," grunted Jim.

"Guess so," said Haymond. He turned and let Pete lead him away.

Jim watched them for a moment, then swung the door closed. "I take it the syringes worked? Is… Is he…"

"Dead? Not when I last saw him," said Gavin. "He really did run off in a panic. If he survives…" He shrugged, then turned toward Debbie. "By the way, half the dose you gave me worked just fine."

She nodded, a little grin on her lips. "Thanks," she murmured. "For what you did for Angel."

"Is she…"

Debbie's grin died a cold death. "She's in bad shape. Malnourished, emaciated. You're the first to come out of it, but I don't have high hopes she'll be any better than John or Larry."

Gavin dropped his gaze. "I'm sorry."

"Me, too." Esteves sighed. "But I'll take her back to Lily's Glen with me." She forced herself to smile. "I'll put her on the same unit and work with her like I did Joe."

"Tom," said Gavin. "His name is Tom Madsen."

"And the others from Millvale?" asked Denders.

Gavin shook his head, then let his eyelids slide shut as the sedation beckoned him again. "Dead. They're all dead."

"Are we safe? Are *you* safe, Gavin?" asked Jim.

Gavin could only shake his head once more and force his eyes open. "Don't know if Glacadairanam survived it. Don't know if he'll be back." He glanced at Debbie and nodded. "But now we know he *exists*, and we know how to hurt him. How to drive him off if he does come back." He nestled his head into the pillow. "He said something…called himself a 'wrath child.' Does that mean anything to either of you?"

"No," said Debbie, but Gavin's eyelids had already slipped closed. He never heard Jim and Debbie leave the room.

Or the peculiar chirp from under his bed.

If you've enjoyed *Wrath Child*, you might also enjoy *Demon King,* book one of my acclaimed horror series *The Bloodletter Chronicles.* You can find it here: https://ehv4.us/4demonking.

Please consider joining my Readers Group by visiting https://ehv4.us/join. Or follow me on BookBub by visiting my profile page there: https://ehv4.us/bbub.

For my complete bibliography, please visit: https://ehv4.us/bib.

Books these days succeed or fail based on the strength of their reviews. I hope you will consider leaving a review—as an independent author, I could use your help. It's easy (I promise). You can leave your review by clicking on this link: https://ehv4.us/2revwc.

AUTHOR'S NOTE

At one point in my life, I thought I wanted to be a physician—a psychiatrist, to be exact—and I took a job working on a psychiatric intensive treatment unit like the three described in this book. I met many different kinds of mental illness during my tenure there and met many different kinds of patients. Some of them, you met in this book.

The Amhain twins, for instance. No, those aren't their names, but they did enjoy Star Trek, often talking to "Uncle Spock" and asking his advice. They were also very religious, being the sons of a Pentecostal minister. TH! William Stedman is also based on a real patient, and that patient did call on the Holy Ghost in the manner Stedman uses in this book—and frequently. Kaspar Anderson is an amalgam of two patients, and the real story of one of them is no less freaky than what happens to Kaspar in this book. That patient managed to get through three key-only deadbolt locked doors, and in a room devoid of any furnishings—well, devoid of anything at all, really—managed to cut himself from elbow to palm. I was the psychiatric technician who discovered him missing and who subsequently found him. When I asked him how he cut himself, he told me, "The Silver Surfer did it." I also met escape artists who found ways off the locked unit, who escaped five-point restraints and either relocked them once free or had somehow slipped out of them (a feat to be sure). I had many hair-raising conversations, and I cleaned up my share of swimming pools, wrestled my fair share of out of control patients, and I have the scars and life-long injuries to prove it.

Some of the behaviors and speech patterns in this book may seem humorous, but the mental illnesses behind these things are not. Many of the patients I helped treat were frequent visitors to the unit, each trapped in their own vicious cycle of stabilization followed by decompensation, and their plight in the world saddened me. It wasn't all grim, and we had our share of success stories, but, looking back, they seem rare and infrequent, compared with those who came to visit us often.

Likewise, some of the staff members portrayed in the book are based on people I knew and worked with. Margie is especially vivid in my memory—a smart-assed, quick-witted woman from West Virginia, who always had a funny simile perfect for the situation. Likewise, Vee stands out in my memory, but for different reasons entirely.

I have taken great liberties with the psychiatric medications used in this book—hell, I made most of them up, and that's the biggest liberty I can imagine. One thing that I feel I must mention is the drug I called Barban—which you may have recognized as a blatant swipe of Narcan. I need to be very clear here, that Barban is a complete fabrication and there is no antidote for barbiturate overdose, which can be fatal.

This book should have been easy to write, but it wasn't. In many ways, my experiences and memories got in the way, and I had to constantly remind myself that the inner workings of a psychiatric hospital had no bearing on the story I wanted to tell. But at the same time, I wanted to do these patients justice, I wanted to give you a peek into their worlds. In the end, the story I told you is not quite the story I set out to tell you, but I think it is better for it.

You may have noticed the odd easter egg in these pages—some from Stephen King's work, some from my own. I enjoy that sort of thing, and I hope you do, too.

Special thanks go out to my readers who have volunteered their names for use in my books. In this work, there are many: Jackson-Barney, Kelly-Ann Malley (and this time, I let her keep her face), Cindi Parker, Julie Ryder, Chanda Curry, Joyce Motes, Patrick O'Hara, Tony DeQuinzio, Joel McCandless, Michael Santoro, David Holmes, John Jenkins, Debra Esteves, Angel Kirk, and, of course, Gavin Gregory. I enjoy this kind of thing, too.

I hope you enjoyed this twisting tale.

Oh, before you ask: I have no idea if there will be a sequel. Glacadairanam hasn't said yet. Visit https://ehv4.us/join to be among the first to know when he does. I have gifts waiting! Exclusive novellas and short stories, plus samples of my Urban Fantasy and Dark Fantasy series, await.

ABOUT THE AUTHOR

Erik Henry Vick is an author of dark speculative fiction who writes despite a disability caused by his Personal Monster™ (also known as an autoimmune disease.) He writes to hang on to the few remaining shreds of his sanity.

He lives in Western New York with his wife, Supergirl; their son; a Rottweiler named after a god of thunder; and two extremely psychotic cats. He fights his Personal Monster™ daily with humor, pain medicine, and funny T-shirts.

Erik has a B.A. in Psychology, an M.S.C.S., and a Ph.D. in Artificial Intelligence. He has worked as a criminal investigator for a state agency, a college professor, a C.T.O. for an international software company, and a video game developer.

He'd love to hear from you on social media:

Blog: https://erikhenryvick.com
Twitter: https://twitter.com/BerserkErik
Facebook: https://fb.me/erikhenryvick
Amazon author pages:
    USA: https://ehv4.us/amausa
    UK: https://ehv4.us/amauk
Goodreads Author Page: https://ehv4.us/gr
BookBub Author Profile: http://ehv4.us/bbub

Made in the USA
Columbia, SC
16 January 2021